BATTLE FOR ASPEN VALLEY

BOOK 4 OF THE *GEMINI GATE* SERIES

STEVEN E. WILDE

Battle for Aspen Valley (The Gemini Gate series, Book 4)
Steven E. Wilde
Hardcover edition 978-1-77342-099-8
Paperback edition 978-1-77342-098-1
Ebook edition 978-1-77342-097-4

Produced by IndieBookLauncher.com
www.IndieBookLauncher.com
Cover Design: Saul Bottcher
Interior Design and Typesetting: Saul Bottcher

The body text of this book is set in Adobe Caslon.

This book is a work of fiction. Names, places, and events are either a product of the author's imagination or are used fictitiously.

*Dedicated to Anna Belle and Porter Steven,
the grandchildren we'll get to know in the hereafter. I love you.*

1: The words of God, which he spake unto Moses at a time when Moses was caught up into an exceedingly high mountain,

33: And worlds without number have I created; and I also created them for mine own purpose;

35: But only an account of this earth, and the inhabitants thereof, give I unto you. For behold, there are many worlds that have passed away by the word of my power. And there are many that now stand, and innumerable are they unto man; but all things are numbered unto me, for they are mine and I know them.

—Book of Moses 1:1,33,35

Prologue

Nathan shuffled, head down, past the door to Aaron's darkened bedroom and heard music. It wasn't the music Aaron usually listened to, but a Rap song, heavy on beat and rapidly spoken words and short on melody.

Was Aaron already home from school? He stuck his head into the room and saw Aaron on his bed, barefoot, in ragged jeans and t-shirt, sitting up and leaning against the wall. A lamp attached to his headboard shone on a CD cover that Aaron studied. The curtains were drawn against the afternoon sunlight.

"Why didn't you wait for me after school?" Nathan asked. "I waited until no one else came out of the building. You've never left without me before."

"I came home early," Aaron replied, setting the CD case down. He sighed. "I'm through with school, but you should keep going."

"What do you mean, 'through with school'? You're only in ninth grade." Nathan was confused. "You know Mom expects us to graduate from high school and get a college degree, like Dad."

"Yeah," Aaron snorted. "You see how well that worked out for Dad."

"What do you mean? Dad's a successful businessman."

"So? He's a failure as a father and husband. When's the last time he spent any time with either of us, playing catch, or going for a hamburger and shake?"

"I don't remember. But he's very busy."

"He's not my role-model."

"He used to be. You used to talk about how you wanted to grow up and be successful like him."

"Well, you can be successful in different ways."

Nathan had to think about that for a minute, not sure what Aaron was implying. He finally gave up trying to understand.

"Then, what are you going to do?"

"Some friends invited me to hang out with them. I'm going to try that for a while."

"I don't get it Aaron. If you don't go to school, what're you going to do all day?"

"We'll find something. We're going out tonight and they'll show me how they *hang out*."

"What's Mom going to say when she finds out? She won't be happy."

"She won't find out, unless you tell her."

"It won't be me who tells her. The school will call and tell her."

"Yeah, you're right. I'll deal with that when it happens. I'm done with idiot teachers and their stupid rules."

❂

Nathan woke and realized he'd been dreaming again. He remembered the dream vividly because it was one of several that had repeated itself regularly over the last five years—hinge points in his life. Until the start of seventh grade, he and Aaron had been best of friends, spending every spare minute together—playing catch on the lawn, basketball in the driveway, riding their bikes around town. Two years younger than Aaron, Nathan idolized his older brother, wanted to be just like him.

Things had changed that autumn. Aaron had dropped out of school two months into the school year. Nathan had later discovered that Aaron had challenged his science teacher in front of the class, during the first week of classes. He had been right and the teacher wrong, but he had no way of knowing that she compensated for her short stature by being extremely defensive. She had spread the rumor among the staff that Aaron was uncooperative and a trouble maker. Thereafter, any time there was a problem in one of his classes, he was blamed, guilty or not.

Nathan remembered being frustrated at Aaron's change in attitude, and they had drifted apart, not because Aaron didn't want his little brother around, but because Nathan no longer felt like he knew Aaron.

But Nathan had recognized immediately what Aaron had meant about their father; he'd had no time for them for years. Mom had tried to cover for him, helping with homework and answering questions. But the truth was, Jason was a lousy father and husband, indifferent to his family's needs and wants.

It hadn't taken Nathan long to begin to change, too. When Aaron started getting tattoos, Nathan wanted one. When he saw all the stuff—CDs, DVDs, games and clothes, all of which required money—that Aaron accumulated, he wanted some, too. He suspected that Aaron and his friends were stealing—he didn't want to get into that—but he was afraid to ask Aaron, for fear it was true. Anyway, Aaron was happy to let Nathan use his *stuff,* anytime.

He knew that Aaron stayed home most days, to catch up on the sleep he wasn't getting during his late nights out with his friends. Mom had given up after a while trying to control him; she just didn't have the energy for it.

When Nathan had finally dropped out of school two years later—he had the same science teacher and was automatically tagged with Aaron's reputation—and started hanging out with Aaron and his friends, he'd discovered that they had a variety of illegal night-time activities. He'd stay in the car while they shoplifted at all-night convenience stores; one of them would distract the clerk while the others lifted merchandise. Eventually, after they'd hit most of the stores in town, they started watching for people leaving on vacation—who didn't have home security—and burglarize their homes.

He knew that Aaron and his friends sometimes picked up girls late at night and spent hours with them before coming home. He never knew for sure where they went or what they did; but he had a pretty good idea.

Nathan had agreed to help pawn their stolen merchandise and was on a first name basis with the clerk at one of the local pawn shops.

Everything had changed when they'd tried to follow the Blunds to their retreat, with its stash of gold, silver and cash. Aaron had died in the car crash and Nathan's world had turned upside down. In a panic, he'd asked his mom for new surroundings—a place to hide from his pain, really—and had confessed all his bad behavior. His mom and sister were going to the Blunds' retreat. Without much more thought than that, he had asked to go with them, and had regretted it ever since.

At first, he'd tried to blend in, but saw immediately that he preferred the habits he'd picked up with Aaron. Now he spent his days exercising or sleeping, and his nights watching videos and eating. He was alone—isolated—and didn't fit in.

He'd tried to start a relationship with fifteen-year-old Rylee Parker, who'd lost her family in the same auto accident that had stolen Aaron from him. They'd had that one thing in common— lost loved ones—but he'd grown tired of her. Then his mother had told him to leave Rylee alone. She was too young, anyway, he'd told himself; but having gained some experience with Rylee, what he wanted to do now was to take seventeen-year-old Rachel

Blund away from her idiot boyfriend, Chris Stephens.

He realized he'd fallen asleep on the couch in front of the TV and missed the end of the movie, but it didn't matter. He'd seen this movie several times and had all the best parts memorized. He considered trying to fall sleep again, but knew it was a wasted effort. He would be awake now for a while. He padded, barefoot, into the kitchen and looked through the industrial-sized fridges until he found cold leftovers that interested him, then took the food back to the community center and started another video.

1

Can we dig our way out?

The Outcasts—Ft. Laramie, Wyoming, 22 February

"It's been six days since the wind stopped howling," Candy said. "Does that mean we can go outside?"

"It may just mean that the snow is piled so high and deep against the house, that sound can't penetrate," Bryce said, smiling at Candy, who carried his baby, a baby that his wife couldn't give him. They'd been trying in-vitro fertilization as a last resort, when she'd died in the shootout at the Johns Creek shelter. Despite all their trials since leaving the shelter, he was happier, with Candy, than he'd been in months.

"Maybe it's time to go upstairs and check the weather again," Beth suggested.

"Okay with me," Bryce said, "but every time we open the door at the top of the stairs, someone complains that we're letting all the heat escape."

"No, we don't," Kerri argued, "we complain about the cold air that comes down from upstairs."

"Same difference," Candy said, defending Bryce. "I, for one, have cabin fever. I'm tired of playing cards and board games, and sick from the bad air in this house." Her cough, just then, emphasized the point. "I want to go outside and get some fresh air."

"Maybe if the wind didn't blow the snow around so much, we could see out the windows on this level of the house," Beth said

"Come on, Ben," Bryce said, his laugh turning to a cough, as he picked up his heavy winter coat, "let's take a look."

Everyone put on their coats, then Kerri and Callie built up the fire, to replace the heat they would inevitably lose when Bryce opened the door.

Watching their playful interaction, Dr. Beth Byron, formerly the doctor at the Johns Creek shelter, was glad that they had stopped in Laramie for the winter. They had become comfortable—yeah, that was the right word—as they got to know each other better; but she worried about their health. They'd been contaminated with the mutated smallpox virus when the government bombed the CDC in Atlanta, Georgia, which had actually improved their stamina and tolerance to temperature changes, but at the same time had intensified their personalities. Callie's change had been Beth's greatest concern, when her shyness had become despondency. When they'd survived the gunfight and slaughter in the shelter, they had run, at first not knowing where to go, then later following Beth's instinct to head for the Rocky Mountains. They'd spent months trying to keep ahead of the soldiers that they supposed the government had sent to find and kill them, breathing air filled with dust, fallout, and the stink of death.

Jared and Pepper had left them the day after they'd left the shelter. They'd lost Karen, Melissa and Suzanne to various accidents along the way, and Lisa now suffered from the lingering effects of hypothermia, including pneumonia and numbness in her extremities. Now, they all suffered from red, watery eyes, and chest congestion that wouldn't clear up. They wanted to blame their winter-long confinement to the house, but Beth was pretty sure these were symptoms of radiation poisoning from spending the winter in a city contaminated by nuclear fallout—eating contaminated food, drinking contaminated water, and breathing contaminated air. Most of them had asked Beth, individually, about the symptoms of radiation sickness. She also wondered what affect this would have on Candy's unborn child.

"No wind, and the temperature is thirty-eight degrees Fahrenheit." Bryce reported when he and Ben returned a few minutes later.

"Can we dig our way out of the house now and get some fresh air?" Candy asked.

"With our improved stamina and good coats, we should be okay outside, shouldn't we?" Callie asked quietly.

"Yes, you should, Callie," Beth agreed, smiling for the first time since Lisa's near-death from freezing several months earlier. "Our changed metabolisms have made us more temperature tolerant. Let's dig ourselves out."

"We'll have to do something with the snow," Bryce said. "We can't leave it on the floor to melt."

"I saw a bucket in the back room," Ben said. "I'll get it."

"Great, and I'll get a shovel," Bryce added.

When they opened the front door, the snow was piled so high and was so compacted, that it didn't collapse inward. Bryce pushed a shovel into the snowbank, about three feet off the floor, and pulled it out again, empty. He inverted his shovel, pushed it in again a foot above his first mark and pried up on the handle. A block of snow—about a foot cubed—fell out onto the floor.

Ben picked it up and laughed at how much it had retained its shape.

"Maybe we should make a snowman," he said. He set the block of snow on top of his bucket—it wouldn't fit *in* the bucket without knocking the corners off—and hauled it to the bathtub.

They continued to carve out blocks of snow until, finally, the top several inches caved in. Fine ice crystals, that formed the top layer, swept inside on a cold wind, and they could see a hazy daylight. They carved steps in the snowdrift that they could climb, and found that the snow wasn't as deep out in the street, once they were away from the house.

"Who wants to be the first to take a walk?" Bryce asked, sniffling, and looking at Candy.

"Let me out of here," Candy said as she waddled over to the door, wrapped in an oversized heavy coat, wool cap and mittens. Seven months pregnant and she looked it. She'd been wandering the small house all winter, climbing the steps to the upper level door—the one they kept closed to keep the cold out—several times a day, as prescribed by Dr. Beth.

Bryce helped her up the snow steps, then they slid down the other side, and strolled off down the street, followed by the others.

They began taking daily walks around the town, waiting for Beth to say it was time to move on. The snow was still deep, blowing back and forth across town, and it seemed like it might never melt.

The Preserve, 3 March

Chris Stephens had his head in a book on the maintenance of artificial environments, the one he'd been studying for days. Living underground in a closed environment that his dad, Terry, and his dad's partner, Amos Blund, had created, Chris had decided he needed to understand the mechanical, electrical, pneumatic and other systems that kept the Preserve—the *Starship Enterprise,* as he liked to think of it—working, and the people alive.

He wondered, not for the first time, if studying the Preserve's life-support systems was a good use of his time. He'd studied political science before coming to the Preserve and didn't really have a scientific inclination; but with the world in chaos, he didn't know if he'd ever have a chance to work for the State Department, his career aspiration.

He felt Rachel's presence before he saw her. They spent so much time together these days that he had become attuned to her. He loved the way she smelled and was distracted by her presence.

"You're lookin' good," he said without looking up, trying unsuccessfully to keep his mind on what he read. He absentmindedly reached out and touched her pantleg, expecting her usual response—squeezing his hand.

When she didn't take his hand, he looked up. She looked shaken.

"What's wrong?" he asked in alarm.

"Nathan hit on me again. That's three times this week and he's getting bolder."

"What did he do this time?" Chris tensed, ready to get up and go after Nathan.

"He cornered me in the bedroom tunnel and tried to kiss me . . . " She hesitated.

Chris sensed there was more. "What else?"

"He said something that wasn't nice."

"Can you tell me?"

Rachel hesitated again, looking around the room, then back at Chris. He followed her gaze and noted that no one else was around.

"He said he was going to have me," she finally said, quietly.

Chris shot up out of his chair, tipping it backwards, but caught it before it fell over. Rachel placed a hand on his arm, stopping him.

"Don't," she said.

"If he hurts you in any way, I'll . . . I'll . . ." He couldn't think of anything he could do to stop Nathan's actions, that wouldn't get him in trouble, but he really wanted to hurt Nathan.

"He may just be trying to get to you, through me," Rachel said, but Chris didn't believe it. He still remembered what Rachel's mom, Lillie, had said to him a few months ago, warning him that she thought Nathan seemed to be following Rachel around and was likely jealous of Chris's relationship with her. Lillie wasn't suggesting that Chris do anything about it, she just wanted him to be aware. Well, he was acutely aware and ready to do something about it; he just didn't know what. He felt helpless.

"I'm sorry Rachel. I'm trying to watch out for you. I just can't be with you all the time. I have chores . . . "

Oh Chris, Rachel thought. *Don't you know what I want?* She wanted Chris to marry her—which should also stop Nathan's advances—but she didn't feel like she could say that; after all, they were only seventeen.

"Maybe I can talk Mom into matching up our schedules better," she said, which was the only other thing she could think of that might work. Lillie prepared the weekly schedule of chores in the Preserve. If anyone could help, it would be her.

"You do that and I'll try harder to be near at all times." Chris smiled at Rachel but there was hurt in his expression.

"Nothing about Greg in either paper," Amos said, disappointed, as he studied the front page of a newspaper through a small opening between his world and its twin. His long-time partner, Terry Stephens, was at the controls of the Observer and had jumped the gate—that's what they called the opening between the twin worlds—from the Smiths grocery store in Logan to the store in Ogden that Mike had set up earlier. Amos was looking for any reference to a relationship between his doppelganger in the twin world, and the president of the United States, Gregory Mc-Cormick. Mike had claimed months ago, before his accident and extended recovery, that he had seen his dad referred to as a presidential advisor.

In this world, Greg had asked Amos to join his administration on numerous occasions, but Amos had refused each request because he placed higher priority on his medical career, scientific interests and family. But if what Mike had said was true, the Amos in the twin world had made a different career choice and joined the president's administration.

"What do you want to do?" Terry asked.

"Let's take this paper. I'll go through it to see if there's a story that didn't make the front page."

Terry laughed. "I used to think that you had more integrity than anyone I know. Now that you're stealing—I mean subscribing for free—to the newspaper, I'm not so sure."

"You know I'd pay for them if I didn't think it would create a paradox in the twin world. Besides, it's after hours and no one else has bought it." Until they knew more about their twin world— it's money, its laws, whether or not they existed in it—he would not intentionally contaminate it with items from their world, like money. He knew he was rationalizing, but he didn't know what else to do.

Terry moved the gate to within inches of the newspaper and opened the gate wider. Amos reached his hand through the opening and plucked the top paper from the pile on the counter and pulled it through the opening. He would spend some time the next day looking through the paper for any stories about the president or himself. Tomorrow night he would get another paper, probably from the other store.

U.S.–Mexican border, 4 March

"Hello, up there," a man called from a small boat in the middle of the Rio Grande River below the International Boulevard bridge connecting Brownsville, Texas and Matamoros, Tamaulipas, Mexico.

"What?" the border crossing guard, who happened to be strolling across the bridge above, asked. Although the president had declared the border to be open before the explosion in Washington, D.C. the previous July, and people had been streaming out of the country ever since—at first by car and truck, then following the EMPs, on foot—the border patrol maintained a presence, to watch for problems unrelated to the migration. Now they took turns walking out to the middle of the bridge, to break up the boredom and monotony of the long days.

"Do you have a way to contact the president, or the director of Homeland Security?" the man in the boat asked in Spanish-accented English.

"Who are you and why are you asking?" The guard wasn't surprised that he'd asked about the president—a lot of people wanted to tell the president what they thought about the war and the turmoil it had caused—but it was curious that he was asking for Homeland Security.

"I'm a Mexican citizen," the man said, looking around nervously. "I was working for your Homeland Security until I lost contact. I need to get an urgent message to them."

"Come up to our customs office and you can fill out a report. Then we'll see—"

"You don't want me up there," the man interrupted. "I have a disease. Just get a message to the president or to Homeland Security that there's a plague in Matamoros that is spreading. If you don't want it to enter the United States, you need to stop all this traffic." The man choked up. "People are dying and there doesn't seem to be a cure. Please help us."

A shot rang out from across the river. The guard recognized the sound and looked in that direction, seeing a puff of smoke rising from the bushes near the river bank. When he looked back at the boat moments later, the man had collapsed, his arms spread wide and a red smear spread across his chest. The guard ducked behind a stalled car and got on his radio.

Prime Bunker—Meeting of the Panel, 5 March

"A new plague?" the president asked, bewildered.

"Or the same one, being spread by someone out of Georgia," Director of Homeland Security Chuck Dickson said. "That wouldn't be impossible."

"But we've been vaccinating people in Georgia and surrounding states for months. Whoever spread it would have had to leave the area shortly after the bombing."

"We bombed the CDC in July," Secretary of Defense James Seymour said, "and we didn't start the vaccinations until November. That would have given someone plenty of time to get out of Georgia."

"I understand," Greg said, "but then we would have heard about a trail of contamination all along the Gulf coast."

"Unless they took a boat," Chuck said.

"I know you found contamination in Alabama, but what about

Mississippi, Louisiana or Texas?" Greg asked.

"We didn't find anything in Mississippi," Chuck said, "so we didn't look farther west.

"Well, look, then," Greg said and swore.

"Yes, sir. What about Mexico?"

"Cy," Greg said to the Secretary of State, Cyril Hutchison, "see if you can get through to the president of Mexico and offer to help, then start sending vaccinations to the border."

"Yes, sir," Cy said.

The Outcasts—Wyoming, 5 March

"I think it's time to leave Ft. Laramie," Beth told Ben, as they lay together under the blankets to keep warm, a habit they'd started when Lisa had nearly frozen to death, after arriving in Wyoming in November, in a blizzard. Beth decided she would tell the group as soon as everyone had returned from their morning walk.

Bryce slammed the door open, rushing into the house out of breath, followed by an equally winded and coughing Candy, who closed the door behind them. Bryce bent over, resting his hands on his knees, and held his hand up, his index finger extended as though telling everyone he had something to say, in a minute. Everyone watched patiently until he caught his breath and could speak.

"They're back," he finally said, breathlessly.

"Who's back?" Beth asked, "The residents of Ft. Laramie?"

Bryce nodded his head. "Or someone else. There are footprints in the snow that don't belong to any of us."

"Maybe it's the government," Candy said, looking frightened. Beth knew Candy's worst fear was that, after all they'd been through, they might still be found by the government and killed for being mutants. Now she had the added worry of an unborn baby.

"Where? And what did the footprints look like?" Beth asked, looking around and raising her hand for quiet, amid general grumbling and expressions of concern. At Bryce's confused look, Beth added, "Were they large boots, like hazmat suits?"

"Oh," Bryce said. "No, they were regular sized boots, or shoes. We didn't stop to look closely. We were out by the highway east of town when we saw what looked like two sets of tracks. We followed the tracks just long enough to see that they kept going north into town."

"Could it be Jared and Pepper?" Ben asked.

"No way," Bryce said. "It's been months since they disappeared. They couldn't have followed and found us after all this time."

Beth hadn't thought about Jared and Pepper since they'd skipped out in the middle of the night, taking all the food and water the Outcasts had found on their first day out of Johns Creek. It had been a struggle for them to find that food, and to replace it.

Both she and Melissa, one of the CDC researchers that had chosen to go to the shelter rather than to the government bunker that she thought was too close to the CDC to be safe from the explosion, had believed that someone was following them after that—maybe the government, maybe Jared and Pepper—but that feeling had eventually gone away as their lives had been challenged by other, natural and manmade disasters.

"Thanks, Bryce," Beth said. "I was going to tell you this morning anyway, but now it's a moot point. We need to leave. Fill your packs and meet back here in thirty minutes."

"Can we take some of the clothes we found?" Callie asked timidly, breathing raggedly.

Beth smiled. She knew Callie had found some pretty tops and designer jeans to wear.

"Everyone," Beth said, "We're not coming back. We don't know who these people are or if any of the owners of these houses will return. But if we saw their tracks, they'll surely see ours. So, take whatever you want, but be ready to go in thirty minutes," she repeated. "We need to put some distance between us and this place."

"Good thing we anticipated this," Bryce said, "and packed the sled last week."

2

Seven-and-a-half months earlier

Johns Creek, 16 July

"Get the backpack," Jared whispered, pointing.

Pepper opened the pack and began removing bottles of water. "What are you doing?"

"Leaving some of the food and water for the others," Pepper whispered.

"Forget that! They'll find more. We need that."

Pepper shrugged, put the water back in the pack and hefted it onto her shoulder. Then they left quietly by the front door, while everyone else slept in other parts of the house, and walked into the black night.

"Where are we going?" Pepper asked after they'd walked for a while, headed southwest.

"Beth is headed for the Rocky Mountains," Jared said, "which is insanity. That's too far away and still in the danger zone. We need to go south, get out of the United States altogether."

"Mexico?" Pepper asked.

"Yeah. What do you think is the best way to get there?"

"We don't have a car. We saw all the cars stalled on the highways. We could walk. That's what Beth was going to do."

"How about a boat?" Jared asked. "You think we can get a boat?"

"How would I know. I wouldn't know how to operate one, anyway. Would you?"

"I did some boating as a teenager," Jared said. "But we'd have to walk to the coast, then hope we could find one."

Pepper realized that they had retraced their steps of the previous day when they passed the Johns Creek shelter. It was early afternoon, with almost no daylight penetrating the dark clouds of dust and nuclear fallout; but she could clearly see the scorched-black front of the shelter, and the total destruction of the building above it. Even the adjacent buildings had been burned, tendrils of smoke still rising from the ashes in places.

"Do you think the military did that on purpose?" she asked.

"What do you think?" Jared asked, defensively. "They're trying to get rid of the virus. We could have been in there."

"It's a good thing Beth got us out when she did," Pepper said. She visualized the massacre that had taken place in the shelter, with the vice president and his security guards shooting at the soldiers and the soldiers firing at everyone. The man who had been standing next to her had been shot in the chest and had collapsed at her feet. He had bled out and died as she'd tried, unsuccessfully, to stop the bleeding. Beth had organized the survivors and coaxed them out of the shelter minutes before a backup team of soldiers had arrived to finish what the first ones had failed to accomplish—the elimination of everyone in the shelter.

The incident had left her disillusioned and angry at the government and everyone else. But Jared had helped her see that maybe there was a way to survive the madness that the government had started. They would go, together, to Mexico.

"Maybe she got us moving," Jared acknowledged grudgingly, "but it's up to us to save ourselves." Pepper agreed.

"We need to detour around this mess," Jared finally said, pulling up his shirt and covering his nose. Shortly after they'd left Johns Creek, he'd realized that they were walking into the destruction from the nuclear explosion at the CDC in Norcross. Houses had been blown sideways off their foundations and damaged. Stronger buildings had suffered structural damage, which looked like it was more severe, the closer they got to Atlanta. And the stench of death had become more pronounced. So, they turned west to cut through a subdivision that was less damaged than what they'd seen toward Norcross; but even here, the houses were damaged, cars were stalled in the streets, and they could smell the rot of dead humans.

"Where are the bodies?" Pepper asked. "I can smell them, but can't see any."

"I don't know," Jared said. "Maybe they're inside the houses. Or, maybe the government came through and cleaned them up?"

"Hah! You think they've had time to do that? They've got to have their hands full with higher priorities."

"Bodies spread disease."

"Yeah. But there's no power, which means there's no clean water, or there won't be for long."

"Do you hear that?" Pepper asked, shortly after they'd started walking on the second morning. They'd passed through several neighborhoods and were now walking through another one. "Sounds like a child crying." Even though it was daytime, what little light was able to penetrate the thick cloud cover made it difficult to see.

"I don't hear anything. How do you know it's a child crying?"

"I've had children, Jared. I know when a child's crying. Sounds like it's coming from that direction," she said, pointing. Then she turned and headed in that direction.

"What are you doing? We can't do anything for it and we can't take it with us."

"A child is not an 'it', Jared. I just need to see."

The child was a girl about six years old, sitting next to a woman's body, between two houses, in the dark. Her shirt was dirty and her jeans were soiled and smelly, as though she had refused to leave the woman's side, even in the distress of having to relieve herself.

A chimney had fallen from one of the houses and landed on the woman's head, killing her. The little one may have tried to move some loose bricks, but several larger chunks were still on top of her. Perhaps they were too heavy.

When the child saw them, she stopped crying.

"Mama," she said, pointing at the woman.

"What can we do for her?" Pepper asked quietly.

"Nothing," Jared said. "I knew we shouldn't have come over here."

"You take the bricks off the mother and I'll give the girl some food. She's probably been sitting here for days. She must be starving."

"You're joking, right? We don't have much food left, certainly not enough to share."

Pepper ignored him and walked slowly toward the girl, making soothing noises, the kind she'd made with her own children when they were hurt or scared. The girl sniffled. Snot ran down her face, and she took a shuddering breath, but she didn't act afraid.

Pepper removed her pack slowly and opened it without taking her eyes off the child. She opened a package that contained some crusty bread that they'd found the day before, tore off a piece and held it out in front of her.

"Are you hungry?" she asked quietly. The girl nodded. "Here. You can have it. Do you want it?" She nodded again, but didn't move from the woman's side, so Pepper cautiously moved toward her, still holding out the bread. When she got close enough, she reached out, opened the small hand that rested in the girl's lap, and set the bread in it.

The girl stared at the bread, then at Pepper, but didn't put the bread in her mouth. Pepper took the girl's shirt tail and used it to dry her eyes and wipe her nose, then took the girl's hand and raised it to her mouth, making chewing motions and sounds with her own mouth.

Suddenly, the girl stuffed the entire piece of bread into her mouth and gagged, nearly choking on it. Before she had finished chewing the first piece, the girl held her hand out for more. She chewed frantically, a hopeful expression on her face. Pepper gave her another piece, which also went into her mouth, before she'd swallowed the first.

"Slow down, Pepper," Jared warned. "She'll eat everything we have."

"It's okay Jared. I have an idea."

"What's your name," Pepper asked the little girl. She didn't answer, but held her hand out for more. "Where do you live," she asked while handing the girl the last piece of bread. The girl pointed to the house on Pepper's left. "Is anyone else at home?" She shook her head.

"Jared, I'll try to get her to go with me into the house and show me where there's more food. You remove the bricks and follow, okay?"

"Good luck with that," Jared said, sighing.

"There's no more bread," Pepper said, making a pouty face, then she smiled. "Let's go into the house and you can show me where there's more, okay?" The girl looked at the woman and must have decided that her hunger was more urgent than sitting by her mother, because she stood up and moved toward the back of the house. Pepper followed, after looking at Jared to see if he would do what she'd asked. He was already moving toward the woman.

They went to a pantry, which was filled with canned and packaged food.

"What would you like?" Pepper asked. The girl pointed to a package of cream-filled cookies, so Pepper gave it to her. She plopped down on the floor, tore the package open, and began stuffing them into her mouth, her cheeks bulging as the treats filled the mouth.

Pepper filled her pack with packaged food that would be easy to prepare, then tried the water faucet in the sink.

"No water pressure," she said, then remembered what Beth had done to get water from the water heater at the restaurant.

Jared walked into the kitchen just as she located what appeared to be a basement door, and she told him what she thought.

"Go downstairs and find the water heater to refill our containers," she told him.

"You go find it," he replied, brushing dust off his hands and glaring at the girl.

"Okay. You stay with her."

"I'll go find the water heater," he said as he walked toward the door Pepper had pointed to.

Within minutes, Jared returned to the kitchen, carrying several water bottles, both those that they had carried, and others he had located in the basement. "What do we do with the rug rat?" he asked when they had finished filling their packs and the little girl had a pile of food and several full water bottles in front of her on the kitchen table.

"I agree, we can't take her with us," Pepper said, "but I think she'll die if we leave her here alone. I cleaned her up and showed her how to open the canned food. I'm leaving the pantry door open. That should keep her comfortable for a few days, but I don't know if it's enough to keep her alive until help arrives. Ohhhh, let's go, before I decide I can't leave her."

Over the next few weeks, they skirted Atlanta, following Interstate 85 to Montgomery, Alabama, then Interstate 65 all the way to Mobile. They turned onto Interstate 10 and walked to Pascagoula, Mississippi. They walked for long hours each day and didn't seem to tire. It took them several weeks, and they had to avoid people and search for food and clean water along the way. Several times they were forced to leave the highway to hide from roaming bands of armed men and women.

Near Pascagoula, Pepper feared that the way the road had turned to the west, they would miss the coast entirely. So, they followed Highway 63 into Pascagoula and worked their way to Beach Boulevard and the Beach Park Fishing Pier, discovering where they were only when they saw the sign on the pier.

"Now what?" Pepper said, standing on the end of the pier, several feet above water level, looking out over the Gulf. "I don't suppose you can see a boat anywhere around here, can you?"

"No, I can't see anything in this darkness. Maybe we need to search along the beach tomorrow."

"I don't know. With the number of people camping on the beach, maybe we need to look elsewhere."

"Wait! What's that?" Jared asked, squinting out over the water.

"What? Where?"

"There," Jared said, pointing. "There's a light out there bouncing on the waves. Do you see it?"

"Yeah, I see it," Pepper said after a few moments. It was a dim light and looked far away. "It must be a buoy."

"No, not out in open water. It's got to be a boat."

"You think it's a boat?"

"What else would it be?" he asked.

"I have no idea," she said, watching him. "What? Are you thinking of swimming out there just to see if it is?" He nodded. "That looks like a long way to swim. Are you that good a swimmer? And if it is, then what?"

"I had to learn how to swim before they'd let me take a boat for a spin. Besides, I've got Smallpox enhanced stamina." He barked a laugh at her confused look.

"Just don't drown," she said. "With it as dark as it is, I wouldn't even know."

"How about we wait until morning, so you can watch me drown?" he asked.

"Very funny!" she said. "I hope it's still there."

It was there. It was a little hard to see, as if it had moved farther away from them; but it was there. Jared reluctantly removed his shoes, socks, and shirt, and swam out from the beach where they'd slept, using their packs as pillows. He wasn't as confident about his swimming ability as he'd said the night before, and worried the entire time. At one point he thought he was tiring, but he pushed through the wall and got his second wind.

In a surprisingly short time, he was at the starboard side of the small craft. It was a daysailer, a seventeen-foot pocket-cruiser called a Sage 17. Although he'd never operated one of these—he'd read a lot about them—he knew it had a carbon fiber deck on a fiberglass hull, with a jib and mainsail. There was a small red light on the bow.

The sails had been lowered, but not tied off.

He swam to the stern, through the gentle swells, pulled himself up the ladder next to the outboard motor, and looked inside the boat. There was a man lying face down on the deck between the benches. Jared was so startled that he fell over backward and swallowed water, came up sputtering, and had to hold onto the ladder until he could stop choking and catch his breath.

When he'd collected his wits, wondering why he hadn't anticipated finding someone in the boat, he pulled himself back up on the ladder and looked at the man again. He was fully clothed and wearing a life jacket. Certain the man was dead, Jared thought he could probably just move him out of the way so he could get to the outboard motor and see if it would start. He climbed into the boat, stepping on the padded bench, then onto the floor at the man's feet.

He reached down, took hold of the life jacket with both hands, and lifted him off the deck. The dead man's head turned and lifeless eyes stared at him.

Jared's heart skipped a beat. It felt like his lungs had collapsed; and he suddenly couldn't get air. He let go and fell backward, saved from going overboard again by slipping on the deck and falling against the transom at the stern. Unable to stop his momentum, Jared finally landed on top of the dead man. He scrambled to get away, panic filling his head. Within moments, he found himself crouched on the starboard bench, his arms hugging his legs as if to protect himself from the deceased gentleman. He wanted to get farther away, but his muscles wouldn't respond to his commands. He breathed heavily, trying to understand what he was seeing.

Smallpox. There was no doubt.

Gradually, his mind focused on something Beth had said--that about one third of Smallpox victims died, but that the mortality rate dropped to about five percent for those who had been vaccinated. That meant Jared was probably fine, since he'd been vaccinated; besides, he figured that he couldn't catch it again since he'd already had it.

When he finally got his breathing under control again, he approached the man and lifted him onto the port bench. It didn't take much physical strength, but Jared had barely been able to muster the mental fortitude to touch the man again. When he finally did, he avoided touching the man's skin as if he was a venomous snake.

Why hadn't the man gone into shore for help? Jared remembered how debilitating the virus was when the fevers started, which may have explained it. Had he come from somewhere else and died before he could get to shore? Maybe he was from here, had been dying when he left, and only gotten this far. Jared realized he had no way of knowing how long the man had been dead; he might have been drifting out here for days.

He wondered if he should throw the body overboard. He briefly considered taking the man back with him, just to see Pepper's reaction. He chuckled. No, he didn't know how she would react, so that wasn't a good idea. He searched the man's pockets, finding some money and ID. A quick look told him the man's name was Thomas Strang, which didn't mean anything to him, and his home was in Norcross, Georgia—there was an ID card for the CDC— so he might have been one of the first people affected by the virus.

Finding nothing else of interest, Jared pocketed the cash and ID, then lifted the man over the side of the boat into the water, where he floated for a few moments, then sank out of sight. Turning back to the outboard, Jared's foot kicked something on the deck—a handgun that had been hidden by Mr. Strang's body. He released the clip to verify that there were bullets in it, check the safety, then stuffed the gun in the deep pocket of his wet cargo pants.

Jared was beginning to feel the euphoria that only seawater could give. He stretched and looked into the sky. Several seagulls drifted lazily on the breeze, and Jared watched them for a few moments, forgetting where he was. But reality soon came crashing back, and Jared lowered his eyes.

He checked the outboard and confirmed that it held some gas. likely enough to get him back to the beach. He didn't know where Mr. Strang had been headed when he died; but assuming that he had been going south, Jared suspected that there must be more gasoline below, in the V-berth. He took a quick look and found a nearly-full gas can, along with a duffle stuffed with food, clothes, and other supplies that Mr. Strang must have felt were important.

The engine kicked over on the third attempt and he turned it in toward the beach. Before leaving, he took a few minutes to straighten and tie down the sails. Looking over to the beach, he could see that Pepper must have heard the engine kick on. He watched as she began walking away from the other people standing on the beach. Within moments, it became clear that some of the others must have figured out what she was doing, since about a dozen of them followed her as she raced down the beach away from the pier. They must have wanted the boat for the same reason he did.

He tried to estimate where Pepper would be by the time he got close enough to pick her up, without grounding the boat in the shallows, and headed that direction. Pepper kept ahead of the others and finally turned into the water, swimming quickly toward the boat. The others followed, but it appeared they couldn't move as fast as Pepper could. Some of them started swimming, but that looked to be slower than running along the beach.

Jared knew he had to slow down enough for Pepper to get in, without the others catching up and overwhelming them. They could easily swamp the boat, then no one could use it. He thought of the gun but was loath to use it. Besides, it was in his wet pocket and he didn't know what affect that would have on the gun's function. Maybe he could scare them off just by showing it, so he did.

As he approached the beach, he yelled, "Stop where you are or I'll shoot!" He hoped his voice would be heard over the engine noise. He was obviously loud enough, since some of them hesitated. But others continued, hurrying faster, if anything. Jared idled the engine just before Pepper reached him, and the others kept coming.

"I said stop, or I'll shoot," he yelled again, sure that they could all hear him this time. More stopped, but three strangers kept coming, moving quickly.

Pepper was still climbing over the side when the first two arrived next to the boat. Jared hit a large man on the side of the head with the gun and he dropped away into the water. The second man, slightly smaller than the first, grabbed Pepper by the arm and started pulling her back out of the boat. She screamed. Jared didn't know what else to do, so he shoved the gun in the man's face and pulled the trigger. The blast from the gun nearly blew his hand off; but the man fell back, half of his face a bloody mask from the explosion. Pepper fell into the boat.

Jared hit the gas, but the pain in his blackened and bloody hand nauseated him. He looked down at the wound and felt his head swimming. The boat swerved back and forth; the tiller arm held loosely in his good hand.

Pepper, obviously startled from the strange movement of the boat, got up and went to him. Seeing Jared's hand, she looked back toward the beach. Jared followed her eyes, and absently noted that those who had been following her had given up.

"How do you slow this thing down?" Pepper asked. "We need to fix your hand. Where would I find a first aid kit?"

Jared was dazed and didn't know how to respond. He watched Pepper as she looked around, then went below deck. When she returned, she opened a first aid kit. Then she reached over Jared and played with the tiller until something she did caused the boat to slow to an idle.

"Sit down and let me look at that hand," she said, then pushed him onto a seat. She cleaned and treated his hand with burn cream, then bandaged it. Then she forced him to lie down on a port bench in the V-berth.

☢

When Jared woke, it was night and the boat was drifting, the engine idling. Pepper was asleep, holding on to the tiller to keep them pointing into open water, roughly parallel to the shore. She wore a life jacket, with another one between her head and the transom.

"Pepper," he said, waking her. "Where are we?"

"You're awake," she said groggily. "That was a nasty burn. We ought to check it as soon as we get a little light, and rebandage it. What happened to the gun? It looked like it blew up."

"I found it in the boat and put it in my pocket without checking it over really good. Maybe it was clogged or something. I didn't know if it would fire at all, but I didn't know what else to do."

She chuckled nervously. "Well, it worked, although it could

have been worse. You could have killed one or both of us. As it was, I was nearly deaf from the explosion for a while."

"So, why are we stopped?"

"I don't know how to sail a boat," she said, frustrated, "and I didn't want to waste gas steering us in the wrong direction, so I thought it was better waiting for you to wake. I didn't know you were going to take the whole day off."

He frowned at her attempted humor. "Maybe you should have woke me up," he said. "Let me spell you. You go below and get some sleep. I'll see if I can catch some wind with these sails."

"Don't you need stars to steer by?"

He turned on a flashlight that he'd bumped his head on when he'd laid down earlier and shined it around the boat, looking for a GPS device. "Got it," he said. "No stars needed tonight."

"Right," she said and traded places with him.

"We're quite a distance from shore. Not a good idea in a boat this small. Keep your life jacket on and I'll try to get us closer to shore. We'll follow the coast. Unfortunately, I don't think we'll have shore lights to guide us."

"Will we be safe?"

"Of course," he said, with more confidence than he felt.

3

I'm sure there's more

The Outcasts—Wyoming, 5 March

Over the winter, Beth and her friends had had time to reconsider the decision to follow the Old Oregon Trail, which led through Idaho to Oregon. They'd heard reports about the destruction along the Pacific Coast, so they had decided, as a group, that they should turn southwest at Fort Bridger toward the Great Basin of Utah. Maybe they would find a place to stop in the valleys of the Rocky Mountains.

They'd spent the winter in Ft. Laramie. Months later, they left Fort Laramie in the snow, on snow shoes, with full packs, heavy coats, hats and gloves. The snow was a dull gray color, as it had been all winter. Much of the soot and pollution from fires and destructive blasts the summer and fall before had been removed from the air. But the snow had been the cleansing agent. They had wanted to melt it for drinking water several times over the winter, but had decided each time that it wasn't worth the risk.

As they left Fort Laramie, Ben and Bryce took turns pulling a toboggan loaded with extra food and supplies. Lisa had gained some strength over the winter, but was still weak, with wracking coughs, so thy made her a bed among the packages on the sled and made her comfortable. They knew they would eventually have to abandon the sled, but for now it was nice to have. It wasn't that difficult to pull across the icy snow. When the weather turned warmer, they would have to find an alternative.

As they walked, a couple hours after their departure, Candy turned to Beth. "Do you think this pregnancy is going to slow me down?"

"I think the walking will be good," Beth said, "and with your virus-enhanced stamina, I don't see a problem." Besides, Beth mused, Bryce was sticking so close to her, there was no way he would let Candy lag behind, even if he had to carry her.

The only thing Beth worried might slow them down was their health. They all pretended they had colds, but Beth was sure they all realized that they had radiation sickness. The nuclear fallout from detonations around Cheyenne, Wyoming, which wasn't far from Fort Laramie, likely affected their health. Beth determined she would need to be even more vigilant. She didn't really know how exposure to the cold would affect their already-flagging conditions.

Near Atlanta, Georgia, winter

CDC Director Anne Lister had informed the president in October that she thought they had a vaccine for the Smallpox K mutated virus. President McCormick had given her thirty days to conduct clinical testing before directing her to mass produce the vaccine. Then he'd ordered SecDef James Seymour to organize the military to begin vaccinating the population, beginning near the former sites of the Level 4 research and testing facilities—Atlanta, Georgia, and FT. Detrick, Maryland.

The military had hastily recorded a message, to be broadcast over a loudspeaker from trucks that carried the vaccine and medical personnel to administer it. They had been accompanied by soldiers, for their protection, who walked next to the trucks in camouflage hazmat suits carrying automatic weapons.

The troops had been given explicit orders by their leaders that anyone who refused to be vaccinated, whether they showed symptoms or not, was to be detained or shot. The soldiers had had so much ground to cover to get ahead of the spreading virus, that quick action had been required so they could keep moving.

When reports had come back to SecDef Seymour that many people were running from the commanding male voice ordering them to voluntarily approach the truck to be vaccinated, he had realized that the recording sounded more like something from World War II or horror movies filled with futuristic invaders. When he'd heard from the medical people that the soldiers were shooting anyone who ran from them, he'd been shocked that his orders had led to this type of massacre, and had immediately halted the vaccinations until the plan could be reviewed.

Since then, the vaccination trucks had broadcast instructions via a pleasant female voice making a polite request, with an explanation for the vaccination. The recording was a little longer, but the response had been much better. Fewer soldiers had gone with the vaccination teams and they had stayed in the trucks until contact had been established with the citizens, always careful to avoid being abrupt or brandishing weapons.

There had still been some resistance. Those who had refused vaccination were detained, taken from the area and given a choice between receiving a vaccination or being shot. No one, so far, had refused the vaccination.

Now, more than three months later, it appeared that the military had made progress at stopping the spread of the disease, at least from the east coast to the Mississippi River and along the Missouri River, from St. Louis to Kansas City. Farther west, nobody really knew.

The Outcasts—Wyoming, 7 March

"If we bypass Casper and turn south toward Interstate 80,we can save several days and get to warmer weather faster." Beth was suggesting leaving the Oregon Trail and following the Mormon Trail into Utah.

"Won't we miss Independence Rock and Devil's Gate?" Kerri asked, sniffling. These were two of the historic sites along the trail that Beth had said they would pass.

"I want to see Independence Rock," Candy said, looking at Bryce for support. "We want to carve our names and a message in the rock." Then, turning to Beth she added, "Didn't you tell us we were pioneers as much as those who passed in the nineteenth century?" Beth had convinced them that since they were travelling across the continent on foot, they were more like those pioneers than anyone in the last hundred and fifty years.

"Yes, but . . . " Beth started to say.

"No buts," Bryce objected, cutting her off. "I say we stick to the plan. We want to see Independence Rock." He looked around at the others for support.

Ben nudged Beth and raised his eyebrows in a 'What would it hurt?' expression.

Beth took a deep breath. "Ok, let's go to Casper, as planned."

"Sweet," Candy said, smiling.

☢

Casper, Wyoming was still occupied. They didn't want to encounter anyone after their previous experiences, so they waited until after dark to pass through Casper.

Passing through town, Bryce noticed a disturbance near the highway and pointed it out to the others. Beth was against getting any closer, but Bryce's curiosity compelled him to check it out. When he was close enough to tell that the noise came from the Wonder Bar, two men flew out the door, landing in the street, fists flying.

"Should I break it up?" Bryce asked no one in particular.

"I think we should leave," Candy said, standing close and speaking into his ear quietly. "Not our business, and we don't need trouble."

Most of the Outcasts passed on the other side of the street, Candy struggling to pull Bryce after her. But they didn't get away fast enough. As Bryce and Candy moved away, they were noticed by the struggling men and the small crowd of men who had come to the door to follow the fight.

"What are you looking at?" one man asked, his voice growling. He stepped out of the doorway and confronted Bryce. "You want a piece of this?"

Candy tugged harder on Bryce's arm, trying to pull him away; but she wasn't quick enough. First one man, then several of his associates, charged out of the bar and chased the Outcasts down the street. It was a hopeless mission. The Outcasts had much greater strength and stamina, and were soon far away. Just as Bryce thought they were in the clear, a gunshot sounded in the distance. Bryce turned to his left as the bark of a nearby tree splintered. He ran harder, yelling for the others to pick up the pace.

Within three minutes, they had turned a corner and were well on their way to safety. Bryce slowed, then stopped. He turned around. Nobody was following, so he called out that they could slow their pace. They were safe, this time; but the danger had been too close. Bryce realized he would have to be more careful. There was nobody to impress anyway.

By the time they reached Independence Rock, Beth had convinced Candy that it was a bad idea to carve their names on the rock, adding them to the names and messages left there by their predecessors.

"We don't want the government to be able to track us," she told them daily. Inside, however, Candy had felt it would be vandalism, and an act of desecration, to carve into the rock, but she still wanted to do it. In the end, Beth's warning gave her the excuse she needed to not carve her name. The group still spent a couple of hours climbing the rock and reading the inscriptions. There was still snow on the rock in shadowy places, so it was slippery and they had to wipe away the snow to see the inscriptions.

A large plaque provided information about the area, and settlers who passed by, and some of the travails they endured.

"This is awesome!" Candy said. "Wouldn't that have been an amazing adventure? Look here. This young couple had no kids. Wouldn't that have been romantic? Like a long honeymoon." She smiled at Bryce. He looked away, but Candy saw his smile before he turned.

The Preserve, 9 March

Rachel had just asked Chris to walk her to her room when his mother called out to him.

"Go ahead," Chris said.

Rachel cast a concerned glance at Nathan, who was sitting a few feet away looking at a book, not paying attention to them.

Chris followed her gaze and whispered, "I'll see what Mom wants and be right behind you."

Rachel left the community center and walked down the bedroom tunnel while Chris hurried over to his mother on the other side of the room.

Moments later, as Rachel unlocked her bedroom door, she heard footfalls behind her. Certain that it was Chris, she turned toward him with a teasing comment on her lips about entering a girl's bedroom.

"Don't you know it's not—"

It was Nathan. He grabbed her by both shoulders and shoved her roughly into her room, kicking the door shut behind them so hard that it bounced off the frame and reopened a few inches.

Nathan continued pushing until Rachel banged into the dresser against the opposite wall, causing her to wince at the pain in her back. In the fraction of a second that her eyes were closed, Nathan had his hands under her untucked shirt, his hands warm against the bare skin of her stomach. As he pressed his face toward hers, likely for the kiss he'd tried to get earlier, she turned her head, so that his lips landed on her ear.

"Now we're going to have some fun," he whispered into Rachel's ear, his husky voice making her shiver, "while your idiot boyfriend is occupied with Mommy." As his hands moved slowly across and up her stomach, she folded her arms across her chest to stop his progress. She knew he outweighed her by at least eighty pounds and had been working out all winter. He was strong and she knew she couldn't stop him. She looked over his shoulder at the door, willing Chris to show up and rescue her. Rachel knew she should call out for help, but for some reason, in the heat of the moment, she decided she wouldn't be heard.

Nathan breathed heavily into her ear and chuckled deep in his throat, as his hands continued their slow progress, obviously in no hurry. Leaving her left arm across her chest, she pushed down on his hands with her right hand, then quickly struck his face and shoulder. He tried to grab her hand, but was unable to stop her before she accidentally poked him in the eye. He growled, then intensified his effort to get what he wanted.

Suddenly Nathan was pulled backward, away from her. Rachel watched Nathan's body spin around, looking off balance. As her eyes cleared from the tears that she hadn't even felt forming, she saw Chris grab Nathan by the throat with one hand and punch him in the stomach with the other. Seemingly unaffected by the blow, probably as a result of his weight training, Nathan pushed Chris away and pulled a steak knife from his belt with his right hand. Rachel watched in horror as Nathan whipped it from left to right in front of him, cutting Chris' shirt and drawing blood on his chest. Chris winced and backed away a step.

Instead of pressing his advantage on Chris, who he could have stabbed and perhaps killed with one good thrust, Nathan took that brief reprieve to turn and grab Rachel with his left hand. He pulled her off balance and partially in front of him, then pressed the knife to her neck.

Rachel didn't believe that Nathan intended to hurt her with the knife, but she really didn't know what he was capable of. It scared her, both for herself and for Chris.

"You want to see your girl get hurt, huh?" Nathan asked. "You just back out the door and leave us to our fun."

"Not going to happen, Nathan," Chris replied, touching the cut on his chest. "Let her go now, man. I mean it; or you and I are going to have a lot of trouble."

"We already have trouble," Nathan snorted. "Its name is Nathan. Now, beat it!"

Chris took a step to his right. Rachel, despite her fear, tried to understand Chris' action. She imagined his movement was meant to get himself away from the knife; but she also imagined Chris was trying to see if he could get her away from Nathan. Nathan countered by grabbing Rachel with his knife hand and pulling her to his right, away from Chris's movement. Rachel resisted, causing Nathan to drag the knife across her exposed collar bone, leaving a trail of blood that dripped slowly down her chest. Rachel let out a gasp and tried to pull away from him.

Nathan must have noticed the blood. He quickly moved the knife hand away from her, throwing his left arm around her shoulders and across her chest. The distraction was just enough for Chris to grab Nathan's right wrist with his left hand and raise the knife up and out of the way.

Nathan reacted by pushing Rachel out of the way and reaching for Chris with his left hand. Rachel quickly moved behind Chris. Nathan stepped in and took Chris' right wrist with his left hand. They might have stayed that way, Nathan pressing down on Chris and Chris pushing up on Nathan, until help arrived. But Nathan was bigger and stronger than Chris. Rachel realized that Chris must have known this too. Plus, the pain in Chris' chest was likely distracting him. Chris had to find a way to distract Nathan and get the advantage, and Rachel knew just how to do it.

Chris' advantage came moments later. Nathan's eyes glanced over Chris' shoulder and a look of surprise registered on his face. In that instant, Nathan let his guard down for just a moment; but it was enough. Chris moved into Nathan, raising a knee into Nathan's groin, hard. Nathan doubled over in pain and fell to the floor, curling into a fetal position.

Nathan should have let go of the knife, but he didn't. So, as both hands moved to protect his groin, he landed on the knife, driving it into his abdomen. He moaned and rocked back and forth slowly.

Rachel didn't know whether Nathan was dying, and knew that

Chris probably didn't know either. But he wasn't a threat anymore. Chris turned toward Rachel. She was pulling her shirt back down, and putting pressure on the trickle of blood running down from her collar bone.

"What did you do?" Chris asked.

"Don't worry about it. But we're safe now."

Chris looked worried, and glanced at Rachel's shoulder, where blood continued to run. "Go get medical help," he said, waving at her to go. Then he knelt down next to Nathan to check his condition.

☢

Chris wasn't a doctor, but living with a doctor—his dad, Terry—had taught him a few things about knife wounds. He knew that the adrenaline rush that accompanied a fight could block out pain from a penetration wound for minutes or even hours. Each situation was different. He also knew that once the knife was removed, blood would have a clear path to exit the body. So, his first priority, if he wanted Nathan to live—and right now he had mixed feelings—was to make sure Nathan didn't try to remove the knife.

To Chris's surprise, Nathan continued to rock and moan, with both hands between his legs, apparently unaware of the knife in his abdomen. There was bleeding around the knife, but surprisingly little.

"Get away from me or I'll kill you," Nathan growled suddenly, apparently becoming aware of Chris kneeling beside him. He tried to straighten out his legs, only to curl up again, closing his eyes in agony. Chris scooted back a little, keeping his eyes on Nathan and the knife.

Seconds later, Chris heard footsteps. He turned to see Rachel's dad, Amos, carrying his medical bag, charging into the room. Amos smiled, carefully, at Chris, then knelt opposite him, next to Nathan.

"What happened," Amos asked with a calm that likely came from years of experience as a medical first responder.

"He attacked Rachel," Chris said, his voice shaking. Now that the problem was in Amos' hands, Chris' own adrenaline started wear off. He felt weak, and was glad he was already on the ground. "I tried to stop him. I put a knee into his—you know . . . But as he fell, he landed on his own knife." All adrenaline drained away, and the pain in Chris' chest came rushing back, making him wince.

"I'm sure there's more," Amos said, glancing at Chris. Chris wasn't telling the whole story; but given the fact that Amos surely knew of his feelings for Rachel and his dislike of Nathan, Chris wasn't surprised that Amos had that insight. "But it will have to wait. Help me get him on his back."

Amos held Nathan's upper torso, while Chris took Nathan's legs, which were still curled in a fetal position. "Take hold of his hips and turn them. Try to keep the legs bent."

Nathan opened his eyes, noticing Amos and Chris. "Get him away from me or I'll kill him," Nathan growled.

Chris let go of Nathan's legs and Nathan's body started to twist. Chris leaned back, closed his eyes and started to lean to the side. Nathan moaned louder with the movement,

"Chris. Don't let go," Amos said urgently, but calmly. He looked at Chris' face, then down at his shirt. Chris followed Amos' gaze. Upon seeing the blood on his own shirt, he felt himself start to black out. His vision blurred.

"Chris, stay with me, okay?" Amos said loudly

Chris felt confused. He was losing focus. He heard the un-mistakable sound of footfalls and wheels turning. He watched his father, Terry, come around the corner pushing a gurney. Then he fell to the floor.

When Terry arrived, he quickly lowered the gurney so it was just a few inches off the floor.

"What have we got?" Terry asked, with a glance at his son. Amos lifted latex gloves out of his medical bag and pulled them on. Amos nodded in Chris' direction. All the blood had drained from his face, his eyelids drooped, and he was leaning to one side; but he was still conscious. Terry helped Chris over to Rachel's bed, where he laid him down.

"Let me check Chris," Terry said, "then I'll help with Nathan."

Amos understood his friend's priorities. He watched Terry check Chris's chest wound. Amos could tell it was more of a scratch than a cut and it had stopped bleeding, though Amos wondered why Chris would have this reaction to a scratch.

"Doesn't look like much of a problem," Terry said. "Rachel, stay here with Chris while I help with Nathan."

Terry moved over and knelt next to Nathan, opposite Amos, while Amos gave him Chris' summary. Together, they moved Nathan slightly to the side so Terry could get the gurney alongside. Then they rolled him onto his back with Terry holding his legs up.

Nathan appeared to have passed out. Terry took his hips and Amos took his shoulders.

"On three," Amos said. "One . . . two . . . three." With practiced ease, they lifted Nathan onto the gurney. Still kneeling, Amos took a moment to look at the wound; it was seeping blood slowly. Amos spread the wound gently with gloved fingers, watching more blood seep from the wound.

"Possible internal injuries," Amos said, speaking aloud out of habit. "Not much blood out here."

Terry released a lever and the two men lifted the gurney to its full-up position as they stood. Amos reached into his medical kit and ripped the wrapper off a large compress. He wrapped it around the knife to soak up the blood and keep the wound from bleeding excessively.

Terry guided the gurney slowly down the tunnel, while Amos kept the compress in place with one hand. After they made the turn into the main tunnel, they began to move a little faster, but Chris caught up with them, Rachel immediately behind him.

"He saw you leave, and got up," Rachel said, apologetically.

"No problem. He can help," Amos said. "Can you walk?"

Chris was shaky, but made it to the gurney on his own power, but hesitantly. "Hold his knees," Amos said, thinking that that would help Chris stay upright. "Don't let them move, okay?" As they passed through the community center, several people stopped to look at them.

"*Is that Nathan?*" Jason bellowed as he stood and charged across the room, shouting. "*What happened?*" He stopped abruptly when Becca Stephens got in his way. "Get out of my way, woman. I need to see what they did to Nathan."

Amos let go of the compress and pushed Chris and the gurney into the Medical tunnel while Becca delayed Jason. He stopped just inside the door, then closed and locked it.

"*Let me in!*" Jason yelled as he banged on the door.

"Come with us, Chris," Amos said as he took hold of Chris again.

They moved the gurney to a location surrounded by machinery and light stands. Terry turned on lights, attached a heart monitor, and started an IV drip in Nathan's arm, all while watching Chris, as Amos washed up for surgery.

"Thanks for your help, Chris," Terry said. "You were a real pro back there. Now, go see Lillie in the Nursery. Let her look at your cut." He would have said 'scratch', but saying 'cut' made it sound more manly. "Go through that door," he added, nodding at a door in the side wall.

Chris had forgotten about his chest wound, but at his dad's mention of it, the stinging returned. He staggered momentarily as he turned and headed for the side passage—the one that didn't require him to go out through the locked door and into Jason's screaming fury.

In the nursery, he could see Rachel lying on her back on a hospital bed, off to one side, with a sheet covering her. She also had an IV drip and heart monitor, and wasn't moving.

Lillie, Rachel's mother and a registered nurse, approached Chris and helped him over to another bed a few feet away from Rachel's.

"I've sedated her, Chris. She just came in, and looked a little sick. There are traces of a foreign substance in the wound and I haven't figured out yet what it is, but we'll check it. Now you come over here and lie down so I can look at you, too."

Chris was torn between the pain in his chest and his concern for Rachel, lying there with an infected wound. What had that creep done to them? He obeyed Lillie reluctantly.

While Amos and Terry operated on Nathan, Lillie went to the community center to help Becca calm Jason.

"You can't go in there Jason," Becca said. "Why don't you go sit down and wait?"

"He's my son. He may be dying," Jason replied in anger and anguish.

"They're doing everything they can for him," Lillie said coming into the room. "Calm down and wait for Amos to come out and talk to you."

Jason turned on Lillie. "If I lose another son, I'm holding Amos responsible."

"We don't know the details of what happened. Why don't you wait until we can get more information?"

"Becca said Rachel told her some cockeyed story about Nathan attacking her with a knife. Then I hear it's Nathan who's been stabbed. Sounds to me like someone else did the attacking. I want answers."

"And you'll get them . . . as soon as the kids wake up and can tell us more. Why don't you go check on your wife? She's probably upset, too, and could use some consoling." Lillie looked around at the others in the room, wondering how much rumor control would be needed. Rylee and Sydney sat with mouths open and eyes wide. She would have to speak with them later.

"She doesn't need anything I have to offer," Jason said.

Lillie looked over at Brittany, quietly playing with the girls, the sad smile on her face likely a mask hiding her pain.

"Nathan's all I have left in the world," he said.

Lillie suspected that Jason was thinking about the auto accident with Tyler Parker's SUV last year while the families were trying to leave Logan. His son, Aaron, and a friend had attempted to follow the families to the Preserve. Nobody really knew why, but the general consensus was that Aaron and his friend probably intended to rob them. The two boys had died in the accident along with three members of the Parker family—all except Rylee.

According to Brittany, Nathan had asked to go with the families to the Preserve to think about what he wanted his life to be like. Brittany also believed that Jason wouldn't have come to the Preserve except that he didn't know how to live without a wife to take care of him. Now his behavior had stressed his marriage almost to the breaking point. Brittany and their daughter, Sydney, had assimilated well into the new lifestyle. But Jason and Nathan were angry, causing commotion and strife at every opportunity.

Jason and Amos had had several confrontations and had come to blows on two occasions. Jason was restless and seemed to be constantly looking for a way to escape the Preserve. If Jason lost Nathan, she could imagine that it might tip him over the edge.

4

Too much information

The Preserve, 13 March

Chris woke and looked over to where he had last seen Rachel. She was still there, with her mother, Lillie, looking at her and holding her limp hand.

"How is she," Chris asked weakly, drawing Lillie's attention. He sat up, leaning on his elbows. His head started to spin, as though he'd had one too many rides on the Tilt-A-Whirl.

"You're awake," Lillie said, smiling. "Good. How do you feel?"

"Dizzy," Chris replied with a hoarse laugh. He noticed that the stinging in his chest had decreased considerably. He looked down at a large white bandage taped to his bare chest.

"Apparently the knife was contaminated with ethylene glycol," Lillie said. "That's antifreeze. We're trying to figure out where Nathan got it, and why he used it. Rachel's been awake once, like you. She's asleep now, but she's out of the woods, so to speak." Lillie smiled at Chris.

Chris smiled back.

"And Nathan?" he asked

"Still too soon to tell. That was a nasty wound. Because of the way he fell, the knife went in and twisted; did a lot of damage to his some of his organs. He was also infected."

Chris could feel himself becoming lightheaded. His eyes lost focus.

Lillie must have noticed. "I'm sorry Chris. That was too much information." She went over and helped Chris lie back down. He must have fallen asleep immediately, because his next recollection was the voices of his mother and Rachel. He decided to lay quietly and listen.

His mother was speaking.

"Chris was holding him off?" Becca asked.

"Yes," Rachel answered, "but he was injured. It looked like Nathan was going to hurt him."

"So, how did Chris turn that around and get the advantage?" This sounded like Lillie.

Rachel hesitated for several seconds and Chris wondered if she was going to answer.

"I stood behind Chris," she finally said, "where Nathan would see me . . . and lifted my top and bra, so Nathan could see my breasts." From the sound of her voice, Rachel was embarrassed by the admission.

Both women laughed sympathetically.

"Oh Rachel," Lillie said. "Did you really have to?"

"I couldn't think of anything else. I thought it would shock him just enough to give Chris an advantage," Rachel was becoming defensive.

One of the women said "shush" quietly. Chris could picture them looking over to see if their voices had awakened him. He tried to remain still. Both women were still laughing quietly, but trying to control themselves.

"It's alright Rachel," her mother said. "I'm sure it's not the first time he's seen a woman's breasts. The internet has made it almost impossible to get to adulthood without having that experience."

"Does Chris know?" Becca asked.

"No," Rachel responded "I was behind him. I didn't want to

distract *him*."

"Are you going to tell him?" Becca asked seriously.

"What would that accomplish?" Rachel asked.

"Good point," Becca said.

"Mature beyond your years," Lillie said.

"Should I tell him, Mrs. Stephens?"

"Please call me Becca, since we're one big happy family now," Becca said sarcastically.

"Thank you," Rachel said.

"What's Nathan's condition now?" Rachel asked, sniffling.

"Amos doesn't think Nathan is going to recover," Lillie said. "He's going to meet with Jason and Brittany in a few minutes to discuss options. Jason is quite upset. He said he doesn't believe Nathan is capable of what he's been accused of, but I think he knows it's true. He's just in denial. He's certainly afraid of losing another son. It probably makes him look a failure as a role model."

"What do you mean by options?" Rachel asked.

Chris could hear Lillie sigh, possibly considering how much to say.

"Nathan is in an induced coma while his body tries to heal itself," Lillie finally said. "The poison that was on the knife seems to have caused some brain dysfunction. They can keep him in a coma until his brain scans look normal, which could be never. Or they could choose to bring him out of the coma and let him live or die on his own. It's Jason's and Brittany's decision . . ."

"But it's only been one day," Rachel complained, interrupting her mother. "Why are they trying to make that decision so soon?"

"Actually, it's been four days," Becca said.

"Four days?" Rachel said loudly, then someone shushed her again.

Chris could imagine his mother looking over at him and

shrugging her shoulders.

"Jason accused Amos of not doing everything he could to help Nathan," Lillie said. "Jason said the coma is Amos' way of keeping Nathan away from you and Chris. Amos assured him that we are doing the best we can with the equipment we have, which really is state-of-the-art, and that the coma is what's best for Nathan in his present condition. Amos is giving them one more chance to ask all the questions they want regarding Nathan's care, then he's going to force them to make the decision for Nathan."

Rachel was quiet for a long time after that. Chris decided this was a good time to pretend to wake up. He stretched, then moaned at the pain the stretching caused to his injured chest.

"Oh, Chris is waking up," Becca said as she walked over to him. He opened his eyes to see his mother's smiling face. "How do you feel?"

"Like I've been cut with a poisoned knife," Chris replied deadpan, trying to make a joke out of it.

"I'm sorry, Chris," his mother said sympathetically, clearly not realizing he was joking.

"No Mom. I'm fine. Really. It was a joke." Chris looked over at Rachel. She was holding a sheet up in front of her, modestly. As he stared, he thought about Rachel's comment that she had shown Nathan her breasts to distract him.

"Of course, you are," his mother said, turning to look where Chris was looking.

Rachel returned Chris' stare. Then her eyes dropped to Chris' bare chest with the large bandage.

In the Office, Amos leaned against his desk, his legs crossed, his hands resting on the edge of the desk. Terry was seated off to the side, by the video equipment. They were waiting for Jason and Brittany to arrive to talk about the incident between Nathan, Chris and Rachel.

"How's the quest coming?" Terry asked, referring to Amos's attempt to find himself in the twin world.

"I've been a little distracted the last few days," Amos said, "but there are a couple of stories about the president that I want to get back to." After that first night, a week and half earlier, when Terry had helped Amos steal a newspaper, Terry had shown Amos how to program the Observer to jump between retail establishments, so he could "steal" his own papers. He'd been doing it, but was so busy, he hadn't had time to look through all of them, and they were stacking up in the lab.

The office door opened and Lillie entered, followed by Jason, then Brittany, holding a tissue to her face. Brittany took a seat against the wall and Lillie left, while Jason paced nervously, three feet in front of Amos. Jason immediately began summarizing the story he'd been told, as if he'd rehearsed it before entering—as if he were a prosecutor and Amos were a reluctant witness in a courtroom.

"So, Nathan follows Rachel to her bedroom, with a poisoned knife in his belt, intent on killing Chris or raping Rachel. Chris appears and confronts Nathan, who inadvertently cuts Rachel with the poisoned knife—he didn't want to hurt her, just molest her—then fights with Chris. Chris overcomes the larger and stronger Nathan, while injured with a poisoned knife, and manages to force Nathan onto his own weapon. Is that what you want me to believe?" Jason asked sarcastically.

"Until we have more information, that's what it sounds like," Amos replied.

Jason snorted, then continued.

"You're either a fool, Amos, or a liar. I'm not buying it."

Amos bristled and tried to calm himself. Terry shook his head.

Brittany began to sob in the background. Jason turned on her.

"Do you believe this nonsense, woman?" Jason asked. Brittany looked down and cried harder.

"What do you think happened, Jason?" Amos asked, forcing himself to remain calm.

Jason spun back around to face Amos.

"I think it was Chris who had the knife. I think he followed Nathan and Rachel into Rachel's bedroom, drew the knife and attacked Nathan with it."

"And how did Chris and Rachel get injured?" Amos asked. "Are you suggesting that Chris intentionally cut himself and Rachel? If you haven't noticed, Chris and Rachel have been inseparable for months."

"Actually, they've been friends since grade school," Terry added, "best friends since Katie's twenty-second birthday, last year. They danced exclusively with each other the entire evening of Emily's and Matthew's wedding."

"They had a falling out," Jason said haltingly, as though making it up on the moment. "Rachel hit on Nathan to make Chris jealous." He continued to pace. Finally, he threw his arms up in exasperation and glared at Amos. "I don't know how she got in the way."

"Let me show you something," Amos said. "Terry?"

Terry got up and turned on the TV monitor as Amos began to explain.

"This is a video recording from four nights ago, immediately preceding the confrontation, in the community center."

"Yes, I know you have cameras set up in the common rooms

and tunnels," Jason commented. "Spying on us," he added. "I bet you're recording this meeting."

Amos glared at him without speaking. He wasn't going to admit that they were recording this.

The video showed Chris and Rachel, hand-in-hand, approaching the bedroom tunnel on their right. Chris turned and looked over his left shoulder, said something to Rachel, then hurried away to the left. Rachel, smiling affectionately after Chris, turned and continued into the tunnel.

After a few seconds, Nathan entered the screen, looking over his shoulder in Chris' direction, then followed Rachel into the tunnel. A couple of minutes later, Chris reappeared and continued quickly into the tunnel. A few minutes after that, Rachel ran from the tunnel, looking frightened, holding her right hand over her left collar bone.

"That poor girl," Brittany said through her tears. She blew her nose. Jason stood stoically watching the monitor, which now showed Amos trotting into the tunnel with his medical bag swinging from one hand.

"Your thoughts?" Amos asked, watching Jason.

Jason jerked, as though waking from a trance.

"Doesn't prove anything," he replied, looking at his wife with distaste.

"You can't tell how much Chris and Rachel like each other, or how suspicious Nathan acted?" Amos asked.

Jason stared at Amos without responding.

"Okay, how about this?" Amos asked. "Terry?"

Terry slid a new disc into the machine. He fast-forwarded for a few moments, then started the new video. It showed someone who looked like Nathan, sitting in a darkened community center, watching TV. There was a glare on the TV screen, so the image was just a blur of motion.

"So, he's watching TV in the dark. So what?" Jason asked as he squinted at the TV screen.

"This was taken five nights ago, at two-thirty in the morning. We think he's watching pornography," Amos said. Brittany gasped. "He's been watching videos after everyone else goes to bed, several nights a week for as long as we've been recording." He wasn't going to tell Jason that Rylee had been joining Nathan in the community center at night until they had broken up. He didn't want to dilute the present discussion, and he didn't really know what Nathan and Rylee had been doing in the dark, since Nathan had always turned the video off when Rylee entered. That told Amos that Rylee was *not* watching pornography with Nathan.

"So what? What does that prove?" Jason asked.

"If you watched the news—" Amos began, but Jason interrupted.

"I don't. The media is biased. There's nothing on TV except nonsense, violence and garbage," Jason said.

"I know you don't watch TV, Jason," Amos continued calmly. "You've made that perfectly clear. So, I'll tell you. What you're missing is that much of the violence that's reported, particularly the violence against women and children, is a direct result of men's addiction to pornography."

"Humph," Jason said nonchalantly. "Why am I not buying that?"

"Oh Jason," Brittany moaned. "Are you so blind?"

Jason turned on Brittany again. "Shut it, woman. What do you know?"

"You can't see the truth when it's right in front of you," Brittany sobbed.

"You believe this garbage?" Jason asked, then turned back to

Amos. "Ok, genius. Where would Nathan get this pornography? Somebody had to provide it to him. Huh?"

"Obviously he brought it himself," Amos replied. "No one else here looks at pornography."

"So you say," Jason said, defiantly. "Prove it."

Amos watched Jason for a few moments, then looked at Brittany. Jason must have mistaken Amos's hesitation for an admission that Amos couldn't prove it.

"Hah!" Jason said. "You can't, can you?"

Amos glanced at Lillie, who had just entered the room. She stood by the door and nodded.

"Okay," Amos said, "it has to be where only Nathan would look. Let's check his room."

Suddenly, Jason didn't look so sure of himself. "Someone could have planted it in his room. Like Chris," he said, "or Lillie. I saw you make eye contact with her just now. She just planted it in his room, didn't she?"

"No Jason," Amos said, holding his temper and pushing off from the desk. "Lillie just came from the hospital. Her nod was to let me know that Nathan is stable, so we have a few minutes before we have to look in on him again. Lillie, maybe Brittany would rather stay here. Will you stay with her?" Lillie moved over and sat by Brittany as Amos and Terry left the office. Jason followed reluctantly a few moments later.

☢

Nathan's bedroom looked like a tornado had struck. Posters of rock bands covered the walls. His bed looked like it hadn't been made since he'd arrived at the Preserve almost a year earlier. There were dirty clothes on the bed, the dresser and the floor. A pair of boxers hung partway out of one of his dresser drawers. The room smelled of dirty laundry. Jason looked disgusted, then hid his emotions behind a serious face.

"Brittany told me she never went in the boys' rooms after they became teenagers," Jason said. "Maybe this is why." He paused, then continued. "She said if they wanted clothes washed, they had to bring them to her."

Amos was partially behind Jason, so Jason didn't see him shake his head in amazement at Jason's ignorance.

"Okay," Jason said defiantly. "Where do you think he would hide pornography, if he had any?"

"In the medical cases I've discussed with the police, they find it mostly on computer hard drives. Did Nathan have a computer or tablet?" Amos asked.

"I never saw him with one," Jason said.

"Since we only saw Nathan watching his videos on the community center TV, I'd say he probably doesn't have one," Amos agreed. "Therefore, he may have it locked up in a box, under his bed or in his underwear drawer." When Jason didn't move, Amos added, "Would you like me to look?" Jason's mouth hung open and he nodded once, possibly fearing what might come out of his mouth if he spoke, possibly not wanting to touch anything in the room.

Amos got down on his hands and knees and looked under the bed. He dragged out more dirty clothes, then a box about six by ten inches and six inches high. He tried the lid, but it was locked. He set it on the bed where Jason could look at it.

Amos searched the remainder of Nathan's room, looking for a key, while Jason stared at the box on the bed. He didn't find a key, so he turned to Jason. "We undressed Nathan before surgery, but didn't check his pockets. His clothes are in a garment bag in the hospital. Should we go check?"

Amos held the box out to Jason, who took it, numbly. Amos left the room, followed by Jason. Terry brought up the rear.

In the hospital reception area, Amos handed Jason the garment bag from a locker. Jason acted like he didn't know what to do with it. Amos leaned against a counter to wait.

After looking at Amos with a mixture of fear and uncertainty in his eyes, Jason laid the box on the counter, then searched and found a key in a pocket of Nathan's jeans. He eased the key into the lock and it turned easily. When he opened the box, his face scrunched up in pain and he closed the lid again. Finally, he got control of himself and turned the box toward Amos, opening the lid in the process. The box was filled with pornographic DVD's in slim cases.

Defeated, Jason followed Amos back to the office. When Brittany asked what they found, Jason turned sad eyes to his wife. Amos and Terry walked to the other side of the room and watched Jason sit down next to his wife. They spoke, but Amos couldn't hear what was said.

A few minutes later, Jason turned his pained eyes back to Amos and Terry. After a few moments of silence, where Amos let Jason figure out what he wanted to say, Jason stammered, "Will you please leave Nathan in a coma? We'd like to give his brain function a chance to improve."

Brittany told Amos later that Jason, likely as a result of the way he'd acted toward his wife earlier, had decided he could not bear to sleep in the same room with Brittany. He was likely ashamed, but his pride wouldn't allow him to apologize or accept responsibility for his actions. So, after straightening up Nathan's room, one of the few times he actually did housework since coming to the Preserve, he packed most of his possessions into a backpack and set it just inside Nathan's bedroom door. Brittany explained that Jason had considered staying in Nathan's room, but he couldn't shake the feel g that it was still dirty—a filth that no cleaning supplies could wash away. Instead, he took a blanket from the bedroom he shared with Brittany and made a bed on a couch in the community center that night.

The Preserve, 14 March

Amos kept Chris and Rachel in the hospital for another night, just to keep an eye on them. Lillie and Becca alternated checking their vital signs every few hours. In between dozing and the interruptions, Chris and Rachel spoke quietly about anything and everything, except the incident with Nathan.

After eating a good meal, they were both released, with instructions to take it easy for a couple more days and to report any unusual sensations or ailments. They deflected questions about the incident, as they had been instructed by their parents, and took some light-hearted ribbing about what some people will do to get out of chores.

5

Have you found what you're looking for?

The Preserve, early morning, 15 March

Rachel heard footsteps behind her and turned to find Chris approaching, a huge smile on his face and a gleam in his eyes.

"Don't you know it's not nice to be alone in a girl's bedroom with her?" she asked, looking down shyly.

"All I see in front of me is a beautiful woman," he replied.

He placed his hands on her shoulders and gently pushed her into her room, kicking the door shut behind him. He continued pushing until she was pressed firmly against the dresser opposite the door. She smiled encouragingly, then took both of his hands and placed them on her stomach under her untucked top. His hands were warm against her bare skin. He leaned in and kissed her.

"Now I'll have you," she heard, and opened her eyes in surprise. It wasn't Chris, but Nathan. She didn't scream, but she fought him, twisting and pushing him away.

She heard her name, spoken softly, and realized it wasn't Nathan's voice, which confused her.

"Rachel," the voice said, more firmly, as she continued to fight. It was Rylee's voice.

"Rachel, wake up. *Rachel!*" Rylee said.

Rachel woke. She was lying in her bed with Rylee leaning over her, kneeling on her legs and holding her wrists, as she struggled, trying to break free. When she realized she had been dreaming, and that she was safely in her bed, in the room she shared with Rylee, she relaxed and started to cry.

"Are you okay?" Rylee whispered, releasing Rachel's legs and wrists. "You were having a nightmare. Do you remember what it was?"

"Rylee, I'm sorry." Rachel cried and dropped her hands to her stomach. That's when she realized her pajama were in disarray and her bedding had been thrown around.

She remembered exactly what the dream had been about and what had caused it. She started to panic. Did it mean that Nathan was going to continue to torment her from his hospital bed, where he lay in a coma? Would she have to fight to be free of him?

"Just vaguely, Rylee," she said and sniffled. "I'm sorry." She wondered how much Rylee suspected.

"Well," Rylee replied, "whatever it was, it must have been a doozy. You were writhing and moaning, all twisted up in the bedding." Rachel looked down at herself, to see what Rylee could see in the dim light of the night light. She could feel the heat of embarrassment rise to her face and was grateful Rylee couldn't see her blush in the darkness. "Thanks for interrupting the dream . . . whatever it was," Rachel said.

"You're welcome. Would you like me to get you a drink of water, or anything?"

"I'll be fine, thanks."

Rylee yawned and moved tiredly away, collapsing onto her bed.

Rachel straightened her pajamas, then tugged at the stubborn bedding until it unraveled a bit. Too tired to do more, she turned toward the wall and lay on her side, thinking about her nightmare, grateful that their parents hadn't divulged any details of the fight with Nathan.

She didn't know how long she could keep the truth from Rylee but she was too tired to think about it any further. She fell into a fitful sleep.

The Preserve, early morning, 16 March

Rachel's nightmare repeated itself in almost exact detail the next night and was again interrupted by a sleepy Rylee. Instead of grabbing Rachel's wrists as she had the previous morning, Rylee just patted Rachel on the shoulder.

"Rachel, wake up. You're having another nightmare." Rachel woke to find Rylee leaning over her, but far enough away that she didn't get hit by Rachel's flailing arms, like she had the night before.

"I'm sorry, Rylee," Rachel cried. She remembered how embarrassed she'd been to know Rylee had seen her pajamas and bedding all twisted up the previous morning, so she felt around and found the same conditions this morning.

"Will you be okay?" Rylee whispered.

Rachel blushed, wondering again how much Rylee suspected.

"I'll be fine. Thanks . . . again," Rachel said, trying to control her emotions.

"You're welcome . . . again," Rylee replied, a smile implied by her voice. "You want me to get anything for you? Maybe hit you over the head to knock you out."

"I'm good, Rylee. Thanks." Rachel was embarrassed, but grateful Rylee was amused rather than suspicious. "If this continues, I'll get my mom to give me something."

When Rylee moved away, Rachel repeated her ritual of straightening herself and her bed as best she could. This time, it took her longer to fall back to sleep; and when her alarm went off a few hours later, she couldn't be sure that she'd slept at all.

"Rachel?" Lillie asked, stopping Rachel after breakfast.

"Yeah, Mom?" Rachel asked apprehensively. She'd been on guard against looks and comments from others ever since the incident with Nathan.

"Are you sleeping well?" Lillie asked.

"Why do you ask?" Rachel asked.

"Some people sleep poorly after a traumatic experience," her mother answered. "I just wanted to make sure you're not bothered by bad dreams."

Rachel wondered if her mother knew about the nightmares or really was just following up like a good nurse. "I'm great, Mom."

Lillie nodded and walked away. But as she did, Rachel felt ashamed that she couldn't confide in her mother.

"Rachel's not sleeping well," Lillie told Amos that night as she prepared for bed and Amos turned pages in the newspaper without reading anything. "Have you found what you're looking for in the papers?"

"Is Rachel suffering from post-traumatic stress?" he asked. "It's not unusual."

"Rylee said she's having nightmares. Wrestling with her bedding." She noticed that Amos had stopped turning pages and had his head buried in the paper, focused on some story. He probably hadn't heard her last comment. "I'll take care of it," she said, smiling.

"Hmm," he said in response.

"What did you find?" she asked pulling the paper down from

in front of his face.

"What? Oh, I found something on Greg. I mean, in the twin world. Does that make him Greg's twin, or Greg Two or what . . . his doppelganger?"

Lillie shook her head and smiled. "He can be whoever you want him to be, since you'll probably never meet him," she said.

"Actually, I've been thinking about Mike's idea. Maybe one of us should go to the twin world."

"Seriously? What for?"

"Well, kinda seriously. I'd have to have a reason for going, and I don't think Mike's reason—to find ourselves—justifies the risks of contaminating one or both worlds. We should be able to find out if we live in the twin world without actually going there."

"How?"

"Well, that's the dilemma. We haven't figured that out. Terry's checked several libraries, but they don't carry newspapers—everything's electronic—and we don't have internet access there. That's why I've resorted to theft." Amos held up the paper he was holding and shook it a bit.

"You're stealing them? How long have you been a criminal?" Lillie smiled, but let it fade quickly as she saw there was no humor in Amos' eyes. He looked ashamed. "We don't know if our money is the same as theirs," he said apologetically. "That's one of the concerns I have about contaminating their world."

"So, what have you found?"

"I've found two stories so far about Greg . . . I mean Greg's twin. They have to do with his efforts to shut down North Korea's nuclear program, the same issue our Greg was working on before the terrorist bombing, and neither story mentions me . . . I mean my twin."

"Maybe you need to work on how to refer to our *twins* before you confuse yourself and everyone else," Lillie said with a smile.

Mike knocked on his parents' bedroom door.

"Who is it?" Amos asked through the door.

"Mike. Do you have a minute?"

"Sure, Mike," Amos said. "Come on in. What's up?" Amos sat on a chair, one shoe off and a sock in his hand. Lillie was sitting up in bed, wearing her favorite 'I'm a Pepper' t-shirt, and reading a book.

"I noticed a stack of newspapers in the lab," Mike said with a nervous smile. He still smarted from his dad's chastisement about his going through the gate and getting himself beat up and hospitalized. "I wondered where they came from."

"Right." Amos said. "I've been following up on your research into the twin world, but I've been too busy to talk to you about it."

"He's stealing newspapers," Lillie said without looking up from her book.

"Dad? Stealing? I don't believe it," Mike joked. He was delighted, but wished his dad would let him help. He had been strictly forbidden to play with the gate following his recovery from his incident in the Smiths parking lot. "Have you found anything interesting?"

Amos told him about the two stories he'd found.

"I've had to let my research slide, Mike, because I've been too busy with Rachel, Chris and Nathan; and Nathan's not out of the woods yet. I was wondering if you'd like to take over for a while."

Would I? Mike exclaimed. "I mean, I would," he added, more subdued.

"I thought that might interest you," Amos said, as he and Lillie both laughed at his enthusiasm. Amos explained how he was alternating between the two grocery stores and made Mike swear he wouldn't do anything else with the gate, as a condition of being allowed to get involved again.

"Maybe I can find additional newspaper sources so we don't draw too much attention at those two stores," Mike suggested. "We don't want them to set up a camera to see where the papers are going."

"Okay, Mike," Amos said. "You can do that much, but no more."

The Outcasts—Wyoming, 16 March

They were close to Devil's Gate and Beth wanted to see what it was. Although it was quite unique, she was a little disappointed to discover that it was just a split in the mountain with a river running through it. But while searching for Devil's Gate, they happened upon the Mormon Handcart Historic Site at Martin's Cove. There were snow-covered paths lined with split-rail fences, a small log structure that turned out to be a museum, and a couple of newer homes that reminded her of park ranger housing.

No one answered their knocking at any of the buildings, and the doors were locked, so they broke in. Beth didn't think anyone would mind—at least not anymore. By the time anyone got around to staffing the museum again, if ever, there was likely to be much more damage just from the weather.

The houses were abandoned and quite barren, as though unused since the last tourist season, and snow had blown into drifts against the outside walls. The museum, however, was filled with interesting things. Murals on the walls showed pictures and told stories about the Martin and Willey Handcart companies, and the many members of their parties who had frozen to death at this site in a freak early winter storm in 1856. Beth immediately thought about Lisa, who nearly froze to death in a severe snow-storm in Ft. Laramie, and teared up at the memory of her failure to help Lisa recover fully. She was sure that Lisa still had pneumonia, and she had no way to treat it. It nearly broke her heart to think that Lisa would have a long recovery on her own, without proper medication, when she had been so full of life and so helpful before that experience.

The visitors' log was filled with expressions of gratitude for the experience of pulling a handcart around the area, to experience some of what the pioneers had endured. There were pictures of handcarts, so there must have been a few around here somewhere, but they hadn't seen any outside. With the power outage, the handcarts would have been a valuable commodity for transporting personal property. Beth was certain they had been stolen by others, before Beth and her friends had arrived.

Glass cases contained artifacts from those nineteenth century pioneers, including worn-out leather shoes, bent eating utensils, and excerpts from personal journals that told of the hardships of their travels. Beth, and others, shed a few tears as they read how the Mormon pioneers had been persecuted and driven from their homes in Illinois by angry mobs, and how most had had to walk the two thousand miles across the plains and mountains to make a new home in the Rocky Mountains.

"Sounds like us," Callie said, obviously holding back tears.

"This historic site was set up to honor those who died in the storm and to tell the story of the miraculous rescue of the survivors," Beth said, summing up what she'd been reading on one of the plaques. "Their religious leader sent a rescue party from the settlement in the valley of the Great Salt Lake."

"Maybe we can finally rest if we go there, too," Kerri suggested.

"Times change, but maybe you're right," Beth said. She was

more determined than ever to turn southwest at Fort Bridger and follow the Mormon Trail into Utah.

The Preserve, early morning, 17 March

Rachel was beside herself with shame when she realized that she had undressed herself in her sleep and was only partially covered by her bedding. She could tell that Rylee could see what she'd done, but Rylee didn't speak after she shook Rachel awake and returned to her bed.

"I'm so sorry, Rylee," Rachel whispered to Rylee's retreating form. Rylee raised a hand in acknowledgement—which Rachel could distinguish in the faint light—but didn't say anything or turn around again. Maybe she was embarrassed, too.

Later, after showering and dressing, Rachel determined something had to be done. "Mom?" she said, stopping Lillie, who had just stood up from the table and started walking toward the kitchen with breakfast dishes in her hands.

"Yes?" Lillie asked as she stopped and looked over her shoulder.

"Can we talk . . . in private?" Rachel asked hesitantly.

Lillie showed no sign of alarm. She handed off her dirty dishes to Mike as he was passing.

"Michael, will you take these to the kitchen? Thanks." Mike took her dishes with a nod.

Settled in her parents' bedroom, alone with her mother, Rachel started talking, not knowing beforehand what she was going to say, but knowing she had to get help before her nightmares became any more embarrassing.

"You asked me yesterday if I was sleeping well," Rachel said, tears coming involuntarily to her eyes, her voice shaky.

"Yes, and you told me you were fine," Lillie replied. "Was that not true?"

"Did you know I was having bad dreams when you asked?" Rachel asked, indirectly answering her mother's question.

Lillie looked at her daughter for a few moments before answering. "As I said, some people sleep poorly after a traumatic experience. However, in this case, a little bird suggested I ask how you've been sleeping."

"A little bird named Rylee?" Rachel asked, tears now running down both cheeks. Lillie handed Rachel a tissue from her nightstand and smiled without answering. Rachel attempted a smile, thinking how compassionate and clever her mother was.

"Do you want to tell me about them?" Lillie finally asked.

Rachel sobbed as she told her mother about the nightmares, leaving out little.

"You don't think I'm making this up?" Rachel asked, appreciating her mother's tenderness.

"No, I don't think so, dear," Lillie assured her, smiling.

"It's so embarrassing to have Rylee wake me up, knowing she can tell I'm naked. She can probably figure out what the nightmares are about. Is there something I can take that will stop them?" Rachel pleaded through her tears.

Lillie opened her arms and Rachel moved over next to her on the bed, leaning into her, crying against her mother's shoulder while her mother rubbed her back. When Rachel finally stopped crying, Lillie lifted her head until they were eye-to-eye. "I'll find something to help you sleep. I'll tell Dad you're having nightmares related to the incident with Nathan without going into detail."

"Thanks Mom," she replied, choking back her tears.

"We'll keep this between the two of us. Let's talk about it again in a couple of days, okay?"

Rachel tried to smile, giving her mom a hug. "Thanks," she said again, then stood to leave.

"Stop by the hospital before lunch and I'll have something for you."

Rachel could feel the knots in her stomach coming undone and her tense muscles relax. Her mouth turned up in a genuine smile. Mom was the best.

☢

"How's Rachel?" Amos asked.

"I gave her something to help her sleep," Lillie replied. "I'll let you know how it goes. Anything new on Greg's twin?"

"Nothing new, except that Terry and I agreed to call Greg, Greg One, and his twin Greg Two, and so on."

"So, should I start calling you Amos One?" she asked with a smirk.

"I don't think that's necessary. I'll continue to call you 'the love of my life'."

"Oh, that's certainly simpler," she said sarcastically.

"Maybe not simpler, but true nonetheless."

6

Who are you?

The Preserve, 18 March

Rachel slept through the night. It was a restless sleep and she was tired when she woke; but she couldn't remember dreaming and Rylee didn't have to wake her.

At breakfast, Lillie sat down next to her

"How did you sleep?" she asked quietly.

"Not well, but no dreams . . . that I can remember, anyway," Rachel replied. "The pill really made a difference. Thanks."

Lillie patted her on the knee, under the table.

"You're welcome. Let me know if anything changes. Ok?"

Rachel smiled tiredly and nodded her head.

"I saw my name in the paper," Amos told Lillie and Terry as soon as he entered the hospital to relieve them. The three of them, plus Matt, had been trading off monitoring Nathan—at least one of them was with him at all times.

"About time," Terry said.

"What did it say?" Lillie asked at the same time.

"Apparently I'm a special advisor to the president . . . or my twin is . . . Amos Two is. Criminy, this is frustrating," Amos said.

"We know what you mean," Terry said. "Don't make it so hard."

"Yeah," Amos said, taking a deep breath and letting it out. "The story said I just got back from a trip to China, where I met with representatives of China, South Korea, North Korea and Japan."

"All by yourself?" Lillie asked.

"No, no. But I led the U.S. delegation and represented the president, who couldn't or wouldn't go—it didn't say."

"That doesn't sound like you," Terry said, "Mister keep-in-the-background-and-don't-draw-attention-to-yourself."

"Certainly not the role I would have chosen for myself," Amos said. "A little out of my comfort zone."

"But you're certainly capable," Lillie said.

"Thank you, honey," Amos said. "Apparently, that's the role Greg chose for me. I'm glad I'm in this world and not that one. How's our patient?"

"No change," Terry said. "No better, and no worse."

"Okay, I'll take it from here. You two take a break."

"I'm glad you got some information, even if it's not exactly what you expected," Lillie said, giving him a kiss. Then she and Terry left.

☢

"Dad," Mike said, looking up from a newspaper as Amos and Terry entered the lab to find Mike reading a newspaper. "you'll never guess what I found." Mike had stacked the papers across the table in three piles. Amos and Terry looked at each other and smiled.

"I told you it wouldn't take him long," Terry said.

"What did you find, Mike?" Amos asked, amused.

"You marked those two stories for me and I read them, just like you did. Then I started going through all of the papers from cover to cover, noting anything that caught my attention. This stack," he continued, pointing to the papers on his right, "has the sections of the papers that contain interesting information."

While Mike was talking, Amos had noticed that many of the pages had corners turned down, with yellow highlights on story titles.

"Right, and I couldn't find anything interesting in these papers," Mike said, pointing to a smaller stack on the far left. "The third stack are the papers I haven't read yet." It was the smallest stack.

"Mike, when are you tending the gardens?"

"I figured the gardens could tend themselves for a day," he said, but Amos's expression must have convinced him to clarify his comment. "Actually, Katie agreed to manage things, and I've arranged lots of help for her. I checked on their progress right after lunch and I'll go back tomorrow morning."

"Okay, Mike," Amos said, shaking his head and chuckling at Mike's enthusiasm. "What did you find?"

"After I read the two stories about Amos Two's China mission, I found other stories about problems in the Middle East, Central and South America and here in the United States. Well, in the twin version of those countries. President McCormick Two has all the same problems we had before the terrorist attack here."

"Are you surprised?" Amos asked.

"No, not about there being global tensions. What surprised me is how he's dealing with them. Many of the stories refer to a special advisor and a team of experts that this advisor has organized to deal with the problems. Do you think Amos Two is his special advisor?"

Amos became thoughtful. He already believed Amos Two was the special advisor. If he had joined Greg's administration, as Greg had requested, what would he have been working on for the president? What skills would he have had to develop that were different from what had made him a good doctor and scientist?

"Is that you?" Terry asked, breaking Amos's train of thought.

"How could it be?" Amos asked. "The skill set required to be a diplomat are . . . " he was going to say 'so different from those of a doctor and scientist', but were they? He would have to think about this.

"You're creative and have great organizational skills," Terry said. "And you're a natural leader."

"Right," Amos laughed self-consciously, "and good-looking—a requirement for being a good diplomat." Terry laughed with him, while Mike quietly studied his dad.

"What do you think, Mike?" Amos asked when he noticed Mike's serious expression. "Could that be me or are they referring to someone else?"

"I don't know," Mike said, as he continued to stare at his dad. "I guess, I'm just trying to picture you in meetings with foreign leaders, speaking through translators, leading discussions, influencing global leaders. That sort of stuff."

"Do you think I could do all of that?" Amos asked, genuinely curious about his son's belief in his old man.

"Yeah, I think so, but . . .." Mike's voice trailed off.

"But what?" Amos asked, trying to hide his smile. He didn't really think he was up to that, so why would Mike have any other perspective?

"Okay, here's the problem I see. The real failure of diplomacy, in my opinion, is that language is totally inadequate for communicating intent. A person can say one thing, and those listening— whether in the same language or some other language—could interpret the words to mean something totally different. You could be at some conference, and it could end with everyone believing they had reached some agreement. But then everyone walks away and nothing changes because the words used had different meanings to different people, based upon their language, their culture, and whatever else differentiates them from each other."

"I agree with all of that, Mike," Amos said, curious about where his son was going with his little speech. "So, you don't think my language would be sufficient to overcome that problem?"

"I don't think anyone can overcome that problem. That's why we're in this mess."

"But I asked you if you though I could be the president's advisor. It sounds like you think nobody could do the job."

"Yeah, I guess you could do as well as anybody. I guess I'm just saying that I'm glad you're not. I wouldn't want my dad, my hero, to be that guy that fails, and gets blamed for the failure, even though nobody else could have succeeded either."

"Well, I appreciate that," Amos said. "I'm glad I'm not the president's advisor too."

The Outcasts—Wyoming, 19 March

They crossed the Continental Divide at South Pass in deep snow. The only hint that there was a sun above the dark clouds was the occasional lighter color in the cloud cover.

They followed the interstate to Fort Bridger, nestled in a small valley with several other small towns. The Fort was at the edge of town and looked like the other forts they'd seen. They didn't bother stopping. They continued into town to find food, but as had happened before, they were scared away by men and women with guns. The danger was too great to proceed, especially since they still had a bit to eat.

They found Interstate 80 and followed it to Evanston. There was a grocery store and several fast food outlets at the first exit.

"Should we try to find food here?" Beth asked no one in particular. She was already heading down the off ramp.

"It's not deserted," Ben warned, following Beth. There were footprints and horse tracks in the snow, and smoke coming from some of the chimneys.

"Ben, why don't you come with me and we'll see what we can find," Beth said. "Maybe the rest of you should wait for us here."

They saw immediately that the grocery store was closed, boarded up and dark.

"Should we break in?" Ben asked.

"I don't think so. The way it's boarded up, it's not likely we'll find anything anyway." As they leaned against a wall, looking around and considering options, they were approached by a very young man in a long overcoat, who stopped before getting too close to them.

"Who are you and what do you want?" the boy asked boldly.

Beth considered her response before answering. The kid, who couldn't be more than sixteen years old, was obviously not afraid of travelers. Perhaps he had food and was the front man for the town. Or, perhaps, she mused, he was the sheriff and wanted to run them off. Only one way to tell.

"We're travelers from the east and we're looking for food and water before continuing on," Beth said.

"What do you have in your packs?"

Beth became suspicious. No way was she going to tell him what she had in the pack. "Only a change of clothes," she said. "We're finding food to eat along the way."

The young man reached into his long coat. Ben quickly closed the distance and grabbed his arm, pulling open the coat with his other hand. The young man had a handgun in his waistband, which Ben took, while the young man struggled uselessly to get out of Ben's iron grip.

"Whoa, there," Ben said.

Beth stepped up and took the kid's other arm. She was aware that she was probably contaminating him by doing so.

"Why?" Beth asked.

"We don't get many travelers here anymore . . . not since the war. You must be thieves . . . or worse."

"Sorry to disappoint you," Beth replied. "We're just passing through, headed for the valley of the Great Salt Lake."

"Only place I've heard Salt Lake City called that is at the fort," the young man said through gritted teeth, his struggling less determined.

Beth smiled. "Well, we've come a long way and haven't been to . . . Salt Lake City before. We'll remember that."

"Oh, you don't want to go to Salt Lake," the young man said. "A missile fell on Hill. It caused a big earthquake in Salt Lake. People came storming through here for days, headed anywhere, to get away."

Beth was confused. "A missile fell on a hill? In Salt Lake?"

"Not on *a hill*, on *the Hill*, Hill Air Force Base, in Ogden, north of Salt Lake." The young man laughed mirthlessly at Beth's ignorance. "The whole Wasatch Fault gave way, destroyed everything from Ogden to Provo and beyond. You go that way and you won't get far." At Beth's discouraged look, the young man added, mimicking, "Sorry to disappoint you."

"Watch your tongue, kid," Ben said, shaking the young man's arm. It made his skinny little body rattle.

"It's okay Ben," Beth said. Then to the boy she said, "Thanks. We'll have to rethink our plan." Beth was discouraged and sure that it showed.

The young man waited expectantly. Ben decided to take the

initiative. "We need food and water. Where can we get some?"

"Well, if you really want food and water, you better have something besides spare clothes in your packs," the young man said, mocking.

"Okay, kid," Ben said, applying more pressure to his grip on the young man's arm, the gun held down to his side. The young man winced at the pressure on his arm. "We have enough money to buy what we need. Where do we get food and water?"

The young man got a cagey look in his eye.

"Let go of me and I'll show you," he said.

"I don't think so," Ben said. "Not when you were ready to pull a gun on us. Just tell us and we'll be on our way."

"Do I get my gun back?"

Beth took the gun and opened it, finding it empty. She gave it back to the young man and they let go of him.

"Okay, so we can't trust you and you don't trust us. Where do we go from here?"

"There's no food in the stores. When the looting began, the Sheriff cracked some heads. They boarded up the stores and sold all the food at a markup. When the people from Salt Lake came through, some of the food got resold at a higher markup. Now, everyone is hoarding the food that's left, 'cause it looks like there won't be anymore."

"So, there's no food?" Ben asked.

"Oh, we got food to sell, 'cause we already had a store of food before the crisis began. But it will cost you."

"Ok," Beth said, "I'm going to call the rest of our group down here and you can show us what you have."

"The rest of your group?" the young man asked nervously.

"There are seven of us," Beth said. We're trusting you not to take advantage of us, so we're asking you to trust us—to not be afraid of us. Beth stepped out where the rest of the Outcasts could see her and waved. She could see the others start to move toward them.

When the others arrived, the young man led them down the street, into a yard. They spread out and moved cautiously, expecting an ambush. The young man noticed and laughed again.

"Stop acting so strange," he said. "There's no threat here, just my folks and older brother."

"You trying to trick us again?" Ben asked.

Beth kicked Ben lightly in the shin. When he looked at her, she motioned for him to let her negotiate with the young man. Ben shrugged and backed off a step.

The young man took them to the back of the house, to a basement door. Beth followed him cautiously inside. A middle-aged man and woman stood on the other side of the room in a doorway. The young man spoke to them. "We have customers," he said, "travelers just passing through on their way west."

"West?" the man questioned.

"That's what they say."

The man started to enter the room, frowning. Beth felt guilty about contaminating the young man and didn't want to make it worse by contaminating the older man.

"Please don't come any closer," Beth said apologetically.

"Why not?" The man asked suspiciously.

"Because we may be contagious."

"Contagious?" the kid shrieked and jumped away. "You touched me."

"Only because you tried to pull a gun on us. We had no intention of touching you before that."

"I don't believe it," the young man cried, clearly agitated.

"I'll explain and tell you what to do about it. First, let us buy some food and water from you."

"No," the young man yelled. "Get out of here."

"Okay," Beth replied as she turned and started walking out the door, "but wouldn't you like to know what we have and what you should do about it?"

"Wait! Okay. What do you want?" He walked over to one side of the room and pulled back a curtain that was covering shelves loaded with food, then over to an adjacent wall and did the same. Beth couldn't believe how much food they had. She realized her mouth was hanging open, so she closed it.

Rather than touch the food herself, she told the young man what she wanted and he piled it on the floor in the middle of the room.

"That's a lot of food," the young man said in surprise.

"We'll pay for it," Beth replied defensively. When she thought she had enough, but not so much that they couldn't carry it all, she asked for the price.

The man had been tallying up the cost on a scrap of paper. She was surprised at how much they wanted for it, but the Outcasts had gathered—stolen, she admitted to herself—a lot of money during their search of Ft. Laramie, so she was willing to part with some of it.

She called in Ben and Bryce to pay the boy and pack out all the supplies. "Okay," Beth said, "I believe you've been fair with us. We have a mutated form of the Smallpox virus. We've passed what would normally be the contagious stage, but we may still be contagious. That's what I meant when I said it was mutated." The woman, still standing in the doorway, gasped. The man gritted his teeth in frustration.

Beth told them what symptoms to expect if the young man caught Smallpox, then offered to vaccinate him and anyone else who wanted to be vaccinated, telling them that the vaccination would reduce the severity of the symptoms. Beth still carried a few of the original vaccinations that they'd received in the Johns Creek shelter, and hadn't used or given away. They wouldn't cure the mutated Smallpox, but they were better than nothing.

"But he may still be contagious. Is that what you're telling us?" the man asked.

"The government is working on a cure," she said, nodding. She really had no idea if they were, but thought they would be, and wanted to give these people a reason to be optimistic.

Beth vaccinated the young man. When she offered to vaccinate the other two, the woman said she would do it.

"Have you had medical training?" Beth asked.

"I help out at the school during flu season," the woman replied, "or, I did. There's no school now." Beth didn't want to ask why not. She thought it better to go quickly.

The woman didn't do too badly.

"We have more vaccinations if you'd like us to leave some," Beth said.

"You mean in case we contaminate someone else?" the woman asked bitterly. Then, after thinking about it for a moment, her attitude changed. "Maybe we should," she said looking at her husband.

Beth brought out a packet containing a few vaccinations and handed it to the young man who passed it on to his mother. "Thank you," the woman said.

"You're welcome. And thank you for the food," Beth said to the young man as she and Bryce turned to leave.

"Sure," the kid replied half-heartedly. Beth watched him turn around, walk to a box in the corner of the room, and sit down.

Apparently, he had decided to quarantine himself in this room for three days . . . or longer.

Once outside again, the Outcasts hefted their packs and started walking back to the interstate that led to Utah, but Beth wanted to talk. They'd walked partway to the freeway on-ramp when she left the sidewalk and sat down under a tree at a boarded up fast-food restaurant. She wasn't sure where to go now. Salt Lake was out, and she had to tell the others; but there had to be other places where they could disappear and settle for a while. She pulled out the map of Utah, which showed the southwest corner of Wyoming in the upper right corner, and found Evanston. She saw Ogden, Salt Lake City and Provo. Those were big cities, but they were all in ruins now, if what the boy had said was true. She wanted something smaller anyway.

Coalville was across the border, in Utah. It was on the freeway and near a junction between freeways that went to Salt Lake and Ogden. The boy had said a lot of people had come from that direction. It made sense that a lot of them would stop in Coalville and the surrounding towns if they weren't destroyed, too. But that might be true of any of the towns in the mountains. She kept looking.

There was a place called Bear Lake, northeast of Ogden and northwest of their present location. A road led directly to it from Evanston, with a couple of small towns on the way and a couple more along the shore of the Lake. It was only fifty miles away or so. They could be there in less than a week, even with Candy's pregnancy and Lisa slowing them down. They talked it over, Beth and Ben telling the others what the boy had said, and they all agreed on the course change.

7

Seven months earlier

Galveston, Texas, 14 August

Wet from being on the water, Pepper had gotten cold; and the drying sea water had made her skin itchy and left her hair a mess. She had gone through Strang's duffle and found dry clothes, which had been tight on Jared and loose on her. She'd rolled up the pant legs and sleeves and wore Strang's light jacket. Jared had left the shirtsleeves unbuttoned, wrapped a blanket around his shoulders and used a ball cap to cover his mostly bald head.

Pepper had also found enough food to last about a week—rationed—which had gotten them as far as Galveston, Texas. Jared had used some of his spare time, when he wasn't sailing the boat or teaching Pepper how to sail, to check out Strang's gun. He'd discovered that it hadn't blown apart, but was dirty and wet, so he'd found a gun cleaning kit and more ammunition, then cleaned and reloaded the gun. He still didn't quite trust it to not explode the next time he fired it—but hoped it would work better, if he were forced to use it again.

They sailed around the windward side of Galveston island until they found what looked like docks.

"Look! There are lights in one of the buildings," Jared said, as they got closer, "It looks like a coast guard station, which makes me nervous."

"What do we do?" Pepper asked.

"Let's go to the seaward side of the island. The water will be a little rougher, but there should be fewer people around."

"Why can't we just stop at the beach we saw at the north end of the island?"

"We need deeper water, so we don't have to worry about the rudder hitting bottom and grounding us."

They had to sail several miles before they found a pier on the seaward side.

"What's that?" Pepper asked.

"Looks like a Ferris wheel. This pier must be an amusement park. Maybe we can tie off and climb the support structure."

They continued until they reached the pier, then tied the boat to a support structure at the deep end. Jared kept the blanket around his shoulders, stuffed a flashlight in his back pocket, and carried the empty gas can in one hand. Although they had sailed most of the way to Texas, they'd had to use the engine periodically to navigate windless seas, and to maintain control in heavier weather and when docking.

They climbed a metal ladder which extended from the base of the pier—partially submerged under water—up to the top, where the amusement park spread out before them.. There were no lights and, from their vantage point, no people in the park. They wound their way through the silent rides and empty food stands to the road that ran along the seashore, crossed the road, and lost themselves in the dark streets. Jared led the way, staying in shadow as much as possible, since they feared their Smallpox marks would attract attention.

Their first priority was finding food and drinkable water, then they would look for gas.

"Turn away," Jared said as a lone man approached. When the man looked up and saw them, he reacted as though surprised to see them, and quickly crossed the street and continued past.

"That scared me," Pepper said, her voice quiet and cautious.

"I don't know," Jared said. "He's the first person we've encountered, and he seemed as nervous about us as we were about him. I wonder what it means."

"Does it mean we don't need to hide our faces? As dark as it is, it would be hard for anyone to see our spots."

"Let's not get careless. If someone takes a good look at us and calls out in alarm, we may have to make a run for it."

"We may be out of luck with food and water. Nothing around here seems to indicate we might find some." Pepper said. They'd been walking past shops, many of which looked like they'd been closed permanently. "I wonder how Beth and the others are doing."

"I don't much care," Jared said quickly, then paused, as if thinking about it. "They're travelling overland, so they're probably encountering more people and damage. They may be facing more threats, but that's their problem; they weren't very nice to me."

Pepper was tempted to remind him that he was the one who had attacked Callie, not the other way around, just to tease him, but she didn't really care either. She had made her decision and had tied her wagon to Jared.

"No lights and no shopkeepers," Pepper said. "Wait. Is this a beauty shop?"

"Looks like it, why?"

"I've been thinking that maybe we could cover our spots with makeup. Maybe we can find something here."

Jared tried the door and found it locked. Pepper tried looking in through the window, but it was too dark to tell anything, and he was loath to use the flashlight.

"Let's try the back," Jared said.

They walked to the nearest street corner and found an alley that led behind all the shops. They found the back entrance to the beauty shop, but it was locked, too. Jared kicked the lock and the door squeaked open a few inches. Once inside, Jared closed the door and turned on the flashlight. He covered the lens with his hand, so that only a little light escaped between his fingers, and turned his back to the front of the shop. From the light of Jared's flashlight, Pepper could see that they were in a back room, with a door between them and the display area. Jared must have realized the same thing because he allowed the light to roam the room.

"Oh, look!" Pepper said, walking up to a counter. There were boxes of cosmetics on the counter, which she rifled through, looking for what she wanted.

"What are you looking for?" Jared asked.

"I liked my red hair. I'm looking for hair die," she said, dragging her fingers through a few strands of hair, "and I'd like to wash the salt out."

"Don't forget the skin makeup," Jared said. "Actually, how about you dye your hair black and use darker skin makeup. We're going to Mexico, right? Maybe you want to look a little less pale."

"Not bad. Let's do your hair, too. Okay, shine your light over here." She found what she wanted and put everything in a bag she found on a shelf. After searching through a small break room in the back, and finding nothing to satisfy their hunger, they left the way they had come.

☢

Pepper and Jared continued their exploration of the Galveston area, winding their way through the streets. They saw very few people and were able to avoid all of them. The city seemed abandoned, and Pepper found that strange. Eventually, they could see houses on the next street. Jared had said that they didn't want to get too far away from the pier, in case they were challenged and had to run for it.

"Now what?" Pepper asked.

"We still need food, and I don't know where we're going to find gas for the boat."

"Do we check the houses, or turn back?"

"I wonder if the houses are as empty as the streets," Jared said. Pepper had turned a corner and stopped.

"What's this?" she asked.

"Looks like a women's clothes store," Jared said when he caught up with her.

"They call it a boutique," she said

"What's the difference?"

"Look at the clothes. This is perfect. Let's go inside."

Pepper rummaged through the racks and found some expensive jeans, long-sleeved tops that looked like Mexican imports, with shoes and scarves that matched, and sexy underwear. She even found dressy, elbow-length gloves that would hide the marks on her hands and arms.

She wanted to change, but didn't want to put her new clothes on over her itchy skin.

"I need to wash this salt off me before I put on clean clothes," Pepper said, looking at Jared, although not for approval.

"I saw bathrooms back there," Jared replied, pointing a thumb over his shoulder.

In seconds, Pepper was in the bathroom, but there was no running water. While she looked herself over in a dark mirror, Jared went to search for a water heater. He returned a few minutes later and poured enough water in the sink for her to wash her hair and take a sponge bath.

"I'm going to look for some clothes in the adjacent shop. Be back in a few minutes."

When Jared returned, he was carrying a huge pile of men's clothes. Pepper had dressed and was adding makeup to her face. "Find what you were looking for?" Pepper asked, laughing as she looked at Jared's arms filled with clothes.

"Maybe. I've got to try them on. I'm a dude. I don't memorize what sizes of clothes I wear."

After Pepper had finished applying makeup and hair dye, she turned to Jared. "Your turn." She winked and moved toward Jared.

Half an hour later, after they had each attempted to rinse out their hair and Pepper had applied a bit of makeup to Jared's face, Pepper turned Jared toward the mirror, shining the flashlight toward the ceiling so that it illuminated the area around them.

"I feel stupid," Jared said, bending closer to the mirror to check himself out. "Now what?"

"You've never worn makeup?" She asked, chuckling.

"Not since I was in a play in high school."

"Well, you look lovely," she said, smiling.

"Okay, let's go find some food," Jared said, picked up the gas can and a backpack, and headed for the door.

"Wait! We better take all of our clothes and the makeup."

"Why?" he asked.

"We have to go back on the water to get to Mexico. We'll need to redo the makeup, I'm sure."

"My stuff is in the bag," Jared said, holding up the backpack. "It's waterproof. I found it next door. Add your stuff and let's go." Pepper stuffed her clothes into the backpack and Jared threw it over his shoulder.

"What's that noise?" Jared asked as they exited the shop onto the street.

"I don't hear anything."

"Shhh . . . listen. There it is again. It sounds like an argument."

"It's coming from that direction," Pepper said, finally hearing it and heading in that direction.

"Be careful," Jared said. Pepper turned and gave him a dirty look. Of course, she would be careful.

Pepper turned a corner and stopped dead in her tracks. There were two men, and they didn't appear happy. She couldn't tell what they were saying—their words were slurred and they wobbled where they stood—but one appeared to want to fight, while the other tried to back away from it. She pressed herself against the brick wall and watched.

One man took a swing at the other, but missed. The other man backed off the sidewalk into the street and staggered, nearly falling over. The momentum of the swing pulled the first man off balance and he fell on his face on the sidewalk and didn't get up. The other staggered away as two more men and a woman spilled onto the sidewalk from the adjacent building.

"We should leave," Jared whispered from behind Pepper, startling her and making her yelp.

The three newcomers on the sidewalk turned toward them, only twenty yards away. "Who's there? What do you want?" one of the men said. Pepper thought he sounded more frightened than angry.

Pepper knew that Jared didn't know what was going on, so she was surprised when he stepped around her and strode toward the three.

"What are you doing out here?" Jared asked in a rather authoritative voice.

"We're sorry," one man said. "We wanted to prevent a fight, so we came out to stop it." He sounded apologetic. What was going on? A curfew? Martial law?

"Pick him up and take him inside," Jared said.

"Yes sir," the man said as the two men took the drunk under the arms and dragged him back through the doorway. The woman stared at Jared.

"You!" Jared said, making the woman jerk. "Come here."

Pepper watched the woman. She stood frozen in place, as if she were afraid for her life. "Now!" Jared said, making the woman jerk again; then she moved toward him slowly. Pepper was worried. What was Jared going to do next? He didn't have any authority out here. The woman would easily realize that Jared wasn't someone she recognized. She had to do something.

"Hey babe," Pepper said, stepping around Jared and between him and the woman. "We don't mean you any harm. We just want to talk."

"You're not going to punish me for violating curfew?" the woman said, hope tinging her words.

Up close, Pepper couldn't see the woman's features or expression, but she thought she could see a tear on her cheek.

"Naw. We're just checking for serious violators," Pepper replied. "We saw you step out on the sidewalk just now."

The woman squeaked in relief and brought her hands together in front of her. "Thank you. I'll get off the street right now." She turned to leave.

"Wait." Pepper said. "Come here." The woman turned, her body visibly shaking. "Don't worry. Maybe you can help us. We've been working all day without anything to eat. What have you got to eat in there?"

The woman paused before speaking. "All they have is cheap liquor and bad sandwiches." She sounded apologetic, like it was her fault and they would take it out on her.

"No problem. Any fruit or vegetables? Water?"

"Yeah. I'll get some." The woman turned into the building and returned shortly with oranges, sandwiches, and bottled water.

"Fine. This will have to do," Pepper said, then walked away, with Jared following.

"Let me know when she's gone," Pepper said.

Jared looked back. "She's gone back into the bar or whatever that place was. That was great thinking back there. Maybe we should have said thank you, or paid her."

"That would have been out of character for enforcers, don't you think?" Pepper asked.

"Enforcers?" Jared repeated. "Yeah, I suppose you're right. Maybe we should have asked her where we could find gas."

"Yeah, but where are we going to get gas?"

As they walked back toward the pier, they passed a gas station. After a quick check, Jared said, "the pumps aren't working. No way the cars are either, but they might have gas in them." Pepper was amused by Jared's sudden excitement.

"We just need to find a length of hose."

Jared rushed into the station, and Pepper followed. She copied his action in setting down their bags, then watched the light from Jared's flashlight as it played across the shelves. Apparently not finding what he needed, Jared went outside. Pepper grabbed all the bags and followed.

When Jared found a water faucet with a hose attached behind the building, he ran back into the station, returning a couple of minutes later with a pair of large scissors. He used to hack and cut at the hose until he'd cut off a section about four feet long.

Moving to the closest car—a small light-blue sedan of some kind—Jared said, "I've only done this once, a long time ago. It was like two o'clock in the morning or something. I ran out of gas and had to get the girl I was with home so her dad didn't beat me."

"You obviously survived," Pepper said, amused at the story.

"Yeah, but the gas is disgusting."

Jared placed one end of the hose inside the gas tank and the other in his mouth. He sucked deeply for a few seconds, then coughed, spitting gas onto the ground as it came flowing from the tank through the He quickly filled the gas can. "I wish I had another one, but we probably wouldn't be able to carry it with all this other stuff."

"Let's get back to the boat, with your hose," Pepper suggested. "We can dump the gas into the boat's tank and find more. There were other cars closer to the pier."

"Good idea," Jared replied. Then he began walking.

Pepper followed him all the way back to the pier, without incident. They dropped their bags inside, then went to find more cars. Within a half an hour, they had topped off the tank. As they settled into the boat to leave, they joked about how nervous they'd been breaking into shops, and how well everything had worked out for them; but when Jared couldn't get the motor to kick over, Pepper began to worry.

8

We have an emergency

The Preserve, 23 March

Amos sat at the table in the lab looking through the stories that Mike had marked for his review. He couldn't get his mind off what he'd been reading the last few days about his role in the twin world. He'd seen his name again, this time associated with tensions in the Middle East. He was convinced that he was the special advisor mentioned in all the stories, but how could he manage so many problems on so many fronts.

He'd seen other names in the stories—not politicians, but scientific and military people, whose names he recognized—who appeared to be working with, or for, Amos Two. Believing that Amos Two had the same personality and temperament that *he* had, Amos suspected that Amos Two had selected this team of experts and that Greg Two had recruited them to help him with diplomatic negotiations.

These questions caused Amos to wonder what resources Greg One had gathered, *in this world,* to help him try to discover their enemies' plans and to prevent war. He knew about Greg's secret, terrorist-fighting Panel—SecDef Jim Seymour, DNI Tom Mitchell, HomeSec Chuck Dickson, and Secretary of State, Cy Hutchison—but were there others?

This line of questioning led to other queries. How had Al-Qaeda managed to bring a nuclear weapon into the country and detonate it in Washington, D.C.? Someone had to have helped them. Certain that Greg had retaliated as he had told the UN General Assembly he would, his attack must have caused other nuclear powers to get involved, resulting in nuclear war. The shaking that they had felt in the preserve several days after the Washington explosion told him that the war had been extensive. Since Greg's original goal was to stop Al-Qaeda, Amos wondered if Greg had succeeded in locating and bombing the Al-Qaeda strongholds.

Now that he had gathered his thoughts, he realized that he couldn't rest until he had asked Greg. No matter what was happening in the twin world, he had to know what was happening in *his* world, right now. He picked up the encrypted phone he had used to call the president before, hoping it was still operational.

"Hello Amos," Greg said tiredly. "It's been a very long time. I've wondered what happened to you. I'm happy you called."

"Hi Greg," Amos said. "I'm sorry to bother you. I've missed our calls. How is everything?" He was anxious to get to the point, but knew that he needed to be polite. It really had been a long time.

"Well, I don't know how much you know Amos, but the world is in shambles, and a lot of it is my fault."

"I've heard and read a lot of it, Greg. I'm sorry it's so bad out there. I don't want to take much of your time, but I've got a couple of questions for you. Do you have a minute?"

"Always have time for you. What do you want to know?"

"How did Al-Qaeda get a nuclear weapon into the country and detonate it? Someone had to have helped them."

Amos had expected some reservation on Greg's part to answer this question, since the information might be considered classified, but Greg was silent for so long that Amos wondered if he'd hung up.

"That's classified," Greg finally said. "Why are you asking?"

"Actually, Greg, it's history. In a few years, you'll write your memoirs and this will be front and center of your experience as president."

Greg was quiet again, but Amos could hear background noises, like a drawer opening and closing, shuffling papers, and tapping fingers.

"I don't know, Amos. I think I should only talk to my advisors. If you were one of them—" Greg left the comment unfinished, likely to remind Amos once again that Greg had asked him to join his administration, and that by turning Greg down Amos had failed to do his patriotic duty and was on the outside, without a need to know.

"That's *generally* a good idea," Amos said, hoping that Greg would decide that their present relationship worked fine. Amos always helped when Greg really needed him, and Greg had frequently shared information that his advisors would consider classified. This wasn't much different.

After another pause, during which Greg must have come to the same conclusion, he relented.

"Oh, what the heck," Greg said. Then he answered all of Amos's questions as best he could. He didn't have all the details about how the Los Zetas drug cartel had helped Al-Qaeda sneak the bomb into the United States, but he offered all he knew. Then he explained the suspected role of Russian Siloviki in supplying nuclear bomb components and technology to Al-Qaeda and North Korea.

When Greg asked, Amos confirmed that he'd seen video footage of the confrontation at the UN General Assembly meeting, so he had no questions about that; but he wanted to know about the escalation of hostilities that led to the war.

Greg explained the sequence of events following the detonation in Washington, D.C.—his retaliation against Russia and North Korea, the nuclear response from China and Russia, the missile exchange between China, Russia, and the U.S. and her allies, and the unintended consequence of inciting other nuclear and non-nuclear countries to launch missiles at each other and their neighbors. He explained the collaboration between the U.S., UK, France, and Israel, with input from Saudi Arabia, to identify, then bomb, Al-Qaeda and ISIS strongholds and weapons caches.

"Anything else?" Greg asked, when Amos didn't follow up with another question.

"No," Amos said after thinking about it for a moment. "That about covers it. Thanks. By the way, how are Liz and the boys?"

Greg hesitated before answering, making Amos wonder if he was going to get the truth or a whitewashed version of it.

"The boys and their families are fine," Greg finally said. "Liz is a little upset with me right now because some of my decisions have caused so much pain and suffering. I'm upset too, but I don't know what else I could have done."

"You mean, you don't know how you could have prevented the hostilities, right?" Amos asked. "How are Tom and Jim holding up?"

"Jim enjoyed orchestrating a no-holds-barred war, but we're all frustrated with the consequences. The national power grid is down and Tom has his hands full trying to figure out how to get the equipment to get the country running again."

"Not an easy problem to solve," Amos agreed. "Are you going to be okay?"

Greg was silent again.

"Greg?" Amos finally asked.

"I'm fine," Greg replied. "How are you all holding up? Is the

Preserve still functioning the way you intended?"

"It is, Greg," Amos said, wondering at Greg's wording—about his interest in the Preserve. "Do you have a question about the Preserve?"

"No, no. Just wondering if everyone's alright. How's Lillie."

"She's fine, Greg. We're all fine."

"Good," Greg said, then the line went dead.

Amos held the phone out in front of him and studied it. He knew Greg wasn't big on small talk, but his hanging up was a little abrupt, even for Greg.

The sedatives left Rachel tired all day, but she would tolerate that, since they enabled her to get through the night without dreaming. She thought again, as she did every day, what her life would be like when—no, if—Nathan ever recovered.

"What's Nathan's condition?" she asked her mother.

"Dad's doing all he can for Nathan," Lillie said. That was the only information she offered.

It was late in the afternoon when an alarm went off in the community center. Rachel and Chris were playing a game of Monopoly with Sydney and Rylee. It wasn't a loud sound, but it was one they hadn't heard before.

"What's that?" Rylee asked. "Is it a fire alarm?"

Chris took Rachel's hand under the table and smiled at her. She assumed his look was an attempt to reassure her

"What does that mean?" Rachel asked, staring at Chris. She could tell from his expression that he thought he knew.

"Wait for it," he replied.

The alarm continued. Others stopped what they were doing and looked around.

It took no more than ten seconds before they could hear footsteps in the tunnel. Lillie appeared from the direction of the kitchen, pulling an apron off over her head. She continued into the medical tunnel, headed for the hospital, and all eyes followed her.

A few seconds later the alarm shut off. Then Amos appeared from the direction of the office, looked around the room briefly, then turned into the medical tunnel.

❂

"Amos," Jason called as he and Brittany entered from the bedroom tunnel at a trot.

Amos stopped in the doorway; he couldn't tell Jason's mood from his tone of voice. Jason generally spoke with anger and attempted authority.

"Yes?" Amos asked with anger and attempted authority.

"Yes?" Amos asked. He know he sounded impatient, but he was, after all. Jason and Brittany must have realized what the alarm meant and why Amos was hurrying to the hospital. It was Nathan. Britany held her hand over her mouth as if holding a scream inside.

Amos could see the eyes of almost everyone in the community center, watching him and Jason. He was sure they were waiting to see what Jason would do next. There was no love between them. Amos was generally tolerant of Jason, but Jason constantly spoke poorly of Amos's leadership in front of others, and that really bothered Amos.

"We have an emergency, Jason," Amos said. "Can it wait?"

"I want to be there," Jason said, not sounding as angry as usual. He sounded more like he was pleading.

"Come along," Amos said. "But I can't promise you can stay. It depends on what we find." Jason nodded and followed Amos into the medical tunnel with Brittany hurrying after them.

"Is that what I think it is?" Rachel asked whispering, her mouth close to Chris's ear.

Rylee leaned forward to hear what Chris would say. She had a pretty good idea that it meant that Nathan's condition had gotten worse. Maybe he had died. She hated him for rejecting her, but she didn't want to say that, so she just listened. She noticed that Sydney had leaned forward as well.

"When I asked about Nathan a couple of days ago," Chris said, "your dad told me they had him attached to a monitor that would alert them if his condition changed for the worse."

"Does that mean Nathan's dead?" Sydney asked.

"Not necessarily," Chris replied. "But I'm sure we'll know soon."

"I'm sorry, Sydney," Rylee said, when she couldn't stand being quiet any longer, "but I hope he dies."

Sydney stared at Rylee with a blank expression, perhaps expecting her to say more—some kind of explanation.

Rylee realized she should have kept her mouth shut. She knew that Sydney didn't have a lot of love for her brother, but he *was* her brother. Instead, she looked at Rachel.

"He's been trouble ever since we got here," Rylee said, "and he's made your life miserable, Rachel."

Tears welled up in Rachel's eyes and spilled down her cheeks, which confused Rylee. She remembered Rachel's dreams. Were they about Nathan and not Chris? Did she secretly have a crush on Nathan instead of Chris? Would Rachel tell her if she asked?

Rylee could see Rachel watching her closely as she spoke about Nathan. Rachel knew that Rylee had had a crush on him. Rylee had talked to Rachel about it a bit. But Rachel didn't know why it had changed. All Rachel knew was that Nathan had lost interest in her about the time he had started coming on to Rachel. Rylee assumed Rachel had figured it out, and that Nathan had rejected her.

✳

Lillie plunged the needle into Nathan's IV tube and watched his vital signs while Amos washed up. Matt had been in the hospital with Nathan when Lillie arrived, but he had not been authorized to take action on his own. Now Matt was helping Terry with his surgical gown and gathering supplies.

"His heart's overstressed. We're trying to stabilize him," Terry said, looking at Amos as he walked into the hospital room. He was going to say, 'we're losing him', but changed his mind when he saw that Jason and Brittany had followed Amos into the hospital.

"Tell us what's going on," Jason grumbled. "Don't gloss it over."

Terry took a deep breath before continuing.

"Cardiac arrest. If we can't get control of it, we'll lose him."

"You're experienced doctors," Jason said sneering, looking at Amos. "You have state-of-the-art medical equipment." These were words Amos had thrown at Jason in anger, in the past, and Terry knew Jason's bruised ego was speaking. Brittany started to cry as Jason continued getting worked up. "If you let him die, we'll all know you're a fraud."

"Get out, Jason," Amos said, as he dried his hands. It looked to Terry as though Amos was barely controlling his temper. "You're not helping. Get out and let us try to save your son's life."

Jason stared at Amos contemptuously for another few moments, then spun on his heels, pushed Brittany out of his way, and left. Brittany recovered her balance and looked pleadingly at Lillie.

Terry spared a moment to glance at Brittany, who appeared to be in agony, likely needing someone to offer her sympathy and understanding. But all of them—he, Amos, Lillie and Matt—had their hands full, and could spare her no more time.

Brittany bowed her head, turned, and slowly walked out.

☢

Jason had been spending a lot of time in the exercise room and the study lately. He would have spent more time in the community center, but everyone else congregated there, and he didn't want anything to do with any of them. His being in the bedroom with Brittany when the alarm went off had been a fluke. He had gone to tell Brittany that he wanted a permanent separation—a divorce—but hadn't gotten the words out.

"I should never have agreed to come here," he had told her. She had just stared at him with sad eyes, not speaking. "Nathan and I could have gone on to Garden City . . . or beyond. We could have found somewhere else that was safe."

Brittany had always been reluctant to confront him—afraid of his temper. Apparently, no longer. Jason was a bit surprised by his wife's response. He assumed that, since Brittany had started making friends here in the Preserve, she didn't need him as much..

"You don't remember those days before we left, do you?" she

had said. Jason had been introspective while she was speaking, but when Brittany had challenged his memory of the crisis they had gone through a few months earlier, he had bristled. "You were as scared as I was, Jason. As mean as you were to Amos and the others, they were still willing to let us come with them. So, what do you want to do now? Go back to Las Vegas, to the bimbos you paid to stroke your ego?"

Jason's eyes had gone wide at her mention of Las Vegas, but he remained silent.

"Hah," she had snorted, "you didn't know that I knew, did you? You can't hide those kinds of things from a wife who does your laundry. I could see the lipstick and smell the perfume on your clothes. I don't know why I stayed with you these last three years; I guess I was weak and scared. Not anymore. If you can't make peace with our current circumstances, take your things and get out of my room—out of my life."

Jason had been found out. He hadn't bothered to deny her accusation—it had been true. Instead, he had faked humility and accepted Brittany's chastisement, "You're right, Brittany," he had said. "I keep forgetting how kind they've been to us. You and Sydney seem to be fitting in nicely. I just need to try harder."

He had loved Brittany once. He had just outgrown her—moved on while she'd been satisfied being a mother, stuck at home, raising snot-nosed kids. Just like she was satisfied now living in this hole in the ground, washing toilets and pulling weeds in the gardens. Not him. His career had shown him his true potential, and his trip to Las Vegas had shown him that he could still attract women.

He had already decided he was going to leave the Preserve, but he wasn't going to let Brittany know; she would just tell Lillie. For now, he would move his things out of Brittany's room and wait for his opportunity to leave.

He also hadn't decided where he would go. Should he go back to Logan and try to get his old job back, if it hadn't been given to someone else by now? Could he pick up where he'd left off or would he have to go somewhere else and start over? Amos wanted him to think there'd been a world war. Hah! He would prove that that was a bunch of bunk.

He still had a set of keys to the van. He'd given one set back to Amos after they'd arrived, but had lied about not having a second set. The gas in the engine may not be any good after all these months, but he was willing to give it a try. He still had to find a way to get through the outer doors. Whatever happened to Nathan in the next few days or weeks would settle it. If Nathan died, he would find a way to get out of here.

Those were the thoughts Jason was ruminating on when the hospital alarm had gone off and all of Jason's professed humility had gone out the window.

Now, as Jason left the hospital, he charged through the community center with his head down, not acknowledging anyone, and disappeared into the bedroom tunnel.

Brittany appeared in the community center next, a tissue up to her tear-streaked face.

☢

"Mom?" Sydney called, starting to stand. Brittany just shook her head and hurried through the room toward the bedroom tunnel. Sydney looked at the others sitting at the table, her eyes beginning to tear up. "Why would Mom not want me to be with me?" she asked, not expecting an answer, and not getting one.

Rachel started to stand.

"Don't go to the hospital," Chris said, placing a hand on her forearm. "Your parents will be busy for a while, and they'll let us know what's going on when they can."

Rachel sighed and sat back down. Sydney sat down too, slowly.

None of them was interested in continuing their game and nothing was resolved before they turned in for the night.

9

Your clothes don't look worn out

The Preserve, 24 March

"Where are my parents?" Rachel asked. She and Becca were eating a small breakfast of orange juice and granola.

"They're in the hospital," Becca replied before stuffing a huge bite of cereal into her mouth.

"Are they coming to breakfast?"

"I think they had a quick breakfast a while ago then went to the hospital. That's all I can say."

That afternoon, Amos sent word through Becca for everyone to gather in the community center at 3:00 pm, with a separate message to Jason, in the Library, and Brittany, in her room, to meet with him in the hospital at 2:30.

When Brittany showed up, Amos asked her to sit while they waited for Jason, who showed up five minutes late, a scowl on his face.

"I'm very sorry," Amos said, his face not doing a very good job of displaying real remorse. "Nathan died of heart failure. I'm sure you're not surprised, but we did everything we could for him. We couldn't stop the infection from spreading."

Jason sat stoically, offering nothing. Brittany, in tears, screamed at her husband.

"Show some kind of emotion, Jason," she said, her voice an octave higher than usual. "Are you so indifferent to Nathan's death that you have nothing to say?"

"I've said my peace," Jason said without looking at her, a snarl coming to his lips. "I have nothing else to say. It's obvious Amos killed Nathan to keep him away from Rachel and Chris. My whole life is ruined because of Amos and his harebrained scheme. I've wasted months of my life hiding underground. What else do you want me to say?"

Brittany stared at her husband, her tears forgotten. She didn't recognize this man. She couldn't believe she had lived with him for over twenty years without seeing this side of him. Brittany realized she would have to take control of the situation, since Jason had absolved himself of any responsibility for his actions or the actions of his sons.

"What happens next?" she asked Amos.

"We have no place to bury him," Amos said, with a quick glance at Jason. There was no reaction from him. "And we have no way to preserve his body until we can go outside. We have a freezer that's big enough, but it's full of food—we can't risk contaminating our food supply."

"So, you want to cremate his body." Brittany said, thinking that was the only other option. Jason got up and walked out without hearing Amos's response.

"We want to tell everyone what's going on," Amos said, nodding his head. "We've called a meeting for—" Amos looked at his watch. "—twenty minutes from now. Would you like to tell them? If you want me to handle it, I promise I'll be discrete."

Brittany had trouble controlling her emotions. She'd lost both sons and was losing her husband. She appreciated Amos's strength and stability, especially for Sydney's sake.

"Would you please handle it for me?" Brittany asked.

Amos nodded.

Everyone except Jason gathered in the community center. Amos sat in the front. Becca sat next to Brittany, holding her hand.

Once everyone had settled into their seats, Amos stood. "I've asked you to gather," Amos began, "to give you an update. You all know that Nathan was injured two weeks ago. Terry and I, with th4e help of Matt and Lillie, operated immediately, then continued monitoring his condition around the clock and adjusting his treatment whenever it was called for. We did everything our combined years of experience told us needed to be done for him. Unfortunately, it wasn't enough. His body could not defeat an infection that arose as a result of the injury." Amos intentionally lied, to hide the fact that the knife had been poisoned. "The alarm you heard yesterday was our warning that his heart was failing. We worked all night in an effort to stabilize him. It didn't work. Nathan passed away two hours ago."

There were several gasps, and a couple of sighs around the room as the news sank in.

"We'll try to answer your questions and will appreciate you respecting Brittany's and Jason's privacy by not asking them about it. Any questions?"

Rylee and Sydney, sitting in chairs, side by side, started whispering. Amos noticed and asked, "Sydney, Rylee, do you have a question?"

"Umm . . .," Rylee stammered, "Nathan's dad said that Nathan got knifed. Is it true?"

Amos decided there was just enough untruth in her question that he could deny it without lying.

"No, Rylee, Nathan *did* suffer from a knife wound, but he did not get knifed. Any other questions?"

"What's the difference?" Rylee asked.

"One is intentional, the other is unintentional."

Sydney raised her hand and waited for Amos to acknowledge her. "Yes Sydney?" Amos asked.

"Excuse me, Mr. Blund," Sydney said, "but it seems like you're not telling us everything. Are you?"

Amos smiled at Sydney's bluntness. He noticed Chris and Rachel look briefly at each other.

"Sydney," Amos said, "I'm withholding some information. It's to protect the feelings of several people. We would appreciate it if everybody would refrain from speculating on the 'who' or the 'why'. Is that acceptable?" The one thing he didn't need was people taking sides and causing more trouble. Sydney reluctantly nodded her head, and others did as well. Amos was sure everyone would know the whole truth eventually. There was no way this would remain a secret forever.

"Anything else? Amos asked.

"What are you going to do with Nathan?" Katie asked, "I mean, with Nathan's body?"

"After presenting options to Nathan's parents, Brittany has agreed to have Nathan's body cremated," Amos said.

"Why?" Katie asked.

"Well, Katie, we're in a closed, controlled environment. Do you understand what that means?"

"We're in the Starship Enterprise, right?" Katie replied, with a look at Chris, who had compared the Preserve to a starship in outer space when they'd had a conversation about life support systems months ago. "I know we can't go outside, and we can't bring anything from outside into the house." Several in the group had started calling the Preserve, 'home' or 'the house'. Amos was not surprised by Katie's use of the word.

"That's right, Katie," Amos said. "It also means that if a disease were introduced into the environment—the house—we could all become contaminated. Does that give you an idea why we want to cremate Nathan's body?"

"If we went outside to bury Nathan—Nathan's body," Katie said with a nod, "we could bring some contamination into the house and make us all sick."

Amos smiled broadly, turning to Becca Stephens, Katie's mom. "She's brilliant," he said.

As they rearranged the couches and chairs into their normal positions, Becca whispered into Lillie's ear, "Have you seen my keys?"

Lillie was immediately alarmed. "Where was the last place you remember having them?"

"I just noticed they were missing. I know I had them when I was fixing dinner because I have to use them to open the big freezer. After that—" Becca shrugged.

"Before we ask the others, I'll help you look for them." Becca would have to adjust her meal menus until her keys were found, but Lillie knew the real concern would be the key to the outside doors, which each of the board members had on their keyring. Becca had been asked not to wear her keys in plain sight, but she used them so often in her meal preparation, that it was difficult to be strict about it with her.

Lillie told Amos about the missing keys as they prepared for bed. Everyone else had gone off to their bedrooms.

"Jason stole them," Amos said accusingly. "Why didn't you tell me as soon as you knew?"

"Becca and I looked for them for a while after the meeting, then I needed to talk to Rachel about her medication, then I needed to console a very emotional Brittany. It just slipped my mind."

Amos started to put his shirt back on. "I'm going to get Terry to change the passcodes."

Lillie grabbed his hand to stop him. "No, you're not. Terry didn't get any sleep last night. He was up with Nathan the whole night."

Amos tried to pull away, but Lillie put both arms around his waist, holding him back. "I heard him tell Becca he was going right to bed after the meeting. Let him sleep. I'm sure Becca just misplaced them. I'll help her look for them some more in the morning. They'll show up."

"Then I'll get Michael to change them." He thought maybe he should do it himself, but he wasn't as familiar with the locks as Terry or Mike. He and Lillie hadn't gotten much sleep either, and he was emotionally drained after dealing with Jason and Brittany.

"Amos, it's the middle of the night. Everyone's gone to bed. Nothing's going to happen tonight." Lillie finally succeeded in getting Amos to remove his shirt. She wrapped her arms around him and started kissing his neck. He chuckled. He couldn't resist her. The problem with the passcodes would have to wait until morning. He was sure Lillie was right. They would show up in the morning, but the problem nagged at him all night.

❁

Jason had made a bed on the couch in the common area between the three bedrooms in his bedroom cluster. With the lights out, he pretended to sleep, as Amos and Lillie passed by, usually the last to go to bed. Using what little light the nightlights gave, he pushed off his bedding and stood, fully dressed. He quietly opened the door to Nathan's room where he had stowed a backpack, filled with all the things he thought he would need to survive for a few days on the outside, at least until he got to civilization. He carried his shoes and coat, so he wouldn't make any noise as he passed through the dimly lit tunnels of the Preserve.

Jason smiled to himself when he thought of how proud Amos was that the doors didn't squeak. That just worked in his favor.

He had been surprised when he'd seen a set of keys on the kitchen counter after dinner, while he was taking his dishes to the sink. He suspected that they were Becca's and that she had only set them down for a minute, while she did something—maybe whip up a topping for her pies. He had been quick to recognize his opportunity, quickly slid them into his pocket while no one was looking, and slipped out of the kitchen.

Now, practically tiptoeing through the preserve, he got all the way to the airlock without encountering anyone. He didn't expect anybody to still be up, but who knew with these people? He put on his shoes, then tried several keys on Becca's keyring until he found the one that worked in the control panel. He punched in the passcode that Mike had used last summer, which he'd memorized, and hit enter. One of the doors swished quietly inward and the lights came on in the airlock.

Jason didn't know if he had to enter the code again, but he tried just pressing the enter button again from the other side. The door swished closed. *Excellent,* he thought. That would give him a little more time before they figured out where he'd gone.

He took the key off the ring and stuffed it in his pocket. Although he couldn't imagine it at the moment, there might come a time when he would want to get back in. Then he threw the keyring, with the rest of Becca's keys, into a corner of the airlock.

He looked briefly at the lockers against the wall, where Amos had said there were hazmat suits to protect the wearer against contaminated environments. He wondered if they would ever be worn. He remembered Amos saying that people could live for years after being exposed to radiation. It made sense, based on what he knew about the *downwinders* in Southern Utah in the 50s and 60s.

"So now I'm listening to Amos, all of a sudden?" he thought aloud, then chuckled uncharacteristically. He didn't believe there had been a war or that the outside was contaminated, but he didn't know how to put one on anyway.

The second set of doors opened just as easily. He looked around but couldn't find a light switch in the tunnel. There were switches on the walls inside the Preserve, and that seemed the most likely place to find them. But they weren't there, so he gave up after a few minutes of searching and left the airlock door open. A light came on in the elevator when the door opened. Jason rode the elevator up to the garage, and, unable to find a light switch in the garage, and couldn't see the van in the cavern of the garage, waited a few moments to let his eyes adjust to the darkness. With only the elevator light backlighting him, he couldn't see the van in the cavern of the garage; but he was certain it was there.

He had to make a quick decision, because he didn't know when someone would notice that he was gone. Even if he found the van, and the gas was still good, he had no idea how to open the garage doors. He could either waste his time looking or leave by way of the secondary exit that they had used last summer when they'd gone out to see the valley. He chose the latter. He rode the elevator back down and followed the dark tunnel, keeping his hand on the wall until he arrived at the exit.

Jason paused before entering the passcode, trying to convince himself that this was really what he wanted. It was. He couldn't stand another day in this hole with these . . .people. Even in the dark tunnel, he was able to enter the passcode by feel—he only got it wrong twice—and had the door open in five minutes.

As the door swung in toward him, a cold blast of air hit him, taking his breath away. He was glad he'd thought to bring a heavy coat. But as he stared out the door, he again wondered if this was the right thing to do. The snow that had piled up against the door, almost two feet deep, broke off and fell into the tunnel. All he could see outside, in the dark of night, was snow and the shadows of snow-covered trees. The sky was totally overcast—no moon and no stars. He stepped out and touched various places on the rock wall to the right side of the door until the door started to close. He only knew to do that because he'd questioned Mike last summer when he'd pressed a certain place on the rock wall to close the door. It was a covered pressure pad, which signaled the door mechanism.

It suddenly occurred to him that maybe that's why he couldn't find light switches in the tunnels. They must have used pressure pads instead of light switches.

Now what? Jason looked around, seeing only darkness. His options were to make a long hike up and over the mountain to Garden City or take an even longer hike downhill to Logan. He knew there were small communities, campgrounds and a river toward Logan. But as he thought about it, he realized Logan was a lot farther away than Garden City; and even with the roads plowed, it would be a long walk to Logan unless he could hitch a ride. He had to get to the road first, then he could decide.

It turned out to be a lot harder to get to the road than he'd expected. Jason knew he was in the clearing above the Preserve and that the dirt road out of the valley was to his right, past the cliff. It wasn't snowing, but the air was filled with small ice crystals that slowly settled on his nose, cheeks shoulders, and hands. He would have expected, this late in the year, that the sun would have come out and melted the top layer of snow to form a crust. But it was soft, as if it had just fallen.

There were no trees in the clearing, so the wind had blown the snow into drifts that he had to plow through to get to the road. The surface of the snow was dark, without shadows to warn him before he stumbled into buried bushes and fallen logs. By the time he got to the paved road, which was only a little over a half mile away, according to Amos—a half mile as the crow flies—snow clung to his coat, soaked through his jeans, and filled his shoes. He was wet, freezing and out of breath from exertion

Jason thought he had finally reached the road when the ground leveled out and seemed more solid. He confirmed it by kicking at the snow until he could see asphalt. He stood on the edge of the road, bent over with his hands on his knees, trying to catch his breath. He looked first right—uphill—then left, weighing his options again. The road should have been plowed but it was covered in deep snow. There were no tracks in the snow either, as far as he could tell in the dim light. *New snowfall,* Jason thought, anger simmering inside.

He'd been thinking about all the stories Amos had told—about a bomb at Hill Air Force Base and an earthquake on the Wasatch Front, as a result of the war. He still believed that Amos had made it all up, but looking around he could tell that something wasn't right. On the slim chance that some of what Amos had said was true, his best option for finding civilization would be going to Garden City. Uphill, then. He turned right and plowed ahead with determination through knee-deep snow.

Garden City, 25 March

It took Jason close to three hours to reach the overlook above Garden City, without a moon or stars to light the way. It was so dark that he couldn't see the edge of the roadway in some places, and it was made worse by the deep snow. Twice he stepped off the road and rolled down the embankment until he could stop himself.

In the parking lot at the overlook visitors' center, he looked down at the Bear Lake Valley. The light from campfires reflected off the ice-encrusted water, outlining the edges of the lake for as far as he could see. Other campfires appeared to be in open fields, surrounded by tents. There didn't appear to be any electric lighting in the valley. There must have been thousands of people down there, possibly tens of thousands. Had he stumbled into a mountain man rendezvous? Or, were these really exiles from an explosion and earthquake on the Wasatch Front? Certainly, this was unnatural. People didn't camp at this time of year at this elevation. How hard was it going to be to find food with all these people crammed into the valley?

With a final look behind him, he started down the hill toward Garden City. There was no sense going back now. By the time he reached the edge of town, the dark night had given way to a gray diffused light. Shabbily dressed people were starting to stir in the camps he saw, in fields and other open spaces, many of which he hadn't noticed from the overlook.

He hadn't anticipated this. He didn't know what he would say or how he would be received. He would try to blend in, but his nice-looking clothes might lead to some difficult questions and envious looks.

"Where've you been all winter?" a young man asked casually from where he sat at an outdoor table in front of the *Quick and*

Tasty, near the corner of Highway 89 and Bear Lake Boulevard. "Your clothes look like they've hardly been worn."

"The sign says they sell raspberry shakes here," Jason said, ignoring the question. He didn't know how to answer it anyway, without inviting more questions. "Do they?"

"Ha! You're hungry? Get in line for work," he said, laughing along with the young man sitting next to him. "But I doubt they'll pay you in raspberry shakes."

The two young men looked about the age of his son, Nathan, and he thought they should have a little more respect for an adult. Maybe this was how teenagers acted when there were no authority figures nearby. He realized he hadn't spent enough time around his own sons to know what to expect.

"You got a name?" Jason asked seriously.

"Isaac," the young man replied nervously. He and his friend stopped laughing.

Not the reaction he was hoping for. He'd have to be more careful if he didn't want to stand out. Maybe he'd have to be nice to these cretins.

"Sorry. That didn't come out right. Maybe you could help me. Where would I go if I wanted to earn a meal?"

The young men visibly relaxed.

"They're assigning work and issuing food vouchers at the convention center," Isaac said.

"Thanks. Isaac, is it?" Isaac nodded. "And what's your name?" he asked the other young man.

"Zach."

"Okay, Isaac and Zach," he said, looking around for a sign that said "convention center" and trying to smile. "Where would I find the convention center?"

"It's back the way you came," Isaac said. "Second street on the right. There's a big sign in the parking lot out front. You can't miss it."

Jason looked back the way he'd come and could see the sign. It was huge, but he *had* missed it. Was Isaac making fun of him?

Now he could see that a few people, mostly men, were walking in that direction. As he was about to follow, Isaac spoke again.

"Have you been in the mountains all winter?" he asked.

"What'd you eat?" Zack asked at almost the same time.

Jason studied them again, wondering how much he should say. He realized he should have been prepared with a story.

"Oh, some food I took with me when I left Logan," he replied. "Supplemented it with roots, berries, and such." He had food in his backpack that he'd taken from the pantry in the Preserve, but he didn't want to use it up if it wasn't necessary. He didn't know how much food he'd be able to get, and he didn't want to have to share it.

The boys looked skeptical.

"You had enough food to last the winter?" Zach asked. "You don't look like you've been starving."

"Your clothes don't look worn out, either," Isaac said, "like they would if you'd been wearing 'em all winter."

Jason realized the boys looked like they *were* hungry and *had* worn the same clothes all winter. He began to feel his nerves tighten. He hadn't thought this through carefully. If he had at least assumed that Amos could have been correct, he might have planned better—or at least waited a couple more months until the snow was gone. This world he'd stepped into was a little worse off than he had imagined, and it was beginning to look dangerous.

"I have a couple of changes of clothes in the pack," he said, "and I've lost some weight." He hoped that would satisfy them and was pleased when they changed the subject.

"What's *your* name?" Isaac asked.

"Jason," he said without thinking, then could have kicked himself for giving them his real name.

"Well, Jason," Isaac said, "ask for my dad at the center and tell him I sent you. Maybe he'll give you a choice of work. His name's Justin."

"Thanks for the information, Isaac. I'll do that."

"I'm looking for Justin," Jason told a man sitting at a desk at the side of the large room. The man was the only person sitting at a desk who didn't have a line of people waiting to talk to him.

The man looked up from his papers and eyed Jason.

"You're new here," he said, studying Jason's clothes and frowning.

"Well, yes, I am. Are you Justin?"

"That's him in the plaid shirt, over there," the man said, pointing. He looked down at his papers again and Jason turned away. Then the man spoke again.

"Where'd you come from? Nobody around here has clothes that look that nice after living in them all winter."

Jason knew he had to answer the man, or he might get into trouble. What kind of trouble? He didn't really know. He said the only thing he could think of, building on the story he'd told Isaac and Zach. "My worn clothes are in the pack. I wore my good ones to come into town." He smiled, hoping it would make him look more believable.

"Hmmph," the man said and looked down at his papers again.

Jason looked at the line in front of Justin, which had grown steadily longer. There were now about twenty people ahead of him, but he'd better get in line and wait his turn.

The line moved quickly, and by the time he'd worked his way

up to second in line, he'd figured out the process. Justin was looking down at what looked like a list of day-jobs and only looked up to glance at the next person in line before giving him or her the next job on the list, then checking it off.

The scrawny old man in line ahead of him must have been the exception. When he got to the front of the line, Justin had his finger on the next day-job, but when he saw the old guy, who probably couldn't lift more than ten pounds at a time, Justin ran his finger down the list before stopping at one.

"You'll sweep the mayor's offices," he told the old man.

"I did that yesterday, Justin."

"Well, it needs it again, George, and I don't have too many jobs on the list that you can handle."

"Oh, alright. Thanks. I'll be back later to get my voucher."

"You do that, George." He looked down at his list again as Jason moved forward.

"Isaac said to tell you he sent me," Jason said.

Justin looked up sharply and studied Jason.

"How do you know Isaac? I haven't seen you around here before."

"I just got into town and Isaac was feeling sorry for me, I guess."

"Where'd you come from and how'd you get here?" Justin asked suspiciously.

"Sorry, Justin. My clothes seem to be drawing a lot of attention. My worn clothes are in the pack. I'm from Logan, but I've been in the mountains all winter." He was making this up as he went, trying to say enough to get what he wanted, without having to defend himself too much. His answer and his soft presentation seemed to have disarmed Justin a little.

"What's your name?"

"Jason Brown," he lied, not wanting to give up his real name.

"So, Jason, Isaac sent you?"

"Yeah. Nice boy. So's his friend Zach." Didn't hurt to drop another name. Made him sound more friendly.

"I suppose he wanted me to give you a choice of jobs, right?"

"He did say that, but I'll take anything you have. Strong back, you know?" he said, laughing.

"Hey, hurry it up, up there," someone said from back in the line.

"Take it easy, Dennis," Justin said, looking back along the line. "Plenty of work to go around, and I'm sure you're in no hurry to get started."

A couple of people in line chuckled nervously.

"Okay Jason," Justin said as he wrote a couple of words on a scrap of paper and handed it to Jason. "Take this up to the corner, across the street from the *Quick and Tasty*. You know where that is?"

"Uh, yeah."

"Okay. Give it to the guy with the orange vest. He'll show you where to go and tell you what you need to do."

"Great, thanks," he said, remembering that the old guy in front of him had thanked Justin.

Jason spent the remainder of the gray day with a crew of seven other men, chopping, splitting and stacking firewood on a snowy, wooded hillside half a mile up the road. They were given warm vegetable soup, bread and water halfway through their short workday, then given a voucher for dinner before walking back to town.

He was so worn out by the time he got back to the convention center, that he didn't think he could eat; but his stomach growled when he smelled food asnd he had no trouble downing the warm meal and Dutch oven raspberry cobbler. There was little talk, either during the workday or during dinner. So, as the other workers went their separate ways, he realized he hadn't thought about where he would spend the night, and hadn't asked anyone for suggestions. He found himself on the corner by the *Quick and Tasty*, looking down the road in three directions, trying to decide what to do, when a familiar voice spoke behind him.

"Where ya goin'?" Isaac asked.

"I don't know," Jason said, turning to look at the two young men. "I need to find a place to sleep. Do you have a suggestion?"

"Well, you probably don't want to sleep in the open. Too cold. There's a barn down the road where a bunch of old men cuddle up to each other to keep warm."

Zach laughed mischievously at Isaac's comment.

"But I suspect you wouldn't like that. You don't appear to be that type. I suggest you ask Zach's mom if you can sleep in one of her cars. The seats aren't really comfortable, but it keeps the wind off ya and it looks like you have a warm coat. What do you think, Zach?"

"Yeah. I already talked to her. We knew you'd need a place to sleep. Follow us if you're interested."

10

What do you want to tell them

The Preserve, 25 March

Jason's disappearance wasn't noticed until mid-morning when he didn't show up for breakfast. That, by itself, wasn't so unusual. But when he failed to show up for his morning work assignment, which was *not* normal, people began to wonder. As much as he complained about the chores in the Preserve not utilizing his management skills, he could usually be counted on to fill his assignments. Lillie had told Amos that she was careful not to assign him anything that the other adults didn't do routinely.

"Terry," Amos said, when Lillie told him she hadn't seen Jason, "check the monitors and the video recordings to see if you can locate Jason. Mike, come with me."

"Where're we going?" Mike asked, as he followed his dad to the lab.

"The airlock," Amos said as he led Mike back through the community center. "After I get a Geiger Counter."

The When they arrived at the airlock doors, they were closed, but unlocked, and the second set of doors stood open. Amos turned on the Geiger Counter, which started clicking.

"There's a slight increase in the radiation level, but it's not dangerous," Amos said.

☢

"Amos," Terry's voice said in Amos's ear. "Can you hear me?"

"What is it, Terry?" Amos replied.

"Jason left shortly after midnight. I've got video of him leaving his common room, fully dressed with a backpack and heavy coat, then passing through the community center and airlock. He didn't find the pressure pads, so I can only see his feet as he passed the night lights. Looks like he headed for the secondary door."

"Thanks, Terry. That's where I am now."

"What are you going to do?"

"I'm going to go out and look around. I'll keep talking so you and Mike can keep track of me."

Mike began putting on a hazmat suit.

"What are you doing?" Amos asked. "There's no reason for two of us to risk exposure."

"Well," Mike replied, "if you run into trouble, I don't want to take time to suit up before coming for you." He attached a radiation dosimeter to a Velcro patch on the outside of the suit and turned on his helmet mic.

"Fine," Amos said.

"Terry, Mike's suited up too, but is going to stay here. He'll come out for me if necessary. I'll keep both of you posted. Leaving now."

He handed the Geiger Counter to Mike and put on his own suit and dosimeter, then picked up a flashlight from a shelf and stuffed it in an outside pocket of the hazmat suit.

Amos and Mike entered the outer tunnel and walked to the outside secondary door. Amos touched the pressure pads that turned on each section of lights as he passed.

"The radiation level's higher here than in the airlock," Mike said into his helmet mic, "but still not enough to cause alarm."

"It means this tunnel has been exposed to the outside," Amos said, taking the Geiger Counter from Mike. "Why don't you stay back by the airlock while I do this?"

"Okay," Mike said reluctantly, "but talk to me constantly about your readings and what you see."

A few seconds later, Amos spoke again, for Terry's benefit. "Okay, there's a puddle of water inside the outer door, probably melted snow from when the door was opened. The door's unlocked. The radiation level is higher here, but still not a problem. I'm opening the outer door."

"I can hear the Geiger Counter clicking," Mike said.

"Yes, the reading's higher outside. It just passed the low threshold and is still rising."

"Do you need to come back in? What do you see?" Amos could tell Mike was torn between his concern for his dad's safety and wanting to know what was going on outside.

"I'm fine for a minute. I'll take a quick look around and come back in. I can see his tracks. Looks like he stumbled once on the way to the trail."

The Geiger Counter started to chatter. "Dad, get back in here."

"Here I come."

The noise from the Geiger Counter dropped off as quickly as it had risen. "I'm inside now. The radiation level has dropped, but it's higher than it was before. Opening the door allowed radiation to enter. Terry, based on these readings and the time Jason left, can you estimate the actual radiation level outside?"

"I can approximate it," Terry said. "Get cleaned up and bring me the Geiger Counter."

Before Amos entered the airlock, they discussed the reading on Mike's dosimeter and decided he could remove his suit and reenter the Preserve without a shower. After Mike left, Amos entered the airlock and locked the door. He turned on the cleansing ventilation and disinfected the hazmat suit and Geiger Counter in the corner shower.

"I found Becca's keyring," he said into his mike. Once he was satisfied that the radiation level in the airlock was in the safe zone, he removed the suit and entered the Preserve.

Mike was waiting, along with Terry and Lillie. They all started talking at once.

"What was it like?" Mike asked.

"Are you okay?" Lillie asked.

"Any sign of Jason?" Mike asked.

"Wait!" Terry said loudly to be heard over the others. That got their attention. "Give me your dosimeter, Amos, so I can record your exposure." As medical professionals, they knew the long-term effects of radiation exposure, so they kept a log.

"Here's the Geiger Counter, too," Amos said, "Terry, I want Mike to go with you to see how you calculate the radiation level."

"Is that important?" Mike asked.

"This is the first time since our outside sensors malfunctioned that we've taken a reading of the elevated radiation outside. I'd like to know how the sensors performed before they malfunctioned. We need to know if they captured the highest radiation level. But I'd also like *you* to know how to run these calculations, in case you need to know in the future."

"I hope you and Terry will be around to do the calculations, if we ever need to do them again." Mike said, then added, "I'm going," when his dad gave him a stern look.

"I'm fine," Amos told Lillie. "No sign of Jason. I think everyone may want to know what it's like outside. Maybe we should call everyone together."

"I think the board needs to talk about it first," Terry said over his shoulder as he walked away. "No need to get everyone thinking about what's going on outside. They'll all want to see for themselves."

"We need to tell them about Jason," Amos said. "But let's have a board meeting first."

☢

"I followed Jason's tracks for about fifteen feet until I saw where he tripped over something buried in the snow," Amos told the board members. "The snow was at least two feet deep and it was difficult to distinguish distances because of the lack of light. The sky is totally overcast with dark clouds. It looked like there were snow drifts, but again, it was difficult to tell without shadows to add perspective."

"What did the valley look like?" Emily asked, likely more concerned about the trees than about Jason.

"The trees look burned, Emily. Not burned to the ground, but the bark was darkened, the branches thinned, maybe burned off. There's snow on the branches. With the exception of Jason's tracks, I couldn't see any signs of life, not even a rabbit track, but I wasn't out there very long."

"Are you going to tell the others that Jason escaped?" Terry asked. He had already told Amos that he thought it was a bad idea. He brought it up in front of the rest of the board to force Amos to discuss it with them.

"I agree with you Terry. We don't want them to know he found a way out."

"You'd also have to tell them that you've been outside," Terry added.

"Yeah, maybe they don't need to know what it's like out there. They might think that, because I'm not dead, it must not be a problem to let everyone go out, right?"

"Brittany, at least, deserves to know what he did." Lillie said

"Why don't you and I talk to Brittany privately. I don't think we should tell her that the board has been discussing this."

"Everyone is going to notice Jason is gone, you know," Mike said. "What do you plan to tell them?"

"Maybe we should talk to Brittany. See how she wants to handle it." Amos didn't really have any better plan.

The rest of the board was happy to let Amos and Lillie handle it.

After the board meeting, Lillie went to get Brittany. The others, except for Amos, left the room by another way, so they didn't encounter her. Once Amos, Lillie and Brittany were alone in the office, Amos asked how she was holding up.

"He's gone, isn't he?" Brittany asked. Amos must have given himself away with his expression, since she didn't wait for confirmation. "You've met with the other adults—with your board—haven't you? That's why I couldn't find anyone. Do you know how he got out?"

"Yes," Amos said with a sigh. "He's gone. He left on foot. It's dark out there—totally overcast with dark clouds—so I couldn't see much. But there was no sign of him except footprints."

"That stubborn, arrogant man," Brittany shook her head. "Where will he go?"

"I don't know. But I'm sure he knows Garden City is closer than Logan. And it's away from the explosion and earthquake, not toward it."

"He said he didn't believe there'd been a war. Would that change anything?"

"Maybe. I don't know, but Garden City is still the closest community."

"How far is Garden City?" Brittany asked

"About ten miles. What did he take?"

"The only things I can tell are missing are some clothes and all of our gold and silver."

"Becca said she could tell he'd been in the pantry," Lillie added, "so he took some food. Do you want to tell the others, Brittany, or should I?"

"I don't really want to be in the spotlight," Brittany replied.

"What do you want to tell them?" Lillie asked, looking at Amos. "That he was distraught with Nathan's death?"

"If we tell them he's gone, they'll know he found a way out of the Preserve," Amos said

"What do you want to tell them," Lillie asked. Her voice was becoming more heated and agitated. "Should we tell them that he committed suicide and we cremated his body?"

Amos was surprised by Lillie's sudden show of emotion.

"I . . . no . . . that's not what I meant." Amos said, trying to excuse himself.

"Amos, this isn't about trying to save face. We should admit that Jason outmaneuvered us and found a way out of the Preserve."

"Lillie, Amos, please don't fight over this. Jason could have been planning this ever since we arrived. It's not your fault." Brittany started to cry.

Lillie put an arm around her. "I'm sorry Brittany. What should we do?"

Brittany shook her head, as if to say she had no idea. Finally, she looked up at Amos.

"This is a problem for you, isn't it?" she asked.

Amos didn't know what to say. It *was* a problem, but he didn't want to fight with Lillie.

"I know you need to keep everyone content to be here," Brittany added. "As difficult as it is for me, you should do what you think will be best in the long run. If that means telling the others that Jason committed suicide, I'll go along with it."

"That isn't what I meant," Amos protested.

"It's okay, Amos. You told us that day in your living room that if anyone were to leave, you wouldn't let them back in because of the contamination they might bring with them. Jason is dead to us now. He won't be able to come back."

"Brittany—" Amos started, then realized that he had nothing to say that would ease her pain. She was right. There was no way he would let Jason back in, even if he brought an army with him.

Lillie gave Amos a dirty look, then led Brittany out.

☢

Lillie returned to the office to find Amos in conversation with Terry. The conversation stopped abruptly and Terry excused himself. "Later Amos. Hi Lillie," he said as he passed her on his way out.

Lillie sat next to Amos, a serious expression on her face.

"I'm sorry, honey. But Brittany's right. I can't let Jason back in. It wouldn't be fair to the others."

Lillie put her arms around Amos' neck and looked him in the eyes. "I know Amos. Brittany wants you to tell everyone that Jason's dead. You can tell any story you want and she'll go along with it. She feels bad for not talking Jason out of coming in the first place." She gave him a quick kiss to let him know it was alright. As she got up and started to leave, she said over her shoulder, "I've called a family meeting. You have fifteen minutes to decide what you're going to say." She smiled mischievously and was gone.

☢

Lillie and Brittany sat on the front row, with their backs to the rest of the group. Amos stood in front of them.

"Thank you all for coming," Amos said. He looked down at Lillie and received a reassuring smile from her.

"It seems like we just did this. I'm sorry for that. But we need to give you a follow-up on Brittany's family. You all know that Nathan passed away yesterday. His older brother, Aaron, died in the automobile accident last summer. Their father, Brittany's husband, Jason, had a difficult time with both deaths."

Amos noticed Mike standing at the back of the room, out of view of the others, making a get-on-with-it motion with his hand.

Amos almost smiled. So typical of Michael, he thought. But it wouldn't do to smile right now. He bowed his head a moment to give himself a chance to regain facial control. That would just look like his emotions were close to the surface.

"We discovered Jason this morning. He had taken something that made his heart stop. We couldn't revive him."

There was a sudden uproar.

"*Not Dad, too!*" Sydney screamed. She laid her face in her hands and started to cry. Rylee, sitting next to her, placed an arm over her shoulders and leaned her head against Sydney's.

Others wanted to know, when? Where? What did he take? Why are you just telling us now? Are you going to cremate him, too?

"Hold on," Amos said, holding both hands up in front of him in a placating manner. It took a minute for everyone to calm down. "As we've said before, too many times already, we want you to respect Brittany's privacy and not harass her about the when, where, what or why. On top of that, I'm not going to answer any more questions tonight."

"You haven't answered any yet," Chris complained. Becca gave her son a stern look. It stopped him but likely didn't satisfy him.

"I'm sorry Chris. There's a lot of tension in the house right now and we need it to settle down. In her own good time, Brittany will share with us what she wants us to know—or not. In the meantime, I want everyone's promise that they will let this go until Brittany feels comfortable talking about it. Okay?" Amos didn't need to get a commitment from the members of the board; they already knew what was going on and were in agreement. He looked at most of the others—the ones that seemed the most unsettled--until he got nods of agreement from each of them. Satisfied, he nodded and motioned toward Lillie.

"Now, Lillie has an announcement," he said.

"Another party?" Chris asked loudly, obviously excited with the idea. That got everyone talking.

"Next week is Becca's birthday," Lillie said after everyone had settled down again. "I want some creative ideas about what to do to celebrate—things that don't require Becca to cook them, like a game night. So, all of you put on your thinking caps and come up with some suggestions. Bring them to me or Emily. Thanks. Now, Becca said dinner will be at the usual time."

☢

"Who is it?" Brittany asked when there was a knock on her bedroom door. She'd been crying and knew she looked terrible. She swiped at her eyes and blew her nose.

"Lillie," Lillie said. "May I come in?"

"Sure. It's unlocked." Brittany looked around the room to see if she needed to straighten anything before letting Lillie in, and decided it didn't matter. Lillie would understand.

The door opened a foot and Lillie stuck her head in.

"Would you like some company?" Lillie asked, looking around the room.

"Oh, Lillie!" Brittany said, then put a tissue to her face and cried into it—quiet sobs that shook her entire body. Lillie took two steps toward Brittany, but didn't touch her.

When Brittany had regained her composure, she added. "What happened, Lillie? He used to be so loving and caring."

"I don't know, Brittany. Maybe life happened." Lillie stepped over to the bed where Brittany sat, with piles of clothes and mementos all around her. Lillie pushed one pile out of the way, sat next to Brittany, and placed an arm around her shoulders. Brittany turned toward Lillie, suddenly grateful for the attention and empathy. She laid her head on Lillie's shoulder and continued to cry. She'd been going through all of hers and Jason's things, trying to decide if she needed to get rid of anything. She'd gotten to a box of family photos and got no further. Now, she was a mess. She wanted to explain Jason's behavior, but wasn't sure she knew what was going on.

Finally, she sat up straight, pulled away from Lillie and wiped her eyes and nose again.

"Here's a picture of us just after we married," she said, picking up a photo from a stack on her other side. "Mount Rushmore became one of my favorite places because of this trip," The picture showed younger versions of Jason and Brittany, in twin t-shirts that read: Mt. Rushmore South Dakota. They stood looking into each other's eyes, with the carved mountain in the background.

"You look so in love," Lillie said.

"We were. He was so big and strong, so ambitious. He had almost finished school—a master's degree in Business Management. I was so proud of him.

"We went on a helicopter ride over Mt. Rushmore. It's the

only time I've been on one. He bought me jewelry to remember the occasion—said the whole trip was the honeymoon we didn't have time for because he couldn't miss classes. We had a candlelight dinner. He was so attentive—and I talked and talked, until it became obvious that I was acting like a nervous newlywed. We stayed in a fancy hotel. He was so tender and sweet.

"I wanted a family and thought he did, too. It wasn't until I was pregnant with Aaron that he told me he had wanted to wait. He'd been told by one of his professors that if he really wanted to get ahead, he'd have to be willing to relocate every couple of years until he got where he wanted to be. Even then, he'd need to be flexible and willing to take whatever was offered. He was so ambitious. It should have been a clue." She paused to think about what she was saying and what else she wanted to explain.

"When Nathan came along," she continued, "I thought he'd take an interest in the boys—teach them sports, take them camping or fishing, anything. But he never showed an interest in teaching them anything. I got them to a piano teacher and signed them up for soccer, but Jason never went to a recital or soccer game." She stopped again and wiped her eyes, then continued.

"We moved a couple of times early on, but when we got to Logan, I fell in love with the people and the rural feel in Cache Valley. He seemed fine staying in Logan, until he got an offer for a promotion if he'd move to Chicago. That's when we started to drift apart. He knew I didn't want to go, so he started looking for other ways to promote himself.

"He'd been on training trips to places like San Francisco and Orlando. Then, he began going to seminars and conventions every few months." She hesitated, thinking about his trip to Las Vegas and trying to decide whether to go on. "When he told me he was going to Las Vegas—that was three years ago—I offered to go with him, something I'd only done a couple of times before. It was a last resort to see if I could keep our marriage alive.

"He told me it would be boring, that he'd be in meetings all day and studying all night, but he'd lied to me. When he got home and I did the laundry, there was lipstick and perfume on his clothes.

"I considered divorcing him, but I had my hands full. Aaron had stopped attending school and Nathan had started going out with Aaron at night. I even spoke to an attorney, but that's as far as it got. I still loved him and couldn't imagine life without him.

"Stupid me!" Brittany said, then leaned into Lillie and cried some more. Lillie patted her on the back without speaking. They stayed that way for some time, until Brittany sat up straight again.

"I'm sorry, Lillie. You didn't need to hear all that," she said.

"I'm sorry, too, Brittany—sorry about the trouble you've had in your life." She smiled. "You can talk to me anytime you want, about anything you want. I'll keep your confidences."

"I know you will. Thank you for everything you've done for us—for Sydney and me. You're a good friend."

"Now," Lillie said with an enthusiastic smile, "are you ready to go play a game?"

"Huh? A game?"

"Yes. When I left the community center, the girls were just starting a game of Rummikub. Go wash your face and I'll tell them you're coming."

11

I came to see if you need anything

Garden City, 28 March

The snow had turned to slush from the constant foot traffic, freezing again during the night. With no electricity, horse-drawn wagons had become the second-most prevalent means of transportation, after walking. Farmers were preparing their fields for spring planting, using horses and old fashioned, rusty plows. Some of the raspberry fields were being plowed under to make room for other crops, like potatoes, corn and beans.

There was plenty of work for someone who wasn't sick. But almost everyone had some medical problem, from colds that wouldn't go away, to radiation burns and internal pains that were debilitating and kept them from doing anything useful. Jason didn't know anything about medicine, except what he'd learned in the Preserve. For that matter, he hated to admit, he hadn't known anything about gardening, food production or cooking until he'd lived in the Preserve.

He continued to work and got paid in food, which was good enough, until it wasn't. He had become a celebrity, of sorts, and he didn't like it. Almost everyone he came in contact with knew who he was and had heard bits of his story, even if they were third- or fourth-hand; and they were either curious for more detail, skeptical, or outright suspicious. He began avoiding contact or saying as little as possible, which only fueled the rumor mill. He noticed the looks and the talk behind his back, more and more.

After three days in Garden City, he'd had his fill of trying to please others and answer their questions. He realized he wasn't good with people, something Brittany had told him often enough, but he hadn't believed it until now. It was difficult for him to have a friendly conversation with strangers. He found himself wanting to respond with biting comments.

He was already missing the Preserve and that fact ate him up inside.

At breakfast, he helped himself to seconds, which was unheard of and which drew the wrath of the kitchen help, so he took his stolen food and left. He knew there was another town—Lake-town—at the south end of Bear Lake, so he left Garden City, with no plan, and not knowing what he would do.

The Preserve, 28 March

"What's going on in the twin world?" Lillie asked Amos as they sat on a couch in the community center after everyone else had gone to their rooms.

This had become a daily topic of conversation for them, Amos sharing his confusion about his role in the twin world and Lillie amused at his discomfort. When he'd told her about his conversation with Greg, she'd questioned why he needed to know about the terrorists and the bombings. He'd minimized the importance of the information, explaining that he was just curious, although an idea was starting to form in his head, that he could trade the information for help from the twin world.

"I've turned the research over to Mike," he explained, "so I can get other things done. I've asked him to keep notes on his findings, analysis and conclusions. I've also asked Terry to review Mike's conclusions and let me know if there's anything that I need to see."

"There's no way you can just turn this over to them and let it go," Lillie said.

"I'm going to try. It's driving me crazy, but I've got to focus on making the Observer function as a medical device."

"Okay," she said, playing with a button on his shirt. "Let's go to bed."

The Preserve, 29 March

Rachel asked Chris to walk her to her room and he agreed, although she felt as though he were hesitant.. They held hands as she led him down the tunnel to their bedroom wing. She felt like she was dragging him, like he didn't want to be there with her.

Their relationship had cooled since the episode with Nathan. She felt guilty, like the whole thing had been her fault. Chris would sit with her and hold her hand whenever they were together, but nothing more than that. He barely spoke to her. She could tell he was holding back, but couldn't tell why. She felt empty inside, going through the motions without living, and now she'd lost his affection and couldn't even talk about it with him.

Chris hesitated at her door; his expression unreadable. She wondered if his hesitation was an indication that he had quit caring about her. Maybe it was the bad memories this place held for both of them. Her mother had asked if she wanted to move to another room, but she had declined at the time. She hadn't wanted to upset the household by making everyone play musical bedrooms. Now, the way Chris behaved, she didn't know what she wanted.

She tugged on Chris' hand, smiling weakly, and drew him into her room. Chris looked around.

"No Rylee," he said. "Is she staying with Sydney tonight?" There was no excitement or anticipation in Chris's voice, like there had been in the past. Just curiosity.

Disappointed, Rachel nodded, not trusting herself to speak. She wanted him to kiss her, but she didn't want to have to ask. How could she encourage him—let him know that she still loved him—without being too forward?

Chris didn't know what Rachel wanted or needed. He had been intentionally holding back to let her get over the trauma of her experience with Nathan, at her own pace, like Lillie had suggested when she told him about the medication. He thought Rachel had invited him to her room to try to pick up where they'd left off—that would be a positive step—but she was acting unsure of herself, not giving him any leads. What should he do?

He had thought that asking about Rylee would have given her an opportunity to open up and talk about things, but she didn't answer him. He returned her smile, not sure if he succeeded in showing his interest, since he was so concerned for her emotional health.

Rachel leaned in to give Chris a quick kiss, then backed off and smiled, this one a little better than the last. That was better. They were still holding hands, so Chris squeezed her hands and leaned into her for another quick kiss.

When they broke apart, they stood inches from each other for several moments, looking at each other without moving. Chris didn't know what else to do.

"Good night, Rachel," he finally said. "Sleep well. See you to-morrow." He smiled again, dropped her hands and left, closing the door behind him. He thought he could hear her crying before the door closed all the way and it broke his heart.

The Preserve, 30 March

"Is Rachel alright?" Chris asked her mother.

Rachel didn't show up for breakfast or her work assignment the next morning.

"I don't know, Chris," Lillie said, "but I'll check on her in a little while."

When Rachel entered the dining room for lunch, Chris took her limp hand in his and asked how she was feeling. He thought she was about to say something, then her face crumpled, she shook her head, and left the room in a hurry with a hand over her mouth.

He considered going after her, but remembered he was going to give her some space and time. He turned back to his lunch, only to notice his mother looking at him with a frown.

Rachel didn't return.

☢

When Rachel didn't show up for dinner, Chris went to her room and knocked tentatively.

"Who is it?" Rachel asked without opening the door.

"It's me." No response. The bedrooms were well insulated, so maybe she had answered and he just didn't hear her. "Can I come in?"

"Okay," she said, less than enthusiastically.

Chris stuck his head around the door and smiled. She was sitting up in her bed, reading. He smiled, but suspected that his concern showed in his face. He was glad to see her and see that she wasn't currently crying because of him. He stepped into the bedroom and left the door open. She watched him without smiling or speaking.

"I came to see if you need anything . . . and to see if you're alright." She still didn't respond.

Chris took a step toward her, but she didn't move. *What does he want from me?* She was confused by his smile, which seemed genuine.

"Rachel, I'm sorry if I've done anything to offend you. Your mother said to give you time to recover and not to press myself on you."

What? What does that mean? Have I misjudged him? Was he really only thinking of me? She started to cry and covered her face.

"I'm sorry, Rachel. I didn't mean to upset you. I'll go if you want me to." Chris turned to leave.

"No! Wait!" she said, putting her book down and rising from her bed. She hurried over, barefoot, and threw her arms around him, crying into his chest. "Please don't go."

Chris placed his arms around her and rubbed her back while she continued to cry. Finally, she pulled away long enough to snag a tissue from the bedside table, wipe her eyes and blow her nose. She knew she must look terrible from her crying, but she didn't care. She threw the used tissue toward the garbage can, not caring if it made it or not, then looked into his eyes. He was smiling!

"Rachel, I love you," he said, "and I'm sorry if my actions haven't shown you that."

"Oh, Chris," she said, as she cried into his chest. "I love you, too."

"Do you want to know what happened that night?" she asked through her tears.

"If you want to tell me." Chris replied. Rachel imagined Chris had already heard the full story from others, but decided that if she told the story in her way, it might release some of the anxiety she was still feeling.

She looked down at the floor. He placed a hand under her chin and raised her gaze to meet his, then smiled. She tried to smile, but it was tentative.

She started slowly, beginning with her thinking it was Chris that had followed her into her room, then filled in the parts that Chris might not know.

"I'm sorry, babe," he said, "but now he's gone and it's over."

She hadn't told him about her embarrassing nightmares. She started to cry again, feeling like maybe it wasn't really over.

"What's wrong?" he asked. "Are these tears of relief?"

"No," she cried. "I've been having nightmares about it. They start out with you and end up with Nathan. Mom gave me some pills to help me sleep and the nightmares seem to have stopped; but I don't know for sure." It felt good to tell him.

"So, now that your mom has given you something to stop the nightmares," Chris said, as he brushed a loose lock of hair away from her face, "hopefully he won't bother you anymore."

"I'm still not sleeping well--I'm an emotional wreck--and I won't know if the nightmares are gone until I stop taking the pills," she complained.

"What can I do to help?" he asked.

"I'm going to stop taking the pills today. Will you stay close by?"

"Of course. We'll get through this, together."

She threw her arms around him and gave him a tight squeeze, which he returned.

The Outcasts—Utah, 1 April

Snow covered the ground in and around Laketown, at the south end of Bear Lake. The group had just arrived in the hills above the town having walked most of the way across the country..

"Look at all the people," Candy said, looking at Beth. The crowds of dirty, skinny poor people upset her each time she thought about them. The pregnancy had progressed so much that she walked with one hand under her large belly to help support the baby's weight. Just then the baby kicked. He or she had been active all morning, but this kick seemed to be a reaction to Candy's negative emotions.

There were groups of people with tents set up all along the lakefront, as far as they could see in both directions, between the lake and the hills that rimmed the valley. They were even set up in the yards of the homes in town and scattered across the hillside. The sky was dark and the air cold. If it seemed that the snow was melting here, perhaps it was the mass of humanity crammed into this little valley.

"There must be thousands of people," Candy said. She was looking at smoke rising on the far side of the valley, on the other side of the Lake.

"I'd guess tens of thousands," Bryce replied.

"I don't know if we should stay here," Beth said, shaking her head. "Maybe we should keep going or go back to one of the towns we passed through on the way here." She set down her pack on a rock and started getting out her maps.

"I don't think I can go any farther today," Candy complained.

"Why don't we get higher so we can see better," Ben suggested, pointing to the hill to the south. "Maybe that will help us decide."

"You think a different perspective will help?" Beth asked. Ben shrugged, then picked up Beth's backpack and helped her put it back on, resting his hand on her shoulder as he did.

They climbed the hill, avoiding most of the town. After passing a tent community, crowded with families of all sorts and sizes, they topped a rise where a lone man sat next to a crude lean-to shelter, made from tree limbs, under a large pine tree. He had a campfire nearby. He wore a warm coat with a blanket over his shoulders and back. He didn't seem to notice them.

"We need to avoid interacting with people," Beth said quietly, "but that might be impossible. Let's try that cluster of aspen trees over there," she said, pointing, "to avoid him." They moved to the east and stood at the base of the trees, on sloping ground.

"Nobody has discovered this spot?" Candy asked sarcastically. It was a marginal spot for camping because of the slope.

"Maybe our neighbor is grouchy," Bryce said, nodding toward the lone man.

"I say we should stay here, at least for the night, and see what we think in the morning," Beth said.

"I'm for that," Candy said, dropping her pack. Bryce laid out a blanket and helped her sit. That settled it.

"We'll discuss options in the morning," Beth said.

12

Six-and-a-half months earlier

Matamoros, Mexico, 12 September

"I'm glad we decided to change back into our old clothes before leaving Galveston," Pepper said as she stepped up onto the small dock and tied off the boat. Jared watched her as he wiped his face with a towel that was almost as wet as he was.

"I don't dare go any farther in the boat," he said. The wind had changed direction constantly in the rough weather, and several times they'd had to drop the sails when it felt like they were going to capsize. "We've used the engine so much that I'm surprised we haven't run out of gas by now."

"Where are we? Do you know?"

"We passed Brownsville, so we're definitely in Mexico. Other than that, I don't know. This is the first place that looked like it would have a dock."

"Well, I'm ready to stop. I need to get my feet on dry, solid ground, so my head will stop spinning. I just want to find a place to wash the salt off my skin and put on dry clothes."

They took their bags and walked up the dock to a small building. A weathered sign over the door read, Municipio de Matamoros, Tamaulipas, Mexico.

"That confirms it," Pepper said as she read the sign, attempting a Spanish pronunciation. Jared thought her accent was pretty good. "Let's see if we can find some fresh water."

"Doesn't look like anyone's around," Jared said. "No lights. Even if the EMP's didn't knock out all the power in Mexico, they might have, this close to the United States."

"The air doesn't seem to be as contaminated here as in the states," Pepper said, "Maybe it will be easier to find food and water."

Jared silently agreed. This looked promising. "But we still need to be careful," he said.

The door to the small building on the dock was locked, so Jared knocked, keeping one hand on the gun in his pocket. When no one answered, he leaned into the door, pushing with his weight. The door gave easily and swung open. A quick search of the building revealed that there was no running water, but they found a rusty water heater in the back and helped themselves to a sponge bath.

"What are you doing?" Jared asked when he'd finished washing and started dressing in fresh clothes.

"Dyeing my hair," Pepper said, standing in her underwear with a towel around her neck. She had leaned over a sink with her gloved hands stirring her hair. "Then I'm going to apply fresh makeup and dress in my brand new, Mexican-style clothes. How about you?"

Jared wrapped his arms around her bare stomach and nuzzled her neck, careful to avoid hair dye.

"What are *you* doing?" she asked, wiggling her shoulders in an attempt to dislodge him.

"Do we have time for . . . you-know?" he asked.

"It's only been three days," she said. "Aren't you getting enough to satisfy your 'male needs'?"

His face reflected his hurt feelings. "Don't you enjoy it, too?" he asked.

"I do, but we need to get made up before someone comes along, don't you think?"

"I guess so, but I've never dyed my hair before."

"I'll help you," she said, smiling.

❂

"That sounds like a truck," Jared said. They were standing in front of the building, trying to decide what to do. "It sounds like it's getting closer. Get back inside." He grabbed her arm and propelled her toward the front door.

The truck pulled around a corner before either of them could duck inside. Someone shouted.

"*Alto!*"

Jared looked and saw an open bed military truck with several coarsely-dressed men standing in the back with rifles aimed at them. He had already dropped his bag when he'd turned away, so he stopped and raised his hands in the air. He noticed that Pepper did, too.

The men jumped out of the truck and ran over, their rifles still pointed menacingly at Jared's and Pepper's chests. One man, holding a pistol, starting yelling at Jared in rapid Spanish. Jared had studied Spanish in school, but couldn't translate quickly enough. He must have had a stupid expression on his face—maybe a look of concentration—because the leader looked frustrated.

"*Inglais?*" he said.

"Yes . . . *si*," Jared said. "Americans." He smiled, hoping that being Americans was a good thing with these guys.

Apparently, it wasn't. The leader motioned toward the truck with his gun. The other men moved back to form a sort of path for them, leading toward the truck. Jared motioned for Pepper to go ahead of him. As he followed, he noticed the lecherous expressions of the men she passed. One reached out and patted her butt, then chuckled when she swung a fist at him, missing as he backed away a step. The leader yelled something and the sound died abruptly. Jared helped Pepper into the back of the truck and the men piled in after them. It was crowded, the dirt road bumpy, and Jared could tell each time someone bumped into Pepper, from her reaction. He attempted to interject himself between Pepper and the men, but was shoved roughly out of the way, a gun barrel pressed up against his throat.

They stayed this way, Jared watching the men and the men watching Pepper, as the truck headed north on winding roads. They passed, through wetlands and small towns, until they hit a straight, modern highway that looked like it would lead to civilization. When Jared could see a large city ahead, the truck slowed and turned off the highway, left the pavement and followed a dirt trail for several minutes. It stopped in front of a large, guarded gate in a long, poorly maintained wall, with armed guards at the gate and on the wall. The driver spoke rapidly to the gatekeepers, then passed into a large compound that housed several buildings. Four additional military-style trucks, like the one they were in, were parked on either side of the largest building. Several armed men guarded the door.

The driver of the truck stopped in front of the building and the men motioned for Jared and Pepper to get out. Some of the men jumped down first and the rest after them, so that Jared and Pepper were surrounded as they were ushered into the building. The leader followed them in, his gun pointed at Jared's back.

An older man, maybe forty years old, sat behind a battered old wooden desk, looking down at some papers, ignoring them. There were four armed men standing around the room, paying close attention, but no one spoke. After a few minutes, the older man sighed, laid down his pencil, and looked up at them.

"*Que es?*" he asked.

Jared understood that to mean that the man was asking what was going on, or something like that. The man who'd brought the prisoners in replied in rapid Spanish. All Jared understood was the word "*americanos*". The older man turned his head and studied them, Jared quickly, then Pepper for a little longer.

"What are you doing here?" he asked them in heavily accented, but understandable English. Pepper looked at Jared, so he took the lead.

"We left the United States because of all the destruction there. We'd like to live here."

"Why here?"

Jared didn't know if the man was asking why Mexico or why Matamoros. He chuckled self-consciously.

"Our boat was running low on gas and we were afraid we couldn't go any farther south."

The man looked at his subordinate and spoke rapidly. The subordinate looked embarrassed and shrugged, then said something that sounded like an apology. His boss barked some order. All the men in the room became alert and the subordinate left in a hurry, still apologizing. There were barked orders outside and the truck started up and left quickly.

"We will find your boat and confirm your story," the older man said. "You may sit over there until they return." Then he picked up another piece of paper on his desk and studied it, ignoring them again.

Jared looked around at the guards, then at Pepper. No one moved. Finally, one of the guards motioned with his rifle toward the seats that the older man had mentioned, so Jared took Pepper's hand and led her to the old wooden, armless chairs in one corner. While they waited, Jared studied the room and noticed what looked like bullet holes in the wooden desk and pock marks in the adobe walls. There must have been a gun battle in here. Was this a drug cartel? What would that mean for them?

Pepper's stomach growled. She didn't know what time it was and couldn't remember her last meal. She looked at Jared, who gave her a sympathetic smile. She wasn't about to ask for food. She was intimidated by being at the mercy of so many obviously affection-starved men and worried what they would do to them—do to her. When her stomach growled a second time, Jared looked like he might say something, so she shook her head at him, slightly, and he settled back into his chair.

She wondered what had become of Beth and the other outcasts. Had they been captured by the military and executed, as they'd feared? Were they being held hostage somewhere? Or, had they made it to the Rocky Mountains and found a place to live in peace? She hoped they'd escaped and found their peace.

Finally, after what seemed like more than two hours, Pepper heard the sound of a truck approaching. Minutes later, the man who had led the group that captured them re-entered the building and stood at attention before his superior, waiting to be acknowledged. When the leader looked up, the subordinate gave his report and the boss excused him. He left after a final look at Pepper, his expression unreadable.

"We found your boat," the leader said. "We also found bags of clothes and makeup. No food. It's too bad you didn't land somewhere else. If you had, you could go on your way. I can't let you go. I must send you to El Jefe. He will decide what to do with you."

Pepper's heart sank. If they'd gone past this particular dock, they could be on their way. Her stomach growled again.

"You're hungry?" the man asked.

"We are," Jared said before Pepper could speak.

The man looked at Pepper, then at Jared. He turned to one of his guards and gave an order. The guard motioned for them to follow him and headed for the door. As they were leaving, the man spoke again.

"I'm sorry. Tell El Jefe the truth and he will be fair. He is the boss"

Pepper wondered what that meant. Would El Jefe, whoever he was, have them shot without torturing them? Is that what being fair meant?

13

We don't need your gold

The Outcasts—Utah, 2 April

They'd discovered from their experience in Ft. Laramie that sharing body heat helped ward off the cold and they slept better. So, when Beth stirred from her blanket the next morning, she had to move Ben's leg, which was draped over hers, before she could rise. She immediately noticed that the stranger had moved closer and watched her. She sat up, thinking about the location of her knife and how quickly she could get to it; then realized that, had he wanted to harm her, he wouldn't have waited until she was awake.

"Hi," Beth said.

"Hi, yourself," Jason said. "You have food to share?"

"Depends." Beth could hear rustling behind her and realized that the others were awakened by their conversation. Good.

"How about I buy some from you? I have gold."

"We don't need your gold. We can share."

"I'll take your gold," Bryce said. Jason chuckled, recognizing the type.

"I'm Beth, this is Bryce. What's your name?"

"Jason."

"Okay Jason, give us a few minutes to wake up and get organized." Jason nodded and sat back to wait.

"I would rather avoid contact with Jason," Beth whispered to Ben as they rolled up their bedding and stuffed it into a backpack.

"We don't know if we're still contagious."

"Letting him join us would answer that question," Ben whispered back. "In three days, we would know for sure."

Beth nodded.

"Ben, Bryce, would you two please find some wood to make a fire?" Beth asked. "It would be nice to have a warm meal this morning."

"I looked around a little last night," Bryce said. He and Candy had gone for a walk before bed, so Beth wasn't surprised. "We might have to cut some." He and Ben retrieved the hatchets they had acquired in Ft. Laramie and walked up the hill.

"Kerri and Callie, when you finish what you're doing, will you follow them and help bring back whatever wood they find?" Beth asked.

"Sure," Kerri said. They finished packing their bedding and walked up the hill, followed slowly by Lisa.

Before long, Bryce had a small fire going and Candy knelt beside him opening cans of vegetables to place in the coals to heat. When the food was hot, they took their cans, with gloved hands, and sat around the fire. Bryce took a bubbling can to Jason with his gloved hand and accepted a small gold coin, then moved back to sit by Candy.

Beth was aware of Jason's questioning look as he stared at their faces.

"I couldn't help but notice the skin condition," he said, watching her.

Beth hesitated involuntarily, then recovered quickly, but she was sure he'd noticed. She wasn't sure what to say. Other times, she had warned people to keep their distance, but she didn't want to warn Jason. Instead of answering, she asked a question of her own.

"Who are all these people?" she asked, sweeping her hand

across the ocean of people surrounding the lake.

"Refugees from the explosion and earthquake on the Wasatch Front," Jason said. To his chagrin, he had learned that Amos had told the truth about the war.

Beth assumed the Wasatch Front meant Salt Lake City, Ogden and Provo, which confirmed what she'd heard in Evanston.

Jason *had* noticed that Beth didn't answer his question about her skin condition. Did that mean that they had been sick and recovered? He believed most women were vain, when it came to their appearance, so maybe she was too embarrassed by her appearance to talk about it. Was it possible that they were still sick? They didn't act like it.

"Will anyone care if we bath in the lake?" Beth asked.

"Does it matter?" Jason laughed. When Beth just stared at him, he decided it wouldn't hurt to give her a straight answer. He thought these might be his kind of people—lonely, independent, maybe a little ornery. He didn't really mind having them around. Besides, a plan had been forming in his head since they'd arrived, and he would need help to make it work.

"The lake water isn't for drinking," Jason said seriously, "but I don't know if they're dumping stuff in the lake, if you know what I mean. I'd say, swim at your own risk."

"Is there someplace we can get drinking water?"

"The towns around the lake have set up places to get drinking water. They're using generators and sand filters to treat it until they get the electricity back on, if ever, and they're trying to control water use."

"Thank you," Beth said. "So, why are you here by yourself?"

Jason thought about how to answer while he continued eating. By the time he swallowed the food in his mouth and could speak without being obscene, he had settled on the first steps of his plan.

"I was staying in the mountains until a few days ago. I don't usually seek the company of other people. I prefer to be alone."

"But now?"

"I was hungry," he replied, smiling and holding up his empty can. He noticed that Beth looked skeptical but didn't push it. Other than the blotchy skin and sniffling, which could mean they suffered from radiation sickness or some sort of disease—he wasn't a doctor—he thought they looked healthy enough. He decided to stay close to them for a couple of days. These were the first people who weren't trying to get his good coat.

He'd been considering trying to get back into the Preserve, where life was easy and food was readily available. Maybe he could, with the help of these people. The only drawback was Amos.

"How did you survive the winter in the mountains?" Beth asked Jason casually. He might have information that would help them.

"I lived in a cave," he lied. Well, a half-lie. He wasn't ready to tell them the whole story; not now, maybe never.

Beth's expression turned hopeful and she looked over at her companions as if eager to share what Jason had said. They must be looking for a place to stay. This could be easier than he'd thought.

"It's such a long story," he added, encouraged, but acting indifferent. "I don't think you'd believe me anyway."

Beth's expression changed again. She looked suspicious.

"Try me," she said.

Jason told himself not to mess this up. He needed to get her hooked and keep her there until he worked out the details of his plan.

"Maybe later," he said.

A cave sounded like the perfect solution to Beth, a place where they could live alone, safely, near a source of fresh water. But was Jason playing some kind of game. If not, why wouldn't he tell her about the cave? Was he telling the truth when he said he came to the valley to get food? Or, was there more to it than that?

The Outcasts—Utah, 4 April

Beth awoke to Jason's moaning, lying in his shelter a few feet away. She went to check on him, and found him with rashes on his hands and face, looking miserable.

"What's wrong with me?" he asked. Beth had told him she was a doctor.

"Looks like radiation sickness," she said, which was true. Smallpox, in its early stages, looked a lot like radiation sickness, but she was pretty sure it was Smallpox. She was no closer to finding out what Jason was hiding, so she decided not to say more until he opened up a little more about his cave. Maybe this would do it. She should know in another day.

"Now? It's been months since the explosion and I've been in the Pre . . . I mean, in a cave for most of the time."

"That's how radiation sickness works." What was he about to say? "The radiation accumulates in the system, then expresses itself when it reaches a threshold. It's different for each person."

"Quite a coincidence that it came on just after you arrived with your blotchy skin," he said.

He was obviously in agony, holding his head with both hands and moaning.

So, he was suspicious about the Smallpox. She decided now was a good time to press him for more information about the cave. "Maybe you would be better off in the cave," she said. "We could help get you there."

Jason's head jerked up, unable to hide his surprise.

Hmm, was Jason just thinking the same thing? What's he hiding in his cave?

"You're a doctor," Jason said angrily. "Give me something that will stop the pain."

He wasn't quite ready to talk. She'd wait and see how strong his resistance was tomorrow.

"I have some aspirin," she said. He took six of them.

"Why don't you give him something stronger?" Ben asked when they were out of Jason's hearing, "or a vaccination?" They had learned at the Johns Creek shelter that a vaccination would reduce the Smallpox symptoms significantly, but she wasn't going to tell Jason that . . . yet. Besides, this might turn out to be radiation sickness, after all. She told Ben what she suspected, that it really was Smallpox, but that Jason was telling her only half-truths, and she needed him to want help badly enough that he would trade medicine for information.

All she told the other Outcasts was that Jason might catch Smallpox from them if they were still contagious. Then she asked them to let her deal with him through the difficult transition stage.

"Gladly," Candy said. "You're the doctor, but do you have earplugs, so we don't have to listen to him?"

"You've forgotten how bad this stage was, haven't you?" Bryce asked.

"Yes, and I don't want to be reminded."

Jason's moaning continued all through the day and into the night, keeping people awake. There were angry calls from adjacent camps.

The Outcasts—Utah, 5 April

Beth waited as long as she could before checking on Jason. It was still dark; not quite morning.

"This isn't radiation sickness, is it?" he asked angrily, then moaned again. "Whatever you have is contagious and you've given it to me. Tell me the truth."

"I'm going to give you a shot that will take away the worst of the symptoms. You'll be sick for a few days, then you can tell us what you're hiding up in that cave of yours. Then we'll all go there."

"Tell me. What did you do to me?" He asked, cursing her.

Beth opened Jason's coat, startling him, but he didn't resist. She pulled his shirt far enough to the side to expose his upper arm and plunged in the needle. It was too dark to tell if his condition had worsened. "How does your tongue feel?" She asked.

"My mouth feels like it's full of cankers. What is it?"

"Tomorrow will be soon enough," she said, letting him fall back onto his blanket. His eyes rolled up in his head and he was out.

Contamination confirmed!

The Outcasts—Utah, 11 April

When Jason's scabs were falling and he was regaining his strength, he was about to tell Beth about the Preserve, when she surprised him by telling him the Outcasts' story; about the family that brought the virus to the shelter, why they ran, and what they were hoping to find in the mountains.

"I'm sorry, Jason," she said, "I feel a little guilty about using you as a guinea pig. Now you're contagious, too. But it has convinced me we won't be safe in public. We need to find a place away from others, where we have the resources to survive, and your cave sounds perfect."

Jason couldn't believe his luck. During the entire time he'd been away, he'd been thinking how good life was in the Preserve.

He'd begun to think that he could almost tolerate Amos's leadership. As sick as he'd been a few days ago, he had even thought he should swallow his pride and ask Amos to help him get better.

Now Beth had voluntarily given him the information he needed to finalize his plan to get back into the Preserve. Maybe, with these Outcasts, as they called themselves—this group of hardy survivors—Jason could even take control away from Amos.

He had severed his relationship with his wife and daughter and had no love for the rest of the people in the Preserve. He'd like nothing better than to contaminate Amos and laugh while he suffered. Maybe these Outcasts would follow him and help him oust the Blunds and Stephenses.

He had always considered himself a good manager, and had thought he was a good leader; but he'd come to realize, since going to the Preserve and watching Amos, that a leader was only a leader if he had willing followers. It made him wonder what it would take to convince the Outcasts to follow him.

He'd have to handle this just right.

He figured he could make them feel guilty about contaminating him, but would that be enough? What did each of them want? He would have to figure that out and see if it was something he could provide.

The Outcasts—Utah, 12 April

Jason started his campaign to take control of the Outcasts—to win them all away from Beth, their apparent leader—by taking hikes across the hills and inviting one or two of the others to go with him each time, "for the exercise", he said. The snow seemed to be melting slowly, so the ground wasn't too slippery or overly muddy.

Jason invited Bryce first, figuring he could influence him with gold. Bryce went willingly, and his pregnant girlfriend—Bryce called her Sheryl, but the others called her Candy, which she seemed to prefer—went with them at first. He thought to impress Bryce by talking about his job as a corporate controller; but found that Bryce knew so little about corporate finance, that he lost interest almost immediately. He was so wrapped up in telling Bryce about himself that he missed the change in mood until Candy asked Bryce to take her back to camp.

"Don't go back now," Jason said frantically, appealing to Bryce. He scrambled to think of what to say to convince them to stay. "The weather's so nice," he said, looking around at the dark, overcast, dust-filled sky, "and I really wanted you to tell me about how you two got together."

Candy and Bryce looked at each other for a moment, and Jason realized that if he paid attention, he could almost tell what their expressions were saying. This was a new experience for him; he'd never tried to understand other people, because he never really cared about anyone else's feelings. He could tell when some message passed between them.

"I think Sheryl wants to go back and rest," Bryce said, "but I'll stick around for a while." Candy excused herself and walked back to camp alone.

With Jason's encouragement, Bryce talked about the Johns Creek shelter, the gun battle with the soldiers and the months-long trip to Ft. Laramie, where they'd spent the winter. Jason's mind drifted and several times he wanted to interrupt and share something about himself. He thought this was the most difficult thing he had ever done, feigning interest in someone else's experiences. He even wondered if it were worth the effort. Then Bryce mentioned saving Sheryl's life, and Jason knew he'd found a nugget that would influence both Bryce and Candy.

At the end of their walk, Jason steered Bry—as he'd started

calling Bryce—toward his campsite, still a little distant from the Outcasts camp, and gave Bryce a gold coin, because, he said, "friends share with each other". He'd decided that Bryce was simple-minded enough to take that at face value and not see an ulterior motive in it.

The Outcasts—Utah, 13 April

He tried Ben next, thinking he would be easier to talk to than the young women. He was still trying to figure them out.

"Tell me about yourself," Jason said as they walked across the hillside.

"Not much to tell," Ben replied.

"Bryce told me about the shelter and his leading you to Wyoming."

"Bryce was not our leader," Ben said defensively. "Beth was, and still is."

"Sorry, Ben," Jason said apologetically, trying to smile. He worried that he might have blown his chance to influence Ben. "Beth must be a strong leader. What is it about her that makes men want to follow her?"

Ben stopped and stared at Jason.

"What?" Jason asked, truly confused by Ben's reaction.

"Beth is a good, loving, responsible person, who cares about others. You make it sound like only a man can be a good leader."

"Sorry, Ben. That wasn't my intent." But he wondered how Ben could be so disillusioned that he thought a woman could be as effective leading people as a man.

"Maybe this wasn't such a good idea," Ben finally said. "I have things to do back at camp."

"Yeah," Jason agreed, thinking that Ben was a wuss. "Let's try it another time, when you're not so busy."

The Outcasts—Utah, 14 April

"I don't think I'd be interested," Kerri told Jason, with a look at Callie and Lisa, when he invited her to go for a walk. The young women were sitting on a tarp on the ground, talking quietly.

Jason thought he noticed a message pass between them. This was amazing. Did everyone except him have this subliminal way of communicating?

"Why don't you all come?" he asked with a forced smile. "It will do us all good to get some exercise."

"Well, okay," Kerri agreed after a nod from Callie. Lisa declined; she was too tired to move and Beth had decided to try to get Lisa to eat some warm soup for her congestion.

"I understand that you two met in a shelter near Atlanta," Jason said after they had walked a while without speaking. Both women looked up suddenly.

"What do you mean?" Kerri asked.

"I don't mean anything," Jason said, realizing that his comment might have more than one meaning. "Bryce told me that you all met while you were in the shelter, but he didn't give me any details about it. I was just curious."

"Sorry," Kerri said. "The shelter was a bad experience for all of us. Did Bryce tell you that there were almost a hundred people in the shelter, and that less than twenty survived? The seven of us are all that's left of the twelve who started out together."

Jason couldn't think of what to say, he was so surprised. Should he apologize for their loss, or tell them he had lost family, too? He had to remind himself that, as much as he wanted to talk about his own problems, this was about them, not him. He'd had no idea how hard this would be! But he had to keep them talking.

"So, is that where you all got sick?" he asked. Beth had told him about the family that carried the virus to the shelter, but still hadn't told him it was smallpox. All he knew was, that whatever it was, it was highly contagious.

"The president bombed the CDC and a mutated version of smallpox escaped."

"*What?*" Jason yelled, stopping and turning to look at Kerri and Callie. Were they serious? "The president bombed the CDC? Now I have smallpox?" Was everything that Amos had told him true? Had he made an ass of himself in the Preserve because he was too fat-headed to believe the governments of the world would tolerate nuclear war, or that Amos had lied about any of it?

"Hard to believe, isn't it?" Kerri said. "Who would have thought the terrorists were stupid enough to start a nuclear war that they couldn't win?"

I certainly didn't believe it, Jason thought, sadly. Now, he may have ruined forever his chance to live in the security of the Preserve. Well, no matter. What was done, was done. He needed to look forward to how he could take advantage of this new information. He might still be able to get back into the Preserve.

The Outcasts—Utah, 15 April

Jason continued his walks, with Bryce eagerly joining him whenever Candy didn't object. He willingly shared information about the other Outcasts each time, knowing there was a gold coin waiting for him at the end of each walk. Candy went with them sometimes, but more often walked by herself or with one or more of the other women, since Dr. Beth encouraged her to get daily exercise. Jason wondered if Candy didn't enjoy his company, or didn't like the things they talked about.

Jason thought he had the two young women, Kerri and Callie, figured out as being lesbians. He made the mistake of asking them, assuming that they would be proud of it—that was the trend nowadays, wasn't it—only to find out that, without denying it, they resented his questions about their personal lives.

Ben finally went with him, once, but seemed to be on edge the entire time. Jason was careful to ask only general questions about the Outcasts' travels—where they went and what they saw—until Ben was ready to talk about other things on his own. He never did, and Jason learned very little about any of the Outcasts from him.

Jason had been trying to identify their weaknesses, so he could exploit them. Most of what he'd learned was from Bryce, either by admission or by inference. He now knew that Bryce resented the government for what they did at the shelter, and thought he was in love with Candy, who would soon make up for his losing his wife in the shelter by giving him a child. Candy wanted to be famous, but had to settle for being fertile, and felt committed to Bryce for saving her life. Kerri had nearly lost her best friend when Lisa got hypothermia, then pneumonia in Wyoming. There was something about telepathy in that story, which he didn't understand. Now Kerri had taken Callie under her wing, so to speak. Callie hated the president for withholding knowledge that might have saved lives, especially those of her parents, who were murdered—her words—in the shelter. Now she was dependent on Kerri for moral support. Ben was in love with Beth and would do anything for her. Beth was a caregiver and the Outcasts were her patients, now that she had failed to protect the rest of the people in the shelter.

So, at a minimum he needed to win over Bryce and Kerri in order to wrest control from Beth.

14

Ahh, that's sweet

The Preserve, 29 April

"Based on the Geiger Counter and dosimeter readings from your little excursion outside," Terry said, "I think it's safe to go out and check the monitors, as long as we don't stay out too long at a time."

"That's great, Terry," Amos replied, "Mike, the locations of all the sensors are marked on this map. I've circled the first ones that should be replaced."

"It looks like a strategic layout; the perimeter of the clearing and the approaches," Mike observed.

"Good eye, Mike. That's exactly what we're doing. We'll take turns working out there. You and Terry get the first turn."

"Since we'll be working from a ladder most of the time, we'll replace each sensor as soon as we take one down," Terry said. "The sensors have both audio and video capability, so whoever is in the lab will test the video, then the audio connection, and report to those outside using the helmet mics. We'll bring the bad sensors into the lab to be tested and repaired, if possible. Any that *can* be repaired will be returned to service later."

At the airlock, Amos helped Terry and Mike suit up.

"I put the tools you'll need, in the center pocket of the utility belts," Amos said. "The left-hand pocket has the new sensors you'll install. The right-hand pocket is empty to hold the sensors you remove."

Mike looked in each pocket as his dad explained. "Got it," he replied.

"Mike, will you carry the ladder?" Terry asked. Terry always had trouble working in the confinement of a hazmat suit. A lot of people wore them daily for their work with no problem. However, anyone who had never done it had no idea how difficult it *could* be to work while breathing canned air. It was easy to become disoriented and nauseated.

"I don't want to vomit in my hazmat suit," he added.

"That's a terrible thought," Mike said.

"We'll take turns climbing the ladder," Terry added, "so one of us doesn't wear out while the other stays fresh."

"I'll keep an eye on you through the sensors and let you know when you've reached your estimated exposure limit for the day," Amos said. "Shout if you have a problem."

The Outcasts—Laketown, 29 April

"I think I know *what* he's doing," Ben told Beth during a quiet moment alone, "I just can't figure out the *why.*"

"Tell me what you think," Beth replied. She had her own idea about his motives. "Maybe, between us, we can figure it out."

"Well, he's bribing Bryce with gold—Candy showed me the pile—obviously to buy his allegiance. He wasn't as successful with the others. He insulted Candy, Kerri *and* me, right off."

"How did he insult you?"

Ben was hesitant to tell her—it would be baring his feelings about Beth, to admit that he was offended because Jason had insulted *her*—but they'd been sleeping together for months now, so she probably already knew how he felt.

"He thought Bryce was leading the Outcasts, not you. I don't know if Bryce told him that or he just assumed a man would be the leader—he seems to think women can't be leaders—but it made me mad."

"Ahh, that's sweet," Beth said, chuckling, as she laid a hand on his cheek. "You defended me."

"Jason calls me Bennie-boy whenever he wants to influence me," Ben continued.

"Is it working?" Beth laughed.

"Oh, it's influencing me, all right. It makes me want to punch him in the nose. But I won't show my displeasure as long as we're still trying to figure out his game."

"So, how did he insult Candy and Kerri."

"Candy said he thinks she's Bryce's cow—a brainless bimbo— only good for her reproductive ability."

"Ouch! That's harsh."

"She hasn't said anything to Bryce or Jason about her feelings, but she's pretty upset about it. When he was with Kerri and Callie, he asked them if they were lesbians."

Beth had to think about that for a moment. It was true that they were sleeping together. So were she and Ben, and Bryce and Candy, but that was to keep warm, supposedly. The young women gave no other indication that they might be gay. She believed that Callie had become very close friends with Kerri and Lisa since Lisa's illness.

"Did Kerri deny it?" Beth asked.

"Well, no," Ben said, "but she was offended that he had the nerve to ask something so personal."

"Hmm, so what does all that tell us about Jason's motives?"

"The fact that he hasn't invited *you* to go for a walk with him tells me that whatever it is, you don't play into the picture."

"Oh, he invited me once, but I turned him down so quickly— possibly a mistake— that he hasn't asked again. So, you think he's planning to challenge me for leadership of the Outcasts? Or, do you think he has something else in mind?"

"Oh, I think you're right Beth, but why? What does he gain by controlling the Outcasts?"

"Followers? Someone to do his bidding? He hasn't told us much about himself, but the one thing he has *refused* to tell us about is the cave."

Jason knew time was running out. He felt stronger and healthier than ever in his life—one of the side effects of the virus, they'd told him. They would demand that he lead them to the Preserve any day now.

He tried to picture how life would be different in the Preserve with him in charge, getting the Outcasts to do all the work to keep it running, while he sat in the office, directing everything —that was his perception of what Amos did. As Beth had said, his cave was the perfect solution.

But trying to win the Outcasts over to his side of the ledger, taxed his abilities. As a corporate controller, he was accustomed to telling people what to do and expecting them to do it—the way he wanted it done. Their jobs depended on making *him* happy. All this politicking was draining him.

But he knew he had Bryce; he'd spent a lot of gold to ensure it. Bryce already followed him like a puppy, and Candy would follow Bryce, he was sure.

He'd finally gotten Kerri to open up about her feelings after nearly losing Lisa. All he had to do was make empathetic noises. He didn't even have to listen to her bleeding-heart story. Callie was the same way about her parents. Act like he was interested, and their simple minds would soak it up. He couldn't be sure that they would take his side, if it came to a battle between him and Beth, so he would have to pretend to agree with Beth, while undermining her authority over them.

"I need to confess," Jason said that night during dinner, "that I haven't told you the whole truth about my cave."

"You haven't told us anything about your cave," Ben complained loudly.

"Well, I've spoken a little about it on our walks, but you haven't gone on any with me," Jason snapped, then caught himself. "Sorry, Benny-boy. It's just that this cave is a special place to me. It's in a beautiful valley and leads to an underground retreat that I spent 15 years designing, building, and stocking with everything needed to survive a crisis like the one we find ourselves in now." As Jason talked, he looked at their faces to see who was buying his story and who was still skeptical.

He figured he knew enough about Amos's Preserve to tell a convincing story—pretending he was Amos—about how he had set it up to be self-contained and self-renewing for years, at least long enough to outlast the nuclear fallout. He made Amos the bad guy, tricking his way into being invited as a guest, then conspiring with the others to take control of the Preserve, and force Jason out.

"What can we do to help you get it back?" Bryce asked excitedly, his hands fisted.

"Thanks for the thought, Bry," Jason said, satisfied that Bryce acted like he was ready for a fight. "That would be too much to ask. It's not your fight."

"I disagree," Bryce replied, smiling at the use of Jason's nickname for him. "If this place is as good as you say it is, it's just what we've been looking for." He looked at his fellow Outcasts and asked "Isn't it?" There were murmurs of support, others just looked back at him.

"Well, I can see it's not unanimous, Bryce. I'm gonna go back there in a few days and try to win back my retreat. If any of you want to join me, you're welcome. If not, no hard feelings." He wondered what else he needed to say to prepare them for what they would encounter and to help ensure their support, then had an idea. "This group could get violent. Anyone who goes with me will have to be prepared to defend themselves."

"Bring it on," Bryce said, as he drew his knife and flashed it around in the air in front of him. Candy beamed at him proudly.

Kerri, Callie and Lisa looked at each other with raised eyebrows, as if asking each other if they should support Jason's plan. Ben and Beth also looked at each other questioningly, but Jason thought their expressions said this retreat was worth checking out, even if they didn't believe everything he said.

The Outcasts—Laketown, 30 April

"What has Jason told you about his preserve?" Ben asked Callie and Kerri, while Jason was out on a walk with Bryce.

"Not much," Callie replied. "Mostly the same things he told all of us the other day."

"Do you think he's telling the truth?" Beth asked.

"His words don't match the look in his eyes," Kerri said, "I met a lot of politicians like that, working at the UN—self-serving and basically untrustworthy. But why would he lie?"

"I've been asking myself the same question. What if he's making this stuff up to get us to follow him?"

"He's trying very hard to convince us that he's a leader," Kerri said, "but he's not showing leadership skills. He's nothing like Ambassador Porter."

"Should we follow him?"

Kerri shrugged. "Does it matter? If this retreat is anything like he said it is, we need it."

The Outcasts—Laketown to Aspen Valley, 1 May

Jason led the Outcasts out of Laketown and into Garden City. People walked the streets or sat on benches or at tables. Seeing the crowds, Jason realized it was Sunday and no one worked on Sunday. He didn't try to avoid them but walked down the middle of the road, the Outcasts following in his wake, slushing through what little remained of the snow.

People moved out of their way and he heard his name mentioned several times. The comments were not kind, the people either remembering his abrupt departure or noticing his disfigured face and those of his followers.

"We should have left yesterday," he said to Bryce, who was a half-step behind on his right. He hadn't wanted people to notice that he was leaving or where he was going, but it was too late to worry about that now. Those who knew he had spent the winter in the mountains probably assumed he was going back, now with friends.

"Why is that," Beth asked, two steps behind, walking next to Ben. It seemed like every time they tried to catch up to Jason, to hear what he was saying, he hurried a little faster; he was always two steps ahead.

"Most of these people still believe they should take Sundays off. If we'd left yesterday, we wouldn't have had to avoid people."

"It doesn't look like we've had to avoid anyone," Ben said with a chuckle. "Everyone is going around us." No one had come within six feet of them.

Jason turned briefly to give Ben a dirty look.

"Today's Sunday, then?" Beth asked, wondering what Jason's problem was. She knew he'd been around Bear Lake for a while, so maybe he had made a few enemies. Her experience with him so far was that he only tried to be nice when he wanted something from you. "They must still believe in God," she added. She believed in God, but she preferred the loving one in the New Testament over the Old Testament one that allowed entire civilizations to be wiped out.

Jason looked at her like he didn't know what planet she had just come from.

"We've been on the road a long time," she said. "Each day looks like the last one after a while." She wasn't apologizing, she told herself, she was explaining.

✴

They reached the turnoff to Highway 89 in the middle of town.

"Hey, Jason," a young voice called from the right. For some reason he couldn't explain to himself, he looked in that direction. "Looks like you found some friends."

It was Isaac and Zach, sitting in their usual place at the table outside the ice cream restaurant. Without acknowledging them, he made the turn and headed up the hill toward the canyon.

"People know you," Beth said to Jason's back.

"They're a bunch of worthless busy-bodies," he replied. "I'll be glad to be rid of this town and back in my cave. The sooner, the better."

"Those two look like pleasant young men," Beth said, but Jason ignored her and kept moving.

✴

The snow on the ground close to town was riddled with foot and hoof prints and wagon wheel tracks, Beth noticed. The fields were mostly plowed under, in the process of being planted, it appeared. Higher up the mountain road, the tracks petered out until there was only one set of vague footprints, and they were headed down the hill, toward Garden City—obviously Jason's.

At the top of the hill they stopped at an overlook. "From up here it looks so beautiful and inviting," Callie said almost reverently.

"Except for all the people," Jason said sarcastically and walked away. The Outcasts followed, tearing their eyes away from the Bear Lake Valley reluctantly. The snow got deeper, the farther they traveled down Logan canyon toward Aspen Valley, and Jason's tracks became more obvious.

"What happened here?" Beth asked when they passed a spot where Jason had apparently stepped off the road and rolled down the hill. She smiled when Jason ignored her question and kept walking. *He can't handle a little teasing,* she thought.

How dare she question me, Jason thought as they continued.

"It was the middle of the night and there was no light," he finally said, trying to speak quietly enough that only Beth could hear him.

Late in the afternoon they rounded a wide, sweeping bend in the highway and came into view of a large valley. The only other time Jason had seen Aspen Valley in daylight had been when they'd first arrived from Logan months ago. Then, it was green and alive, thick with growth. Now, under the cover of snow, with most of the trees blackened from fire and no growth apparent between the naked trees, it looked dead.

He stopped abruptly in the road as an inexplicable wave of sadness washed over him. The war had done this. Even Garden City, with its masses of people, had avoided this much damage.

"This was obviously a beautiful valley before the fire," Beth said, startling him.

"My valley was beautiful," Jason said, using this as an opportunity to reinforce his position with the Outcasts. "It might be again if I can regain control of it." He could see that the others were moved by the sight. Candy leaned against Bryce and cried. The others looked sad as well.

"The entrance to the retreat is at the base of that cliff," Jason said, pointing to the cliff across the valley. "I have a key." He held the key in the air in case anyone questioned his right to be here.

"It looks like someone's down there," Bryce said.

"Where?" Jason asked, frantically searching for any sign of people.

"The base of the cliff."

It could only be one of the men—Amos or Terry—but Jason couldn't see any movement against the backdrop of the snow and rock, probably because whoever was out there was wearing a white hazmat suit.

Amos was probably trying to fix the sensors! This was perfect. Jason had promised his new followers a confrontation—Jason wanted a confrontation—but he needed to hurry. He didn't know how long Amos would remain outside.

"We follow this trail around the edge of the valley," he said, pointing to his left and hurrying forward. "We need to get closer. With luck, we'll be able to walk right up to the cliff and catch him off guard." He would tell Bryce to attack Amos. Then, with Amos out of the way, he could walk right in to the Preserve and take over.

15

Looks like you'll need some help

The Preserve, 1 May

Amos checked the video and audio feed on the sensor that Mike had just finished attaching to the cliff face and noticed color across the valley where there should only have been blackened trees and gray-white snow. He squinted at the screen to make certain of what he was seeing, then picked up his radio and called Terry and Mike, who were wearing helmet mics and headphones.

"Terry, there's someone in the valley with you," he said, now noticing movement, too.

Mike was on the ladder with his back to the valley and Terry was on the ground. They both looked around slowly, limited by the bulky hazmat suits.

"Where are they?" Terry asked. Amos wasn't surprised by the question, since the helmets on the suits limited visibility. "They're coming around on the trail. It looks like six or seven people."

Terry started moving in that direction as Mike cautiously descended the ladder.

As Jason came into the clearing ahead of the Outcasts, he saw that there were two men in hazmat suits. Amos and Terry? The one on the ladder, the one he guessed was Amos—he couldn't be sure, and decided it didn't matter—had his back turned and was doing something on the cliff face. The other one, Terry? was standing on the ground. Both men turned before Jason could get close to them, as if they had eyes in the back of their heads. The video sensors must be working. He turned to Bryce.

"Kill 'em," he said.

⊛

Beth had expected some sort of surprise from Jason—he'd been so secretive that she was suspicious of his real objective—but "kill 'em" was not it. Regardless, she had stayed close to Bryce just in case. She grabbed Bryce's arm, the one that wasn't holding a knife.

"Bryce, stop," she said. "These people haven't shown any aggressive behavior."

Bryce saw the two men in hazmat suits with utility belts around their waists and remembered the soldiers at the shelter, who had drawn weapons from their belts and started shooting innocent people. He decided Jason must be right. These people were hostile.

Bryce shook Beth loose and charged.

⊛

Terry watched the interplay between the intruders. When the man with the knife shook the smaller woman loose and started running toward them, he took a quick look at Mike, who was still trying to get off the ladder without falling, and placed himself between Mike and the charging man.

"You go inside. I'll talk to them," Terry said.

"Looks like you'll need some help," Mike replied, as he picked up a tree limb, as thick as a baseball bat, about three feet long and comfortable in his hands, that he had kicked out of the snow earlier. "This guy looks dangerous."

Bryce heard Jason screaming for him to throw the knife, but he didn't. There were two of them and one of him. One of them picked up a tree limb and stepped away, so he must not have another weapon.

Then the other one moved his hand to one of the pouches on his utility belt. That must be where his weapon was. His heart began to pound. Would it be a gun? Since he didn't know, Bryce had to stop him before he got the weapon free of the pouch. Then he could throw the knife at the one with the club.

Jason couldn't believe Bryce wouldn't throw the knife. Frustrated, he started to run across the uneven, snow-covered ground. It wasn't slippery, but he knew from experience that there were hidden obstacles under the snow that could trip him up if he stepped wrong. Still, he moved as fast as his virus-enhanced abilities would allow. He had to get into the Preserve, and he didn't know if he would get another opportunity like this.

Mike wasn't a fighter, and the hazmat suit limited his movement, but as he thought about his last encounter with bad guys—in the parking lot in the twin world—he felt his pulse quicken and his temper flare.

The man with the knife headed directly for Terry, moving fast. Mike moved awkwardly in the hazmat suit and wasn't sure he could get there before Terry got hurt. Then the man stumbled in the deep snow, which slowed him down momentarily, and gave Mike the precious moments he needed.

Just as the man swung his knife, Mike arrived from the side, swinging the tree limb like a baseball bat, just like he had in high school. It hit Bryce in the stomach, knocking the wind out of him. He lost his footing and fell, his knife flying out of his hand and barely missing Terry.

Amos watched the confrontation in silence, wondering if he should go out and help. No, he couldn't get suited up in time. It would be better to be where he could warn Terry and Mike if it looked like they were blindsided because of the limited visibility provided by their hazmat suits.

As he watched, Terry and Mike looked down at the man on the ground, who wasn't moving.

"He's out for the count," Amos heard Terry say, "but here comes his tag-team partner." They turned to face the large man who was now charging them, who also had a knife.

As Amos studied the man, he thought there was an uncanny resemblance to Jason Carlsen, but there was something off about him, and Amos couldn't tell what it was at first.

"You're too close together," Amos said, then watched as Mike took a couple of steps away from Terry. That was better. It would force the charging man to choose between them.

Then another man and woman started running. Were they trying to stop the Jason look-alike or were they also attacking Terry and Mike?

As the second attacker got closer, Amos could see him better and made a decision.

"It's Jason," he said. He didn't know how Terry and Mike would respond to this new information, but he wanted them to know who they were facing.

The man who Jason had identified as Terry held up a hand toward him and started calling his name. How had he identified him so quickly? He thought his disfigurement would hide his identity for a while. The other one—who he was sure was Amos—took a couple of steps to the right, turned to his right, and put the club on his shoulder in a baseball stance.

He heard everyone calling him, but ignored the voices. His vision had gone red with rage as he charged Terry, who stood his ground. Why didn't he run, or at least defend himself, unless he was a decoy? The one with the club—Amos, he thought— was more dangerous, as he'd demonstrated with Bryce, and it was Amos who he really wanted to kill. At the last moment, he abruptly turned toward Amos and swung his knife.

Mike's swinging club hit Jason on the shoulder, spinning him around and driving him to the ground, where he lay still. Mike had considered aiming for Jason's head, to end it all, but at the last second changed his mind—he couldn't intentionally try to kill him. As Jason fell, his knife hand swung around and sliced through Terry's sleeve, cutting his arm.

Mike looked around at the intruders. He had two on the ground and five more standing off at a distance, watching, but not moving.

"Terry. How ya doin'?" he asked, glancing briefly in Terry's direction while he stood with the club poised, ready to swing it again.

"I'm cut and it stings," Terry said, holding a hand over the hole in his protective suit.

"Okay. It looks like we have a standoff. Let me check on Jason and his friend, then we'll get inside."

Beth held out a hand to stop Ben. If Jason was right, the two suited men would take this opportunity to kill him and Bryce. They didn't. One had obviously been cut by Jason's knife—ample reason to want revenge—and held a hand over the cut. The other one lowered the club to his side, looked around and settled his gaze on Beth and Ben, then went over to Jason, who wasn't moving. He felt for a pulse, then did the same with Bryce. Maybe they were both dead, after all. Still watching Beth and Ben, he dropped the club and helped his injured friend as they backed farther away. Then they turned and walked quickly to the cliff face.

To Beth's amazement, a doorway opened in the rock face of the cliff and the two men disappeared inside the mountain.

Mike could hear his dad saying something to him on the radio, but the sound of his heart beating in his ears was louder than his dad's voice, so he couldn't tell what it was. He turned his back on the intruders and helped Terry walk to the secondary door, finally able to hear what his dad said.

"I'm on my way to the door," Amos said again. "Don't let Terry sit down. They're not moving toward you. Don't let Terry sit down."

As they reached the door, it opened, and Mike helped Terry push his way through the doorway. Amos was at the control panel, without a hazmat suit, closing the door behind them. Amos had the radio up to his mouth, talking to them. Even though they were standing within feet of each other, Amos's voice was louder through his headset.

"Don't take your hazmat suits off—either of you," Amos said, then he turned and ran down the passage away from them. He was still talking into the radio.

"Get Terry to the airlock. Disinfect both of you, then get him to storeroom three before you take off his suit."

"Storeroom three," Mike repeated as he helped Terry down the hall to the airlock.

"Yes. Take the tunnel that bypasses the community center. The storeroom is almost empty. Your mother is in there now removing anything that would be difficult to decontaminate. We'll quarantine Terry there."

"Quarantine? What's going on?"

"Just a hunch right now," Amos said. "Keep your suit on, Mike. She'll leave food and a medical kit in the storeroom. When you get Terry's suit off, treat his wound—"

"That will be difficult to do with my suit on," Mike said, helping Terry into the airlock. He had him sit in the corner under the disinfectant showerhead and turned it on. He also turned on the ventilation system.

"Do what you can," Amos said.

"I can help," Terry said. "I have one good arm."

"What did you see?" Mike asked his dad while helping Terry stand and scrubbing his suit.

Ignoring Mike's question, Amos said, "So, the knife cut through the suit?"

"Yes," Mike replied, wondering why his dad wouldn't answer his question.

"And Terry's cut as well?"

"Yes, I am," Terry said.

"What's going on Dad?" Mike asked again, becoming agitated.

"In a minute, Mike. I need to deal with the people outside. Make sure your mother is out of the storeroom before you enter."

"They're alive," Beth said to Ben as the outcasts gathered around. Beth had just checked Bryce and Jason, finding a strong pulse.

"What happened?" Kerri asked.

"Why didn't the men fight back?" Callie asked.

"They could have killed Jason and Bryce, but they didn't," Ben replied.

"Jason lied to us," Beth said. "The one with the club could have killed Jason with that club, but he didn't. These aren't the killers Jason said they were. We need to know why." She looked around for a place to set up camp. "Let's drag Jason and Bryce over there," she said, pointing to a spot on the edge of the clearing, still within sight of the rock face. "We'll set up camp for the night, then decide what to do next."

In the office, Amos watched them collect Jason—if it was Jason—and his friend, and drag them to the edge of the clearing. A woman seemed to be their new leader, now that Jason was out of commission. A man tied Jason's hands and feet. A pregnant woman had laid the second man's head in her lap and stroked his forehead while the man tied his hands and feet, too.

Amos went to the monitor that showed him storeroom three. Terry's hazmat suit had been removed and he sat on a cot while Mike sat on a chair next to him. Terry held a gauze bandage in place while Mike taped it to his arm. Then Mike gave Terry some pills and a cup of water.

"How are you doing Terry?" Amos asked.

"It stings," Terry said after he handed the cup back to Mike. "Do you think there was antifreeze on the knife?"

"Chris and Rachel survived, so you should too," Amos said.

They were referring to the knifing incident that ended Nathan's life and Amos knew it was Terry's way of joking sarcastically about something that had scared him. That violence, and today's, were too personal.

"Mike, are you okay?" Amos asked. Mike had one hand on his stomach and fidgeted.

"Now I know what you were telling us about how hard it is to work in a hazmat suit. As long as I take my time, I'm fine. But when I was exerting myself out there, and again helping Terry in here, I almost lost my stomach."

"Okay. Get out of there and get it off."

Mike stood slowly, holding his stomach, and walked mincingly out of the storeroom.

"What did you notice about our visitors?" Amos asked Terry after Mike had left.

"You mean the splotches on their faces and hands?" Terry asked.

"Yeah," Amos thought he knew what they were, but wanted Terry to confirm it.

"Looked like Smallpox. But the splotches mean it's past its contagious stage."

"My thoughts exactly. We'll need to take some precautions until we know for sure. Terry, will you be okay if we set you up in the storeroom with food and water for a few days?"

"You mean two weeks?" Terry said. "Yeah, I'll be fine."

"If I'm right about this being Smallpox," Amos said, "you could be in for a rough time."

Terry lay down on his good side and closed his eyes. His mouth was twisted in a grimace.

"How do you think Jason got hooked up with the others?" Terry asked, not opening his eyes.

"I'd say they met wherever Jason's been for the last few weeks—maybe Garden City—and fed them some story to get them to follow him to the Preserve."

"And convinced at least one of them to attack us?"

"Go figure," Amos said. He was worried about his good friend. His mind was on afterburner trying to figure out what was going on and what to do about it. It looked to him like President Gregory McCormick didn't take his advice about preventing the virus from escaping the Level 4 facilities. If there were Smallpox victims this far west, how bad was it in the east? Why did Greg let it get this far out of control?

✹

Late that night, Jason woke to find Beth staring at him. His shoulder hurt where Mike's club—he'd recognized Terry and Mike through their visors during the confrontation—had struck him. He tried to sit up, but his hands and feet were tied. He lay there, waiting to hear what Beth would say.

"Why did you lie to us?" Beth asked.

"What are you talking about?"

"They could have killed both of you, but they didn't. You said they would, given a chance. Why didn't they?"

"Too many witnesses?"

"Ha!" Beth said, but didn't say more.

"Where's Bryce?" he asked, craning his neck to look around with his limited mobility. The others were sitting around a fire a little way off.

"Bry. Sheryl. Come and untie me," he called. Bryce and Candy looked up. He could see their faces. They weren't happy. "We can get in the retreat while it's dark and take it over. They'll never expect it."

"It's over, Jason," Beth said.

"You're a stupid woman," he said with venom in his voice. Then he called again.

The others ignored him.

Jason continued calling out. "Bryce, why didn't you throw the knife. We could control the retreat by now. What's wrong with you?" He struggled with his bonds. "Get over here and untie me."

Nobody moved. Bryce and Candy looked back down at the fire.

Jason struggled some more, then gave up. Bry must have tied the knots, but why? Bry had been on his side until he ignored the order to throw the knife. Eventually he lay still, thinking that if he pretended to sleep, Beth might go away and he could talk to Bry alone—convince him to untie him—but Beth didn't leave before he fell asleep for real.

16

How far could he really trust these men?

In the morning Ben was watching Jason when he woke.

"You're my morning baby sitter?" Jason asked.

"Maybe you need a baby sitter," he replied, looking past him.

"Are you going to untie me?" Jason asked.

"No."

"Then you're as stupid as that woman."

Ben just shook his head, stood, and walked away.

"Hey, get back here. You can't walk away from me."

Ben kept walking. Beth spoke to him from behind.

"You really have a way with people, don't you?"

"Shut up or I'll shut you up."

Beth chuckled humorlessly. "You're a real work of art, Jason."

"What's that supposed to mean?" When she didn't answer, he asked, "What's for breakfast?"

"Humble pie. Let's hear it."

"Hear what?"

"Why did you lie to us?"

"What do you want me to say?"

"Tell me the truth. That's not your retreat, is it? Why did you leave?"

"You're so smart, you tell me." When she didn't respond, he said, "I didn't like the people. Satisfied?"

"Didn't like the people," she repeated, testing the sound of it, "so you were willing to kill them? That's some serious dislike." She waited again, but Jason didn't continue. "I'd say you couldn't handle the regimented lifestyle, living under someone else's control, but you did like the convenience of a full pantry. So, you tried to convince us to help you take it over. Did you picture yourself as the boss—take it over—convince us to be your servants . . . or slaves?"

Jason didn't answer. His face contorted with hatred as he stared at her.

"Okay," she said. If looks could kill, they might all be dead. She stood and walked over to where the others were sitting around a small campfire that Ben worked on. Bryce had his head down. Sheryl sat by him with her arms folded across her ample belly, her face unreadable. Lisa, Kerri and Callie were just waking.

Jason called out. "Hey Beth. They'll trick you. They'll slit your throat when you're not looking." She ignored him, so he continued. "I'm the one who lived here. I know what's going on." He was becoming more agitated by the minute. He was pulling on his bonds again.

Beth went over and looked at his bonds. Jason must have misunderstood her intentions. He smiled. "Good girl, just untie me and I'll take care of everything."

"Good girl?" she asked, giving him a dirty look. "You pig. I should turn you over to them and let them do what they want with you. You've screwed up enough. You don't get another chance."

"What about Bryce?" he asked. "Why isn't he trussed up like Thanksgiving dinner? He attacked them, too."

Beth chuckled. "You don't deserve an answer," she said, "but I'll tell you anyway. We *did* tie him up, until he explained himself. You see, we had one run-in with hazmat-suited soldiers who said they were doctors, then pulled guns out of their utility belts and started shooting. Over eighty percent of the occupants of the shelter died in the gun battle.

"You bribed and lied to a vulnerable, innocent man to get him to do your dirty work. I blame you for Bryce's actions and so does he."

Beth sensed a very different situation here than what Jason had told them was going on. What she saw was two innocent men trying to get some work done when Jason attacked them. There was no dialogue and no retaliation—that man could have clubbed Jason to death, but he didn't. And that door in the rock face! She wanted to know more about that. As she walked away, ignoring Jason's foul language, she wondered what was going to happen next.

Amos entered the lab where Mike was looking at the monitor.

"What's going on?" he asked.

"Can't hear what they're saying. But it looks like Jason's trying to get someone to untie him."

"Any takers?"

"Nope. Looks like he's on his own. The woman seems to have control over the others."

As Amos watched, the group talked around the fire. The woman in charge was doing most of the talking, but the others spoke as well, all except Jason, who was still tied up, and the other knife wielder, who was sitting in their circle with his head down, next to the pregnant woman. Finally, the leader and the one other man in the group stood and approached the cliff.

Over a warm breakfast, Ben reminded the others that the two men in hazmat suits had turned to looked at them before they were close enough to be heard or seen.

"I think someone inside can see us," Ben said. "Maybe we can communicate with them."

"And say what?" Beth asked, but Ben didn't have an answer.

"Say that Jason fooled us into thinking he had been wronged," Candy said.

"Oh, and we came to take over and kill them all?" Beth asked. Candy had no reply.

"We should apologize and tell them we thought this was a place where we could be safe," Callie said in an unusual show of confidence.

"Very wise advice, Callie," Beth said and nodded her approval, which made Callie smile. "Come on Ben. Let's try it. Maybe they can tell us where there's another shelter we can use."

Beth and Ben walked toward the cliff. When they were twenty feet away, Beth spoke. "Hello in the retreat. I'm Dr. Beth Byron, a medical doctor from Georgia. This is Ben Schick, a nurse who worked with me in a shelter near Atlanta. If you didn't recognize him, that was Jason, from your retreat, who attacked your associate with a knife.

"We want to apologize for our interference. We were misled by Jason into thinking we could come here and get away from other people. We don't know if you can hear us. If you can, will you please talk to us? I feel kind of stupid talking to a rock." She chuckled. "If we don't hear from you, we'll repeat this message every hour until we do."

Silence—

"Michael," Amos said, "are you sure the speaker on this monitor is working?"

"I'm pretty sure if you can hear them, they can hear you."

Amos decided to talk to them.

Beth had just turned away when she heard what sounded like static coming from the rock face in front of them. A voice said, "This is Amos Blund. I thought that was Jason. His name is Jason Carlsen, if he didn't tell you his last name. But there was something off about his appearance. When you said you were from Atlanta, it clicked. All of you have had Smallpox . . . and survived."

"Thank you for responding, Mr. Blund. I'm so sorry for what happened. We were misled—"

"I understand, Dr. Byron. How did you contract Smallpox?"

"Are you a doctor?" Beth asked, his question taking her off guard. She wondered how he had made such a quick connection between her mention of Atlanta and Smallpox.

"Among other things."

"It's a long story," Beth said.

"I'm listening."

Beth summarized the events at the Johns Creek shelter, up to, but excluded the part about the military coming to kill them all.

Amos jumped ahead, surprising her. "The virus mutated," he said. "You're still contagious. That's why Jason has Smallpox. Correct?"

"You're very good, Dr. Blund. We . . . we call ourselves 'the Outcasts'. We've travelled a long way to get here, hoping to find a remote place to hide from the military. They want to kill us. We're sorry we got you involved in this."

"Thank you for your candor. We've already quarantined Terry. We'll just keep him in quarantine a little longer. The incubation period is about two weeks, isn't it?"

"Three days."

"Three days?" Amos asked, amazement in his voice.

"Yeah" Beth chuckled self-consciously. "Bummer, huh? That's one of the mutations."

Dr. Blund went quiet, making Beth wonder if he was still there.

"Terry's the one Jason cut?" she asked after a few moments. "Is he okay?"

"Yes, Terry's my good friend and business partner. He's okay." He hesitated again. Beth could think of nothing else to say. "I need to think about this, Dr. Byron," he finally said. "You're welcome to stay in the valley. What do you need?"

Beth hadn't expected that offer. She thought frantically. "We realize you can't let us come inside."

"Potassium iodide pills," Ben whispered. Beth looked at him, amazed that she hadn't thought of that, then turned back to the wall.

"Some of our people have radiation sickness. Is there any chance you have potassium iodide pills?" Beth asked.

"Yes, we do. We'll place them outside the door in a few minutes. Please stay back until we deliver the pills and return to the Preserve."

"We'll do that," she said. By the way, one of our women has pneumonia. Do you have anything to help her?

"We do. We'll give you that as well."

"So, they call their retreat 'The Preserve'," Beth said. When she turned to leave, she noticed that Kerri and Callie had come up behind her. She immediately ushered them back to their campsite on the far side of the clearing.

A half hour later—Beth had been staring at the rock wall the entire time—that amazing door opened and someone in a hazmat suit placed two large containers and several smaller ones outside the door. Then the person disappeared back inside, closing the door. It disappeared again, as if by magic.

Beth wondered at the size of the packages. There was more than a few pills there.

"Ben, Kerri, Callie," Beth said, "will you help me retrieve the packages?"

They studied the rock face for a few moments before returning. "It's ingenious," Ben said. "You can't tell where that door is without knowing it's there and looking for it. The seams for the door match perfectly with the cracks in the rock face."

When they'd all gathered around, Beth opened the two large packages first, to find two boxes of pills on top of fresh fruit and vegetables. The smaller packages were sealed bottles of water. Beth looked up at the wall.

"Thank you," she said, with tears in her eyes. "Thank you so much."

"You're welcome," came the reply. "No need to ration the food. If you need more, we'll give you more."

"How?"

"Ask Jason."

Prime bunker, 2 May

The President sat alone in his office, thinking about how the crisis had progressed across the country. The extra cold winter, on top of radiation sickness, diseases and violence, was killing a large portion of the population, while they were still trying to get a handle on the mutated Smallpox virus.

His encrypted sat phone started to ring. "Hi Amos," he said when he answered.

"Hi Greg. How are things going in your neck of the woods?"

"I'll be honest with you, Amos. This is the coldest winter on record. People are dying."

"What happened at the CDC, Greg?"

Surprised at the sudden change of subject, the president made the connection immediately. "Are the people from the Johns Creek shelter in Utah?"

Amos summarized what Beth had told him about the Outcasts, the part about the CDC bombing, the escape of the mutated virus and the military attack on the shelter.

"Outcasts, huh? What do you want me to do, Amos?" Greg asked. Elated to finally know where the missing people were and surprised at how far they had traveled, he started making a mental checklist of things that he needed the military to do: get a detailed description of where the Outcasts had been and who they'd interacted with; pick them up and have them eliminated for the trouble they'd caused; identify others along their path that had been contaminated and vaccinate or eliminate them.

"I want to talk to the CDC Director, Greg. Is that still Anne Lister?"

"It is."

"Good. I want to know everything she can tell me about the mutated virus. Terry may be infected. We have him quarantined until we know."

"I'm sorry Amos. We'll come and take them off your hands. Tell us where you are." He added one more item to his mental list: decide how to deal with Terry, and what to do with Amos and the rest of his group.

"Nice try, Greg. You know I'm not going to tell you how to find us. Do you have a cure yet?"

"We think so," Greg said, wondering how he was going to get Amos to reveal the location of his retreat and the Outcasts. "We're testing it on everyone we can find from Florida to Maine and as far west as Kansas City."

"What do you mean you're testing it?"

"I suppose 'testing it' isn't exactly correct. Director Lister wanted four months to run clinical tests, but I told her we didn't have that much time. I gave her thirty days, then she began mass producing the vaccine. I told her she could continue studying her subjects and improving the vaccine if she needed. That was months ago, so now we're vaccinating everyone we can find."

"And how's that working out?"

"At first some people reacted to the vaccine. Now, I think we've got the formulation right. Those that've spent the winter outside are dying from the cold, or disease, or violence—or they're getting sick from radiation poisoning—but they're not contagious as far as we can tell."

"I'm sorry, Greg."

"You're all okay? Other than Terry?" Maybe he could trick Amos into revealing his location.

"We're fine Greg."

"Look Amos, I can get you some vaccinations. Tell me how to get them to you. I won't try to figure out where you are."

"I've got an idea how to make that work. Let me get back to you in a bit . . . and let me know the earliest you can be in the area."

"Great Amos. There's no telling how many people have been contaminated by them. See if you can find out the route they took to get to Utah."

"Will do, Greg."

17

Five months earlier

Matamoros, Mexico, 1 December

"You! Come!" the guard said. He'd given up trying to have a conversation with Jared, since Jared could barely understand a thing he said, his accent was so strong.

They hadn't been taken to El Jefe. Jared had been locked in a room by himself for seventy-nine days—he'd kept track with scratches on the wall beside the bed—with only a thin, hard mattress on the floor, no pillow or blankets (although he didn't get cold, likely because of the virus), and a chamber pot. A meager meal of gruel and tepid water was slid into the room twice a day by a guard. Since the first week, no one would enter his room and he hadn't seen the same guard for more than a few days at a time.

He'd even given up trying to find out about Pepper, since no one could speak enough English to understand his questions.

The guard stood outside his prison holding a gun on him. He wore a mask over his nose and mouth and backed away as Jared approached the door.

Pepper was sitting on a wooden chair in the main room when he entered.

"Pepper?" he said. She stood and ran to him. One of the guards—there were six of them in the room, all wearing masks—made a move to stop her, then backed away suddenly and allowed her to continue. "Are you okay?"

"It's been a nightmare," she said, on the verge of tears. "They're animals."

"Did they hurt you?" She looked like she was okay, other than being upset.

"No, just humiliated me. I can't wait to get out of here."

"What did they do?" he asked with concern.

"Oh, never mind. They didn't hurt me. I'm fine."

"You! Go now!" one of the soldiers said, waving his rifle toward the outside door.

Jared continued to watch her as they walked out of the small building. A truck was waiting, a lone driver in the cab, also wearing a mask.

"Have you figured out what's with all the masks?" Jared asked as they climbed into the back. None of the guards got in the back with them, but two of them climbed into the cab next to the driver. He'd thought it was just his guards responding to his body odor, since he hadn't bathed in over two months, but this was something else.

"I think they're all getting sick," Pepper said. "After we'd been here about a week, the guy who was their leader when they captured us visited me a couple of times." Her face suddenly flushed, as if she were embarrassed. "He asked if I had a disease, because the first two guards who'd watched me had gotten sick. Now, I haven't seen him either since then. Are we still contagious? That's the only thing that makes sense."

"Is it possible?" Jared wondered aloud. "We were told the virus had mutated, but we were vaccinated like everyone else in the shelter." Was it possible?

It took them four days, driving mostly south, to arrive at their next destination. They sat with their backs against the truck cab and talked about anything except how Pepper had been treated by the guards. She refused to answer his questions about that. After two days, they didn't have much left to talk about, and their voices were ragged from having to speak loudly enough to be heard over the truck engine, which needed an overhaul badly.

The driver stopped the truck every few hours to stretch, smoke and get something to eat out of a cooler in the space behind his seat. Jared and Pepper received one bottle of water a day to share and a couple of thick slices of crusty bread spread with some kind of vegetable spread. It tasted terrible, and the water barely washed it down, but it was more than nothing.

The first night, a guard motioned for them to lie down in the bed of the truck, while the guards slept on mats on the ground about ten yards away. They had nothing to lay on, so Jared folded his light jacket to use as a pillow and had Pepper lay her head on his stomach.

The farther south that they traveled, the clearer the air became. When they woke on the fourth day, the sun cast shadows and it was bright enough that Jared had to shield his eyes. The truck left the highway and spent the day climbing into a jungle. They could see snow on the mountains to the west. Their destination was a plantation in a clearing, with peasants working in fields, guarded by men with rifles, on towers around the perimeter of the fields. There were five buildings in a row on one side of a dirt courtyard. The middle one looked large enough to be a warehouse, the two on the far end looked like single-story bunk houses and the near two like small offices. All five were covered with netting that must have been an attempt to hide them from overhead surveillance.

The truck stopped in front of the second office, which Jared noticed had bars on the windows—a new prison, it seemed. The driver spoke with a guard in front of the prison building, while the other two hopped out of the cab and ran around back, pointing to Jared and Pepper to get out and go to the building. Jared noticed the surprised look on the prison guard's face as he looked from one of the guards to the other, perhaps reacting to the face masks. He let the guards usher them into the building, then locked the door behind them.

The interior was divided in two by a low, cinderblock wall and iron bars extending to the ceiling and across the front of both. There was a door on each half of the barred wall, but the doors stood open and Jared suspected that no one would enter the prison in an attempt to separate them.

"We seem to be a lot of trouble for them," Pepper said, sarcastically. "Why don't they just shoot us and be over with it?"

"Maybe they're as curious about this virus as I am," Jared said. "I wonder if this is where El Jefe lives . . . or works. This has got to be a drug cartel. I think the plants in the field closest to us are poppies and the trees in that farther field are coca."

"You mean for heroin and cocaine? How would you know?" Pepper asked in alarm.

"I'm not positive, but I've seen pictures and that's what they look like. Considering how we've been treated, it fits."

No one brought them food before the sun went down and they had to figure out their own sleeping arrangements.

18

It's a gut feeling

Prime bunker—Meeting of the Panel, 2 May

The president sat at the table in the Prime bunker situation room. His advisors—SecDef, DNI, HomeSec and State—were connected to the meeting by secure communications, images of their situation rooms arrayed on wall monitors in front of him. In addition, Ambassador Daniel Porter and CDC Director Anne Lister had joined from the VEEP bunker. The other three monitors had been dark since the bombing of the bunkers by the Chinese, months ago.

"Director Lister, I need to patch you through a secure line to an associate of mine out in Utah. He's a medical doctor who has a need to know everything you can tell him about the mutated virus. I've arranged for secure rooms in your bunker and mine where we can make that happen. I need it taken care of immediately."

"Alright. Is he a virologist?" she asked.

"Cy," the president said to the Secretary of State without answering her question, "have you spoken with her about Mexico?"

"Yes, sir," Cy said. "President Obrador accepted our offer to loan them military and medical professionals to determine the extent of the problem and a possible solution."

"And I've spoken to the scientists at the government run Level 3 Biohazard facility in Mexico City," Lister said. "We've given them the information they need to set up a Level 4 containment facility and they say they're ready to receive the vaccine and begin vaccinating their populace."

"Greg," HomeSec Chuck Dickson said before the conversation could move on, "we've sent people to the Gulf coast to see if the virus spread in that direction. You were right to question it. We found a large population of contamination in Galveston, Texas, and we've asked Director Lister to provide vaccinations and people to help Jim distribute it." Greg looked at Jim, his eyebrows raised.

"We've got the vaccinations," Jim said, "and I've sent troops to Texas to take care of it."

Greg looked back at Chuck. "Anywhere else, Chuck?"

"Nope. That's it."

"So, whoever did this, they probably took a boat from the Georgia coast as far as Galveston," Greg said, "then bounced back out and landed in northern Mexico. Is that our conclusion?"

There were nods of agreement.

"Thank you, director," Greg said. "Please go with Captain Nichols to prepare for that phone call. I'll join you shortly."

"Sir," she said, still sitting. He looked at her, a little annoyed at her delay.

"What is it, director?"

"I want to thank you for authorizing me to give the vaccine formula to the Russian scientists. They've succeeded in duplicating the vaccine and are saving lives."

"That's great," he said quietly. "So, some of the Russians will survive and we can expect to deal with them again in the future."

"What's going on, Greg?" SecDef Jim Seymour asked, drawing the president back to the conversation. "You're talking about Amos Blund, aren't you?"

"The Johns Creek survivors are in Utah," Greg said. "I told

Amos I'd let him talk to the director. I also told him we'd get him some vaccinations."

"Thank you, director," Greg said. Anne got up and left, then Ambassador Porter disconnected and his monitor went dark.

"Greg," Jim said, "those survivors have already cheated death once. They're probably responsible for all the contamination we've found west of the Mississippi River. Now you're telling us they've gone all the way to Utah. We've got to stop them. If I get my hands on them, I'll wring their scrawny necks."

"You might get your chance," Greg said. A plan was forming in his head and Jim was the key to making it work. "Amos is going to get back to me with a plan to get him the vaccinations without giving away his location. I want you to prepare a team to meet him in an as-yet undisclosed location near Logan, Utah."

"With the vaccinations?"

"Or something that looks like vaccinations."

"Yes sir," Jim said. "I'll get a helicopter in the air immediately. I'll get you an ETA as soon as I have one."

"Great Jim. Thanks. Anything else gentlemen?"

"What are you thinking Greg?" HomeSec Chuck Dickson asked. "You told Amos you'd give him vaccinations but you're not going to?"

"I need to bring Amos in. His partner needs a vaccination, so I'll trade it for his cooperation. I'll let Jim deal with the Outcasts."

"Hasn't he been cooperating so far?" Chuck asked.

"Yes, but I need something from him that he's possibly not willing to give me."

Jim smiled deviously. "So, you're going to trick Amos into giving himself up?"

"I'm going to try, Jim. It won't be easy."

"Hasn't Amos been a friend since you were in school?" Chuck

asked, becoming agitated.

Greg made eye contact with Chuck, then each of the others. How far could he really trust these men? He'd known Jim the longest and was fairly confident he would cooperate. He wasn't as sure of the others.

"Chuck—all of you—we may have the survival of the human race in our hands. That is paramount. If Amos has something that will help, we need it. Is that understood?" He waited for each of his advisors to say 'yes' or nod their agreement, Chuck last of all, and reluctantly. "That's all gentlemen," Greg said. "Jim, will you stay for a minute?"

Jim nodded and the others disconnected.

"Jim, we have a problem. You remember Chuck saying that we're running out of fuel and parts for the generators?" Jim nodded. "I'm worried that these bunkers won't last long enough for us to get through the environmental crisis."

"They were built a long time ago," Jim said.

"Yes, they were. When I was in the Senate, as head of the Senate Committee on Commerce, Science, and Transportation, I received an unsolicited report about these bunkers. At the time, I didn't do anything with it. I dug it out recently because I remembered it stating something about the survivability of the bunkers. Because of the age of the bunkers at that time, the power supplies were projected to last less than five years."

"That's why you want to talk to Amos?" Jim asked. "Chuck said his people didn't expect it to be safe to go outside in some parts of the country for at least five to ten years considering the amount of contamination we put into the atmosphere."

"Exactly. Chuck did a patent search on Amos' power source. The patent's there all right, but there's insufficient information in the application to duplicate it. We need to know the secret of

Amos's power supply. Do you get my drift?"

"Loud and clear, Greg. We get the Johns Creek mutants *and* Amos's secret power source at the same time."

"Don't forget, we believe Amos has vehicles in his hardened bunker, too," Jim said.

"Oh yeah, what did we find out about . . . what did you call them? Preppers?"

"I think that's a dead end Greg. We've talked to a dozen groups and none of them have the technological expertise to build a nuclear reactor except the one we already discussed—the former submarine mechanic, and we've already determined that his reactor isn't compatible with an electrical distribution system like we need; but we already know Amos's works, so that's the one we need."

"And who knows what other secrets he has that we need?" Greg asked, not expecting an answer from Jim.

Jim was thoughtful when he disconnected his link with the President.

The Preserve, 2 May

Amos called an emergency board meeting to tell them about his conversation with the president. Terry participated by video monitor from his isolation in the storeroom.

"I'm suspicious," he said. "I trust Greg, but his advisors have been fighting this disease for months. No telling what they might try to do, with or without Greg's permission. I can't lead them to the Preserve."

"You said we can trust the President," Terry said. "So why are you worried?"

"I don't know. It's a gut feeling. I've thought this through several times. He'll probably have Jim Seymour handle the drop, since Jim's over the military. Greg may be sincere, but he seems too anxious to get us the vaccinations. They're not even properly tested."

"You know, Amos," Terry said, "if they'd taken time to test the vaccine according to protocols, everyone would be dead before the cure was ready."

"You're right, of course. But Jim could have a military team on the way to Logan right now, with instructions to capture us when we show up." That made everyone stop and think. "I need to get back to Greg with a plan soon."

"Beth said the president wanted to kill them," Mike said. "Is he lying about the vaccine in order to get to the Outcasts?"

"Or," Terry asked, "does Greg want to know where the Preserve is for some reason? And if so, what's his interest?"

"Good questions," Amos replied.

"How much does he know about the Preserve?" Terry asked.

"He knows we planned to outlast a nuclear winter and he knows we're totally self-contained," Amos replied.

"What is it about the Preserve that Greg would want?" Becca asked.

"I'm sure they have medicine and hydroponic gardens," Lillie said.

"What about the Observer?" Mike asked.

"All Greg knows is that it allows us to see things at a distance," Terry replied.

"However," Amos added, "he may suspect there are other applications."

"There's no way he can guess it's real capability," Terry said. "We didn't even know until recently."

"We still don't know if we've seen its full capability," Amos said. "We may just be touching the surface."

"Alright. What's their highest priority right now?" Terry asked.

"Clean water?" Lillie asked.

"Electricity?" Terry asked.

"Weather control?" Mike asked.

Amos barked a laugh.

"Maybe he thinks the Observer can control the weather," Mike said.

Amos and Terry made eye contact and Terry nodded. "I think his highest priority now is survival," Amos said.

"Meaning?" Lillie asked.

"Power is out across the country," Terry said. "Without electricity, nothing works."

"Millions of people are without food, water and medical help," Amos said. "He may be worried about the government bunkers lasting long enough for the radiation to drop to safe levels. If he doesn't survive, he can't help anyone else, and he *really is* concerned about the country and the people.

"The one thing we have that he doesn't," Amos continued, "is a long-term supply of power. He may want the secret of our reactor so he can start building local power supplies to get the country running again. I'm guessing he wants the plans for the nuclear reactor."

"Can we tell him how to build his own?" Lillie asked.

"Yes," Amos replied, "but next to the Observer, the reactor is our most valuable intellectual property."

"Can't the government steal the patent information?" Mike asked.

"Normally they could. But in this case, there's insufficient information in the patent application to allow them to duplicate it," Amos answered.

"Okay," Mike said, "we're not sure the president wants the reactor or the Observer. He may just want the Outcasts. How do we keep him from getting any of them?"

"Amos," Lillie asked, "would Greg try to capture one of us to use as leverage to get what he wants?"

Prime bunker—Meeting of the Panel, 2 May

SecDef General James (Jim) Seymour did what he did best; set up Covert Ops. In this case, he planned to place an elite Special Forces team in the vicinity of Logan, Utah, to capture Amos Blund or one of his family members to use as leverage to obtain the secret to the Preserve's power supply.

Jim and his staff had selected a plan from their operational manual—one that had worked many times in the past. Their team was selected from a pool of well-trained soldiers, some of whom had worked together before. Unfortunately, because the current crisis had spread their forces far and wide, they were limited to those who were available and could be gathered together on short notice.

Jim had the Op initiated within 30 minutes of Greg's request with all the fire power and equipment called for in the plan and anything else they could think of that they might need.

The Preserve, 2 May

"What do you think the president will do?" Terry asked Amos as the seven members of the board sat around the table in the office trying to outthink the government.

"He has the military—what's left of it," Amos said, "which includes soldiers, planes and helicopters, hardened communications, night vision and heat sensing equipment, satellite surveillance and who knows what else."

"They could have a team on the way now," Terry said. "They know we're close to Logan. They could set down within minutes of knowing the drop location."

"What chance do we have against that?" Mike asked.

"We need to take all of those things into consideration," Amos said, "and look at our advantages. We can select the drop location and get there ahead of them. We also have some assets that we haven't needed before now. If we can anticipate their actions, maybe we can out-maneuver them. Here's my idea." As Amos explained, there were several questions and suggestions, and a lot of skepticism about how well the plan would work; but they agreed it had the best chance of success.

At dusk Amos and Mike walked their eBikes—electric bicycles that they'd been keeping in the garage—across the snow-covered ground to the path leading to the highway. The bikes had over-sized, deep tread tires, which they'd deflated just enough to ensure good traction in the snow. They pedaled like a bicycle until extra power was needed to climb, then a throttle engaged a battery to add the extra boost needed. They were quiet, generated little heat, and gave off no emissions that could be spotted from the air using heat sensing equipment.

Their hazmat suits were baggy enough that they could pull their arms out of the sleeves to reach their vest pockets, which held food, the straw to their water bag, and the Sat phone that connected Amos to the president. They'd applied quick drying, flat-finish, spray paint to the suits to prevent any reflection from the little ambient light that penetrated the overcast sky, and the suits naturally masked their body heat in the cold air.

They wore catheters to collect bodily fluids and had enough compressed air to last about 12 hours. They had spare batteries in their saddlebags to get them back to the Preserve. Amos wore night vision goggles that fit in his hood and Mike's goggles were heat sensing.

As they rode out of Aspen Valley that evening—they needed darkness for their plan to work—Amos noticed the Outcasts watching them from across the clearing. They were a curious sight, and he chuckled, trying to imagine what they might be thinking.

Garden City, 2 May

Amos and Mike arrived in Garden City about an hour later. They weren't too worried about the locals, since Beth had told them everyone in Garden City went to bed with the sun. They *were* concerned about the military. They needed to verify their plan to get in and out, and get set up without interference.

They rode to the medical center—their first choice for a drop site—paying attention to the layout of the town as they passed. They were familiar with Garden City, but only in its pre-war condition. The added population had changed the town significantly. They drove a mile past the drop site to observe the approach from that direction. Then, after riding around the medical center and parking lot, they rode to a shop 100 yards back toward the turnoff to the Preserve. The shop advertised rentals—bicycles, ATVs, boats and other outdoor equipment. Some motorized equipment was still there—items that would no longer work without power—and three bicycles padlocked to a rack. They left their bikes there, with simple combination locks, for a quick getaway.

After walking back to the medical center, they checked the proximity of the lake to the parking lot. Satisfied that the lake was a good backup plan—they could get to it quickly, if needed—they separated to opposite ends of the parking lot, on the lake side, and hid in the bushes. They'd agreed that if their communications became blocked, they would move to a central location by the lake and decide how to proceed.

"Terry," Amos said into his helmet mic, "are you reading us?"

"Loud and clear," Terry said. "What's your plan if the military disrupts our communications?"

"In that case we're on our own. We'll have to decide whether to proceed or abort based on existing conditions. We'll get home when we can."

"Don't take chances Amos. We need you. You have a limited clean air supply"

"Understood, Terry."

When they were set up, Amos called the president. It was midnight, local time, two a.m. in the east.

Garden City, 3 May

"You have a location for us?" the president asked as soon as he answered the phone.

Amos could tell the President had him on speaker so others could hear. He guessed Jim would be one of them.

"Yes, Greg," Amos said. "Tell Jim to locate the medical center parking lot in Garden City. That's on the western shore of Bear Lake, in Utah. We should be there at two a.m. local time," Amos added to intentionally mislead Greg and Jim. "Have someone meet us there."

"Great," Greg said immediately. "A helicopter is already in the Logan area. Jim tells me we can be there in time."

Greg's quick response made Amos wonder if Terry had been right to question Greg's motives. Jim had two hours to make a trip from Logan to Garden City that should take no more than a few minutes. It was a perfect opportunity for him to set a trap to catch Amos, if that was his plan—something that Amos needed to know.

"How will we know if the vaccine works?" Amos asked—a second test of Greg's sincerity. If they really had the vaccine, there should be no problem answering Amos's question.

"Your visitors can either test it on themselves or find someone to use as a guinea pig," Greg said after a moment.

"That will have to do," Amos continued, thinking that Greg had successfully avoided that trap, and the thought of Beth offering up Jason as a guinea pig to test the vaccine made him smile. Now he just wanted to get off the phone. "We'll meet your team at the medical center in a couple of hours."

"How's the Preserve holding up?" Greg asked quickly, before Amos could hang up. "Is everything working like you want it to?"

Amos's first thought was, *he's trying to delay us from getting to the drop site before his team,* immediately followed by another, *he wants the reactor design!* He knew exactly what to say to end the conversation. If Greg was going to set a trap, he would try to beat Amos to the drop site.

"We're fine for now," Amos said. "Hey, Greg, we need to go so we can get to the medical center on time."

19

Are you threatening me?

Prime bunker, 3 May

Greg was ecstatic. Jim's special ops team could beat Amos to the drop site and set up the ambush that they'd prepared; but he was so intrigued with the concept of a nuclear power source that could last for thirty years, he couldn't resist asking another question.

"Didn't you say the Preserve was designed to hold up for 30 years?"

"That's the design," Amos replied, sounding anxious to get away.

Greg gave Jim, who was listening to the conversation, a 'thumbs-up', but Jim frowned at the President and shook his head.

"Greg, why are you asking about our power supply?" Amos asked, sounding suspicious.

Greg realized that his question could easily give away his reason for wanting to meet with Amos in Garden City.

"Just making sure you'll be okay," Greg said, trying to cover for his faux pas. Amos would either accept it as Greg's sincere concern for the family's safety, or he would figure out Greg's real motive for cooperating and back out of the meeting. Greg hoped he would do the former. "Take care and call after you get the package," he added, then disconnected.

Garden City, 3 May, 12:35 a.m.

Amos considered cancelling the meeting and returning to the Preserve, but they needed those vaccinations, so it was worth a little risk. He hoped his preparations would keep them safe. Besides, he and Greg had been friends for many years and Amos instinctively trusted him.

Amos picked up the sound of helicopter rotors, and mentioned it to Mike over his headset. Within minutes, a helicopter hovered two feet above the asphalt of the parking lot not far from Mike.

"It's amazingly quiet for a helicopter," Amos said. "It must have some stealth capability. Otherwise it would wake the whole neighborhood this close to the ground."

"I count eight soldiers jumping out of the helicopter and scattering to compass points," Mike said.

"Yeah," Amos said, looking through his night-vision goggles. "They appear to have goggles and rifles."

Two of the soldiers moved to the side of the parking lot where Amos and Mike were hiding in the bushes.

"Move back into the brush," Amos said. "If they keep coming, keep backing up. Go all the way to the water if communications are disrupted."

"Will do," Mike replied.

The soldiers, dressed in camouflage clothing, entered the bushes and virtually disappeared. Then everyone settled in to wait.

If Greg wanted the secret of Amos's reactor, Amos wondered, why didn't he just ask for it.

At two o'clock, another helicopter—it may have been the same one, it was quiet enough—hovered over the parking lot, then landed. As the rotors slowed to a stop, two soldiers got out unhurriedly. One lifted a box out of the helicopter and set it on the ground. The other soldier, holding a rifle, looked around, as if protecting his partner.

Amos's sat phone vibrated. He had set it to vibrate so it wouldn't give away his location.

"Hello Greg," Amos said quietly.

"Hi Amos," the President said. "The package has been delivered. When will you arrive?"

After a slight pause, Amos asked, "Why did you send soldiers in advance of the delivery?"

Greg didn't respond. Amos started to ask again, when Greg interrupted him.

"What do you mean, soldiers?" Greg asked defensively, confirming to Amos that the satellite hadn't picked up the electric bikes.

"No games, Greg. Why did you send soldiers? To set a trap for us? What are you afraid of?"

"How do you know I sent soldiers? Is your Preserve in walking distance of the medical center?" There was excitement in Greg's voice, as though he believed he had discovered something.

"No deal, Greg. Pull your soldiers out and tell me what you want. We've been friends too long for you to be playing games. I'm not your enemy. You know I'm not unreasonable. But you have to be honest with me."

Suddenly Mike's voice came over Amos's headset. "The soldiers are moving around. They're looking for us. We need to go to Plan B."

Amos had been focused on his conversation with the President and had let his guard down. Now he could see the soldiers moving. He hung up on the President and he and Mike backed away from their hiding places as stealthily as possible. They made their way to the lake and entered up to their necks. Eventually, two soldiers cleared the brush next to the lake about 40 feet apart and crouched low, looking around the beach and out across the water. If they had heat sensitive goggles, the cool water was hiding Amos and Mike from their sight. The soldiers stayed that way for a couple of minutes, then turned back and disappeared into the brush.

They stayed in the water, waiting for the President to make the next move. Suddenly, there was a high-pitched squealing in Amos's ears as his communications were jammed. Amos shut off his headset and waited.

Finally, the sat phone vibrated. Amos didn't answer. He wanted Greg to come to his senses and stop the games. But maybe Greg had been playing these games for so long that he didn't know how else to get what he wanted. It vibrated six times before it stopped.

When it vibrated again a few minutes later, he decided to take a chance. He couldn't see any movement in the bushes, but he could see Mike in the water—through his night vision goggles—twenty feet away. He moved closer to Mike until Mike noticed him, then pointed two fingers at his head then toward the shore. Mike nodded, understanding that his dad was asking if he saw anything with his heat sensing goggles. Mike looked along the shore, then shook his head slowly.

Amos motioned for Mike to move closer to shore and began moving, himself.

"Hello Greg," Amos whispered. "That wasn't very nice of you."

"Amos," Greg said in a commanding voice. "Show yourself and let the soldiers escort you to me so we can talk."

"Not going to happen Greg." Playing a hunch, Amos added, "I can't let you harm the Johns Creek survivors."

"The Johns Cre . . . " Greg started to ask, apparently surprised, confirming Amos's belief that Greg was not after the survivors, but something at the Preserve.

Greg must have realized Amos had tricked him. "Amos," the President started again, "this is a matter of national security. I insist, as your president, that you cooperate."

"Greg, if you're blocking communications, why can I still hear you?" He knew the answer, but he wanted to see how much Greg was willing to reveal. He was also trying to distract Greg from his demand that Amos reveal himself.

"I've had all communications but this frequency blocked. You can no longer direct your people. You must cooperate."

Amos laughed quietly. "Greg, we're so far ahead of you, you never had a chance." In reality, Amos was worried about their chances of getting away, but he wasn't going to let Greg know that. "Get your soldiers out of here and tell me what you want."

Greg was quiet for another minute. Amos could visualize Greg meeting with his secret Panel of advisors, trying to figure a way to outsmart Amos.

"Ok Amos. You tell me what I want to know and we back away."

"No good Greg. Get the soldiers out of there before one of them gets hurt." Amos was pushing his luck, but Greg didn't know he was bluffing. If Amos had a secret power source, who knew what it was capable of doing. Amos and Mike had reached shore and had started crawling through the bushes toward the parking lot.

"Are you threatening me?" Greg asks, anger in his voice. "That could be classified as treason."

"Cut it out, Greg. I'm just stating a fact. By the way," he added, before Greg could respond, "are the vaccinations worth anything?

Or were they just a bluff to get your soldiers near us?"

"Okay, Amos, against the advice of my closest advisors, I'm calling the soldiers back. Then we'll talk." Had Greg given up the charade?

"Stop blocking communications."

"Done. Soldiers are on their way to the helicopter."

Mike was slightly ahead of Amos. When the two soldiers in the brush broke cover and ran back toward the parking lot, Mike followed cautiously, until he was at the edge of the parking lot. Amos turned his headset back on. Mike's voice sounded anxiously in his ear. "Six of their eight soldiers are in the open, headed for the helicopter. And I can barely hear." He must have left his headset on, listening to the interference.

As the helicopter blades started to rotate, it appeared that the other two soldiers were planning to stay behind. The package was still on the ground where it had been set.

"Not good enough, Greg," Amos said. "Get the other two soldiers back to the helicopter before something bad happens." He had moved up so he could see the helicopter, the soldiers and the box on the ground. He was thinking about what might happen to him and Mike, but wanted Greg to think he was threatening the soldiers. "And have them take that worthless empty box with them."

The helicopter skids were lifting off the ground, but the helicopter didn't leave right away. A few moments later, the remaining two soldiers ran, crouching, from the brush on either side of the parking lot, loaded the package into the helicopter and jumped in. Then the helicopter lifted off, quietly, turned toward Logan and disappeared into the night sky.

"They're gone," the president said.

"Are they truly gone? Or do we have a repeat performance in

a few minutes?"

"They're gone," Greg said with resignation. "Will you keep your side of the bargain, Amos?"

"When have I ever given you reason to doubt me, Greg?" Amos replied seriously.

There was a pause, during which Amos could picture Greg thinking over how to phrase his next comment, or during which he was getting input from his advisors.

"We need the secret of your power supply," Greg said with a sigh.

"I thought so. Why didn't you save us both a lot of grief and just say that to begin with?"

When it was apparent that Greg had no answer that he was willing to verbalize, Amos continued.

"Greg, that power supply is one of my most valuable intellectual properties. I suspect you've already checked the patent office and discovered that you can't duplicate it from what was submitted."

After another pause—and more silence on the sat phone—Amos continued.

"If you'll get your best nuclear engineer on the phone, I'll explain what they need to do to copy it." Amos thought he could hear a collective sigh of relief over the sat phone. As much as he wanted to keep the secret of the reactor, nothing was worth risking the safety of his family members.

After what seemed like an eternity, Amos spoke again.

"Greg, are you still there?" he asked.

"Yes, Amos. We're just trying to figure out who that would be. Let me get this underway, then I'll call you back with the latest on the vaccinations. Sorry about the drama." He sounded truly contrite.

Amos debated how wise it was to say what was on his mind while he was upset. In this case, he was so angry he couldn't resist. He was giving up a lot because of the dangerous situation Greg had created. "Greg, you were ready to attack members of my family with deadly weapons. I won't forget it, no matter how long we've been friends."

Prime bunker—Meeting of the Panel, 3 May

There was nothing Greg could say. Amos was right, again. The President of the United States disconnected the phone call.

"This is a mistake, Greg," Jim said angrily. "If we go back right now, we can catch them while they're trying to escape. You can't let him talk to you like that."

"No Jim," Greg replied. He was embarrassed and humiliated. He couldn't have felt worse if Amos were standing in front of him pointing a finger in his face. "It was a mistake. I should have just told him what we wanted. Who do we have from the Nuclear Regulatory Agency in the bunkers?"

Jim didn't respond. Greg hadn't seen Jim this angry in a long time.

"The vice chairman is in our bunker," Cy Hutchison, in the STATE bunker, said.

"The chairman's here," Chuck Dickson, in the HOME SEC bunker added.

"Good. Chuck, get the chairman to find the right person. Then set it up with Eric Epstein to use my sat phone to connect him with Amos. Let's get this done immediately."

"Now, sir?" Chuck asked. "It's after four thirty in the morning." They had agreed that all references to time would be Eastern time.

"Oh, alright. Wait a couple of hours before waking him. But let's get this done quickly. Chuck, has Director Lister spoken with

Amos about the virus yet?"

"Uh, no sir. You just asked today . . . well yesterday now . . . a few hours ago, for that to happen."

"Well, make it happen, then," Greg said tiredly. He felt like he hadn't slept in days. Sleeping in his office, ever since Liz had kicked him out of their bedroom, was having that effect.

"Yes sir. Right away."

"What else do we need to do? Oh yes. Chuck, we also need to know the status of the vaccinations. If the director has a positive report, I want to get some to Amos."

"How are you going to do that, sir," Jim snapped. "He's not going to trust you a second time. He's going to think we have soldiers waiting for him in Garden City."

The President didn't hesitate. "*Do* we have soldiers waiting for him in Garden City, Jim?" he asked, glaring at Jim as though the entire fiasco in Garden City was Jim's fault. He wondered if Jim would act on his own, without authorization.

"No sir," Jim replied emphatically.

"Would you lie to me if you did?" Greg asked, trying to read Jim's face. He was good at reading people, but Jim was equally good at hiding his thoughts and emotions.

Jim was startled, which was clear in his normally expressionless face. "I don't know sir. I was just asking myself the same thing."

"I'll tell Amos we don't and hope it's true . . . and hope he believes me." He paused, making meaningful eye contact with Jim. He would hate to see Jim violate his trust and force him to take action against him. Jim was too valuable to him and to the nation.

"Ok, gentlemen. Let's get a couple of hours sleep." He looked at his watch, then at Chuck. "Let's meet again at 8 a.m. Chuck, see if you can have an NRC name for us and a report from Director Lister." Chuck nodded and they all shut down.

The Preserve, 3 May

Amos and Mike had waited almost an hour before leaving the medical center to retrieve their bikes. Amos hadn't known if he could trust the president not to trick them by sending the soldiers back to Garden City while they tried to escape.

Amos was already regretting his closing remark to Greg. He had anticipated that Greg wanted the secret of the reactor and had decided to give it to him. He had even anticipated the attack. But in the end, he had felt betrayed. It was a spontaneous reaction; one he might regret later.

He had confessed and apologized to Lillie and Terry over the radio all the way home, which didn't give Lillie a chance to ask him anything about the confrontation.

After he and Mike disinfected the bikes and hazmat suits and vented the airlock, they found Lillie and Katie waiting in the tunnel outside the airlock to greet them, at about 4 a.m. Terry would have been present to congratulate his friend, had he not been in quarantine.

Amos immediately started to apologize, but Lillie placed a finger to his lips, gave him a hug and kissed him.

Katie was right behind Lillie. She grabbed Mike in a tight embrace. Her tear-filled eyes expressed her gratitude for his safety. He wiped her tears away and kissed her.

"You defeated the United States Special Forces, Mike," she said. "You're my hero."

"It was a little scary, I gotta tell ya," he said, chuckling nervously and shaking his head, "and my hearing may never be the same."

"What's Greg going to do now?" Lillie asked, holding onto Amos's arm as they walked to their room, as if she were afraid he might disappear if she let go of him.

"I don't know," Amos complained. "He'll probably do what we

asked. I hope he feels guilty enough to not try any more tricks. We need to come up with another plan."

"A plan for what?" she asked.

"For another drop. We still don't have the vaccinations."

"Right now, you need to get some sleep," Lillie scolded. "You won't be able to think clearly if you don't."

"Of course, honey."

She took the sat phone out of his hand.

"I'll wake you if he calls," she said, "or not," she added with a mischievous smile.

20

What's our highest priority?

The Preserve, 3 May

"Has he called," Amos asked when he came into the dining room for breakfast.

"A couple of times," Lillie replied. "But I thought your rest was more important than talking to him."

"I better call him."

"What are you going to say?"

"I don't know. Maybe I'll just listen, then put him off a couple of hours, so the board can talk about it."

"I think that's a good idea."

"Hi Amos," the President said tiredly.

"Hi Greg. Did you get any sleep?" Amos asked.

"A little. Are you ready to talk?"

"I'm listening."

"We have Dr. Floyd Jerman lined up to talk to you about your power supply when you're ready. He's the Chairman of the Nuclear Regulatory Commission. We also have Director Lister ready to talk to you about the mutated virus and the vaccinations. What do you want to do?"

"I'll get back to you." Amos hung up first.

"What do you want to do, Amos?" Terry asked over the monitor from the storage room. The rest of the board was in the office.

"I want the board to decide. What's our highest priority?"

"Getting Terry vaccinated," Becca said, "and that means getting the Outcasts vaccinated."

"Don't give them the reactor design until we know Terry's going to be okay," Lillie said.

"Don't let them find us . . . or the Outcasts," Mike said.

"How do we get the vaccinations without them finding us?" Amos asked. "I don't think we can use the same plan twice."

That made them all stop and think. What other resources did they have?

Just then, a voice called from one of the outside sensors. "Dr. Blund. Dr. Amos Blund. Can you hear me?"

Amos suddenly had a novel idea.

"I'm here," Amos said, speaking through the sensor that Beth had called him from. "What can we do for you Dr. Byron?"

"We have Jason tied up," Beth said, "but I don't think it's healthy for him to stay that way for long. We don't want to just release him because he's been threatening. What do you think we should we do with him?"

"Thank you for not releasing him. I think we can help you there. How are the rest of you doing? Are you warm enough? Do you have enough to eat?"

"You've been very kind Dr. Blund. We don't seem to get very cold and the food you've supplied has been wonderful. We're fine, thank you. What is your plan for Jason?"

"Excellent. Let me run my idea past the others and I'll get

right back to you. There may be another way we can help each other. I'll let you know."

"We'll be here."

Amos spent a few minutes explaining his idea to the board and they agreed unanimously to proceed.

"Dr. Byron," Amos called.

"I'm here Dr. Blund."

"Here's what we propose." Amos told her.

A short time later, Amos and Mike, dressed in hazmat suits, began stacking supplies outside the door of the Preserve. It took several trips. When they were almost finished, Beth met them at the door and delivered one of her remaining vaccinations to Amos, for Terry, who had started to show signs of smallpox. Amos gave Beth a couple of diagrams and a set of instructions. The other Outcasts also came forward and helped Beth carry the supplies to the edge of the woods.

Before the end of the day, the Outcasts had built a metal cage in a clearing among the trees, from the materials provided by Amos. They bolted poles together for a frame, then bolted heavy wire screen on the sides and bottom and a solid cover for a roof. They placed Jason inside the portable dog run and locked him in with a heavy padlock.

The remainder of the material, they used to build a similar frame—without the heavy screen—large enough to give them shelter for themselves near Jason's cage. This gave the Outcasts some protection from the weather. It also hid them out of view of the military, should they come looking.

In exchange for the shelter, the Outcasts agreed to go back to Garden City and watch for an advance team from the military. Beth decided to take Bryce and Callie. She wasn't quite ready to trust Bryce alone with Jason. She left Ben in charge. Ben and Beth each now had a radio and instructions on how to contact Amos to report their findings.

Prime bunker, 3 May

"Hello Amos," the president said anxiously on the first ring.

"Hello Greg. I'm ready to talk to Director Lister and Chairman Jerman."

The words were barely out of Amos' mouth when the president replied. "Director Lister is standing by. Just a second."

There was clicking on the line, an indication to Amos that Greg's technical people had prepared for this call by linking Greg's Sat Phone to another line, since he was certain Greg wouldn't let his Sat Phone out of his hands. A female voice came on the line, speaking tentatively. "Hello? This is Dr. Anne Lister, director of the—former—CDC."

"This is Dr. Amos Blund," Amos said without responding to her attempted humor. "I would like you to explain to me everything you know about the mutated virus."

"Everything?"

"Take your time. Leave nothing out."

Director Lister spoke for a couple of hours, with Amos asking questions to make sure he understood her explanations. He had also piped the conversation to Terry in the storeroom so they could discuss it later. It was also being recorded.

She explained how the researchers—Dr. Thomas Strang and his associate at the CDC—had tried to modify the virus to make it safer, and how she had later discovered that they and their associates at the other two Level 4 facilities had conspired to protect the virus by removing it from the facilities. They didn't know the facilities were scheduled to be bombed or they might have handled it differently. She then explained what she'd learned about the mutation of the virus, by combining the research data from the three facilities with the testing she'd done on the contaminated people the military had brought to her.

"A family of three carried the virus to Johns Creek," she said, "where it was mistaken for radiation sickness, and was spread through the shelter, contaminating almost a hundred people. My team prepared a vaccine to reduce the symptoms of the disease and the military delivered it."

"Later," she continued, with an effort to control her emotions, "the government sent more soldiers, pretending to be doctors, to kill everyone in the shelter." She explained what she knew of the ensuing gun battle that resulted in the death of eighty-two men, women and children—all of the children that had been in the shelter.

She briefly described as much as she knew about the government's attempt to stop the spread of the disease, starting near Atlanta and Ft. Detrick, using elimination squads, as well as the role the vice president and the Outcasts had played in spreading the disease throughout the east and along the Mississippi River. She also mentioned her efforts to help Russia and stop the outbreaks in Texas and Mexico. Finally, she explained her team's months-long effort to find a cure and the government's campaign to vaccinate the country's population.

"So, you don't know if there was a conspiracy to release the virus, just to protect it?" Amos asked.

"I'm satisfied that they meant only to protect it, although I could be wrong." Lister said.

"Let's hope you're right," Amos said. "Have you been observing any of the vaccinated people?"

"We have," she said tiredly. "There have been no adverse reactions in several months and the patients appear to be no longer contagious."

"That's good. Can you think of anything else to add?"

"No, nothing."

"Thank you for taking time to speak with me, director. Will you please put the president back on?"

"May I ask, Dr. Blund, why you want to know all of this?" She already suspected she knew the answer, but wanted confirmation.

"It seems, director, that your virus has spread its wings," Amos said. "I want to know how to fight it."

"Oh," she said. The way Amos said it made her feel personally responsible for the virus's spread.

☢

"I'm here, Amos," Greg interrupted, thinking their discussion had ended. He'd kept his phone connected and on speaker, while he had been studying reports from his advisors, so he could jump into the conversation, if needed. "Did you get what you needed?"

"We'll discuss it and let you know if we have more questions," Amos said. "I'd like you to prepare to send us some of Director Lister's vaccinations."

"The same place as last time?" Greg asked.

"I'll let you know. Now, is Chairman Jerman ready to talk?"

"He's been waiting. One minute."

☢

An older voice came on the line. "This is Dr. Floyd Jerman, Chairman of the Nuclear Regulatory Commission. Who am I speaking with, please?"

"This is Amos Blund."

"Dr. Blund," the Chairman said, "your reputation as a medical professional and scientist is well known. Pretending humility doesn't cut mustard with me."

Amos laughed out loud, surprising Jerman.

"I'll be blunt," Jerman continued, affronted by Dr. Blund's mockery. "President McCormick tells me that you have a revolutionary nuclear power supply that he wants me to understand and recreate for him. How do you want to handle this?"

"To be honest, Mr. Chairman, I think you're the wrong person to deal with this."

"And why is that?" Jerman asked, bristling.

"Now I'll be blunt. With your ego, Dr. Jerman, we'll spend most of our time together arguing about whether or not my system will work."

Jerman huffed but didn't interrupt. Actually, he didn't know how to respond to Dr. Blund's arrogance.

"The system already works," Amos continued. "I don't need you telling me all the reasons why it *won't* work."

Jerman found his voice and tried to object, but Amos cut him off. "Shut up and listen, Mr. Chairman," Amos said. "Find your best up-and-coming junior scientist—the one with the most revolutionary ideas—and make her available to the President. If you have any reservations about this request—no, this demand—tell Greg that you're sorry, but you can't help him."

"He'll do exactly as you've demanded, Amos," the president said. He must have been listening on the line, which surprised Jerman.

"You said she," Greg continued. "Why does it have to be a woman?"

"Just a guess, Greg. I expect that the NRC has, or knows of, some excellent young nuclear scientists who would like to reinvent the nuclear power industry. I also suspect that those brilliant young scientists are being beaten down by the know-it-alls in the NRC who defend all the regulations that make nuclear power so expensive. I suspect that there is at least one among them who is humble enough to be willing to learn from me and follow my instructions. Finally, I expect that she is a she. Any other questions?"

"We'll find her Amos," Greg said.

Amos disconnected.

Dr. Floyd Jerman, Chairman of the Nuclear Regulatory Commission and head of the country's nuclear regulating Agency, was dumbfounded that anyone would talk to him—or the president—the way Dr. Blund had. He had read everything he could find on this Dr. Amos Blund in the last few hours and this was not the quiet and reclusive physician/scientist described on the internet and in the literature. More surprising, he was on a first-name basis with the president of the United States and the president bowed to his demands.

Garden City, 4 May

"Dr. Blund," Beth said.

"Please call me Amos," Amos said. "Only my patients call me Doctor."

It was an old joke, and a rather stupid one, Amos thought, but it still made Beth laugh. "Okay, Amos. We're in Garden City. We see no sign of soldiers with hazmat suits."

"I suppose that if they were dressed as soldiers with hazmat suits, they would stand out. I learned today from the director of the CDC that some soldiers intentionally allowed themselves to be contaminated, in order to capture the vice president. So, they have the same appearance that you have. I believe you know Art Klemp. I understand that he spent some time with you in the Johns Creek shelter."

Beth shivered at the thought of the time spent in the shelter with Vice President Klemp. "That's a polite way to say that we're freaks," Beth laughed. "But yes, we know him, only too well. They captured him then?"

"They did. What's important is that if those soldiers were to show up in Garden City in civilian clothes, you should still be able to pick them out of a crowd because of the Smallpox splotches on their faces and hands."

"Hmm. We'll do a little more looking. I think we could pick them out just by their bearing. The people here are pretty beaten down. The soldiers would have to be good actors to not stand out, even in civvies."

"Okay. You do that and let's talk again tomorrow. Are you good until then?"

"We're avoiding direct contact with people because we're still contagious. But the home-made energy bars you gave us are great and we have enough water. We'll be okay."

"Just a thought," Amos said. "Soldiers might give themselves away trying to hide their skin condition."

"Good point. We'll watch for it."

Prime bunker, 4 May
"Hello Greg," Amos said.

"We found her. Her name is Dr. Chandra Robertson. She's two years out of graduate school and anxious to change the energy world. Is this a good time?"

"As good as any. Put her on."

"Hello? Dr. Blund?" A young female voice said.

"Please call me Amos, Dr. Robertson."

"Then will you call me Chandi?"

"Agreed. Will you please give me a brief summary of your

background with nuclear reactors, so I know where to begin?"

The president, listening in on a conference line with several scientists, pumped the air with his fist. *Yes! We were right,* he thought. They were talking about a nuclear reactor.

"Yes," Chandi said. "But first, may I say that I'm honored to talk to you? I've read several of your papers on nuclear energy regulations and the need for what you called structured deregulation. Several of my graduate professors at MIT insisted that your work was going to revolutionize the nuclear energy field."

Amos chuckled. "I'm surprised anyone's reading those papers. I know the NRC didn't like them. I received a couple of nasty responses from them."

When Chandi finished her summary, Amos gave her a list of reports and research papers to look up and review, some of them his own.

"I recognize some of those," Chandi said.

"Good. Those documents will give you the background to understand my development. But don't jump to any conclusions. The answer isn't there. Once you've read them, call me again."

"Thank you, Dr . . . Amos."

"You're welcome, Chandi. Just so you understand my position, this is one of my most valuable intellectual property assets and I'm giving it away for free."

"Thank you, Amos," Chandi said, obviously in awe of Amos. "I'll keep that in mind."

☢

Greg wondered if Dr. Robertson's reaction to Amos's revelation was the same as his. If this was only one of his most valuable assets, what else had he done that was of a similar value? *If he makes her doubt the need for us to duplicate his invention, I'll* . . . but he couldn't imagine what he would do.

"Blast you, Amos," he said under his breath.

Garden City, 5 May

"No sign of soldiers, yet, Amos," Beth reported.

"Have you found an acceptable drop location?" Amos asked.

"We have. It meets all of your criteria. It's open enough for us to see comings and goings. There's a way we can observe without being observed, as long as it's at night. And there's someplace close by where we can disappear quickly if someone shows up before or after the delivery."

"You've practiced with the night vision goggles?"

"Those are terrific. Although we're trying to avoid contact with people, we've been able to spy on them. Some of the things we've seen . . . hoo boy."

Amos chuckled involuntarily at the thought of Beth and her friends spying on lovers in the middle of the night. "Okay, give me the location and I'll pass that on to the President. When do you want the drop?"

They discussed the drop for a few more minutes, then Amos concluded the conversation. "As soon as I give the President the plan, things could change dramatically in Garden City. Watch for any kind of change that could indicate the military has been hiding out, waiting for instructions, or that there is an early drop of soldiers or tracking instruments."

"Understood. We'll also check the package before we come back to make sure there's nothing inside that could be a tracking device, including the packaging itself."

"Good. Beth, don't take a chance on being captured. If anything goes wrong, leave the package and get out."

"Are you sure?"

"Absolutely. They tried to trick us before. It could easily happen again. We can try again another day if we have to."

"Okay," Beth said, but there was doubt in her voice.

"Your safety is important, Beth. Please make sure your friends understand."

"I will."

Prime bunker, 5 May

"Hello Greg," Amos said.

"It's Chandi, Amos. I'm ready."

"Do you have any questions about what you've read?"

"None. Most of what is discussed in those research papers is theoretical and inconclusive. And I didn't see anything in the papers that demonstrated real experience with the theories they purport."

"Good. That's exactly what they want you to think."

"But there's more, isn't there? That's what you're going to tell me. Right?"

"Right. Do you have paper and pencil?"

"Yes. This conversation is also being recorded."

"Of course. But you need to be able to visualize what I'm going to explain. Draw a diagram as I talk. Here's what you need to do."

Amos explained what to do with the information she had just read. By the time Amos finished talking, with Chandi asking clarifying questions, three hours had passed, and she had a diagram and instructions on how to build a nuclear reactor that would fit in a bedroom sized room.

"Built correctly, with the proper safety and monitoring features," Amos assured her, "it will operate safely for a minimum of thirty to fifty years and it's scalable. It's also renewable. In other words, as the fuel cells reach a point where they are no longer effective or safe to operate, the reactor can be taken offline and re-charged. The monitoring equipment will tell you when that needs to be done."

Chandi was exhausted, but exhilarated at the same time. Some of the research pointed toward this design, without giving anything away. She could see that in hindsight but she never could have figured it out on her own. She was even more impressed with Amos than before.

"Amos," she finally said, knowing the president and others were listening, "now that they have the design, they don't need me. Someone else could take your design and build the reactors. I was just a tool to get the design from you. What does the President have over you, that you were willing to give away this technology?" She fully expected to be cut off and not hear his answer. When he didn't answer right away, she thought that that was what had happened. Then Amos spoke.

"You're a brave and intelligent woman, Chandi," he said. "I hope Greg recognizes how valuable you will be in rebuilding the country."

Greg, listening on the line, nodded his head. Dr, Robertson had been located in one of the shelters and brought to the bunker to talk to Amos. If not for Amos paying her that compliment and making his recommendation, she probably would have been returned to the shelter and the reactor design given to Jerman to build. Amos may have just saved her life.

"Let's just say," Amos continued quietly, "that my family and friends are my greatest treasure, more valuable than any knowledge. I will do anything to protect them."

Greg understood the implications in that message as well. Amos would go to great lengths to protect his family. The United States government might be impotent against him and his technology.

They said their good-byes and Chandi disconnected.

"Amos, Greg here," Greg said.

"Did you get all that?" Amos asked.

Greg knew Amos meant the reactor design, but also his closing remarks, which were meant for him more than for Chandi.

"We got it recorded, Amos," Greg said. "Thank you. Now, what about the vaccinations? Are you ready for them?"

"We are, Greg. Do you have a military team in the vicinity?"

"Amos, the vaccinations are at the Logan airport, along with a Special Forces team, waiting for my instructions."

"And what are your instructions going to be?"

Greg took a deep breath and let it out. "Amos, I want those people from Johns Creek. We need to know where they've been and who they've contaminated."

"And . . . ?"

"Amos, they've caused a lot of trouble for us. Jim wants to strangle them personally."

"That's what I thought, Greg. I can give you their route, in detail, including where they stayed every night and every time they came in contact with people. That should satisfy one of your concerns. As for the other, I can't in good conscience let you kill them. There's no need for it."

"There's justice in it," Greg said angrily.

Amos didn't reply immediately.

As Greg thought about Amos' comment, he realized that, once again, Amos was right. There was nothing to be gained by killing these people. The only thing they were guilty of was being in the wrong place at the wrong time. Everything they had done since then, was driven by their will to survive. And wasn't that what he'd done when he'd tried to trick Amos?

He felt guilty for the way he'd behaved and realized that his good friend might never trust him again. It was sad, he thought, that their friendship might be another casualty of the war.

"Here's the deal Greg," Amos said, interrupting Greg's thoughts. "We're ready for the vaccinations. In fact, we're anxious for them. Terry has Smallpox and is contagious. I don't want things to stay this way. I'll give you a drop location and time, and trust you to respect our agreement that you won't try to find the location of the Preserve.

"We also made an agreement to exchange the vaccinations for the reactor technology, which you now have and which, against the better judgement of my family and friends, you received before we received and tested the vaccine."

Greg realized that Amos was saying he was protecting the Outcasts, possibly at the Preserve, and that Greg would be violating their agreements by coming after them.

"Blast you, Amos," Greg said, still not certain what he was going to do.

"I think that works both ways, Greg."

Amos gave Greg the location and timing for the drop. It would be that night. Amos had dragged out the conversation with Chandi to ensure that it was dark outside by the time they had finished.

21

I'm considering lying to you

"The drop is tonight at midnight, local time," Amos told Beth over the radio. "The President threatened to try to capture you and your friends, but I think I talked him out of it. He doesn't know your role in the drop, so he won't be watching for you; but I thought you deserved to know. They have a Special Forces team at the Logan airport down the canyon. You should be very careful that you don't get caught."

Beth told Bryce and Callie what Amos had said. They decided to go to their protected location near the drop point and watch for any changes in the daily routine in the area.

The drop point was a nearly empty parking lot behind some condos where there was enough room for a helicopter to land. If there had ever been cars there, most had been moved, but there were people staying in the condos. Beth knew, because she had observed their movements during their two-day reconnaissance of the area. She also knew, or believed she knew, that they didn't come out after dark. A helicopter landing might change that.

Bryce told Beth that he could see stealthy movement north of the parking lot through his heat-sensing goggles,

"Okay," she said. "Stay out of sight." She called Amos and

quickly relayed the situation. Then the three of them hunkered down in their hiding places.

Prime bunker, 5 May, 11:38 pm local time (9:38 pm Mountain Time)

"Hello Amos," the President said as he answered his Sat Phone. He had been expecting and dreading this call. It might be the end of a long friendship. It all depended on Amos.

"Hello Greg. You couldn't resist, could ya? Had to send in the troops."

"How do you know what we're doing?" Greg asked in frustration. "Your Preserve must be in walking distance of the drop point. We should come after you in force and dig you out," he said in anger.

"There are tens of thousands of refugees here, Greg. It could get real ugly, real fast. Besides, we have an agreement," Amos said. "I gave you the technology in exchange for you leaving my family alone."

"But I didn't agree to leave the Johns Creek escapees alone."

"Same difference. You find them, you find us. Your integrity is on the line, Greg."

"I may have to break that promise Amos."

"What would Liz say about—"

"You leave my Liz out of this, Amos," Greg yelled into the phone, interrupting Amos.

"No Greg," Amos said calmly. "My family is as important to me as yours is to you."

Greg tried to calm himself.

"But your family is in a nice, safe little hole where the bombs and earthquakes and diseases don't impact you" Greg said in a more reasonable tone. "I have the whole country to worry about and I don't know how long our bunkers will keep us safe."

"I've given you the solution to your problems, Greg. Use it and leave us alone. And, if you've forgotten, the reason you agreed to give us vaccinations is because we've been impacted by the disease *you* let escape, after I warned you about the risk."

Greg winced at the reminder that Amos had warned him about the CDC doctors and their escape plan.

Before Greg had a chance to reply, his desk phone rang. "Excuse me Amos. This may be important." The president picked up the desk phone and listened as SecDef Jim Seymour shared the bad news.

Garden City, 5 May, 9:42 pm

Bryce identified six figures, presumably soldiers, dressed in black with black hoods and goggles, moving stealthily through the trees on the other side of the parking lot. If not for the goggles that Beth and Bryce wore, they would have been totally caught off guard, but with Bryce's warning, they were able to hide behind a couple of cars on the far side of the paved area and observe the soldiers' movements. The metal and asphalt had been warmed slightly during the day and had yet to cool off sufficiently to reveal their heat signatures.

There wasn't much protection for the soldiers, so two of them laid down on the ground and began to slither across the asphalt. Two more moved in the trees that bordered one side of the parking lot and the last two crept along the front of the condos, trying to stay in shadows. As the lead soldier sneaking along the condos passed in front of a doorway, the door opened inward and a man stepped out, bumping into the soldier.

The surprised soldier spun around, probably thinking he was being attacked and shot the man three times with his silenced hand gun. That might have been the end of it, except that the man had been talking to a woman right behind him. His bloody and limp body collapsed backward into the woman, who screamed.

Beth's first thought was that the soldier would shoot the woman, but then he might have to kill anyone else who came to investigate. Instead, all the soldiers began a quiet retreat to the north. A few condo lights came on, and a few doors cracked open far enough for someone to look out; but they all closed again quickly, including the one that had been opened, where the man had been shot.

Prime bunker, 5 May, 11:57 pm local time (9:57 pm Mountain Time)

"What do you recommend, Jim?" Greg asked after Jim summarized what had happened in Garden City.

"What I'd like is for my team to go in and get whoever's waiting for them, regardless of the collateral damage," Jim said. "They've got to be close to that parking lot."

"That's a given. What *should* we do?"

"It depends on how much you value your relationship with Amos."

"Or my integrity?" Greg asked, thinking about what Amos had said. "I made a promise."

"If they're all dead, who'll know besides you and me?"

"I won't be able to look myself in the mirror, or look at Liz again."

"Look, just leave it with me. Better yet, tell me to leave them alone, but don't ask me whether I followed directions or not. You don't have to know a thing."

"Sorry Jim, there's got to be another answer. How important is it to you to get those Outcasts?"

"You should know that I'm considering lying to you and going renegade," Jim said. "The only reason I'm not going to is because my own integrity is worth more than a vendetta."

"As I would expect, Jim. Please call the team back to the helicopter and ready the vaccinations for delivery."

"I will, Greg. But I'm doing it under protest."

"Just as long as you do it. Thanks, Jim." The President disconnected.

The Preserve, 5 May, 10:10 pm

"Are you still there, Amos?" Greg asked.

Amos had been trying to hear Greg's conversation. He thought he heard Jim's name a couple of times, which meant something had happened in Garden City. He hadn't heard from Beth, but maybe she couldn't call. He decided to hear what Greg had to say.

"I'm here, Greg," he said.

"I'm calling our soldiers home. The vaccinations will be delivered as agreed."

Amos didn't know if that meant Beth and friends had been captured or that something else had happened. He didn't know what to say. Suddenly the radio came to life and Beth whispered, "They're leaving."

Amos was so relieved, he almost shouted into the phone.

"Thank you, Greg," he said quietly, restraining himself.

Garden City, 5 May, 10:13 pm

"That should be the end of it," Amos told Beth.

"They've really gone then?" she asked, relieved. She was actually excited about being part of a secret mission, as she thought of it. But seeing that man shot without hesitation let her know how serious and dangerous this situation had become. She wondered if they should back out.

"Don't let your guard down," Amos said. "They've tried to trick us before."

So, Amos had been through this before. Beth knew he was depending on her, and they really needed those vaccinations. She couldn't let him down when she was this close. She squared her shoulders, took a deep breath and let it out.

"We'll be careful," she said.

"Thank you, Beth."

Beth waited to see what would happen next. Bryce hadn't alerted her of movement and she hadn't heard any noise, including from the condo where the man had been shot. She was sure that he was dead. She'd seen the blood splatter from his head against the dim backlighting of the open doorway—not from electric lights, because there were none, but from some kind of flickering light source.

☢

Two minutes before midnight, Beth heard the beating propellers of a helicopter. Moments later, she saw the sleek silhouette of a military helicopter cruising just above the treetops from the north. It came in fast, amazingly quiet, hung in the air, and dropped to within a foot of the asphalt. A soldier dressed in black dropped lightly to the pavement from the open side door. In one smooth motion, he turned and reached inside the helicopter, brought out a box and set it on the ground, then leapt back into the helicopter effortlessly. Six other soldiers ran from the trees to the north and jumped into the helicopter before it lifted into the air, rotated one hundred and eighty degrees, and disappeared the way it had come. The entire process took less than two minutes.

She heard doors creak open and saw a few heads poke out and look around briefly, then disappear—neighbors curious about the helicopter noise. When she heard the doors close again, one after another, she waited a few more minutes, then sent Bryce out to the package. He picked it up and headed off in a direction that allowed Beth to see if he was followed, which he wasn't.

When Beth and Callie caught up to him, Bryce had opened the package and was looking through the contents for anything that might be a tracking device. Beth turned a flashlight on the contents and they all searched. They found nothing on the package, but as they were moving the vaccinations to another container, Callie said, "There's something on this syringe."

"What is it?" Beth asked.

"A small lump," Callie said, rubbing her finger back and forth on the side of one of the syringes. "I would have thought nothing of it except you said to note anything that didn't seem right."

"Shine the light over here," Bryce whispered. When Beth did, she saw that the bump was clear plastic like the syringe. "What is it?" he asked.

"Check the other syringes," Beth instructed quietly.

"Again?" Bryce asked. "All of them?"

"All of them," Beth said. "Look for anything that's out of place. Good catch, Callie."

They found two other bumps on over a hundred syringes. Without a thorough search, they certainly would have missed them. When they were finished, they loaded all of the good syringes into backpacks.

"What do we do with these?" Callie asked, holding the three suspect syringes.

"Break the needles off and leave them here," Beth said.

"I'll bury them," Callie said.

"Be quick about it, then. We need to get out of here."

Prime Bunker—Meeting of the Panel, 8 May

"I haven't heard from Amos," Greg said. "Are we finished in Garden City?"

"As far as I'm concerned, Greg," Jim said. "Are you ready to hear what's going on in Texas and Mexico?"

Greg nodded.

"As with everywhere else, about a third of the contaminated are dying.

"In Galveston, we're vaccinating, then interviewing everyone we can find. We traced the source to a group of partiers who said they encountered a couple—a man and a woman—who showed up one day last August, passed themselves off as curfew enforcers, then disappeared again, the same day. The partiers started getting sick two days later and the virus spread from there.

"We ran into problems getting information in Matamoros. Turns out, the Los Zetas drug cartel basically owns the city. Finally, one man who had lost family to the virus and feared for others' relatives gave us the information we needed, plus more. He said a man and a woman—he thought they were Mexican from their appearance—were captured sneaking into the country last September."

"Were there Mexicans in the Johns Creek shelter?" Greg asked.

"None that we know of," Jim said. "When the interviewers asked him about spots on their skin, he looked confused and said 'no'. He said they had dark skin and dark hair, but no noticeable spots on their skin. He said their boat was confiscated, along with a couple of packages that they'd brought with them. One contained spare clothes and the other, cosmetics and hair dye."

"Makeup," Greg said, "to hide the disease."

"That's my conclusion. Anyway, he said they were confined for two or three months, then transported to a Los Zetas cartel plantation in Chiapas, where they were to be turned over to El Jefe—the drug lord. And before you ask—yes—he gave us a description of the location. I have people headed there now."

22

Three months earlier

Chiapas, Mexico, 8 February

"What are these rumors I hear about the prisoners?" El Jefe asked his guard captain, Luiz. He sat behind a desk in his spartan office, while Luiz stood at attention in front of it. El Jefe's personal guards stood against the walls and outside the door. Luiz had been summoned, then relieved of his weapons before entering the office, to remind him that no one was above suspicion around El Jefe.

"It's hard to believe," Luiz said, "but they seem to be true. There's a plague in Matamoros that started shortly after the prisoners were captured. We've been careful not to get too close to them since they arrived."

"But they're not sick?"

"We don't have a doctor here to check them, but they don't appear to be sick." Luiz wondered nervously where this line of questioning was going. He'd never known El Jefe to engage in casual conversation.

"Then, how do you know they're the cause and not something else?"

"I . . . I don't know. I'm just repeating what I've been told. Sir, everyone who got close to them in Matamoros caught the plague. It spread from there to the city. I just assumed—"

"Never assume!" El Jefe interrupted angrily. "Find out."

"How?" Luiz asked nervously. Suddenly, his stomach rebelled and he had a sour taste in his mouth. He swallowed a couple of times to keep his lunch down. He had seen El Jefe personally shoot one of his guards to make an example of him, to keep the others in line.

"The woman is pretty, I hear. You will deliver their next meal and get close enough to her to kiss her. Then we will see if she is contagious."

"Sir," Luiz said softly, his knees shaking, "a third of the people who caught the plague, died."

"But two-thirds did not, correct? You will do it, then you will quarantine yourself."

"Quarantine, sir? Where?"

"Let's see. It can't be in any of the buildings, unless you want to stay with the prisoners in their building. Or the trucks. The poppies are close to harvest, so it can't be near them. Use the far guard tower, beyond the coca plants."

☢

Pepper was startled when a guard opened the door and entered the room with their meal. She and Jared had always been warned away from the door by a guard, calling from outside, before the door would be unlocked. Then, the door was only opened a few inches—far enough to set a plate on a table next to the door— then the door would be quickly closed and relocked

This guard entered without warning while they sat at the table by the door. Pepper instinctively looked for a gun, but his holster was empty and all he held in his shaking hands was a bowl of soup and half a loaf of wheat bread, which he set on the table.

He glanced at Jared, who was closer, then stood looking at

Pepper. He licked his lips nervously.

"Do you need anything else?" he finally asked in his accented English.

Pepper shook her head. She felt like asking for their freedom, but expected that was not on the menu. She wondered what had changed and what this man really wanted. She was sure he was not here to see if they were comfortable after being held prisoner in abysmal conditions.

She realized that one thing she wanted, which he might be willing to give her, was to go outside and get some fresh air. They'd been cooped up in this room for over two months, their only exercise walking in circles. She opened her mouth to say so, when she noticed Jared shake his head slightly. She was sure he knew what she wanted because she talked about it regularly, but she didn't know what worried him. Maybe he feared they would be separated permanently. She wanted to ask him about his warning, but didn't dare ask with the guard standing so close.

Her eyes went involuntarily to the window, which the guard must have noticed.

"You want to go outside?" he asked. He smiled and leaned forward encouragingly.

Although she didn't trust him, he sounded sincere, maybe just wanting to give her a break from the monotony, so she looked pleadingly at Jared. His jaw clenched; his expression turned serious.

"Can he come with me?" she asked.

"One at a time," he said, still smiling, and moved toward the door.

As she moved to go around Jared, he reached out and took her hand. The concern in his eyes touched her, but she wanted to go outside and she wanted him to understand. She continued around him, not sure if her expression expressed her feelings, and approached the door.

The guard took her by her upper arm, causing her to turn toward him. What she saw in his eyes scared her, not because she feared for her safety, but because the guard looked scared; of what, she had no idea. He leaned in close to her face; he could have kissed her if he'd wanted, then the moment was gone and he led her outside.

She stopped and looked around, seeing the fields with peasants working between the plants, the buildings with their rusted gray aluminum siding and overhead netting, the guards watching them, but not moving toward them. She wondered what would happen if she ran for the jungle, then decided that even if she could get away—she didn't think she could outrun the guards—Jared was still locked in their prison.

The guard released her and she walked a few steps away from him toward the fields. She looked back at him, then walked farther. Looking back again, she saw that he was becoming nervous, so she thought it better to return rather than make him angry.

When she entered the building, having been gone only a few minutes, Jared was pacing in front of the window. He hurried over to her.

"Are you okay?" he asked, looking into her eyes, and glancing toward the guard, standing just outside the door. "I couldn't see you for a minute. He didn't hurt you, did he?"

"I'm fine," she said, her mind dwelling on the moment the guard had leaned in close enough to kiss her. She didn't understand what that was about. Had he intended to kiss her, then changed his mind? Was he nervous because he was afraid of Jared? Nothing else made sense.

The guard allowed Jared to leave the room, but for only a few moments. When Jared took a few steps toward the fields, then turned and looked at the jungle, the guard bristled.

"That's enough," he said and shooed Jared back toward the door, and into the room.

"What do you think is going on?" Pepper asked after the door had been locked and the guard left.

"No idea," Jared said, "but this may have something to do with the truck that arrived this morning. The guy who got out of the truck must be important, from the way everyone groveled before him."

Luiz took a supply of food and water and went to the far guard tower. He sat on a wooden bench in a dark corner, his shoulders slumped, his arms resting on his legs, and thought about his family a few miles away. They depended on the money he regularly sent them, for their survival. He wasn't fond of El Jefe—if he were honest with himself, he'd have to admit that he loathed him—but this plantation provided most of the paying jobs in the region. He had been blessed to have this job. If he died, what would happen to his family. He felt a drop of water land on his hand and realized it was a tear that had fallen from his cheek.

23

Would you love me less?

The Preserve, 21 May

Everyone met in the community center for a family meeting. Terry joined them for the first time since his quarantine, the splotches on his skin, partially concealed by makeup, still attracting stares. Becca had seen him at his worst, by video, and had discussed the makeup idea with Lillie, who'd encouraged it. As he watched the reactions to Terry's condition, Amos thought about what they had gone through over the last two and a half weeks.

☢

Beth and Ben had vaccinated the Johns Creek and Garden City refugees—the Outcasts, as they liked to call themselves—immediately upon their return from Garden City. Three days later, when none of them had experienced negative effects from the shots, Amos had left the Preserve and intentionally exposed himself to them.

"I'm pleased to meet you in person, Amos," Beth had said, "but I wish you hadn't done it this way."

"Someone had to be the test subject," Amos had replied as Beth had given him his shot, "and I wasn't going to ask anyone else to do it." Amos had immediately quarantined himself for four days, had experienced a mild fever for the first two days, then had felt fine again.

"I'm going to vaccinate myself," Lillie had told Beth over the radio when she'd reported on Amos's condition. "and join him in quarantine for another four days."

"I'm glad he had no side effects," Beth had replied. "Thank you, Lillie. I hope we'll get to meet in person sometime."

"So do I," Lillie had replied. "You've been a great help. Amos told me what you went through in Garden City. Thank you, from all of us."

"You're welcome. Please keep us informed."

"We'll do that. Are you getting enough to eat?"

"Yes, yes. You've been very generous. I'd love to see those gardens of yours."

"We'd love to show them to you," Lillie had said.

Amos had been in quarantine for five days when Lillie had literally thrown herself at him, craving his affection. Even getting Smallpox—as long as it was curable—would be better than being separated had been.

"I'd hate for you to have those ugly blotches all over your beautiful face and body," Amos had said.

"Is there still a risk of that?" she had asked.

"I don't think so. From Anne Lister's report and from our experience so far, I think this vaccine is pretty good."

"Would you love me less if I had those spots all over my body?"

He had tilted his head to one side as if he had had to think it over. "Oh, stop it," she'd said, smacking him on the chest with an open palm. "You should be worried about what *I* think. You haven't had a bath in almost a week."

"There is that," he'd said, "but I have brushed my teeth."

She had taken his face in her hands and kissed him affectionately.

Lillie had stayed in quarantine with Amos for another four

days, a mild fever the only ill effect, then they'd vaccinated every-one else, including Terry.

Now Amos was following up to see if there were any lingering issues. "Any complaints today?" he asked.

Chris looked at Rachel, then at her dad and asked, "You went outside, right?"

"Yes," Amos replied.

"Does that mean we can go outside now, too?"

"No. Next question?" Knowing that his answer wouldn't satisfy Chris, Amos smiled and waited for Chris's response.

"Hey, that's not fair," Chris complained.

Mike, sitting next to Chris, grabbed him around the head with an arm and knuckled the top of the head, affectionately. "That's enough, Chris," he said.

"Okay, okay. Let go of me," Chris said, breaking out of Mike's headlock and running his fingers through his hair. He looked at Rachel.

"It's beautiful," she said, likely just reassuring Chris that his hair was straight.

"Okay everyone," Amos said, holding up his hands, trying to regain control of the meeting. "We have one item of business to discuss." He had discussed this with Lillie during their quarantine.

"There are people in the valley who have been very helpful to us. We need to decide what to do about them."

"You mean like should we kick them out?" Chris asked.

"That would be one option, Chris, except that we'd probably have to go out there in order to evict them. Maybe we didn't tell you, but their exposure to the mutated virus gave them extra endurance. I personally don't want to go one-on-one with any of them, with or without a HazMat suit. Any other suggestions?"

"Dad," Mike said, "you've already thought this through, so why are you asking us? Why don't you just tell us what you want to do?"

"Because I want to know what everyone thinks before I say anything. You may have a better idea, or an improvement on my idea."

It seemed like everyone felt the way Mike did. No one would express an opinion, only to be shot down by Amos.

"Okay," Amos said, prepared to share his suggestion, when Rylee raised a hand.

"Yes, Rylee?"

"I think," Rylee said, "you should let them stay, and build permanent homes in the valley, if they can get the materials." Everyone looked at her, which probably explained why she suddenly stopped talking and looked embarrassed.

"That's good, Rylee," Amos said. It was apparent that she had more to say. "Please continue."

She started hesitantly, turning to look at Sydney. "I think some of us might want to live in the valley with them and we should be allowed to."

Her comment caught Amos off guard. Lillie gasped. Several others started talking at once, commenting or asking questions. Then, just as suddenly, everyone stopped talking and looked at Amos, to hear how he would respond.

"Do you know what it's like out there?" Amos asked Rylee kindly. He had trouble believing she was serious about leaving the Preserve, but she didn't know what he knew.

"Not exactly," Rylee replied, "but they're breathing fresh air and they can see the sky."

Amos steepled his fingers and placed them to his lips. He had not foreseen this development. He let the silence continue for several moments.

"Thank you, Rylee," he said. "I had not considered that. I'll give your suggestion serious consideration. Are there any other thoughts or suggestions?" he asked, looking over the group.

Eventually there were several other suggestions, mostly variations of 'let them stay in the valley'.

Finally, it looked like everyone who had something to say, had said it.

"What I recommend," Amos said, "and I'm asking you all to vote on it, is that we provide them tools to cut down and shape trees, to build a log cabin and stay in the valley."

"I thought the trees all burned," Emily said.

Trust Emily to be aware of the trees, Amos thought.

"The fire went through the valley so quickly, being pushed by the nuclear wind, that most of the trees suffered only surface damage. Some of them already have new leaf buds on them."

"Thank goodness," Emily said.

"You're going to let them cut down all the trees to build cabins?" Mike asked.

"Just one cabin," Amos said. "We've already given them poles to make a shelter framework. I propose to provide concrete to form a floor and shingles to make the roof more permanent."

"We have all that stuff?" Chris asked.

Amos laughed. "We do, Chris. We anticipated the need to eventually go out and build one or more small structures in the valley. The metal frame has already established the size of the cabin they can build. We'll ask them to cut down only as many trees as they need to complete the walls, only trees away from the clearing—so they don't disturb the soil over the Preserve—and to not take all their trees from the same place. Well, we'll let them make one small clearing so they can try to raise crops if they want to.

"They seem to have an immunity to the cold, and unusual endurance, all resulting from the mutated virus. So, I'm not worried about how long it takes them to build a cabin that will keep out the cold. It will keep them busy for a while.

"I also recommend we provide them with seeds and tools to plant crops and take care of the fruit trees that we planted." Emily's eyes got wide at that suggestion.

"Yes, Emily, the fruit trees are starting to leaf. There are buds on the apricot tree," he said with a smile.

"I don't know how contaminated the water is," Amos continued. "But I wore a dosimeter out there and can tell you there's a lot of radiation in the air."

"Won't that hurt them?" Emily asked.

"Yes, over time. We've given them potassium iodide pills, to help prevent the thyroid from absorbing radioactive iodine. There's still an impact to other organs from the radiation. Any other questions?"

Amos noticed Rylee sit up straight in her chair. "Rylee, I'm going to table your suggestion for another time, but I won't forget it. I promise. The board will consider it and we'll discuss it at another meeting, after we know more about what's going on outside. Is that okay?"

Rylee nodded her head, but looked disappointed.

"Okay," Amos said, "let's take a vote. What we're voting on is whether or not to do what I suggested. It doesn't mean we won't consider other options. If you don't like this idea, vote against it. The vote requires at least a two thirds majority to pass. Is that clear?"

"Why two thirds and not a simple majority?" Matt asked.

"Ideally, we should have everyone in agreement, but I know

we won't get that," Amos said. "Let's make it a three-fourth ma-jority—nine people—in favor to pass. Sydney and Rylee, do you understand what we're doing here? Do you have any questions?"

"You know how I feel," Rylee said quietly.

"My baby is seven months along," Emily said with a smile. "Does my vote count for two?"

"Nice try," Lillie replied with the polite sarcasm her children knew well.

"Sydney?" Amos asked.

"I get it," Sydney replied.

Amos called for a vote. Rylee was the only one who voted against it and there were no other suggestions.

When Lillie found a few minutes to relax that evening, she re-membered that she wanted to do some research on smallpox vac-cinations during pregnancy, since Emily was pregnant and Katie might be. She was pretty sure that the advice would be against it, but she wanted to know what the experts said, so she wouldn't be surprised. She was not comforted by what she found in a CDC Weekly Report from May 2003.

> *In the absence of circulating smallpox, pregnant women should not be exposed to live vaccinia virus contained in the smallpox vaccine. The smallpox vaccine should not be administered to women who are pregnant or might become pregnant within 4 weeks after vaccination because of the risk for fetal vaccinia, a rare but serious infection of the fetus. In addition, persons who have close contact (e.g., household contact or sexual contact) with pregnant women are advised to forego vaccination.*

So, not only did Lillie have to worry about Emily, who was seven months pregnant, and Katie, who might be as well, she also had to worry about Matthew, Michael and everyone else in the house. She confided in Amos that they needed to begin testing everyone on a regular basis, until the baby—or babies— were born.

HOME SEC Bunker, 21 May

"That's not what Amos . . . I mean Dr. Blund said to do," Dr. Chandra Robertson said. She worried about trying to correct the chairman, but was afraid that if they didn't follow Amos's instructions explicitly, the reactors might not work properly. They might even be dangerous.

"Dr. Blund is an idiot or a trickster," NRC Chairman Jerman said. "There is no way that step will give the results he promised. I know what to do."

"Maybe we should ask Dr. Blund—"

"We'll do no such thing. I've seen enough to ascertain what's right and wrong with the design. We'll finish this step on all six prototypes and you'll personally take the other four to the other bunkers. I've already asked the President to provide transportation for you."

"But one of the bunkers is in California," she complained.

"Then you better get going," he replied. "When you get a little more experience, you'll be able to intuit these things as well as I do," he said condescendingly. Then, under his breath, but loudly enough for her to hear, he added, "if you last that long."

The Preserve, 22 May

"Mike, what do you mean by"—Amos looked at the notes in his hand and read— "we should contact Amos Two and tell him what has happened in our world?"

Mike rested his arms on the stacks of newspapers in front of him and faced his dad. Terry sat to one side and watched. Mike had expected this question when he'd chosen to include that statement in his notes.

"Dad," Mike said confidently, "I'm convinced that the twin world is facing the same crisis that our world did prior to the terrorist bombing. The information you've received from the president could be exactly the information that Amos Two needs to prevent a world war in their world. Don't you agree?"

Amos considered Mike's words for a few moments.

"You sound pretty sure of yourself, Mike," Amos said. "Have you thought through the possible ramifications of contacting Amos Two or Greg Two?"

"You mean, what's the downside, right?" Mike asked. Amos nodded. "I made a list of everything I could think of and prioritized them. Here's the list. See if I've missed anything."

Amos looked at the page of lined paper that Mike handed him. At the top of the page were the words: *Problem Statement: Possible implications of contacting Amos Two.* There was a vertical line down the middle of the page with a numbered list of comments on either side of the line. The list on the left was titled: *Pros.* The one on the right read: *Cons.*

The number one item on the *Pros* side was: *Save millions of lives/prevent unnecessary misery and suffering.* The top item on the *Cons* side was: *Reveal to Amos the existence of a parallel world.*

"Mike," Amos said "I'm glad you used the word 'possible' in the heading, since we have no idea what the impacts would be."

"You're right," Mike replied with feeling. "We don't know, but wouldn't it be worth the risk if we could prevent their world from suffering the way ours has?"

"I'll have to think about this, Mike. Why would Amos Two believe anything we told him? We've had difficulty believing everything that's happened and we've lived through it."

Mike looked down and gritted his teeth, but had no answer for his dad.

"Because he's you," Terry said. "That means he would believe it if he were confronted with facts."

Amos stared at Terry, thoughtfully, and Mike's mouth turned from a grimace to a broad grin.

"Because he's me," Amos repeated, thoughtfully.

Aspen Valley, 23 May

Beth was in the best mood she'd been in since . . . as long as she could remember. When Amos had explained the group's decision to allow them to stay in the valley *and* to provide tools and material to build a cabin, the Outcasts had actually cheered. Well, all except Jason.

She didn't know what she would do with Jason. At night he was still hogtied, but during the day, they tied him to a tree on a rope that allowed him limited movement. Every time he tried to untie the rope, someone prodded him with a stick, so he had mostly stopped trying to escape.

Now, with tools and materials, they selected a spot that was basically clear of undergrowth—it had been burned away—cleared away the snow, and moved the dog run and shelter. Amos had provided a book on how to build log cabins by cutting down and shaping trees to interlock at the corners, then mudding the cracks.

"If I didn't feel like a pioneer before," Ben told Beth, "I sure do now." Then he laughed happily. The laughter was contagious. Before long they were all laughing and teaching each other campfire songs that they remembered from their youth. Amos, periodically checking on them from the office, had to smile at their carefree behavior.

Prime bunker, 23 May

"President McCormick," an aide said, "that nuclear engineer, Dr. Robertson, is in the bunker. You said you wanted to be notified when she arrived."

"Thank you," the president said. "Please ask her not to leave until I have a chance to talk to her."

"Yes, sir." The aide left.

Greg finished reviewing a report he'd received from HomeSec Director Chuck Dickson regarding the sorry state of the country's infrastructure. People were getting sick and dying from waterborne diseases now, because he couldn't get power to the water treatment plants and clean water delivery systems.

He still had a lot of work on his desk—more reports, requests for services, that sort of thing—but decided he needed a break. In reality, he realized he was excited to get Dr. Robertson's report, hoping she had good news for him about the power generators, or reactors, or whatever they were being called.

He left his office in search of Dr. Robertson and was directed to a service room where she had been meeting with a couple of technicians since her arrival. Mechanics were setting a metal cylinder in place on a pedestal. The cylinder was four feet in diameter and stood about five feet tall. It had cables, reinforced metal hoses and other protuberances that the technicians were in the process of connecting to other boxes set up around the cylinder. All together, they took up most of the room. They had the main circuit breaker box, in the next room, open in preparation for connecting the cylinder to the main power.

"Hello Dr. Robertson," the president said.

"Hello Mr. President," Chandi replied.

"I thought I had asked you to call me Greg," he said conspiratorially, feeling positive for the first time in months, "but not when anyone else is around." He winked at one of the technicians.

Chandi was flustered by the president's friendly manner, but regained her composure quickly. "Thank you . . . Greg. And you had better call me Chandi."

Greg nodded. "Is this the reactor? I've been so excited to see this work. Amos is brilliant, so there's no doubt in my mind that this will solve our energy problems." Greg was smiling, but Chandi was frowning.

"Is there a problem?" Greg asked, becoming concerned.

Chandi opened her mouth to speak, then hesitated.

"Come on Chandi. What is it?" Greg coaxed good-naturedly.

"Sir . . . Greg, I mean . . . Chairman Jerman strictly forbade me to bother you with my concern. I know you have more pressing issues."

"This power supply is my most pressing concern," Greg said seriously. "What did Chairman Jerman not want me to hear?"

"Well," Chandi said apologetically, "he modified Amos's . . . I mean Dr. Blund's design. He said Dr. Blund didn't know what he was doing and the Chairman was fixing it."

Greg gritted his teeth, but didn't interrupt. He wanted to hear what Jerman had done.

"Chairman Jerman specifically directed me to say nothing about my petty concerns to you during my travels to install the units. He said you have much more pressing issues on your mind. He said if I bothered you with my concerns, my career might be on the line."

"But you disagreed with what he did?" Greg asked.

"Yes, I thought you had a right to know what was being done without your knowledge. It created a professional conflict for me."

Greg swore. "Do we know what impact the change will have on the function of the unit?"

"I have no idea and the Chairman forbade me to contact Dr. Blund to ask about it."

"This is wrong," Greg said. "What's the status of the other units?"

"The Chairman is assisting with the installation at the HOME SEC bunker. I've delivered and helped install the units at the other three locations in the East and Midwest. When I leave here, I'll go to California to install the last one."

"What's the schedule for testing them?"

"Test? There is no test. We install them and turn them on. The Chairman said there's no need to test them and time is of the essence."

It was Greg's decision to put the first six units in the bunkers. He had explicit faith in Amos's design . . . as long as it was copied exactly. If the Chairman had changed the design without consulting Amos, there were bound to be problems, especially if they weren't tested before being started. Hopefully, those problems wouldn't be fatal.

The President turned to the technicians. "Stop working until we get back to you." Then to Chandi, he said, "Come with me." They started walking hurriedly. "What's the schedule for turning on the power supplies that are installed?"

"The HOME SEC and VEEP bunkers are set to go live today," Chandi said, hurrying as fast as she could to keep up with the President and his security detail. "The Chairman is anxious for the others to follow as quickly as possible after that."

"What time today?"

Chandi looked at her watch. "In about five minutes."

As Greg started to run, he called over his shoulder to his lead security agent.

"Jeff," he said, "give me your radio." The agent raced to catch up with him, so he could hand him a radio. "Red alert. Red alert," Greg called into the radio. "HOME SEC and VEEP bunkers, stop the nuclear reactor startup, on my orders." He repeated the order three more times on the way to the Prime situation room. Chandi and the agents followed him, jogging to keep up.

As they approached the situation room, people gathered from all directions at a run. Greg began calling out orders before he reached his chair at the table.

"Screens up. Notify the other bunkers to come online. Get me Chuck Dickson in HOME SEC and Ambassador Porter in VEEP."

As the screens on the wall of the Prime bunker were turned on, people could be seen entering the situation rooms of the other bunkers. Chuck Dickson entered, chewing something, and sat in his chair. He must have been at lunch. The ambassador and other advisors entered their situation rooms as well.

"Yes, Mr. President?" Chuck said.

"Stop the reactor startup, immediately," the President said.

Chuck turned to someone off-screen for a moment. "I'm told Chairman Jerman started it up about a minute ago. He's down there with the technicians seeing to its . . . " He never finished the sentence. The HOME SEC bunker was rocked by a strong explosion, which knocked out power to the monitor.

Ambassador Porter got a panicked look on his face and turned quickly to his right to say something. He didn't get it out. The explosion in his bunker knocked out his monitor as well.

The President turned to Jim Seymour in the SecDef bunker.

"Jim, send rescue teams to the HOME SEC and VEEP bunkers. See what they can do to help."

Jim already had a phone to his ear, urgently giving orders. He nodded and kept talking.

Greg looked around the room and noticed that it was the military people who calmly gave instructions over radios and phones. Chandi stood behind him, staring at the now-blank monitors with a sad expression on her face. A tear ran down her cheek and her frame shook slightly. Good for her, he thought. She can still feel sorrow for others amid this madness.

24

Support her in every way possible

Prime bunker, 24 May

Greg had gathered the highest-ranking military and civilian leaders in the Prime bunker, to the situation room, along with his Chief of Staff, Eric Epstein and Dr. Chandra Robertson, who sat next to him. The other situation rooms were similarly attended. The president had specifically requested that Secretary of State Cy Hutchison invite the vice chairman of the NRC to participate, and to sit next to him in the State bunker, where Greg could see him.

Greg noted the confusion on the vice chairman's face, on seeing Dr. Robertson. He would have known of Chandi, but would have had only the former chairman's opinion about her credentials and capabilities, which, according to Chandi, weren't positive.

"Thank you all for being here," Greg said by way of introduction. "As you know, yesterday there were accidents at the HOME SEC and VEEP bunkers. The new nuclear reactors that were installed by former NRC Chairman Floyd Jerman malfunctioned. Although the amount of radioactive material was very small, the explosion was, in effect, a nuclear explosion.

"Everyone in both bunkers is dead. Their deaths are a great loss to their families, the country, and to our efforts to rebuild the infrastructure. I ask you, as a personal favor to me, to pray for their families.

"Dr. Chandra Robertson spent most of yesterday on the phone

with the inventor of the reactors, Dr. Amos Blund, trying to understand what went wrong and how we can test the reactors before going live—as they say—with any more of the units.

"Unfortunately, the facility where these were being built was in the VEEP bunker. We've been able to reproduce the instructions for building the units, but we've lost all of our parts and our supply of radioactive material. It's fair to say that the radioactive material stored in the VEEP bunker added to the intensity of the explosion there.

"As you know, technicians are removing the reactors that were installed in your bunkers. They will be sent to the SEC DEF bunker for rebuilding. I'm placing Dr. Robertson in charge of the project to build as many units as she can, until she runs out of material." Greg glanced at Chandi and thought she looked like a heavy load had just been dropped on her shoulders. There were worry lines on her face that he hadn't noticed before, and she appeared to have aged years since yesterday. He smiled at her and she smiled back, but she didn't look comfortable. She was no longer the engineer who simply followed someone else's instructions. She would have a team of engineers and technicians who would do exactly as she directed, or else.

"The NRC, Mr. Vice Chairman," Greg continued, looking directly into his eyes, "will support her in every way possible. That includes providing radioactive material, insulating material, people of her choosing, and anything else she needs, in whatever quantities she needs. Is that understood?"

A cowed vice chairman, pre-warned that his career was on the line, submitted humbly, if not gracefully.

"Yes, Mr. President. Very clear," he said.

"Jim," the president addressed SecDef Jim Seymour, in whose bunker Dr. Robertson would be working, "Dr. Robertson will have requirements for the safety of the SecDef bunker while she's working with radioactive material there. Anyone who violates any of the safety procedures that she requires, will be accountable to you, and through you, to me." Jim nodded.

"Any questions?" the president asked.

"Do you want to tell them whose mistake caused the explosions?" Jim, who already knew the answer because Greg had discussed this meeting with him beforehand, asked.

"No need to say who was at fault," Greg said, believing that they would all find out eventually, anyway. "For the record, I'm leaving the chairmanship of the NRC open for the time being. After successfully completing this project, Dr. Robertson will be in line to fill that vacancy, and I will offer it to her."

Chandi gaped at the president, as did the vice chairman.

"With the current world crisis," Greg continued, "we will need strong leadership in the energy field to bring the world back to life. I'll be keeping a close eye on this and other projects."

The Preserve, 24 May

"I'm sorry to hear about the explosions," Amos said. "I had a lot of respect for Chuck Dickson. Did you know he was one of Greg's principal advisors?"

"I didn't," Chandi said. "I just know that he was in charge of trying to get the national power grid back in operation. I was supposed to work with him to prioritize—after we got reactors working in the government bunkers—where to place the next ones. Water management is supposed to be the first priority."

"That makes sense. I'm sure Greg will find someone else on Chuck's team to take over."

"Did you know Dr. Anne Lister was in the VEEP bunker when it exploded?" she asked. "Greg said her associate in the SEC

DEF bunker will take over medical research. I guess you know the vice-president died."

"Was it smallpox?" Amos asked.

"He volunteered to be a test subject and had a reaction to the vaccine."

"From what Greg told me about his relationship with Art Klemp," Amos said, "I'd be surprised if Art ever volunteered for anything that included personal risk. Greg probably volunteered him. Where are you getting all this information?"

"Greg has been quite open about what's going on, when I'm around."

"I think that means he trusts you, Chandi. Anyway, congratulations on your assignment in the NRC. You'll do well."

"How can I? I have no idea how to run an organization the size and complexity of the NRC."

Amos chuckled. "It won't be as big or complex as it was. And you can decide what it's focus will be. You're perfect for the job. Gather intelligent people around you, whose advice you can trust. Get rid of the old stuffed shirts and bring in young, creative talent."

"You make it sound so simple," Chandi complained. "Will you help?"

"Keep it simple. Don't let it out of your control. And yes, I'll be here as long as Greg . . . the president wants me and I'll help any way I can."

"You're on a first-name basis with Greg, aren't you? There's history between you two, isn't there?"

"There is," Amos chuckled again. "Not always nice, but we go back a long way. Now he has his world and I have mine. I don't know when, if ever, they will meet again. Good luck, Chandi. Don't let the alligators get too close."

"Thanks Amos, for everything."

"You're very welcome. Call anytime."

Chiapas, Mexico, 24 May

"Do you hear that?" Jared whispered. He lay next to Pepper with his arms wrapped around her while they slept. There was yelling and moving around outside, that started suddenly and sounded urgent. Jared unwound himself, pulled on his pants, and went to the window.

"What is it," Pepper asked.

"Looks like the boss is leaving. His guards are loading crates and packages into one of the trucks." Having been in the Los Zetas camp for as long as they had, they had figured out some things, even though no one actually spoke to them—no one since that one guard let them go for a short walk months ago.

A short while later, the boss jumped into the passenger side of the cab, then a driver, then four guards climbed in the back, and the truck sped away, kicking up gravel. The guards had to grab onto the side of the truck to keep from being thrown around.

The Outcasts, 25 May, early morning

"Dr. Blund, Dr Blund. Can you hear me?" Ben called anxiously, without getting a response, then repeated the call a few minutes later with the same result. He returned to the Outcasts' camp and reported to Beth. "He's not answering," he said.

"That's what I was afraid of," Beth said distractedly as she coached Candy, who was in labor. "It's too early or he's busy with other things. Bring me the radio. It's in the side pocket of my backpack."

When he returned with the radio, she showed him how to call Amos. It still took two tries before he answered.

"I'm here," Amos finally said, to Ben's relief.

"This is Ben, Beth's . . . friend," Ben said. "Candy is in labor and Beth wants to know if you can spare anything to help with the delivery."

"It's okay, Ben," Amos laughed. "You can relax. Tell me what's happening now."

Ben gave Amos a quick summary in medical terms. Being a nurse, speaking to a doctor, seemed to calm him.

"I'll have Lillie collect some things," Amos said when he was finished, "and call you back in a few minutes. Stay by the radio."

"Fantastic! Thank you," Ben said and hung up.

A few minutes later, Ben was back on the radio with Lillie, who told him that sterile blankets, medical and emergency supplies, and surgical tools were being taken to the secondary door as they spoke. There was even a tent, for protection against the weather—it had started to rain—and a portable oven, for warming the blankets. When Ben saw the door open, he yelled at Kerri and Callie to help him get the supplies and almost forgot to thank Lillie.

He realized Lillie was still talking to him. "I'm sorry," he said. "What was that last bit?"

"Tell Beth," Lillie said, laughing, "to call Amos if she needs another doctor and he'll come out there."

"Oh, we don't want him to do that, but I'll tell her. Thanks."

☢

Beth showed Candy how to cradle her baby girl in her arms, while Ben sponged Candy's face and swept her damp hair off of her forehead. As worn out as Candy was from her seven hours of labor, she smiled and cooed as she looked down at her little miracle.

"She's beautiful, Candy, and healthy," Beth said. "We took a blood sample and had Amos test it for smallpox, among other things. I'm happy to say she's immune."

"She's a miracle," Candy said, without looking up.

"Have you decided on a name?"

"We're going to call her Lisa Beth."

Beth choked up, thinking about their Lisa, who had nearly died of hypothermia in Wyoming. Lisa had had an obvious zest for life and a love of people. Now, it was all she could do to keep herself going, from day to day, with Beth doing what she could to help.

"That's a wonderful choice," Beth said, when she trusted herself to talk. "You know; the name Lisa means *God is bountiful.* You have a survivor of smallpox, a new life and a new generation in a new world."

"And a wonderful doctor," Candy said, finally looking up. Her eyes were moist. "Thank you, Beth. Please call me Sheryl."

"Really?" Beth asked.

"Yes. Candy's gone. The *new me* is Sheryl, the person I was meant to become when I finally grew up. The *me* that is loved by Bryce and who loves Lisa Beth."

Beth was brought almost to tears. "I'll tell the others," she said.

☢

"Amos, thank you for making all those resources available," Beth said when Amos met her at the door to return the unused supplies and tools.

"I'm glad everything went well and you didn't need the surgical tools," Amos replied.

"Yes, well, we did have one complication, but it wasn't related to Sheryl and the baby." Beth felt like she couldn't look Amos in the eye as she spoke.

"Oh, what was that?"

"While we were waiting for the baby to decide to join us—everyone was there—Bryce left for a while. He said the waiting was too intense for him—which I interpreted to mean that he was bored—so I didn't worry about it.

"I'm so embarrassed, Amos," she continued. "A few minutes ago, I went to check on Jason and discovered that he was missing."

"How did it happen?" he asked after a slight pause to see if Beth would continue.

"It was obvious to me that Bryce had let him out while we were occupied. I confronted him and he admitted that Jason had promised him gold and silver. But Jason took off without giving him any because, he said, he'd hidden it in Laketown, south of Garden City."

"Are you concerned for your safety? Didn't Jason threaten you?"

"Yes, he said that I had double-crossed him—his words—but he was angrier with you. I didn't tell you because I thought we would have time to resolve the issue while he was our captive."

"What did he say, exactly?"

"I'm very sorry, Amos," Beth said, pleadingly. "Bryce said that as Jason was running up the trail toward the road, he yelled back that he was going to raise an army and come back to kill you and anyone else who tried to stop him from taking control of the Preserve."

The Preserve, 25 May

"We need to find out what Jason's up to," Mike insisted, looking from his dad to Terry and back again. The rest of the board was present, but Mike seemed oblivious to them. He was focused intently on his argument. "If he's planning to build an army and come back, we have to be prepared for them."

"What do you propose?" Terry asked.

"Beth and her friends helped us get the vaccinations. Maybe they could go to Garden City to find out what he's doing."

"The only problem with that idea," Matt said, "is that Jason knows what they all look like."

"He knows what we look like, too," Mike said. "Maybe we could spy on him using the gate,"

"Mike," Amos said, in an attempt to get control of the conversation and prevent Mike from revealing the latest discoveries about the gate. He hadn't had time to consider the impact on the others, of revealing them.

"You mean watch him from here?" Terry asked, so focused on Mike's comment that he was oblivious to Amos's effort to cut into the conversation. "You know we can't allow airborne contamination into the Preserve."

"Terry," Amos said, a little louder, trying to get Terry's attention now, and stop the conversation.

"Then let's find a way to send this end of the gate outside, so Beth could spy on him instead of us," Mike said.

Amos was so surprised and intrigued by Mike's suggestion that he forgot he was trying to stop the conversation

"Do you know how to do that?" Amos asked.

"I'm not sure," Mike said, "but I could look at the programming. Right now, we have a fixed location on this side of the gate and a floating location on the other side. That's why we can select a destination and jump there. If we can reprogram it so both sides have a floating location, we should be able to move this end out of the lab, to the valley, and have Beth jump to Garden City."

"What do you think, Terry?" Amos asked.

"If the engineer thinks he can do it," Terry laughed, "I think it's worth a try."

"What are you guys talking about?" Emily asked, interrupting them. "It sounds like gibberish. Gates and jumps and floating locations?"

Mike looked at his dad for permission to explain. Amos realized that, not only had he failed to stop Mike and Terry from talking about the gate's capabilities, but had become distracted and joined in the conversation. He looked around and saw that everyone was curious, except Lillie, who held a hand over her mouth to cover her smile.

"We need to tell you what we've discovered," Amos said, looking around at those who wouldn't know what they were talking about because they'd been intentionally left out of the discovery process, "so that this discussion makes sense." Amos started with an explanation of their original purpose in building the Observe as a medical diagnostic tool, then went on to explain their discovery, that what they thought was an image on the wall was really a gate or door to somewhere or some-when. There were exclamations of astonishment and doubt, so Amos promised to give them a demonstration. He was about to continue his explanation when Lillie interrupted him.

"Maybe you should give them a demonstration now," she said, "so the idea can grow on them. I think some of them are finding it difficult to believe you."

"Okay," Amos said with a sigh. "I'm sure you're right. Let's go to the lab. Some of you should bring a chair."

Some sat on chairs in front of the gate and others leaned against the table, so they could all see. Mike operated the Observer while Amos explained. They showed each incremental discovery leading up to their conversation about jumps.

"So, what happened to the idea of the Observer being a medical diagnostic tool?" Matt asked, frowning.

"Great question, Matt," Amos said. "That's still my goal. Since we've passed the gate through living animals and Mike and I have both put our hand through the gate."

"Really?" Emily asked, and Amos nodded

"We've decided to begin testing on living people."

"Who?" Emily asked immediately, concern in her voice.

"We think a good place to start is with members of the family who've been injured," Amos said with a mischievous smile, "to check the healing process."

"That means me," she said, her voice cracking. Her face reflected her horror at the prospect.

"Don't worry, Emily," he said, reaching over and patting her on the shoulder, "We'll check your mother's injury first." Emily looked at her mother, who smiled innocently at her.

"These jumps that you showed us," Katie said. "These are what you called . . . what was it? Floating locations?"

Mike, standing behind the Observer, smiled and nodded encouragingly at her.

"That's correct, Katie," Amos said.

"So," Katie continued, "it's like having a mathematical equation for a curve with one *fixed* end point and the other end moving as the variables in the equation change. Is that a close approximation?"

"Brilliant, Katie," Mike said, laughing, which made Katie smile. "That analogy is so close to reality that I may have to hire you to help me figure out how to disconnect the other end of the curve."

"Let me see if I understand this," Matt said. "Right now, the fixed end of the curve is here in the lab and the floating end can be anywhere. Right?"

"Within a reasonable distance," Mike replied. "So far, we've taken it from the north end of Bear Lake, all the way down to Ogden. We've actually taken it farther, but we lose some stability when we do."

"Okay, and you want to change your programming so you can move the fixed end point out of the lab, to . . . where? Anywhere?"

"Mike's earlier suggestion," Amos said, "was to move it out to Aspen Valley, so we can ask Beth to use it to spy on Jason."

"That would be great," Katie said. "Then you and Mike wouldn't have to go back to Garden City."

Amos was sure she was thinking about their dangerous and aborted trip to Garden City to pick up the vaccinations, and he agreed.

"So, what's next?" Matt asked.

"I'll continue to map coordinates in the twin world around Garden City and Laketown," Mike said, "based on Beth's information about where Jason was hanging out when they met him."

Everyone seemed to be following Mike's explanation, and Mike was enjoying himself, so Amos let him continue.

"I've already loaded the location coordinates from the twin world into the database for our world. Since the only coordinates we have for our world are from the original testing we did before the radiation alarms went off, we'll have to make some assumptions about how closely the coordinates, in the two worlds, match.

"We don't want to risk letting airborne contamination into the lab, but if I can reprogram the Observer, we can unfix the endpoint on this side and move it out to the valley. Then we can ask Beth for help."

The Outcasts, 25 May

"What can I do for you Amos," Beth asked when she answered the radio.

"I've spoken with the board about Jason," he said. "We'd like to ask for your help, if you're willing."

"Anything within my power, Amos." She felt obliged to help Amos any way she could, if she could work it around helping take care of little Lisa Beth and answering Sheryl's questions about how to take care of her. She'd been trying to convince Sheryl that mothering was natural—although she'd never been a mother herself, she'd heard it often enough. "You're the mother," she had said a number of times, "you'll know what's best for her."

As Amos explained what he wanted, Beth saw that there was no way out of helping.

"Be careful, Beth," Amos concluded. "He'll recognize you if he sees you."

25

Where is everybody?

Garden City, 25 May

"Where is everybody?" Jason asked himself as he hurried to catch up to the only person he could see. He had assumed that he'd have to keep a low profile until he'd determined the mood of the people toward him, but he'd been surprised when he couldn't see anyone from the overlook. When the man stopped and turned around, Jason was shocked to see that he had smallpox markings on his face similar to his own and was obviously in pain.

"Where . . . is . . . everybody?" Jason stammered, as he thought frantically about what might have happened. Had he and the Outcasts inadvertently spread the disease just by passing through the town?

"Where have you been?" the man asked, then looked startled. "Wait, if you weren't here when the plague spread, maybe you're the one who started it. They said a group of people passed through here"—he thought for a moment— "four days ago, with splotches on their faces."

Jason involuntarily backed away two steps before stopping. He hadn't brought the smallpox, the Outcasts had.

"It wasn't me," he said and tried to go around the man, who was smaller and probably fifty pounds lighter. The man reached out as Jason passed and grabbed his arm—his grip was strong— but Jason shook him off and hurried on, taking long strides. The man followed, yelling at him to stop, then shouting for help. Jason didn't worry about him—one small man in what appeared to be a ghost-town—until other people appeared from both sides of the road as they passed, adding to the growing cacophony.

He heard his name, first from one person, then others, until it sounded like a dozen or more people were chasing him, getting louder and closer. Curious and a little concerned, he looked back and confirmed that there were, indeed, at least a dozen people following him.

He spun around to face forward again and was startled to see several people gathering in front of him as well. Surprised by this unexpected development, he skidded to a halt, trying to decide what to do. He was sure he could bust through the line of people, but by the time he started to move again, strong hands wrapped around his arms from behind, and he couldn't shake them all off.

Everyone spoke at once, accusing him angrily of bringing the plague. Among the shouting, certain words registered in his brain—sickness, pain, wailing, panic, black death, corpses, and kill him.

"Wait! Wait!" he shouted as loudly as he could. The roar of the crowd decreased a little, so he continued. "I didn't bring the plague!"

The shouting increased again. Much of it he couldn't under-stand, then one man, close to him, said, "I saw you pass through here last week, already contaminated."

Then another man shouted, "I remember working with you weeks ago, before you got it, now you have it."

Others joined in with similar comments, among renewed shouting. Some started chanting, "Kill him! Kill him!"

"If you didn't bring the plague, who did?" someone finally asked, giving Jason a direction to focus the crowd.

"I didn't do it!" he shouted again. "But I know who did." That caught their attention. The chanting died down and several people asked "who?"

"I was contaminated by the people who brought the plague," Jason said, "just like you. It's a mutated version of smallpox and it remains contagious even after it shouldn't be. Your doctors should have been able to tell you."

"The doctors were among the first to catch it," one man said, "when they were called to care for the sick. They've all disappeared—gone into hiding or dead—along with their wives and children. I heard one of them say it was a plague."

"Let's hang him," someone shouted from the back of the crowd.

"If you kill me," Jason said, "you won't know who did it."

"Who did it?" someone else asked angrily.

"The people who brought the plague are hiding a few miles from here in the mountains. They've been immunized, so they're no longer contagious."

"Have you been immunized?"

"Yes, I have, and you can be immunized, too," he lied. He didn't know how many vaccinations they still had, certainly not enough to immunize the entire community, and he didn't know if they could get more. He'd heard the Outcasts talking about the president's subterfuge and attempts to catch them. "They're hiding in a retreat that I built. You need to go there with me and help me take it back."

"What are you talking about?" someone asked angrily.

As Jason told his story, the crowd calmed to hear him out. Some just walked away.

"They're in a retreat that *I built* and supplied with food, water and emergency supplies," Jason said. "I got kicked out by my partners when they became jealous, and they took it away from me. I was here licking my wounds, when the smallpox survivors—they call themselves outcasts—came along and offered to help me get it back."

The crowd became restless again and the noise level increased, competing with his voice.

"What a crock," one man said.

"No. Wait. I'm telling the truth. I swear it."

The crowd quieted again, but Jason could see that his control over them was tenuous. He had to make this good. "The outcasts turned on me and joined with my former partners. They put me in a cage, but I escaped and came back here to build an army to win it back, by force if necessary." The noise level increased again, so Jason had to raise his voice again. "Who'll help me?"

"What do you mean, 'win it back by force'?" someone asked.

"We take guns, and use them if we have to," Jason replied.

"I don't know about guns," one man said and started to walk away with his head down.

"I'll have to think about it," another said and walked away, followed by several others. The crowd started to disperse, until only a few people remained, looking at Jason thoughtfully.

"You do that," Jason said to their retreating backs. "I'll stick around until I gather enough people who want access to immunizations, good food and clean water, then I'm outta here, and I'm not coming back."

The remainder of the men wandered off, talking quietly among themselves or deep in thought. At the back of the crowd, Isaac and Zach leaned against a building and watched Jason with interest.

Garden City, 26 May

Mike hadn't figured out how to move the gate out to the valley, so Beth and Bryce had walked to Garden City while it was still dark, to avoid being seen, and scouted out the area. Amos had offered to let them take the eBikes, but they didn't know where they could hide them, that they would be certain no one would stumble onto them.

"We have the stamina to walk," Beth had said, "and this might be a quick in-and-out."

Almost immediately after a dim sun tried to penetrate the heavy clouds, the talk around them was about the guy—Jason—who claimed to know where they could get immunized from the plague, what he'd called 'mutated Smallpox'. Some people said he was crazy, but others were intrigued by the possibility of having good food and clean water at his preserve. He'd told them that he was trying to raise an army to go take back his retreat by force.

"Sounds like he's using the same line on them that he used on us," Bryce said.

"He could be successful in raising his army," Beth replied.

They worried about drawing attention to themselves by being too curious, but they needed to know more about Jason's recruiting effort. They reached an intersection and saw two young men sitting at an outdoor table in front of an ice cream restaurant called the *Quick and Tasty*. Smallpox markings decorated their faces and hands. Beth thought they were the same two who had called out to Jason the last time they had passed through on their way to the Preserve.

"Let me talk to them," Bryce whispered as they sat down at the next table.

"We heard that a crazy man is trying to raise an army," Bryce said. "Who is he and where do we find him?"

"His name's Jason," one of the young men said, "and I think he's gone up north today to do some recruiting. You should be able to recognize him because he has a small following."

"You sound like you're not interested," Bryce said.

"Hah! Are you?" one of the young men asked.

When Bryce didn't respond, the young man continued.

"What he's saying sounds too good to be true. My dad says 'be skeptical of people who promise the impossible'."

"You think he's lying?

"Or crazy. Maybe both. Maybe neither. Regardless, we're thinking we may go with him just to get outta here. Everybody's sick, too many are dying, and nobody wants to take care of them. Dad says it won't be long before we start seeing diseases spread from the decomposing bodies."

"Yeah, that sucks," Bryce said. "Anyway, what's your name?"

"Isaac," he said cautiously. "What's yours?"

"I'm Nick," Bryce said. "And this is Britta," he added, pointing to Beth. No use giving away their real names, especially if the boys were going to be talking to Jason—he might figure out who they were.

"Britta's a funny name," the other boy said, studying Beth.

"I had funny parents," Beth said.

Bryce looked at the second boy expectantly.

"I'm Zach. Our parents thought that would be funny," he said with sarcasm. "They could call Zach, and both Isaac and I would come running."

"You're brothers, then?" Bryce asked.

Isaac and Zach looked at each other and frowned. They didn't look like brothers. Then they laughed.

"You're joking, right?" Isaac asked. "We're cousins."

Bryce shrugged and changed the subject. "He has a following, does he? I mean, this Jason has a following?"

"Uh-huh," Zach said. "My dad's one of them. When my mom turned black and died, screaming, he was so mad, he tore up the inside of the house, until he wore out. Then my sister died; she didn't turn black, but she must have been in a lot of pain. Now, he seems angry at everything and everybody. It's eating him up inside. I think he'll go with Jason just so he can shoot somebody."

"What about your family?" he asked Isaac.

"Zach's mom was my dad's sister," Isaac said. "Dad's sad, but says violence doesn't solve anything. My mom and two sisters are still sick—a lot of people are sick, because the plague didn't hit everyone at once. Dad's considering going with Jason because I want to, just to see if anything Jason said, is true."

"And to keep an eye on us," Zach added with a smirk.

"Hey, are you going to go with him?" Isaac asked Bryce.

"I don't know," Bryce said. "We need to learn more first. Where can we find you guys if we have more questions?"

"Aren't you from around here? You have the spots so we assumed you were."

"Yeah, we're from Laketown. This is our first trip up here since the plague hit. We heard the rumors and came to see what we could find out."

"Well, we're usually around here during the day. We don't seem to get as cold as we used to, since we caught the plague, and it's nice to be outside"—he looked up at the dark sky and frowned— "where we can see and hear what's going on."

"Good. See ya 'round then. I think we'll head up north to see what else we can learn."

They went north, then looped around through the foothills to get back to the highway, but before they left, they found a good hiding place for the eBikes—for next time.

The Preserve, 26 May

Beth called Amos while they were walking back to Aspen Valley, to report what they'd learned in Garden City.

"Everyone's sick or dead from smallpox," Beth said. "I guess we created a plague when we passed through."

"I'm sure it's that way all across the east," Amos said. "The president's pretty upset about it, but I reminded him that he's the one who let the monster out of its cage."

"I still feel guilty about it."

"I would expect you, as a doctor, to feel bad about people's suffering," Amos said, "but you shouldn't become depressed over it. There's nothing you could have done differently.

"So," he continued, "Jason might actually be able to raise an army and show up before I can plan for our defense. Okay, Beth. I'll discuss options with the board. Let me know when you're back in the valley."

Chiapas, Mexico, 26 May

Suddenly the air was filled with men's voices shouting and the sounds of automatic weapons all around them. Bullets struck the outside walls and shattered glass. Jared and Pepper ducked into the cell that held their mattresses, where Jared forced Pepper onto a mattress, then lay on top of her. The shouting and gunfire continued for several minutes. Truck engines started, then tires exploded and men screamed in agony. Finally, the sounds of battle slowed, then stopped.

"Alpha squad, check the trucks and buildings. Bravo and Charlie, go after the men who fled. Delta, collect the peasants from the fields and bring them to the clearing."

Jared raised his head and looked toward the door. Suddenly the lock on the door was blown away and the door swung open.

"Don't shoot," Jared yelled. "We're Americans."

Two soldiers, in full battle gear, ran into the room in a crouch and fanned out to either side of the doorway, panning their weapons left to right.

"Don't shoot," Jared yelled again, raising his hands in the air. "We're Americans. We've been held prisoner for months." Pepper sat up next to Jared, holding her top in front of her to hide her nudity.

"Come out here where we can see you better," one of the soldiers said.

Jared helped Pepper dress quickly, then they stood and walked, side by side, toward the soldiers, who kept them covered with their rifles. The soldiers allowed them to pass and exit the building ahead of them, then one of the soldiers frisked them quickly. Jared noticed the American flag on the shoulders of their uniforms.

"Okay," the soldier said, "you can lower your arms, but stay here for a minute, while we secure the camp." One soldier stayed with them while the other went to the office, which the soldiers must have turned into their headquarters.

"Come with me," the soldier said casually when he returned. "I'm Sergeant Jensen, by the way. I think Captain Swasey will be interested to hear your story."

At headquarters, Jensen told them to stand to the side of the door until it was their turn, Soldiers entered, then exited, giving Pepper and Jared a quick once-over, but not speaking, before continuing. After a few minutes, a soldier stuck his head out of the building and motioned to Jensen.

"Our turn," he said with a smile and motioned them inside.

Captain Swasey looked up from his notes when they entered, leaned back in his chair, and spoke softly, belying his tough demeanor.

"You're American?" he asked, looking at Jared.

"We are, sir," Jared said.

"Where did you catch the virus?" Swasey asked, causing Jared to flinch and Pepper to gasp in surprise.

Jared didn't answer immediately.

"Come on man," Swasey said. "It's obvious you have it. Where did you pick it up?"

"I'm sorry, sir. You just surprised us," Jared said with a look at Pepper. "We caught it in Georgia."

"The Johns Creek shelter, or somewhere else?"

"The shelter. You know about the shelter?" Suddenly, Jared was afraid for his life. Beth had said that if the military caught up with them, they would finish the job that they had started at the shelter. Pepper must have been thinking the same thing, as she took his arm with hands that had become cold, likely from her own fear.

"We were briefed. I'll need the details of how you got here, where you've been, and who you've been in contact with. Sergeant Jensen will record your story, as well as make notes. Please go with him now."

"Will we be . . . taken back to Georgia . . . after we've complied?" Jared asked nervously.

Swasey eyed him for a few moments before answering, then smiled.

"You're worried about whether or not you're in trouble, aren't you?" Swasey asked.

"Well," Jared said, not knowing how to go on.

"What's your name?" Swasey asked.

"Jared."

"Well, Jared, it's not for me to say. However, in light of the fact that your joyride led us to El Jefe—one of his guards told us where to find him—I will recommend to the president that he go easy on you."

"Thank you, sir," Jared said, relieved and placing his free hand on Pepper's hands as she bounced excitedly next to him. Jensen took his arm and led them out to one of the trucks, where he set up his recording device—a tablet—between the front seats.

"Go ahead," Jensen said, "start from when you left the Johns Creek shelter. One of you take the lead and the other insert details that the first one leaves out."

☢

"The captain would like to see you," a soldier said as they were exiting the truck. He held out his hand, took Jensen's tablet and notes, and led them back to Swasey. The captain looked over the notes, nodded his head a couple of times, then set them next to the tablet on the desk.

"According to your story," Swasey said, looking at Pepper, "you were visited by a guard several weeks ago, one who entered your room and touched you, correct?"

"Yes," Pepper said cautiously, looking at Jared and wondering where this was leading. She had left a lot out of the story that she had told Jensen. She hadn't even told Jared how she feared that the guard was going to kiss her.

"Do you know why he entered the room, when no other guards had done that?"

"No," Jared said. "We wondered that ourselves."

"Do *you* know?" Swasey asked again, looking directly at Pepper.

"I thought he wanted to kiss me," she said after squirming for a few moments, "then changed his mind." She looked at Jared to see his reaction, but he hid his feelings in a bland expression.

"Did it cross your mind that he might have been ordered to get close enough to you to determine if you were still contagious?"

"Contagious?" Pepper was shocked at the suggestion. She looked questioningly at Jared, but he shook his head.

"I see that you haven't been told, or haven't figured it out for yourselves," Swasey said. "In Galveston, you represented your-selves as curfew enforcers, but contaminated the group of people you interacted with."

Pepper stared at Jared. They hadn't told Jensen that they had escaped Galveston by telling the woman that they were curfew enforcers.

"In Matamoros, you left a third of the Los Zetas cartel dead and many in the city contracted Smallpox as well. The survivors are so happy to finally get relief, that they're singing like little birds. That's how we found out you were here.

"We think that guard was ordered to get close to you because we found a guard in one of the towers surrounding the fields. He'd been dead for some time. We suspect he'd been in some pain, because of the condition of the body, but he'd been locked in and left to die, so we're not positive he died from the disease.

"We also know that El Jefe left here a few days ago, possi-bly because he suspected that we were coming for him, but more likely because he realized the virus had been transmitted to others here at the plantation and he was abandoning it to its fate."

Pepper was overwhelmed. She looked at Jared, but didn't speak, and neither did he. When Swasey was finished speaking, he studied them for a few minutes, in silence.

"I'm convinced that all of this is new to you," Swasey finally said. "Do you have any questions for me?"

"You said a few minutes ago that you know where El Jefe has gone," Jared said.

"I did, and we do. When a cartel member in Matamoros gave us this location, we set up satellite surveillance, and knew when his truck left. Since he was here, according to some of the guards, but isn't here now, we know it was him, and we've been following him. Anything else?"

"Can we go home?" Pepper asked, with tears in her voice.

"You probably don't want to go home to Georgia," Swasey said, "but maybe you'd like a vaccination, so that you're no longer contagious. Then, we'll decide where to take you. For now, you're safer here than anywhere else. We'll get you some decent food and talk to our people back in the states, then we'll get back to you."

The Preserve, 27 May

The board members raised lots of questions. How many men would Jason bring? What time of day, or night, would he come? What kind of weapons would he bring? Would he bring guns? Would he attack without warning, like he did last time?

What were their resources? They had guns, although they were loath to use them. They had the Outcasts, but they might be more of a liability than an asset in a gun fight. Jason might not hesitate to shoot them.

"Don't forget we have the Observer," Mike said.

"Yes, we do," Amos agreed. "Jason doesn't know it's capabilities, but if we use its known capabilities, we risk contamination in the lab."

"That's why I'm trying to reprogram it to work from the valley."

"How's that coming?" Amos asked.

"You'll remember that we discovered that the Preserve doesn't exist in the twin world, because our doppelgangers never built it. We've successfully combined the location maps for the two worlds, so now we can move between the Preserve in our world and Aspen Valley in the twin world. Our problem has been that if we opened a gate between the lab and the valley, in our world, radiation would enter the lab.

"What Katie and I have been working on," Mike said with a smile at Katie, "is to reprogram Panel B, the one that shows our world, to unfix the base location and move it from the lab, to the valley. We finished the programming this morning, and just need to test it inside the Preserve before we ask for a volunteer from the Outcasts to help us test it outside the Preserve."

"Once Mike and Katie finish testing it in the Preserve," Amos said, "I'll speak to Beth about trying a jump from one part of the valley to another, then from the valley to Garden City. If it works, that will be our secret weapon. We can have Beth and her friends track Jason and let us know when he's ready to attack the Preserve, how big an army he has and what kind of weapons they're bringing."

"That would mean we'd have to let Beth know about the Observer and the gate," Lillie said. "Are you prepared to do that?"

"What do you think?" Amos asked Terry, who was smiling.

"I think that if it comes down to a choice between keeping our secret and protecting our families," Terry said, "there's no real choice."

Garden City, 28 May

"Where have you been?" Isaac asked.

"Hi Isaac and Zach," Bryce said. "What's going on?" They'd hidden the eBikes and walked into town before sunrise.

"Jason's got his army," Isaac said. "Haven't heard when they're leaving, but we're going with them. So's my dad, and a few other men. You want to come? I know Jason's disappointed with the lack of interest. He's had some pretty heated arguments with some people who think he's crazy or a liar or both. He almost came to blows a couple of times. I think if he'd had a gun, he would have used it, and that would have been ugly."

"Interesting. Nah, I think he's blowing smoke. I don't think there's any such place as he described. He's going to lead you all up into the mountains to freeze to death."

Two men approached. There was a strong resemblance to the boys. "Hi dad, Uncle Andy," Isaac said. "This is Nick and Britta. They're asking about Jason's army."

"You interested in signing up?" Uncle Andy asked excitedly. "Jason says there's plenty of food and water, even some gold and silver."

"You believe him?"

"I do. He described this underground retreat in so much detail that I figured he couldn't be making it up. He said it's stocked with everything we'd need to survive for at least thirty years. Besides, I'm itching for a fight. He said those that brought this plague, that took my wife"—he choked up— "and daughter, are hiding up there, and I aim to pay 'em back."

"I'm sorry to hear about your wife and daughter. So, you'll be taking guns?"

"I will and I have one for Jason, too. I didn't think he should have one while he was so worked up."

"What about you?" Bryce asked Isaac's dad.

"I'm Justin," Isaac's dad said, holding out his right hand and shaking hands with Bryce and Beth. "It's too bad that everyone got so sick and some lost family, like Andy here, but I don't see any purpose in the violence. Jason said he's going to get his Preserve back, or he's going to destroy it so no one can have it."

"Destroy it?" Bryce asked

"That's what he said," Justin said "but that seems a little radical to me. I'm not sure he's got it all together"—he pointed at his head— "if you know what I mean."

"He found a miner who has dynamite," Andy said, apparently oblivious to Justin's comment about Jason, or not caring, "who's willing to go with him. He lost a family member, too, and he's as angry as I am."

26

What planet did you come from?

Beth radioed Amos to tell him what they'd learned. Then Beth and Bryce returned to the valley by a route that wouldn't reveal their eBikes.

Amos tried to explain the capabilities of the Observer to Beth, who held the radio up, at full volume, so the other Outcasts could hear. "The board has agreed to share one of our secrets with you, since we need your help," Amos said, then tried to explain the capabilities of the Observer.

"You're teasing," Beth said.

"He's crazy," Bryce said.

Suddenly, a round door opened up in front of the Outcasts and Amos stepped through while talking into his radio.

"I can't stay," he said, his voice coming from his mouth and from the radio, simultaneously. Then he stepped back through the gate and it closed.

"What was that?" Ben asked.

"What just happened?" Bryce asked.

"That was Amos," Beth said, recognizing Amos from their previous meeting in the valley.

"I just demonstrated the gate for you," Amos's voice said from the radio. "We can transport ourselves anywhere between here and Garden City."

"Unbelievable!" Beth said. "Who are you and what planet did you come from?"

"Amazing, isn't it?" Amos said, chuckling at their reaction.

"You stepped right through that hole, didn't you?" Beth asked. "I could see the room you're in, behind you."

"We call it a gate, and yes, I did."

"Why didn't you do that when we were trying to get the immunizations from the president?"

"This technology is so new," Amos said, "that we didn't know it would work until today. Now we know, and we want to use it to tell us when Jason's coming."

"And you're telling us about it now because you want us to use it to check on Jason?"

"It may seem selfish to you, but I'm trying to limit our exposure to the radiation, and you're already exposed."

"I don't think you're being selfish at all," Beth said. "I think that's very practical. What do we do?"

"Wait," Bryce said, "you just exposed yourself to radiation by opening that . . .gate."

"I did," Amos said, laughing, "to make a point. But it was a short exposure and I'm in a storeroom where we've removed anything that we can't decontaminate, and I'll go take a shower as soon as we're finished here."

"Amazing," Bryce said.

"Beth, until today, we could only use the gate from our lab, but we've made some modifications so that we can move our side of the gate—what we call the base location—out to you, so that you can go to Garden City from where you are, and not have to come inside the Preserve. If one of you is willing to test it for us, we'd like to try it."

"I'll do it," Bryce said without hesitation.

"No Bryce," Beth said, "you need to think about Sheryl and little Lisa Beth. I'll do it."

"We need to do two tests," Amos said. "The first will transport you from your present location to a spot about thirty yards closer to the cliff. The second will take you from Aspen Valley to Garden City."

Amos warned her about the tingling sensation she would feel passing through the gate, caused by a mild shock to the nervous system. Being a doctor, she was familiar with the nerve bundle in the heart called the sinoatrial node, or SA node, and asked him to explain everything he knew about the impact on her body.

He made sure she had her radio with her and turned on. He planned to make that part of the test as well, since they didn't know what impact the gate would have on the radio. For the first test, he would be able to see her on both sides of the gate, through the sensor on the cliff.

"Are you ready?" Amos asked as a hole, about six inches in diameter, opened in front of Beth. She could see the cliff in front of her, but it was like looking through a magnifying glass, which appeared to bring the cliff closer to her.

She took a deep breath and let it out, then looked around at her friends.

"I'm ready," she said.

"Go ahead and put your arm through."

"It tingles, just like you said it would. What happens next?"

"Terry is adjusting the Observer settings to compensate for the expected electrical discharge when you pass through the gate. Just a moment."

"Look over there," Bryce said, pointing toward the cliff face and laughing.

Beth looked in the direction Bryce indicated and could see her arm floating in the air about thirty yards away, in front of the cliff. She wiggled her fingers and started to laugh. The other Outcasts, who had been watching nervously, joined in.

"It's like a magic trick," Kerri said.

"Your arm's been sawed off," Callie said, laughing.

"Amazing," Bryce said.

"Amos," Beth said.

"I see it," Amos said, chuckling. "How do you feel?"

"Disembodied," Beth replied.

"Okay," Amos said as the hole expanded, the bottom edge touching the ground and the top extending slightly above Beth's head. "We're ready. Go ahead and step through."

Beth took another deep breath and took a large step. As she disappeared from one location, she appeared at the other. For a moment, she was split in half, then she was through, standing thirty yards away, facing the cliff. She spun around to look at her friends and threw both fists into the air.

"Fantastic!" she shouted. The other Outcasts, who had been watching intently, returned her shout.

"I can still see you through the gate," Ben said, grinning at Beth, "but you look closer. It's like a space warp, or something."

"My turn! My turn!" Kerri and Callie shouted together, jumping up and down.

"Unbelievable!" Bryce shouted as he hugged Sheryl to him, while Sheryl held on to Lisa Beth so she wouldn't drop her in the excitement.

"How did it feel?" Amos's voice asked from the cliff.

"As advertised," Beth said, turning to face the cliff and grinning ear to ear. "That's the strangest feeling ever," Beth said, "but I'm fine, I think."

Suddenly, she was surrounded by her friends, who had rushed the thirty yards over to her. It took several minutes for her to answer all their questions and assure everyone that it was really her, not some alien shape-changer, and that she felt fine.

"One more thing," Amos said from the monitor on the cliff, once everyone had settled down. "Let's test the radio."

Beth spoke into the radio for a minute.

"I can tell what you said," Amos said, "but there's a lot of static. It appears that the electricity may have damaged the circuitry. I'll have Mike meet you at the door to get the radio, so we can check it, and give you another one for the second test. We'll see if we can figure out what happened to that one."

The Preserve, 28 May

"They're all pretty excited," Amos said with a smile. "What do you think about letting them all go through the gate to the overlook?"

"Do you think that's a good idea?" Terry asked.

"It will be a good test. I hate to use them that way, since we don't understand the long-term effects, but it will help us learn the capabilities of the gate."

"Okay, as long as you warn them of the risks and they go through one at a time," Terry said. "I don't know what will happen if they all go through together."

"You'll want to calibrate it for each one of them, won't you?" Amos asked.

"Absolutely," Terry said.

☢

"We have another option," Amos said. "Seeing how excited everyone is, we can run the second test now, and send any of you who want to, to the Garden City overlook. Does that sound interesting to you?"

The others began shouting, "let me try it," until Beth raised both hands into the air to get their attention. Then, looking at the cliff, she asked if they could go now.

"Or, we can wait until after dark and send you directly into the city," Amos added. "There's no data on long-term risks of going through the gate, so you'll be taking a health risk."

"No problem," Beth agreed, "Can't be worse than what we've been thorough already, but maybe Bryce and Sheryl should stay behind—Sheryl, because Lisa Beth needs her, and Bryce, because Sheryl needs him—but the others could try it." Bryce and Sheryl reluctantly agreed.

Amos made them promise to go through one at a time and stay only a few seconds, then step back through. He asked Beth to be the first one through the gate and the last one to return, and to keep the radio with her.

He also pointed out that the overlook wouldn't be a perfect test, since he needed to know if there was a problem sending them all the way to the city, which was a few miles farther and down the other side of the mountain. He wasn't concerned about them being seen at the overlook in daylight, since there wasn't much light to see by, and they could look around the area through the gate before going through; but he would want one more test after dark.

The Outcasts, 28 May

Terry opened the gate about three inches while Amos explained how to verify that no one was watching.

"It can be disorienting," Amos cautioned Beth.

She placed her eye up to the opening, as though looking

through a monocle and could see the snow-covered grass and weeds of the overlook, extending a few feet in front of the gate, and the Bear Lake Valley below, with an overcast sky.

"Terry, you can rotate the gate," Beth said into her radio. While she stood still, the view in front of her started to turn to the right, until it had rotated past the visitors' center, the parking lot and back to the view of the Bear Lake Valley. She became dizzy, reached behind her, and Ben took her hand to steady her.

"All good?" Terry asked.

"Wow," she said, pulling away after a few moments. "I see what you mean. That was disorienting. I knew I was standing still, but the movement of the gate made it feel like I was turning in a circle, like I was on an amusement park ride."

"Thanks for that observation," Amos said. "Did you see any people?"

"All good. No people are around."

"Okay, let's enlarge it," Beth said. The gate opened to just over six feet in diameter, a hole in the air in front of Beth. It stood out against the backdrop of the burned, wooded, snowy, Aspen Valley surrounding them.

She stepped through the gate onto a snow-covered sidewalk. She looked around briefly, then faced the gate, where Ben stood in front of the others, waiting for permission to continue. Seeing his smile and the love in his eyes, her heart beat faster, and she returned the smile. "Terry," she finally said, "I'll have Ben put his arm through the gate. Tell me when you have what you need."

"Okay, Beth, all calibrated. Ben can proceed," Terry said a few moments later.

Ben stepped through the gate directly into Beth's arms and kissed her. Then, with one hand on Beth's waist, he looked around at the scenery.

"It's beautiful," he said, then looked back at the gate, where the others stood waiting, huge grins on their faces. "It's a strange feeling, ladies. Be prepared."

He gave Beth another kiss, then reluctantly let go and stepped back through the gate and out of the way, to one side.

They repeated the process with Callie, Kerri, and Lisa, one at a time, who rubbed their arms and chatted excitedly about the tingling sensation of passing through the gate. It was more animation than Beth had seen in Lisa since they'd arrived in Laramie, months ago.

Beth looked around one last time and was about to return through the gate, when Bryce let go of Sheryl and hurried toward the gate from a few feet back.

"Sorry, baby, but I've got to do it, too," Bryce said to Sheryl. "Beth, please?" he begged.

Beth looked to Sheryl, who nodded. "Okay, big boy, come on," she said and waved him forward. When Bryce returned to Aspen Valley, he went right to Sheryl and gave her a kiss.

"Thank you," he said. "It was great." Then he turned to Beth. "Don't you think it would be alright for Sheryl to try it?" he pleaded.

"Maybe she should wait. Amos said he still doesn't know what long-term impact it might have on us," but she could see that Sheryl was anxious to take part in the fun. "Oh, alright, but we may regret this later."

Sheryl carefully handed off Lisa Beth into Bryce's inexperienced embrace and approached the gate, where Beth repeated the process with her.

"All accounted for," Beth called on the radio as she stepped through the gate into Aspen Valley and hugged Ben, who was waiting for her with outstretched arms.

Amos, who'd been watching their activity on a monitor in the lab, chuckled.

"What do you think?" he asked, his voice coming from the cliff.

Kerri and Callie talked excitedly about the strange sensation.

"Who would have believed it was possible?" Ben asked. "There's no doubt where we were. The same furrowed fields, the same mass of campsites surrounding the lake. It's amazing Dr. Blund. Congratulations."

"Thank you, Ben. Please call me Amos, will you?"

"Certainly, Amos."

"Beth," Amos said, "the static on the radio was as bad as with the first test. Let's get you another radio and we'll run one more test, after dark. I'll have you turn the radio off while you step through the gate, and we'll see if that makes a difference. You decide where you want us to send you."

"I think the second drop location would work well."

☢

Beth gave Amos the address for the condos where the second drop had taken place and Mike, who operated the Observer this time, estimated and entered coordinates for the parking lot.

Amos had Beth look through a small opening to see if they had the correct location and Mike rotated the gate for her to make sure it was clear of people and other surprises.

"It's dark, but I can tell it's the right place." Beth said.

"You have the radio?" Amos asked.

"Yup," she said.

"Good. Also, as a safety factor, if we can't hear each other within ten seconds after passing through the gate, I want you to step back through. Is that acceptable?"

"Absolutely," Beth said. "Let's do it."

The gate opened for Beth.

"Oops," she said, "Looks like you need to drop the gate about a foot, so I don't trip getting out and back in." The gate shifted down slowly. "Stop there," she said. "That's great. I'm turning off the radio."

She stepped through the gate and immediately called Amos.

"I'm here. All clear," she said.

"I hear you," Amos replied, "and there's almost no static."

"Great. I'm coming back through. Radio off," she said, then. "I'm back."

"Good. Go ahead and keep that radio. I'll get the board in here to have a conversation with you over the outside speaker on the cliff face."

"You want everyone there?"

"Anyone you want to help with the plan."

The Preserve, 28 May

A few minutes later Amos had the entire board in the office and Beth had all of the Outcasts except Sheryl and Lisa Beth near the cliff in the dark. They discussed possible scenarios and outcomes of Jason showing up with an armed army, for almost two hours. Beth thought it best for her to meet Jason in the open, unarmed, and ask him to leave. Amos thought that was foolhardy, because Jason would be armed, had already threatened her, and could be unpredictable. In the end, no one could talk her out of it, but Bryce, Ben and Kerri had agreed to carry guns. Amos would be watching through the gate, to help out if needed.

Garden City, 29 May

After verifying that they wouldn't be observed, Beth and Bryce stepped through the gate, into the parking lot that they had chosen for their entrance point. There were no lights in the condos as the gate closed behind them. They walked the mile into town. From a distance they could see that a small crowd had gathered at the intersection. Isaac and Zach were there, sitting at a table with Isaac's dad, Justin. Several other men stood, including Zach's dad, Andy, and Jason, who had his back turned. Jason was talking loudly, waving his arms and pacing back and forth in front of the group. Several of them carried handguns or rifles.

Beth and Bryce got as close as they could without being seen by the group, especially Jason, who would be upset at their presence. They also worried that Isaac or Zach might notice them and draw attention to them, thinking they had come to join up. Their dads, Justin and Andy, might even recognize them. They stopped at the corner of a building and waited, peeking around the corner to check on the group every few minutes.

No one else was in sight, possibly because they didn't want to be associated with Jason, or with what this group planned to do. After waiting nervously for over thirty minutes, worried that someone would come along and question them, they heard shouting. They waited a few more moments, then checked again. The group had left and the three sitting at the table had stood, looking toward the west, toward the canyon that led to the Preserve.

Beth and Bryce stepped out of hiding and moved to where they could see the group walking up the road toward the canyon.

They hurried toward the three, who had just started following.

"Isaac," Bryce called quietly, drawing Isaac's attention without alerting the group ahead of them. Isaac stopped, and so did Zach and Justin. "Got a minute?"

"Change your mind?" Isaac said, laughing. "You almost missed it."

"Naw. Just wanted to know what's going on. Is Jason really taking weapons to start a fight?"

"That's what he says. And he's got nineteen men with guns and dynamite." The three held up handguns to show Bryce and Beth.

"Would you really shoot someone?" Bryce asked Isaac.

"I can't imagine it," he said, looking at his dad and cousin, who shook their heads, too. "Not unless I was shot at. Even then . . . " he shrugged his shoulders, "I don't know."

"Do you know the others who are going with Jason? I mean, are they friends?"

"Just Uncle Andy."

"I know a couple of them," Justin said. "The others are transients. And no, they're not friends. Just acquaintances."

"Why don't you tag along and see what happens?" Zach said.

"No. Don't like violence. We'll pass, thanks."

"Okay, see ya then."

"Be careful. Don't shoot any friendlies," Bryce said, thinking that he and Beth would be among the friendlies they would see.

The three men looked at Bryce curiously, as Bryce and Beth turned and walked back the way they had come.

27

Something strange is going on here

The Outcasts, 29 May

"They're on their way," Beth told Amos on the radio after asking him to open the gate. Terry had shielded the radios against static electricity, so the reception was better this time.

"Are you sure I can't talk you out of confronting Jason?" Amos asked.

"If he shoots me, the worst that can happen is that I live," she said, trying to jest.

"Okay, we'll try to protect you, but I won't shoot first. So, if it looks like he's going to shoot, duck."

"I'll remember that . . . duck," she said, in a teasing way.

"Have you figured out how you're going to stop Jason" Terry asked Amos.

"I thought we could watch them through the gate and decide what to do as the situation developed," Amos said.

"Are you worried about radiation coming through the gate into the lab?"

"What if we hang a lead-coated barrier in one corner of the room and you open the gate behind it."

"That should work, but we need to act fast." They hurriedly hung a barrier, that Terry had brought from a store room, from the ceiling; and Terry, working the controls, opened a small gate for Amos to observe the coming confrontation.

When Jason appeared above the valley, Beth and Bryce were waiting for him, a few feet apart, in the clearing in front of the cliff, where Jason and Bryce had unwisely attacked Mike and Terry weeks earlier. Beth warned Amos that she could see his group at the top of the curve in the road.

Jason strode boldly along the path that curved around the valley and emptied into the clearing above the Preserve, while his followers spread out through the skeletal trees and crept from one tree to the next, gradually getting closer, The trees weren't thick enough to hide behind, as they had supposed, but they offered some protection from whatever weapons they thought Amos and his people might have. As Jason stepped into the clearing, forty yards away and closing, Beth called, "Jason, there's nothing here for you. Why don't you just go?"

"Get out of my way, Beth. I'm going in."

"They've changed the locks. You'll have to blow down the Preserve to get in. Then what will you have—nothing."

Jason waved a man forward from the trees, who removed the backpack from his back and set it on the ground. At Jason's urging, he opened it and started removing what looked like sticks of dynamite.

"We have dynamite," Jason said. "If I can't have the Preserve, nobody gets it. I'll kill anyone who stands in the way."

"He called her Beth," Isaac said to Zach. They stood together just inside the tree line, Isaac, Zach, Jason and Andy. "She told us her name was Britta."

"You're right. Then her friend's name probably isn't Nick," Zach said.

"Weren't they the ones we were just talking to in Garden City?" Isaac's dad, Justin, asked.

"Unless they have twins," Isaac said.

"How'd they get here before us?" Justin asked, turning to face his brother-in-law, Andy. "They didn't pass us. Something strange is going on here. Maybe this situation's not what Jason said it was. Maybe we need to learn more before we follow him blindly."

"What do you mean?" Isaac asked his dad.

Before his dad could answer, something Jason said caught their attention. Isaac watched in horror as Jason raised his hand and fired his handgun, from about forty feet away.

Beth—or Britta—dropped to the ground, apparently hit, but he couldn't tell how seriously injured she might be. The man with her, Nick, or whatever his name was, pulled a gun from behind his back and fired three shots, one of them hitting the man with the dynamite, in the chest. He dropped the dynamite and collapsed onto his back, not moving again. Bryce turned his gun toward Jason, and he and Jason fired at each other, simultaneously, while moving sideways. Nick fell, and Jason remained standing, although he started bleeding at the waist, the blood running down the side of his pants.

It happened so quickly that everyone else seemed to freeze for a moment, then they all scattered, dropping to the ground or finding hiding places behind trees and bushes.

☢

Sheryl watched Bryce and Beth fall, from the front door of the partially-constructed cabin on the far edge of the clearing. She had no way to know if they were injured, or dead, since they'd been instructed to play dead if Jason shot at them. Nevertheless, she handed Lisa Beth to Callie and turned, as if to go to them. When Callie, then Kerri, held on to her arms and whispered "think of little Lisa Beth", Sheryl stopped and turned back, bawling at the helplessness she felt. Lisa Beth started to fuss and cry, being jostled by Kerri's effort to restrain Sheryl, so Sheryl took her, placed her over her shoulder, and patted her back gently, while rocking back and forth.

Ben, hiding behind a fallen log near the cabin and to the right of the invaders—that's what he called Jason and his army—raised the handgun that Amos had loaned him and that Bryce had tried to teach him to shoot. As he took his time aiming it at Jason, he saw Jason waive another man forward to pick up the dynamite. Jason must have assumed that Beth and Bryce were dead and that no one else would try to stop him, since he didn't even try to hide. Ben followed the new man with his gun and fired, missing him, but making him duck. Jason waved at him impatiently to come forward, perhaps thinking that whoever was shooting couldn't hit them, and the man resumed his effort to prepare the dynamite. Ben assumed that he had missed because he hadn't followed Bryce's instructions properly, so he tried again—two deep breaths, hold the second one, line up the sights, finger on the trigger, pull gently, resist recoil—and hit the man in the rib cage. "Aim for their center of mass." Bryce had coached him. Ben was elated as the man dropped the dynamite, and fell, then realized that he may have just taken another person's life, and debated with himself if he should feel badly about it.

"Over there," someone shouted, and Ben had to duck as bullets flew over his head and into his log. He'd noticed how the invaders had mostly spread out and hidden as best they could, all except two teenagers and two older men who might have been their fathers—the ones they'd met in Garden City. Hunkered down behind his log, he felt as if he were out of the game; then the bullets stopped flying around him, although he could tell there was still shooting. He raised his head far enough to look over the log and saw that some of the men were firing in the opposite direction. The teenagers and their fathers had dropped to the ground and covered their heads with their hands. He raised his gun to sight on a man nearest his position, when something hit him in the right shoulder, twisting him sideways, and a numbing pain in his atm suggested to his brain that he might have been shot. Looking down at the offending arm, he saw the hole in his shirt surrounded by blood and felt the blood running down his arm. In anger, he tried to raise the gun again, but his arm wouldn't respond to his instructions. He took the gun painfully from his dangling right hand, with his left hand, and tried again to aim over the log. He found that if he rested his hand on the log, he could aim pretty well, but when he fired the gun, his shots went wild, nowhere near where he was aiming.

The Preserve, 29 May

Amos had watched the exchange through the gate, the opening only two inches in diameter, from the left side of the group of invaders. When they started firing at Ben, he raised his rifle, rested it on the lip of the gate and sighted on Jason. Then he realized what Ben and Bryce had done. By shooting the one carrying the dynamite, they lessoned the chance that anyone else would pick it up. Another invader was just picking up the dynamite, so Amos shot him, then the man right behind him, in rapid succession. The first didn't get up, and the second appeared to be hit in the arm; but he fell back to hide behind a clump of aspen trees.

Amos called to Terry to move the gate opening to a new position, so he could make Jason think he and his followers were surrounded. Terry, in the lab, but on the other side of the partition, tried to guess which way to move the gate. As he moved it to the left, Amos said, "Other direction, Terry," so Terry quickly moved it back to the right, a few feet past his original position. When Amos looked down his rifle sights and through the gate opening, he could tell Jason was frustrated, by the set of his jaw and his clenched hands, something Amos was familiar with from their numerous confrontations.

Amos was now positioned behind several of Jason's followers, with a clear shot at some of them. He set the muzzle of his rifle on the lip of the opening and was lining up a shot, when an alarm sounded in the lab, surprising him.

"Radiation alarm," Terry called through the partition. "You must be catching a large dose if it's setting off alarms out here. Do you want to put on a dosimeter?"

"Bad timing, Terry," Amos said, "It'll have to wait for a minute." Amos looked down his sights again and could tell that he was in the middle of the invaders, near one man who looked around for a target to shoot at. Amos called 'invaders' through the small gate opening, getting the man's attention, and he turned, just as Amos fired, hitting him in the face. He was sorry immediately for doing it, not that he didn't intend to shoot him, but by hitting him in the face, the blood and gore that exploded away from him was sickening. Amos turned his head and swallowed his bile to avoid throwing up. The other consequence of his position in the middle of the invaders was that one of those behind him must have thought that his own people were firing at him, since he fired back and struck one of his own men in the back of the head, killing him instantly.

Amos could see Ben raise his head and fired off a couple of rounds, but had no idea where his shots had gone and it didn't appear that he'd hit anyone.

"Terry," Amos said, "again." Terry must have understood Amos's intent, since he moved the gate again, circling to the right. When he looked out again, he was almost directly behind Jason, but there were several trees between them. He didn't have a good shot. He fired at a couple of the other men, but apparently missed. Someone called to Jason and pointed in Amos's direction. Jason spun around and fired off a shot carelessly, then noticed where the smoke from the barrel of Amos's rifle floated on the breeze, and fired in that direction. Suddenly, several shots were fired in his direction, so he backed away from the opening and called to Terry to move the gate again. Amos noticed a small amount of smoke entering the lab through the small gate opening, letting him know that he was not totally invisible. He turned his head to tell Terry to rotate back to the left, but as he was turning back to look out the gate again, a bullet came through the small opening in the gate, blew the front sight off his rifle and hit him in the jaw. He fell hard and the rifle clattered to the ground next to him.

☢

Mike, periodically checking on his dad behind the partition, heard him fall and his rifle clatter to the floor. He looked around the edge of the partition, saw his dad on his back on the floor and the pooling blood under his head, and yelled frantically to Terry. Terry shut down the Observer, then joined Mike, who had knelt down next to his dad. There was blood on Amos's face—it looked like his jaw was broken—and blood on the floor under his head. It looked like he was dead.

"Terry, get Mom . . . Lillie," Mike yelled in frustration. He had no formal medical training, but he'd been through CPR training and knew he should check for breathing and pulse and stop the bleeding. He couldn't check his dad's pulse in his neck, because of the damage to his face and neck, so he ripped off his shirt and pressed it against the entrance and exit wounds on his head.

Terry, being a medical professional, calmly pushed Mike aside and made his own quick assessment of Amos's injuries. The bullet had gone through his mouth and exited out the back of his head, at the base of his skull. Blood and tissue had sprayed around the room and blood pooled on the floor under his head.

AS he worked to stabilize his best friend, he thought of Lillie and what this would do to her, but he needed her help.

"Mike, let me take this. You go get your Mom and a gurney, so we can get your dad to the hospital."

"What about Jason?" Mike asked, looking at his dad's rifle lying on the floor a couple of feet away. He wanted to pick it up and go shoot everyone out there.

"Secondary priority," Terry said, "Now get going."

In frustration, Mike stood and ran out of the lab, while Terry performed triage on Amos. As he ran through the community center, Brittany asked what the emergency was.

"We're under attack," he said and continued into the hospital tunnel. As he hurried back moments later, followed by Lillie, and Matt pushing a gurney, Brittany asked who was hurt.

"Dad . . .Amos has been shot."

"It was Jason, wasn't it?" she asked sadly. "He brought his army, didn't he?"

"How do you know about that?" he asked.

"I overheard Em and Rachel talking about it. They said Jason had an army, with guns. I'm sorry, Mike."

"Me too," Mike said and hurried on.

When Lillie arrived, followed by Matt pushing a gurney, then

Mike, Terry told them quickly, in medical terms, what Amos's injuries looked like. Lillie became nearly hysterical, paralyzed with grief. Terry took a moment to comfort her, pulling her to him and letting her cry against his chest, then asked if she thought she could help him.

"I have to," she said. "There's no one else who can help." She physically calmed herself, being coached by Terry. Matt looked confused, as if none of it registered, and Terry realized that Matt's inexperience would be a problem. Having left his residency to join them in the Preserve, Matt's experience with medical emergencies had been limited to the simulated training Amos had given him, when they weren't involved in some other crisis. Matt didn't know instinctively what to do to help. Terry realized that he might have to take care of Amos by himself.

"Sorry, Mike," Terry said to Mike, who was standing off to one side, fidgeting and looking around, unable to help and wanting to do something, "you're on your own. Stop him!" Mike knew Terry meant that he should stop Jason, but he needed to help with his dad first. Terry lifted Amos onto the gurney, told Matt to take one end of it and ushered Lillie ahead of him out of the lab. Lillie walked alongside the gurney holding Amos's hand in both of hers, and cried.

Mike looked around the lab after they'd left, feeling lost. His heart pounded in his chest and neck. His fists clenched ad unclenched at his sides. He had no idea how his mom, Terry and Matt were doing with his dad, and he didn't know what he could do to help. If his dad died, everything changed. He realized that he needed some way to focus his energy and anger. His eyes settled again on his dad's rifle on the floor. He knew he had to take his dad's place and help end the fight. When he picked up the rifle, with its broken sight, he knew he couldn't trust it to shoot straight. He quickly retrieved another rifle from the gun safe and loaded it. He moved toward the opening his dad had used, then realized that if they'd been able to shoot his dad because they'd spotted his location, as unlikely as that seemed, Mike needed to change it. He stepped over to the Observer, and with shaky hands moved the opening to another location.

When he looked down the gun sights, he could see that he'd moved the opening to a spot behind a tree. He shifted the opening about six inches to the right and looked again. Now, he was just to the right of the tree trunk—perfect. They might think he was behind the tree and waste ammo shooting at the tree, while he picked them off. He looked around and spotted the top of Jason's head as he lay behind a log. He needed to get Jason to expose himself so he could get a better shot.

Jason, 29 May

Jason was furious. He'd lost six men, quickly, and the others didn't know which direction to defend. It was an ambush. How had Amos known he was coming and when he would arrive?

He thought he'd killed Beth and Bryce, and whoever was shooting from the log on the right must have been hit. Even the shooting from the left had stopped. Where had that shooter been? The shots had appeared to come out of nowhere, so he must be well hidden. Maybe they'd killed him, too.

He was down on the ground, as were the rest of what remined of his army, waiting for his instructions. At least three of them had dropped their weapons and had their hands on the backs of their heads. Giving up? Just then he heard a voice coming from his left. It sounded like Mike.

"Give it up, Jason. We don't have a fight with you, but you've burned your bridges here. Go away."

"What does he mean, 'you've burned your bridges'?" the man closest to him asked.

Instead of answering, Jason screamed profanities and started shooting at the voice, not knowing exactly where to aim. Maybe it was just a speaker with a remote aiming device of some kind. That thought stopped him.

Then he heard a shot and saw smoke coming from a tree to the left of where he'd been shooting. Before he could return fire, he heard the man next to him groan and collapse against the log he was hiding behind, He took a quick look and saw that the man had been hit in the head, obviously dead.

Another shot, from the same tree, and another man went down. Jason started firing, emptying his handgun into the tree.

Mike, 29 May

Bullets started coming in Mike's direction. He could see the flashes from the barrels and vaguely see the bullets flying around him, expecting them to punch holes in the lab walls, but they didn't. It was like there was an invisible force field in front of him that the bullets couldn't penetrate. He knew, intellectually, that the bullets were flying past the spot in space where the gate intersected the valley, but it was a surreal feeling.

He thought about the freak possibility of a random bullet passing through the small opening he had made in the fabric of space, like the one that had hit his dad. He quickly backed away from the opening, went to the Observer and moved the gate, then checked the opening to see if anything had changed.

Ben must have fired at someone, because Mike could see that Jason and the rest of his army had turned in that direction. Then the shooting stopped and Mike wondered briefly if that meant Ben had been hit.

"He's not going to quit," Mike thought out loud as he thought about his dad, lying in the hospital, possibly dying, and an unusual calm settled over him. "Let's finish this." He estimated where the opening needed to be to be in the midst of the invaders and moved it there. When he looked out again, he was closed to a couple of them He hesitated, considering if shooting them would be considered murder. He believed that in wartime, soldiers had to shoot or be shot and believed that God would forgive them for protecting their families and way of life. He decided the same applied to him in this situation. So, he shot them, one at a time, from close range. He systematically rotated the gate so he could see each of the invaders and shot each one from close range, bypassing the three who had already dropped their guns and lay on their faces in the snow with their hands on the backs of their heads. He bypassed two more who had dropped their guns as well. As he approached Jason, the last of the hostiles, he could tell that Jason was confused and afraid, watching his men drop. He heard Jason shout 'Amos' and wondered if Jason was planning to give up; but realized that Jason would never change, he would always be mean, aggressive and uncooperative, and continued toward him. The gate opening was within inches of Jason's head when Jason turned and looked directly into the opening. Whether or not he knew what he was seeing was irrelevant to Mike; he pictured his dad as he had last seen him, lying on the gurney on the lab floor, his face a shattered mess, and hesitated only a moment before firing, hitting Jason in the face. His head exploded like a ripe watermelon; it made Mike sick to his stomach, and he had to rush to the bathroom to throw up.

Ben, 29 May
Ben watched the invaders falling like flies from his log. Some-

thing had changed; these were explosions, as if each was shot from close range.

When the shooting had stopped earlier, he had waited to see what would happen. Then he'd heard a voice telling Jason to go away and the shooting had started again, aimed away from him. He had fired one more shot, drawing their attention back to him, which forced him to duck. He'd felt like a coward for not facing their fire, so he'd looked up again.

Finally, he saw Jason looking around, possibly to see what men he had left. His face was a rictus of hatred, pain and fear. There wasn't much left of the attack, but Ben saw one invader taking careful aim, as if he knew where Mike was shooting from. Ben fired with his left hand and hit the invader in the back. He noticed Jason turn toward him and raise his gun, then the gun flew from his hand and he turned back around. That's when Jason was shot in the face, his head exploding.

When no one else moved, Ben hoped the battle was over. He knew there were still invaders out there, three of which had dropped their guns and had their hands on their heads, but he thought the fight had gone out of them.

"You . . . out there . . . invaders!" Ben called. "Put your hands behind your heads and stand up where we can see you. You're surrounded, so don't try anything." He hoped that would convince them to surrender.

Five men stood up, awkwardly, with their hands behind their heads. Two of them were young—teenagers. The man next to them pushed them behind him, in the direction where there had been no gunfire, protectively. He looked like one of the men he'd met at Garden City, one of their fathers. The other two looked to be in their twenties or thirties. All of them looked scared.

"Don't shoot," one of them said.

"Is there anyone else out there?" Ben asked.

"They look . . . dead to me," one of the teenagers said, choking on his words.

"Bryce? Beth?"

"I'm hit, Ben," Bryce said. "Beth?" When she didn't answer, Bryce struggled to his knees and moved over beside her. "She's alive, Ben. I don't see any blood."

"Kerri," Ben called. "cover me while I check on Beth and Bryce." He didn't wait for a reply, but scrambled toward Beth, stooped over to present the smallest target possible.

"Got it!" Kerri finally said, but Ben didn't look to see what she was doing. All his attention was on Beth. By the time he reached her, Bryce had his gun back in his hand, pointed at the invaders, while he held his other hand over the wound in his shoulder, blood seeping slowly between his fingers.

Ben couldn't see any injuries, and concluded that Beth must have bumped her head when she fell down, pretending to be shot, judging from the goose egg on the back of her head. He left her and went to Bryce, ripping his own shirt and pressing it against Bryce's shoulder.

"Go to the cabin and I'll take a closer look at it when I finish with the invaders," he told Bryce. Bryce didn't move right away, then staggered as he tried to stand.

"On second thought, Bryce, you better sit down, before you fall down," Ben said and helped Bryce lie down.

Ben took a quick look toward the cabin and saw that Kerri had her gun pointed in the direction of the invaders, whose attention was split between her gun and what Ben was doing.

As Ben walked boldly toward the five men still standing, he aimed his gun at one of them, menacingly.

"Don't shoot," the man said. He was the one with the two teenagers. "We didn't intend to hurt anyone. We just came along to see what would happen. We just wanted to get out of Garden City."

"You're complicit with Jason. I ought to shoot you all, right now."

"Wait Ben," Bryce said, raising to a sitting position. "Amos," he yelled, turning toward the cliff. "Amos, can you hear me?"

"This is Mike," the wall replied. "What's your status?"

"This is Bryce. I've been shot. Beth's unconscious. We've got five invaders who've surrendered and . . . we don't know the status on the others."

"Can you hold on until I can get a suit on and come out there?"

"I think so. But I may faint from blood loss." Then he chuckled humorlessly and lay back down.

"This is Ben," Ben yelled from where he stood facing the intruders. "I'm here. We've got guns on them." As he thought about Beth, who could have been killed, it was all he could do not to shoot someone.

"Okay, Ben. Hold tight. I'll be right there."

"Ben," Sheryl called. "I need to help Bryce."

"Just a minute Sheryl," Ben replied. "Let me make sure it's safe." Ben carefully approached each of the downed men, waving his gun at those who were standing, to drive them together toward the center of the clearing. It took some time because of all the downed trees and snow. He checked each one for a pulse—all dead. "You're clear, Sheryl."

Almost before the words were out of his mouth, Sheryl raced across the clearing, knelt and pressed a compress against Bryce's wound, then cradled his head in her lap.

A few minutes later, without anyone noticing, a man in a white hazmat suit appeared in front of the cliff, as though he had come right out of the rock face, or descended from an invisible flying saucer. He wore a utility belt around his waist and carried a rifle, which he'd aimed at the invaders.

"Mike," Ben said, "I need to get Bryce and Beth to the shelter."

"Go ahead, Ben," Mike said, "I'll keep an eye on them."

Ben tried to pick Beth up and quickly realized he needed help. "Sorry, Mike. I need help. Kerri," he yelled, "can you keep an eye on them?"

"Just a sec, Ben," Mike said. "Let's get the invaders out here where we can control them better."

"Right," Ben agreed.

"You five," Mike said, "kneel over here in a circle, facing each other, with your hands on your head." When they had done what they'd been told, and Kerri had her gun on them, Mike helped Ben carry Bryce, then Beth, to the cabin and laid them on cots.

Mike went back out to the clearing while Ben cut away Bryce's shirt and dressed his shoulder wound.

"Looks like a flesh wound," he told Bryce, talking as he worked. "The bullet entered and exited the arm. I'll leave him with you," he said to Sheryl, as he turned toward Beth. He quickly gave instructions to Callie about caring for Beth, then stood and left the cabin.

Mike and Kerri had herded the five surviving invaders into the pen where they'd kept Jason.

"I checked them for weapons," Mike told Ben. "Now I've got to get back inside. Dad's been shot." He started to amble away, as though he were having difficulty moving in the hazmat suit.

"Oh no," Ben said. "Are you okay? What can I do to help?"

"We've got it, thanks," Mike said without turning around, "and you've got your hands full out here, anyway."

"Kerri," Ben said, "help me gather up their weapons." Kerri followed him around as he checked on the invaders that had fallen. She held the weapons they'd dropped in the snow while he dragged the bodies into the clearing. He found one man alive, with a faint heartbeat, and carried him to the pen. He'd been shot in the side and the bullet had exited out his stomach, Ben didn't think he would live very long. He gave one of the teenagers a bottle of water and told him to take care of the guy.

"What am I supposed to do?" the young man asked. "I'm no doctor."

"Move out of the way, Zaac," the older man said. "Let me see what I can do for him."

"You called that guy Bryce," the other young man said to Ben. "He told us his name was Nick."

Ben didn't answer. He was still angry that it could have been worse. He could have lost Beth.

"And the woman, she said her name was Britta. Why?"

"What's your name?" Ben asked as he relocked the pen.

"Isaac," the young man said.

"Be quiet," the older man said to Isaac. "Don't upset him."

"They didn't want Jason to hear their real names," Ben said as he rattled the lock to make sure it would hold, "or he might've figured out who they were and guessed that we were on to him."

"And you thought we might use their names and give them away?" Isaac asked after looking at the older man.

"That was one possibility."

"You're Ben?"

"I am."

"And that other guy is Mike?" Isaac asked, looking around for Mike. "Hey, where'd he go?"

"Yes, his name is Mike." Ben started walking away. He was tired of listening to Isaac and needed to check on Bryce.

"How'd he get here?" Isaac asked, "He wasn't here and then he was and now he's gone again. It's like when Nick and Britta,

I mean Bryce and Beth, beat us here from Garden City. How'd they do that? And how did Mike make his voice sound like it was coming from over there?" Isaac pointed in the direction they had last heard Mike's voice.

"You ask a lot of questions," Ben said, and walked away.

28

What am I going to do without him?

The Preserve, 29 May

Lillie had to get through this. She buried her emotions beneath layers of cold professionalism, the way she'd done on numerous occasions, when attending victims of child abuse, auto accidents, explosions and other serious physical suffering. But this was different; this was Amos. Watching Terry operate on him, seeing the severe damage the bullet had done to his head, she fought to stay focused.

"Lillie!" Terry said when Lillie bent over and rested her head on the operating table, "stay with me."

"I'm okay," she said, raising her head and seeing concern in both Terry's and Matt's eyes. "Just a little light-headed."

"I need you to stay focused."

"I know, Terry. I'm trying." She had helped Terry and Matt get Amos into surgery, holding the compresses on his jaw and the back of his head, seeing and feeling the damage to his beautiful face. She had prepped him for surgery and now assisted Terry by handing him instruments as he asked for them, at the same time watching closely the monitors and IV that Matt had hooked up to him. She knew she needed to remain focused if she were to be of any use to them.

"I know this can't be easy on you," Terry said, his look of concern turning to sympathy. "I think I need the Observer in here."

As Terry had surmised from his earlier assessment, the bullet had entered the side of Amos's jaw and exited out the back of his neck below the skull. His brain had swollen and he had lost a lot of blood. It was too early to tell if the spinal cord had been damaged.

His immediate concerns included Amos's low blood pressure, due to blood loss, the swelling, which he had been watching and might have to drain, and bone fragments in the brain, which he meticulously searched for and removed.

As soon as they'd arrived in the hospital, Terry had sent Matt to get four units of whole red blood and four units of plasma from the medical freezer, bring them to room temperature, and begin a blood transfusion. He didn't know how much blood they would eventually need, but they had a little more in storage, if needed.

Terry knew that only he could save his partner's life, but without telling Lillie, he was certain that if Amos lived—which wasn't certain—he would have diminished brain function.

He could tell Lillie was a wreck. She tried to hide her pain, but her periodic lack of focus let him know that her mind was elsewhere—he hoped she had pleasant memories, but doubted anything would rescue her from this living nightmare.

Matt helped when he was told what to do and how to do it, even going to the medical library twice to check the medical books, and holding incisions open while Terry tried to control bleeding and put Amos back together.

"Can I do anything to help?" Mike asked, sticking his head around the hospital door at one point.

"I don't think . . .wait, yes, you can," Terry said. "Take Matt to Logan Regional Hospital or McKay D, in Ogden, and help him rob their blood bank."

Matt looked up sharply, his eye showing his surprise at the suggestion, the rest of his face hidden by his surgical mask.

"Through the gate?" Mike asked.

"Yes," Terry replied, "and be quick about it."

"It's the middle of the day. There are bound to be people around."

"Your dad needs blood," Terry said. "If you're worried about being stopped, take a gun." Terry stopped abruptly, realizing how stupid his suggestion about the gun sounded. "Forget the gun," he corrected. "Just make a quick exit through the gate. No one will believe that you just disappeared into thin air."

"Won't the blood be contaminated with radiation?" Mike asked.

"Not necessarily, mike," Terry said. "Either way, there's no help for it. We need that blood."

"Maybe there's another hospital that's in a less contaminated location, that we can get to." Matt suggested.

"Do you know of one?" Terry asked.

"I think there's one in Montpelier, Idaho," Matt said.

"Come on, Matt," Mike said. "We'll try Montpelier and use McKay D as backup." Matt started to remove his surgical gown. "No," Mike said, "keep the gown on; you look like a doctor, so our chances of success will be better."

While they were gone, Terry had Lillie sit down twice, for a few minutes each time, to give her time to collect herself. He worried that if she fainted, or lost focus and couldn't recover he might not be able to continue without her help.

☢

"Mike," Terry said when he and Matt had returned with the whole blood, "I want you to try something. Will you send the gate over here so I can see if that makes this easier?" Without looking up, he could feel everyone's eyes on him. He took a quick look to confirm that all three of them questioned what he was about to do. "I want both sides of the gate in here. I'll also need a headset with microphone so I can direct you how to move the gate around."

Mike just stood there with his mouth open. They had talked about looking inside the human body, but aside from the practice on Emily's arm, they hadn't used it. Terry suspected that that was Mike's question. Lillie's question was probably whether or not it would be desecrating Amos's body.

"*Now!*" Terry said forcefully, which startled Mike and got him moving.

It worked just like Terry wanted it to. He put his eye up to the gate, blocking out ambient light, like he was looking through a microscope. He had Mike manipulate the other side of the gate through Amos's face, neck and brain, looking for damage, leaky blood vessels and bone fragments. It was awkward at first, coordinating his hand movements with the gate, but he'd had experience with normal surgical magnifying glasses, so the adjustment was quick and accurate. He fixed everything he could see that needed fixing, but wondered if it would be enough. When he was finished, he sutured up the incisions and bandaged Amos's head, making sure that he had stopped all the bleeding. He even had Matt help with the closure, to give him a little experience with the gate.

At some point in the operation, Terry had taken a few minutes to instruct Mike on building a portable control panel for the gate, so Terry could operate it himself, without having to rely on Mike to operate the controls from the lab. Things progressed faster from that point on.

Prime Bunker, 29 May

"Chandi," the president said, "I'm delighted with the performance of the reactors in the bunkers. Are you ready to start installing them for the public?"

"We're very close, Mr. President," Dr. Chandra Robertson said. "The electric utility coalition that you established shared the initial list of priorities with the utility companies affected and they've been restringing power lines to the water treatment plants and industries that we need online first. We have three secure facilities set up for building the reactors and I have seven more under construction. Now that we're scaling up, I've requested a report on exactly how much nuclear material we have so I know how many more reactors we can build."

"What do you need from me?" Greg asked. He was impressed with how well Chandi had grown into the assignment in such a short time. Amos was right to influence him to keep her.

"It might help if you emphasized the importance of getting me that information. It would also help if we raise the priority of that uranium enrichment facility."

"I can do both of those. Anything else?"

"No. I have a question for Amos, but I'll call him directly. No need for you to worry about it."

"Oh?"

"I think I know the answer already, but I thought I'd get confirmation from him," she said self-consciously.

"What's the question?"

"It has to do with ring versus radial power distribution. With radial distribution, if one piece of hardware is shut down for some reason, like transformer maintenance, the customers on the line lose power, but with ring distribution, power can be delivered through a secondary route, using switches. We don't have switches and transformers yet, so I need Amos to confirm how we can provide power if a reactor is shut down. We won't have the luxury of building ring distribution for some time, but I want to be planning ahead, so we don't build limitations into the system."

"I won't pretend to know what you're talking about," Greg laughed, "but it sounds important and I'm impressed that you're thinking about it."

The Preserve, 30 May

"Hello," Mike said, answering the sat phone on the fourth ring.

"Amos?"

"This is his son, Mike."

"Oh. This is Dr. Chandra Robertson, with the Nuclear Regulatory Agency. Is Amos available? I have a question for him."

"Uh . . . " Mike couldn't decide how to respond. He wasn't sure he should reveal his dad's condition. Besides, he was having difficulty holding himself together. "Uh . . . no . . . he's not available right now."

"Can you tell me when would be best to call back?"

"Uh . . . maybe I should have him call you when he's available."

"Okay. I need to get some other things done," Chandi said apologetically. "If I'm not immediately available, please ask him to leave a time when I can call him back."

"Sure."

"Thanks."

"Who was that," Katie asked after he'd disconnected. They were alone in the gardens. He wasn't sure why he'd decided to keep the sat phone with him, but now he needed to decide what to say in case they called again. He didn't know when he'd have a chance to talk to his mother or Terry. He may never be able to talk to his dad again. The thought made him choke up.

"Are you going to be alright?" Katie asked, wiping a tear from his eye. She must have noticed that he was blinking in an effort to clear his vision.

"I may never be alright again," he choked. "How could this have happened? I *know* the gate opening was only large enough for dad to see down his rifle sights. That shot was a fluke. Nobody can shoot that accurately."

Brittany and Becca met Lillie as she exited the hospital tunnel, on her way to her bedroom, and asked if there was anything they could do for her or Amos. She started to cry immediately, and nearly collapsed. Becca caught her and the two women helped her to her room.

"Thank you, but there's nothing any of us can do for Amos," Lillie cried. "Terry is still with him, but I need to go to rest."

They wanted to help her undress for bed, but she just collapsed onto the be, fully clothed. They left her and returned to the community center.

"Poor Lillie," Becca said. "This has hit her hard."

Just then, Terry appeared, so Becca stopped him.

"How's Amos?" she asked.

"I've lost him," he said. "If we'd had a large hospital, with a staff of surgeons and nurses, maybe it would have turned out differently."

"This is Jason's fault," Brittany said. "Is he still out there?"

"According to Mike, Jason and most of his army are dead. The five that survived have been placed in the pen the Outcasts built."

"Will you be okay?" Becca asked Terry.

"I'll be fine, Becca," Terry said. "What about you, and what do you plan to tell Sydney about her dad?"

"Jason made it clear that he doesn't love me anymore," Brittany volunteered, "and I accepted the fact that he was dead to me when he left the Preserve. I've shed all the tears I have in me for him already. I'll be fine, but thanks for asking. Sydney already believes her dad is dead, so nothing has changed there."

In the end, neither Lillie's lack of focus, nor Matt's inexperience, had made a difference. Even the blood bank hadn't helped. Terry couldn't save his best friend. He believed he had utilized every ounce of knowledge and experience in his long career, in addition to their phenomenal new technology, but all of it combined hadn't been enough.

When the heart monitor had flat lined for the third time in almost six hours of surgery, and he couldn't restart Amos's heart, he had finally admitted to himself and to the others that the battle was over and they'd lost. He'd cursed Jason for killing his best friend, calling him a murderer.

"Lillie," he'd said. He was going to try to comfort her, but she wouldn't look at him. He'd reached out and pulled her to him, smearing the blood that was on his gown onto hers. She'd gone limp in his arms and bawled against his chest.

"Amos," she'd cried. "What am I going to do without him, Terry?"

He hadn't answered. He didn't know what any of them would do without Amos.

Prime Bunker, 31 May

"What did you find out from Amos," Greg asked Chandi conversationally, just to have something to say. Chandi sat at the table in the Prime situation room with both hands on the laptop keyboard, typing her notes. She stopped and looked at him.

"Amos was busy, so I didn't talk to him. His son said he would have Amos call me."

"Mike answered the phone? That hasn't happened before. If Amos isn't available, Lillie usually has the phone with her. I wonder what's so important that neither of them are available."

"I didn't think it was my place to ask."

Chandi's hands twitched, perched above the keyboard, as if she had something she wanted to type and the president was interrupting. Greg decided to let her get on with her work, especially since what she was doing was the most important thing on his agenda.

"I'll give them a call and let you get back to work. Thanks, Chandi."

The Preserve, 31 May

"Hello," Mike said nervously, wondering if this would be Dr. Robertson again, or the president this time. He hadn't been able to talk to his mother, because Becca and Brittany stood guard over her bedroom and wouldn't let him disturb her. They had only interrupted her one time, to verify that she had, indeed, gone to bed. When he'd tried to see her, they'd shooed him away. Terry had been almost as difficult to see, but Mike had caught him for a five-minute conversation, during which Terry had suggested that he stall the president until they had time to figure out what to do.

"Is this Mike?" the president asked.

"It is, Mr. President. What can I do for you?"

"Can I speak to your dad?"

"I'm sorry, but he's unavailable," Mike said. He choked up, thinking about his dad's death, and he had to fight to regain control of his voice.

"Hmm . . . can you tell me when he'll be available?"

"Sorry, sir, but I don't know. I'll be sure to tell him you called when I speak to him again." But it won't be in this lifetime.

"Can you tell me what he's doing or where he is, Mike?"

"Sorry, sir, but you know how he is when he's working on something." Although that doesn't apply in this case. "Can you tell me what you need?"

"I don't know all the details, but Dr. Robertson has a question for him about the reactors."

"I'll be sure to tell him."

"Okay, Mike. Thanks." The president disconnected and Mike took a deep breath, letting it out raggedly.

Prime Bunker, 31 May

"That's strange," Greg thought aloud. Amos had never put him off before. Maybe he had burned his bridge with Amos, after all. He found Chandi, still typing away in the situation room. "Maybe you had better use your best judgement and move forward. I don't know when we'll be able to talk to Amos."

"Is something wrong?"

"I don't know."

Chiapas, Mexico, 4 June

The military had tracked El Jefe to a hacienda in a small town near the plantation. They transmitted a satellite image of the Layout to Captain Swasey, who organized an OP to attack the hacienda and capture him. The hacienda consisted of a large open courtyard, surrounded by a large villa at one end and single-story buildings, that looked like small cottages, closing in the other three sides. The courtyard contained large flower beds, filled with colorful flowers, and small fruit and citrus trees. There were armed soldiers in front of some of the cottages. Captain Swasey's plan was to surround the hacienda and storm the courtyard from the three openings in the outer wall, overwhelm the soldiers quickly, then storm the villa through the main entrance, while watching the back wall, where there were several second story windows.

The OP was executed perfectly. The first three Mexicans encountered in the courtyard drew weapons and were shot before they could get a shot off. The others in the courtyard dropped their weapons and were rounded up without a fuss. The cottages were searched, and a few more men, women, and children rounded up without a problem. Then all that remained was the main villa. When Swasey approached the villa, his soldiers parted to let him through. He was directed by Jensen, and a team of three of his best men, to the master suite, at the top of the broad staircase, where, he was told, he would find El Jefe. At the top of the stairs, he followed directions from a soldier to large double doors.

"Is he in there?" Swasey asked the soldier. "Have you been inside?"

"No, sir. We've stayed out here, as directed. His housekeeper told us he's been in his room all day and her instructions were to not disturb him. In fact, she said he hasn't left his room for three days."

Swasey paused to consider whether this latest information was significant. He had been instructed to capture El Jefe, if possible, and bring him to the United States to be interrogated about the terrorist and nuclear bomb and to stand trial for his part in the terrorist attack on Washington, D.C., where he was expected to be found guilty and hanged for crimes against humanity. If he couldn't capture El Jefe, he was to ensure that he didn't escape—kill him, in other words.

Swasey withdrew his service revolver and knocked on the bedroom door.

"*Adelante*"—come in—a deep voice said. If I was El Jefe, he probably thought it was one of his men with a message. He tried the door handle. It moved, so he pushed it all the way down and pushed the door open, prepared to defend himself against attack. El Jefe sat at a desk, facing the door. He looked up, unsurprised and unruffled by the sight of five American soldiers filling his doorway.

"Welcome to my home," Jose Mendosa said in slightly accented English. "Please come in. I trust that you have been kind to my people outside."

"No one has been harmed," Swasey confirmed. "We ask that you come with us now."

"And where are we going?"

"To the United States. We have a few questions for you."

"Can you not ask your questions here, where we can all be more comfortable? I really dislike travel and the United States is so far away."

"Sorry sir. It can't be helped. There are people who want to talk to you. It will be easier for all of us if you come along now."

Mendosa's hands, which had been resting in his lap behind the table, suddenly shot up and he had a gun aimed at captain Swasey's chest. Before anyone else had time to react, Sergeant Jensen fired his gun from Swasey's left and Mendosa's gun flew across the room.

"That hurt," Mendosa said, shaking his hand. "Good shot, Sergeant. Did you learn that from Wild Bill Hickok?"

Jensen looked at Swasey with a "Who's that?" expression on his face.

"I'll fill you in later," Swasey said, aiming an unbelieving expression at Jensen, then he waved his men forward to take Mendosa into custody.

29

I will always love you

The Preserve, 4 June

Lillie told Mike that she believed she could finally control her emotions long enough to participate in a board meeting, so Mike called them all to the office, including Matt. Everyone sat silently, probably out of respect for Lillie's feelings, then Mike started the meeting.

"You all know that Dad was shot during the gunfight in the valley. You should also know that Mom, Terry and Matt did everything they could to keep him alive. His death"—Lillie started to cry, which started Emily and Rachel crying— "will have a major impact on our lives, but I know he would want us to move forward." Mike paused to regain control of his own emotions.

"We need a new chairman and we need to decide if we will add another board member," Mike continued.

"Does this have to be done today?" Matt asked as he tried to comfort Emily.

"Actually, Matt, it does," Terry said. "President McCormick has been calling, to talk to Amos, and we need to decide how to respond. Mike has been stalling him so far, but we don't know how long that can continue. If the president guesses what happened, he may feel like he has carte blanche to come looking for us . . . and the Outcasts."

When no one else spoke up, Mike continued.

"Okay," Mike said, "nominations are now open for a new chairman. I nominate Mom."

"I decline," Lillie said. "I couldn't do it."

Mike felt like he'd been slapped in the face. As many times as his mother had joked with his dad about her being chairman—or chairperson, as she'd clarified—he thought she would welcome it.

"Mike," she said, "I think you should do it."

"I second it," Terry said immediately. "All in favor?" Everyone raised their hands.

Mike was shocked. He didn't know how to manage the Preserve. He felt like he did a mediocre job managing the gardens.

"Do you accept?" Terry asked.

"I . . . I guess so," Mike said, thinking that this vote showed that everyone had a lot of confidence in him. "What if I mess something up?" he asked, just to test their confidence.

"Oh," Terry said, "you think it's possible that you're human, after all." Katie smiled and choked out a laugh, which got the others smiling.

"Okay, then, I accept, on a couple of conditions; one, I want Matt to be a board member. All in favor." They all agreed. "Two, I need your input on what to tell President McCormick."

"Mike," Terry said, "you're doing fine. Amos didn't want the president to know where we are, so don't tell him. Keep stalling him."

No one else had an opinion. "Okay, anything else?" Mike asked.

"Yes," Lillie said, "I'm resigning from the board and turning over my role as house manager to Emily." Several members began to object, but Lillie raised a hand to stop them. "I'll still help on the work teams and help any way I can, but my heart's not in it. Can you all respect that?" Mike watched her look around at the sad, but loving and understanding faces.

"Maybe I'll feel differently in a few weeks or months, but right now, I can barely function. I need to get feeling more like a human being before I accept more responsibility."

No one wanted to continue the meeting, so Mike excused everyone and went to the lab.

Terry asked Lillie to stay.

Lillie had a lot of respect for Terry. She'd known him for many years, as Amos's good friend and partner; but she wasn't in the mood for a discussion and was a little short with him,

"What is it Terry? Can it wait?" she asked.

"Lillie," Terry said, understanding the source of her frustration and having the same respect for her, "When we heard that Jason was coming to the valley with a small army," he said, "I reminded Amos that Jason had threatened to kill him. He blew it off, thinking there was no way Jason could get to him in the Preserve, even with explosives. But before Jason arrived, Amos told me he had recorded a video message to you, since none of us knew what would happen, and in case he couldn't tell you in person how he felt.

"It's in the machine. I haven't seen it. I'm going to the lab to keep Mike occupied for a while, so he won't interrupt. When you're ready to watch it, just press the play button."

"What am I going to do, Terry? I don't know if I can go on without him." Lillie cried.

"Like the rest of us, you'll figure it out," he said.

She apologized for her short fuse, thanked him, and let him go. She knew that whatever Amos had recorded was going to make her cry again, so she sat quietly for a few minutes, trying to prepare herself for what she expected to see, then hit the play button.

Amos's smiling face—his beautiful face, not the broken one she'd seen in the operating room—appeared on the video monitor. His loving expression—so familiar—comforted and lifted her spirit. She could almost believe that he had come back to her—almost. Her body ached to feel his arms around her. She hugged herself and pretended it was him, tears coming, unrestricted, to her eyes.

She knew how he felt about her—he'd shown her often enough—and she felt the same way about him. When he started to speak, she cried silently, tears running down both cheeks and dropping into her lap.

"My dearest Lillie," the Amos in the video said, his smile turning sad. "If you're watching this, it means I'm either dead or so disabled that I can't tell you in person how I feel. I hope it's the former, since I wouldn't want you to be tied down to an invalid for the rest of your life.

"You are my special angel—the love of my life."

Her body shook—wracked with agony—at his familiar habit of quoting lines from his favorite old love songs.

"I worry about you feeling sorry that I took you from the bright, beautiful, aboveground world to live in the Preserve," he continued. She shook her head and mouthed the word 'no', as if he were there to see it. "Perhaps we would have been better off to die in the war. But I don't believe that. I've made some mistakes, like allowing Jason to come with us to Aspen Valley, but I don't believe for a minute that it was a mistake to build the Preserve and move to it to avoid the chaos of the war.

"We set up the board to survive me. Elect a new chairman—or chairperson." He smiled and she smiled with him, through her tears, knowing that he was referring to her teasing; that maybe she could run the Preserve better than he could.

"And keep the family looking toward the future. You are a strong matriarch and loved by all of them."

"But I need you," she cried aloud, her cries turning to sobs.

"Terry will want to continue his medical experiments with the Observer, to perfect its capability to view inside the human body. Mike will want to continue looking for us in the twin world. Maybe you should let them—maybe I should have let them. Maybe some of what we've experienced and learned would help the twin world.

"You have shown our children the right way to live and they are following your example."

She sighed and nodded her head in agreement.

"I've thought a lot about the Outcasts. Beth and her people will make a contribution to the community if you encourage them. Knowing that Sheryl's baby was born immune to smallpox, there's no reason not to allow Rylee and Sydney to find partners on the outside, if that's their choice. We don't know how long the radiation level will be too high to allow free movement in and out of the Preserve, but Terry can figure that out. Maybe the world will heal itself in your lifetime and you can all go home to Logan. I hope so. Either way, find joy in loving our grandchildren."

Amos paused and his expression became even more serious.

"If I'm allowed, I'll watch you from the other side. I'll try to let you know that I'm alright. Be comforted in knowing that we'll see each other again."

They had often talked about their belief in an afterlife and being together again with their loved ones. Now she wondered if that belief would sustain her for the rest of her life, or if she would despair without Amos to bolster her.

"I will always love you," he finally said, then ran his hand through his hair in a way so familiar to her that she wailed.

The message ended. She stared at the blank video screen and thought about her life with Amos. From the day she had seen him in the hospital, her in a candy-striped skirt and top, and he in green scrubs, she had never loved, or even had an interest in another man. She had called him 'Doc', first as a tease, then with affection. The way he'd said 'Lillie' had made her shiver. He was so handsome, so romantic, so attentive, so sincere, so full of life. They were a team, they were 'one', now half of her was gone and she would never get it back in this lifetime.

Suddenly, she thought of what she had said to a woman who had lost her husband of twenty-plus years after he'd died in a skiing accident. Sitting in the family room in the hospital, holding the inconsolable woman's hands in hers, she had said, 'You're young. You have a lot of life ahead of you. You'll find happiness again. The woman had looked at her with disbelieving eyes and had cried harder. It had made Lillie feel stupid, trying to tell this woman what to feel and what to think.

She never found out what had happened to the woman, but she'd never tried to give advice to a grieving wife again. There were no adequate words of consolation. There were no words for her now. Even if the world hadn't exploded in thermonuclear war, even if they weren't buried in the earth in Logan Canyon, she didn't believe any man out there could replace her 'Doc'.

"I know I'll never find another you," she cried, subconsciously calling up a line from one of Amos's favorite old love songs, then rested her head on her arms on the table. That's where Terry found her sometime later, sleeping restlessly.

Preview:

The Door Between Twin Worlds

(Book 5 of the Gemini Gate series)

Mike placed his eye up against the small opening in the Gemini gate. It made him think of a submarine periscope—up periscope, rotate 360 degrees, down periscope—except that, instead of merely seeing what was around him, the gate rotated on a vertical axis that allowed him to see what was in the space he occupied, as well. He was looking through the gate at the security checkpoint in the lobby of the Grand America hotel in Salt Lake City, Utah, in the twin world.

"The guests have invitations," he told Terry, who stood at his side holding the portable Observer control, "but the staff is collecting them before they pass through the metal detectors, and giving them a program on the other side. It looks like hotel security is monitoring the check-in process and the Secret Service is monitoring hotel security. So, I just need to get a program and step through on the inside of the security perimeter where no one can see me, and mingle with the guests."

Mike and Terry had discussed the possibility that he would

need an invitation and how to get around that. They'd also discussed the chances of Mike getting into the lobby without being seen and what to do if he was found out. Now, it looked like all he needed to do was get his hands on a program. All of their planning, hours of it, might pay off. Mike found himself getting excited about trying to meet Amos 'Doc' Blund—not his dad, but the man his dad would have become if he'd made different life choices.

"Sounds too easy," Terry said. "Where can you get a program?"

"I think I saw an open box of them on a counter, to the left. Let's look over there."

Sure enough, all Mike had to do was have Terry move the gate into the box, open it about six inches, then reach through, pick up the topmost program and slip it through the gate. The gate was open for only a few seconds, so anyone who happened to glance that way, would think they saw something, maybe a disturbance in the air, but by the time they looked again, it wouldn't be there, and they would only see the program move if they were looking inside the box at the exact time when he took it.

"One hurdle overcome," Mike said. "How do I look?" he asked Terry. In his dad's black suit, black bowtie, white shirt with cufflinks and polished black shoes, he knew he looked good, but he was nervous, and wanted Terry to confirm it.

Terry looked him over and gave him a thumbs-up.

"Do it," Terry said and smiled.

Mike made another 360-degree scan of the area through the gate, nodded to Terry to open it, and took one step forward, through the gate. He looked quickly to his left, where the coat check girl was taking coats and hats, then a second step into the cloak room. From there, he identified his target, a secret service agent ahead and to the right, about twenty feet away. He took a deep breath, let it out, stepped out of the cloak room and walked deliberately up to the agent.

☢

"Are you there, Terry?" Mike asked quietly, with his hand to his mouth to hide the movement of his lips.

"Present and accounted for," Terry replied through the small earbud in Mike's ear.

Mike had a fleeting image of himself in one of those secret agent movies and had a sudden urge to laugh. He looked down at his shoes and kept his hand over his mouth until he could control himself, then looked around the lobby, checking the position of the security guards. He walked up to the Secret Service agent that he'd identified, holding his program in front of him with both hands. When he saw how the program shook in his hands, he realized how nervous he was and dropped his hands to his sides.

The agent had already spotted him approaching before he arrived.

"Excuse me," Mike said, nervously. The agent didn't respond. "Will you please tell Amos Blund that his son, Michael, is here and would like to speak to him?"

The agent continued to stare at Mike for a few moments, then did a double take as Mike's comment seemed to register. He looked Mike up and down, studied his face hard, then spoke into his collar mike.

"JP, this is Digs. There's a young man in the lobby who says he's Doc's son, Michael. I know," Digs replied to something JP said in response, "but he's the right age and looks just like him. He wants to talk to his dad."

"Wait over by that column," Digs told Mike shortly, then went back to watching the crowd, periodically glancing in Mike's direction.

Mike figured that JP, who must be someone on Amos Two's security detail, must be delivering the message and waiting for a response. Mike expected to be arrested at any moment and hauled away for being part of a scam. Mike Two was probably already in the building.

"Are you there, Terry?" Mike asked quietly, hoping Terry could get him out on short notice.

"I heard what happened," Terry said. "Hang in there. I'm ready if you need me."

Digs straightened up as another agent appears. He nodded toward Mike and the agent approached.

"Michael Blund?" the second agent asked. When Mike nodded, the agent continued. "Come with me," he said, and started to move away.

"Are you JP?" Mike asked, then wondered where he found the nerve to ask.

Without answering, the agent looked at Mike for a moment, then led the way around a corner and down the hall to a small room. He stepped aside to allow Mike to enter, then followed him and closed the door behind them.

"Do you have photo ID?" the agent asked.

Mike pulled out his wallet and removed his Utah driver's license, handing it to the agent. He didn't carry his wallet anymore, not since they'd moved to the Preserve, but Terry had thought of it and had suggested he might need identification.

After studying the license and comparing it to Mike's face, he returned it.

"I'm Agent Ty Morgan," the agent said. "JP's my nickname. I don't know how you got here, but you appear to be who you say you are. If you'll wait here, Doc will be here shortly."

"Doc?" Mike asked, with raised eyebrows.

"That's what Mr. Blund goes by. I would have thought you'd have known that." He studied Mike again, perhaps wondering if he was other than what he appeared to be. After a few moments, he turned and stepped to the door. "Wait here," he said and left, closing the door behind him.

"This looks bad, Terry." Mike said. He looked around the room and realized this was set up as a meeting room for side conversations. There were three chairs around a small table, with place settings, coffee cups and a carafe of coffee, in the center of the table.

"Be still. I'm watching," Terry said. "Sit down and relax. It will look more normal."

"But I'm nervous."

"Then don't sit. Act nervous. That works, too."

Author's Note

This story is a work of fiction. All of the characters in the book are from the author's imagination and any resemblance to known persons is purely coincidental. Location names, government organizations and functions and the effects of man-caused and natural disasters mentioned in the story are accurate to the best of my ability to determine.

About the Story

One of my goals in writing this story was to give each character a unique and believable personality. So, many of the characters in the series are patterned after people that I know or have known. Just to be sure that I don't offend anyone, let's just say that if you identify with one of the characters, he or she was meant to resemble you—except for Jason, who is a composite of all the bad character traits I could think of.

I mentioned in *World in Chaos* (Book 3), that I've been to and loved many of the places I've written about. With members of my family, I've travelled much of the Oregon and Mormon Trails. One of our favorite experiences was visiting the *End of the Oregon Trail* museum in Oregon City, Oregon, where the museum buildings are built in the shape of over-large covered wagons-Conestogas. Probably our favorite memory of the trails was reenacting the role of handcart pioneers at the Martin's Cove historic site in Wyoming. Marilyn and I played Ma and Pa to a group of young men and women who pulled a handcart seventeen miles over three days, experiencing some of the hardships that the original pioneers might have gone through—well worth a visit.

About the Cover

In the *About the Story* section of *World in Chaos*, I mentioned that I found my mental image of Aspen Valley in Logan Canyon in 2017. It is the inspiration for and was used to design the cover of *Battle for Aspen Valley*. But there's more to the story.

In June, 2019, Marilyn and I vacationed in Scandinavia with a tour group. During one of our rest stops, I was discussing *Omega Crisis* with another couple, and our lovely and enthusiastic tour guide, Ali, overheard our conversation. With her usual witty humor and winning smile, she asked if I was going to write about our Scandinavia trip. Frankly, I hadn't thought about it. I already knew the cover of *Battle for Aspen Valley* would include some view of Aspen Valley, so I began looking for a wooded meadow that reminded me of my valley in Logan Canyon. I found it near the city of Bergen, Norway, during a rest stop. Norway is a beautiful country, with lush, green, wooded mountains, scenic waterfalls, winding highways around expansive fjords and gorgeous architecture. If you're interested, you can see some of our photos from that trip on my website, *stevenewilde.com*.

Acknowledgements

I need to thank the people who've helped me develop, edit and publish the books in the Gemini Gate series. Steve Brown, Kevin Cook, Dan Duvall, David Noble, Felicia Osborn, Chris Palmer and Dan Wilde reviewed one or more of the volumes and provided valuable feedback on content and grammar. The people at IndieBookLauncher.com: Nas Hedron for editing the first two books and educating me on writing styles; and Saul Bottcher, for painting the book covers, setting up the books for publication, and putting up with all my questions. I couldn't have gotten this far without all of you pitching in to make me look good.

Most of all, I need to thank Marilyn for putting up with my obsession to tell this story. She's been my best critic and greatest supporter through the long hours at the computer.

For your patience at all the interruptions, to run my latest ideas past you, and each time I jump out of bed to finish a scene that has suddenly come to me, I love you.

About the Author

I grew up in Salt Lake City and graduated from the University of Utah with a bachelor's degree in engineering. My wife, Marilyn, and I have five children and fifteen grandchildren. Together we enjoy camping, hiking, travel, and family get-togethers. I love to read, and enjoy most genres, particularly murder mysteries and science fiction. In my quiet time, I enjoy reading, writing, gardening, genealogy, and emergency preparedness.

My career as a project manager took me to several countries around the world, and multiple industries and specialties, including electric utilities, nuclear power plant construction, water management, global mining, and aerospace, with each of those experiences contributing to my interest in, and the broad perspective needed to write this story.

Feel free to contact me with questions and suggestions.

This story about the Battle for Aspen Valley is meant to entertain. I hope you enjoyed it. Don't miss the sequel *The Door Between Twin Worlds* (Book 5 in the Gemini Gate series), and visit me on StevenEWilde.com for more information about the characters, story and facts-in-the-fiction.

Thank you.

Steven E. Wilde

Facebook: StevenEWilde_GG
Email: StevenEWilde@gmail.com
Website: www.StevenEWilde.com